A Journey in Southern !

[1909]

PREFATORY NOTE

JEREMIAH CURTIN took the degree of Bachelor of Arts at Harvard College in 1863, having been a member of the last college class that studied their required mathematics under me as Assistant Professor. I found young Curtin's personal appearance and his mental processes unusual and interesting. He was a good scholar in general, with an extraordinary capacity for acquiring languages. In his autobiography (unpublished) he states that seven months and a half before he entered Harvard College he did not know one word of Latin or Greek, but at the admission examination he offered more of each language than was required. At the time of his death, 1906, he knew more than sixty languages and dialects, and spoke fluently every language of Europe and several of the languages of Asia. He was Secretary of Legation of the United States in Russia from 1864 to 1870, during which period he was acting consul-general for one year, 1865-1866. He was connected with the Bureau of Ethnology in the Smithsonian Institution from 1883 to 1891, and later was employed from time to time by the Bureau for special work.

In Siberia, during the journey which this volume describes, he studied the Buriat language with a Buriat who knew Russian, and hard as it was to acquire a strange language without the aid of books, he accomplished the feat in a few weeks. At sixty he learnt a new language as quickly as he did when a Harvard student. Having acquired a language, Curtin always wished to learn the history, principal achievements, myths, folk-lore, and religious beliefs and usages of the people who spoke that language. Hence his great learning, and his numerous publications on myths and folk-tales. Curtin is also known to the learned world by his translations from the Polish of *Quo Vadis* and eight other works of Henry Sienkiewicz. He published many valuable translations from the Russian and the Polish.

In the year 1900, between the 19th of July and the 15th of September, Curtin made the journey in southern Siberia which is the subject of the following volume, his object being to visit the birthplace of the Mongol race, and to see for himself the origins and survivals of a prepotent people which once subdued and ruled China, devastated Russia, conquered Burma and other lands east of India, overran Persia, established themselves in Asia Minor and Constantinople, and covered Hungary with blood and ashes, thus occupying at different epochs most of Asia and a large part of Europe.

The Buriats, who are the surviving Mongols of to-day, inhabit three sides of Lake Baikal and the only island therein. Lake Baikal is the largest body of fresh water in the Old World. From the regions south of Lake Baikal came Jinghis Khan and Tamerlane, the two greatest personages in the Mongol division of mankind.

The volume opens with a brief sketch of the physical features and the history of Siberia, a comparatively unknown and dreary country, which covers about one-ninth of the continental surface of the globe. The long journey in southern Siberia is then amply described, the landscape, the institutions, the dwellings, and the mode of life of the people he met being set forth with vividness and philosophic appreciation. An important section of the book relates to the customs of the Buriats—their customs and ceremonies at the birth of a child, at a marriage, and in sickness, and their burial rites. It then deals with the origin of the shamans or priests, with the sacred trees and groves, and with the gods of the Buriats. The myths connected with the Mongol religion are next recorded, just as Curtin heard them from the lips of living Buriats. A collection of folk-tales completes the volume. It is a book of very unusual character, which only an extraordinary linguist and scholar could have written, so difficult was the gathering of the material for it. The journey itself was one of considerable hardship and exposure; and the linguistic, historical, and anthropological knowledge required to produce the book has seldom, if ever before, been possessed by any single scholar.

The manuscript of this volume was finished a few months before Curtin's death, but it has been published posthumously without the advantage of his revision.

CHARLES W. ELIOT.

OCTOBER 20, 1909.

MAP OF SIBERIA

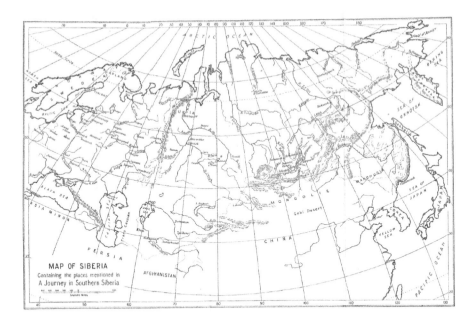

Map of Siberia

CHAPTER I. THE BIRTHPLACE OF MONGOL ACTIVITY

THE Buriats whose myth-tales I have collected, and whose beliefs, modes of worship, and customs I have studied at their source and describe in this volume, are Mongols in the strictest sense of the word as men use it. They inhabit three sides of Lake Baikal, as well as Olkhon its only island. The place and the people are noteworthy.

Lake Baikal is the largest body of fresh water in the Old World, being over four hundred miles long and from twenty-four to fifty-six miles broad, its total area covering about thirteen thousand square miles. The Buriats living west of that water, and those inhabiting the sacred island of Olkhon, are the only Mongols who have preserved their own race religion with its primitive usages, archaic beliefs, and philosophy, hence they are a people of great interest to science.

The region about that immense body of water, Lake Baikal, is of still greater interest in history, for from the mountain land south of the lake, and touching it, came Temudjin, known later as Jinghis Khan, and Tamerlane, or Timur Lenk (the Iron Limper), the two greatest personages in the Mongol division of mankind.

From the first of these two mighty man-slayers were descended the Mongol subduers of China and Russia. Among Jinghis Khan's many grandsons were Kublai Khan, the subjector of China, together with Burma and other lands east of India; Hulagu, who destroyed the Assassin Commonwealth of Persia, stormed Bagdad, and extinguished the Abbasid Kalifat; and Batu, who covered Russia with blood and ashes, mined Hungary, hunting its king to an island in the Adriatic, crushed German and other forces opposed to the Mongols at Liegnitz, and returned to the Volga region, where he established his chief headquarters.

Descendants of Jinghis Khan ruled in Russia for two centuries and almost five decades. In China they wielded power only sixty-eight years.

From Tamerlane, a more brilliant, if not a greater, leader than Jinghis, descended the Mongols of India, whose history is remarkable both in the rise and the fall of the empire which they founded.

These two Mongol conquerors had a common ancestor in Jinghis Khan's great-great-grandfather, Tumbinai; hence both men were of the same blood and had the same land of origin,—the region south of Lake Baikal.

That Mongol power which began its career near Baikal covered all Asia, or most of it, and a large part of Europe, and lasted till destroyed by Russia and England. The histories of these struggles are world-wide in their meaning; they deserve the closest study, and in time will surely receive it.

When the descendants of Jinghis Khan had lost China, the only great conquest left them was Russia, and there, after a rule of two hundred and forty-four years, power was snatched from them.

The Grand Moguls, those masters of India, the descendants of Tamerlane, met with Great Britain, and were stripped of their empire in consequence.

The British conquest of India and its methods mark a new era in history,—the era of commercial invasion, the era of the "drummer" in politics; that drummer who, in addition to the wares which he offers, has statecraft behind him, and when the need comes he has also cold steel and hot cannon-balls.

The Grand Mogul and his counsellors could not suspect danger from this man. They considered him, at first, much as rich ladies in great country houses far from cities might consider a humble and toiling pack-peddler. But, though he might seem insignificant, this man was really a conqueror. The Grand Mogul, Jehargir, could not see, of course, that Hawkins and Roe would bring after them servants such as Clive,

Warren Hastings, and others, who would take from his heirs whatsoever they valued,—land, dominion, and treasures.

Mongol rule was abolished in India by the British because it did not accord with their methods and objects. It was destroyed by the Russians because it was foreign, oppressive, and hateful. They simply freed their land from aliens. The conflict in Russia was what people call patriotic. It was carried on through sacrifices and struggles of many kinds.

There is a third Mongol history which affects greatly the actors in the two histories just mentioned. This history had its origin at Lake Baikal, though indirectly. When Jinghis Khan was hunting the Kwaresmian ruler, Shah Mohammed, to his death on an island in the Caspian, a group of Turks, or western Mongols, fled before him, and found refuge in Asia Minor. The time for them proved favorable. They fought; they obtained land, and prospered. They grew great by accretion, as does a snowball rolling down a long mountain slope, till at last they won the empire established by Constantine.

This Mongol group, four hundred and forty-four families in number, became known as the Ottomans, and after the destruction of the Kalifat at Bagdad they were the heirs of Mohammed, and a terror to Europe. In time, however, they weakened, and Great Britain came to be the defender-in-chief and mainstay of those western Mongols, and Russia their main and chief attacker. So the spoilers of Tamerlane's descendants in India became the active allies of the Mongols on the Bosporus, and the enemy of that Russia who had pushed Mongol rule out of northern Europe.

Had Jinghis Khan never lived, those Turks, or western Mongols, known afterward as Ottomans, would never have left Asia and ruled on the Bosporus.

The Mongols have played an immense part in the past, and they bear in them at the present the great mystery of the future,—a mystery of deep import to all men. The birthplace of that mystery was the mountain region south of Lake Baikal. In view of this I visited that central land of Siberia where the family of Jinghis had its origin.

I think it well to give here a brief outline sketch of Siberia, a country which covers an area of fourteen and one half million square kilometres; that is, about one ninth of the whole continental surface of the globe, but which to the mind of most readers is an unknown, boundless, cold, dreadful wonderland. I shall mention a few of the chief events in the history of the country up to the time when the Buriats first recognized Russian supremacy.

Though the name "Sibir" appears in Russian chronicles in 1407 for the first time, Russians knew the country east of the Ural Mountains much earlier. Southern Siberia was visited by Russian princes in the middle of the thirteenth century, when they were forced to do homage to the Grand Khan at Karakorum, his first capital, not very far to the south of Lake Baikal.

Western Siberia was known as early as the eleventh century to merchants of Novgorod, who had dealings with the people of that region which they called Yugria or Ugri. Those people had furs of various kinds which they were ready to barter, and of all sources of income for Novgorod the chief, and the richest in those days, was the fur trade. That great territory between Novgorod and the Ural Mountains, and from the Volga to the Frozen Ocean was one vast preserve, one immense hunting ground for fur-bearing animals.

In the Middle Ages the wearing of furs was universal. Every one wore them who had the wherewithal to purchase. Wealthy persons wore mantles and coats made of the most costly skins, and at that time Great Novgorod purveyed for all Europe—found furs for every one who would buy. This demand impelled Novgorod to subject, and in cases to colonize, places far north and east of its own territory.

At first fur-bearing animals abounded in all the lands under Novgorod, but in time they decreased in more western regions, and fur hunters searched through the forests on the Kama, Petchora, and northern Dwina, as well as on streams running into those rivers.

Furs were obtained both in payment of tribute and in return for goods furnished the natives. The government of Novgorod sent out its collectors at intervals. The tribute which they took was paid in furs usually, if not always. Traders also went from various points on the Volga to the Arctic, and besides furs they obtained whale and walrus oil, walrus tusks, sea fowls, tar, and potash, but fur was the chief and most valuable article of commerce. From Perm these men received also silver, but this silver had been brought from beyond the Ural Mountains, which in those days were called Kamenyet Poyas (the Stone Girdle).

Though the country west of the mountains was great in extent, the country east of them was enormously greater. It was also richer in furs of a high quality, and had besides the master metals,—gold and silver.

When regions west of the mountain range had become well known to collectors of tribute and to traders, men began to seek wealth in regions east of it. The fame of that eastern land soon spread throughout all northern Russia, and in 1032 an expedition from Novgorod set out for the "Iron Gates," that is, a pass in the Ural, through which they intended to enter Yugria.

This expedition met failure and was crushed by the natives. Only a few of the men went back to Novgorod; most of them perished.

In 1096, sixty-four years after that first expedition, according to a statement in the *Chronicle of Nestor*, a Novgorod merchant named Rogóvitch sent a man first to the Petchora, where the natives paid tribute, and afterward to Yugria, "where the people are shut in by sky-touching mountains, in which there is a small gate with an opening. Through this gate men look out and talk from time to time, but no one understands them. If any person shows a knife or an axe to these people they offer furs in exchange for it. The Yugrians were confined in this region by Alexander of Macedon. While on his way to the sea, called 'The Sun's Place,' Alexander discovered these people, and, seeing their terrible uncleanness,—they did not bury their dead, they ate snakes, flies, and every other vile thing,—he feared lest they might increase and defile the whole earth by their practices, so he drove them to that great north-eastern corner and fenced them in there firmly. He asked the Lord, and high mountains closed in on the Yugrians. Still the mountains did not meet altogether, a gap of twelve ells remained, and there a bronze gate was formed of such quality that fire cannot burn it, or iron cut it."

'Under the year 1114 it is noted in the Chronicle that "old men who had gone to Yugria saw a cloud touch the earth, and then fur-bearing animals came out of it, and rushed away through that country in myriads. Another cloud came down, and reindeer sprang out of it."

These tales are like those told by Pacific coast Indians. There are tribes on the Klamath River who tell of animals coming from the sky. I have several such myths which I took down in California. This account in Nestor's *Chronicle* is beyond doubt a Siberian myth-tale given to some Russian who told it at home as if he had been an eye-witness, or who was reported as so telling it.

Toward the end of the twelfth century Yugria paid tribute to Novgorod, though there was resistance at first, as there had been west of the mountains, where in 1187 one hundred men were killed while collecting tribute. In 1197 a party east of the Ural lost a still larger number.

After 1264 Yugria was counted by Novgorod as a possession of that republic, and tribute was collected there. In 1364 an expedition from Novgorod, made up of young people, sons of boyars, and volunteers, led by Alexander Abakúmovitch and Stephan Lyápa, reached the Ob River, one of the mighty rivers which embrace that vast plain called western Siberia. There they separated into two parties: one, sailing down to the mouth, conquered all tribes to the Frozen Ocean; the other, sailing up the river, was equally successful.

Forty-three years later, or in 1407, Tohtamish, once khan of the Golden Horde, the man who burned and ruined Moscow, was murdered in Sibir, a town on the Irtish some versts below its junction with the Toból. The name "Sibir" was used then for the first time, as the chronicler informs us.

In 1446 a new expedition to Yugria was made, but it failed; and this seems to have been the last expedition sent by Novgorod. Nineteen years later Ivan Veliki (the Great) of Moscow, afterward the conqueror of "Lord Novgorod," as the proud people called their city, commanded Vassili Skryaba of Ustyug to subject Yugria. This was done, as it seemed for the moment, since Kalpak and Tekich, princes of Yugria, were brought to Moscow, where Ivan Veliki confirmed their titles, and appointed a tribute which they were to pay for all Yugria. Thenceforth Ivan must have considered himself master of the country, for in 1488, when writing to the King of Bohemia, he added Yugorski to his other titles.

But in reality the northern part of Yugria showed no desire for subjection to Moscow. And years later three commanders, one of whom was Prince Kurbski, led five thousand men into northern Yugria and conquered it, capturing forty-one towns and taking, as prisoners, more than one thousand people, with fifty-eight princes or elders.

Fifteen years after this Vassili, son of Ivan Veliki, divided northern Yugria. The region on the Lower Ob he called Obdoria, and that on the river Konda, Kondia, and to his titles he added Prince Obdorski and Kondinski. A little later the southern part became known as Sibir, which was the name of the capital of the native khans, and in time became the name of the entire country.

In a letter, written in 1554, to Edward VI of England, Ivan the Terrible, as Karamzin states, entitled himself "Commander of all Sibir."

In 1558 Tsar Ivan granted Grigori Stróganoff unoccupied lands, one hundred and forty-six versts in length, on the Kama and Chusóva rivers. No taxes were to be paid on those lands for twenty years. Ten years later lands extending twenty versts along the Kama from the mouth of that river were granted to Grigori's brother, Yákov. These lands were to be free of taxes for ten years. In return the brothers were to build stockades and maintain troops at their own expense. On both these grants the Stróganoffs showed great activity.

In 1563 Khan Kuchum, said by some writers to be a Nogai, who lived near Lake Aral, and by others to be a simple Usbek, captured Sibir the capital, and after killing the ruling khan, Ediger, and Bekbúlat his brother, termed himself Tsar of Sibir, probably calling all the country in that region Sibir, to signify that it belonged to his capital. When established firmly he subdued many northern tribes and refused to pay tribute to Moscow.

In 1569 Ivan the Terrible sent Kuchum a message reminding him of his duties as a vassal; and in 1571-72 Kuchum despatched two envoys, Tamas and Aisa, to Moscow with tribute, and a letter in which he asked to become a subject of the Tsar, and promised to pay the tribute in future.

The envoys took oath for Kuchum and his chief men, but not knowing how to write and having no seal they were unable to sign an oath paper; hence Ivan sent Chabúkoff, the son of a boyar, with envoys to Sibir, and there Kuchum and his chief men took the oath to Ivan, and put their seals to the oath papers.

Mahmet Kul, mentioned variously as son, brother, nephew, and relative of Kuchum, was enraged that his people should bend before Russians. He attacked those who were willing to pay tribute to Moscow, captured their wives and children, and ended by assaulting Chabúkoff while that envoy was returning to Moscow; but learning that troops on the Chusóva were preparing to attack him he fled.

In 1574 the Stróganoffs, Grigori and Yákov, were granted the privilege to build posts on the Toból and Takhcha rivers; to use guns and cannon; to enlist men and employ them in warfare; to restrain every uprising; to establish iron-works and fisheries; to cultivate land on the Toból and streams flowing into it. Settlers on those lands were freed for twenty years from taxes and services of all kinds. The Stróganoffs were to put down robbers, thieves, and vagrants; they were to protect native tribes and other people from Kuchum, and bring Kuchum and his subjects to true obedience.

In Moscow there was great complaint touching robberies on the Volga, and in 1577 Ivan Grozney (the Terrible) sent a strong force with an order to capture Yermak, the chief ataman, with four other atamans, and send them in irons to Moscow, that he might make an example of them by a painful and ignominious death.

Some of the robbers, or Cossacks, as people called them, were captured and hanged straightway, but most of them scattered and saved themselves; among these was Yermak Timofieff, with his associate atamans, Ivan Koltsó, Yákov Mihailoff, Nikíta Pan, and Matvéi Mestcheryak, and other men to the number of five thousand, or five hundred as some historians state.

The following year these men reached the land of the Stróganoffs. Grigori and Yákov were dead; their heirs were Simeon, a third brother, Maksim, son of Yákov, and Nikíta, son of Grigori. There are in Russian Chronicles two versions of what happened at this time. One is that Yermak planned the subjection of Kuchum and the conquest of Sibir, and induced the Stróganoffs to aid him; the other is that the Stróganoffs planned the conquest and got Yermak to assist them in the undertaking. Either version may be true, or it may be that the Stróganoffs and Yermak had the same plan and agreed to co-operate. But the glory of being the first real conqueror of Siberia is given to Yermak, and he is therefore the popular hero of Siberia.

Kuchum had shown clearly that no success in Sibir was possible for the Stróganoffs or others till his power was crushed thoroughly. Yermak undertook to crush it.

Of Yermak and his origin accounts are also conflicting. One *Chronicle* calls him Vassili, and says that he was a native of the Ural country, who worked on a boat navigating the Kama and the Volga; that he was pot-boiler, that is, cook, for the boat-men. Yermak was the name of a company's pot on such boats, and instead of calling him Vassili the boatmen nicknamed him Yermak (Pot). Yermak was ambitious, hence he grew dissatisfied and restless, and, seeing a chance to win wealth on the Volga by robbery, he deserted his employers, formed a company of young, daring boatmen, put himself at the head of it, and began business. He did what he pleased, and above all what gave profit. At last he and Koltsó with a few of their associates grew so bold that they robbed the Tsar's envoy; and then came the order to bring him to Moscow. In another account Yermak is made a Cossack of the Don; and in a third, that of Kostomareff, he is described as an ataman in the Tsar's service on the Ural, and has no connection whatever with Don Cossacks or with robbery on the Volga.

Yermak's first hostile meeting with the natives of Sibir was with the Tartar prince, Epancha, whom he defeated. In a second battle, somewhat later, he captured Epancha's chief stronghold, which stood where the town of Tiumen is now situated. Yermak and his forces spent the winter of 1580—SI at this place. Early in the spring he sailed down the Tura. Near the mouth of the river hostile princes were awaiting him. A battle ensued, which after some days ended in the defeat of the native forces, and Yermak captured so much booty that he was forced to abandon a large part of it. He now entered the Toból River, and with ten hundred and sixty men, his whole army, sailed toward the Irtish.

In spite of continual attacks by the enemy the small army reached Isker, or Sibir, Kuchum's capital. At that place there was another engagement, and though few of Yermak's men were killed many were wounded. October 1st a battle was fought in which the Russians simply held their own, but on October 23d a merciless hand to hand conflict took place; Yermak lost one hundred and seven men, but he won a decisive victory. A few days later two tribes deserted Kuchum, and he fled with his troops to the steppes, taking with him everything that it was possible to carry.

October 26, 1581 is memorable in the history of Siberia, for on that day Yermak entered Sibir, the capital, as master. Four days later a chief of the Ostyaks appeared bringing provisions and tribute.

Early in 1582 Mahmet Kul was captured and taken to Moscow. Yermak now sent Ivan Koltsó to lay the Tsardom of all Sibir at the feet of Ivan Grozney. Koltsó was attended by fifty Cossacks, and took with him two thousand four hundred valuable skins, two black foxes, fifty beavers, and a letter from Yermak to the Tsar announcing his conquest.

The Tsar received Koltsó with honor, and so great was his gratitude that he sent Yermak a fur mantle from his own shoulders, a magnificent goblet, and two rich suits of armor, besides much money. He also sent one of his most valued leaders, Glúkhoff, to assist him.

Yermak now extended his authority in every direction. In September, 1583, a messenger came from Karacha, a murza who had formerly been devoted to Kuchum, begging Yermak for aid against Nogai Tartars. Yermak, not thinking of treachery, sent Koltsó with forty Cossacks. Karacha slaughtered the entire party.

In November came the first government officials to Siberia from Moscow, Prince Bolhovski, with two associates and five hundred sharpshooters. The following winter there was a terrible dearth of provisions. Prince Bolhovski and many of his men died from hardship and lack of food. While the Russians were in such straits Karacha tried to anticipate Yermak in action, and prevent him from taking revenge for the murder of Koltsó and his Cossacks. He invested Sibir, the capital; but the Russians made a sally, defeated him, and drove off his warriors, who fled, leaving their supply of provisions behind them.

During the summer of 1584 Yermak made his last expedition. He sailed up the Irtish to subdue the various tribes and force them to pay tribute, and to punish Karacha, if he could find him. With the tribes he succeeded, but Karacha eluded every search, and escaped.

Near the end of July Yermak returned to his capital, but in August sailed again up the river to rescue, as he thought, Bukhara traders, reports having reached him that Kuchum had seized them on the Irtish. Finding that these reports were false, he turned and sailed homeward.

One night, when it was so dark and stormy that Yermak thought it unsafe to continue the journey, he stopped at an island near the bank of the river. The weary Cossacks were soon sleeping soundly. The enemy, who had followed very sharply and cautiously, stole onto the island during the rainstorm and darkness and killed or drove into the river every man except one; that man escaped and carried the tidings to Sibir.

Yermak was either killed by the natives or drowned. His body was borne down the river and found, seven days later, by a Tartar fisherman, named Yanish.

After Yermak's death Siberia was lost to Russia for a season. In Moscow no one knew what had happened in far-off Siberia. The entire force of men left there was one hundred and fifty, the remnant of Yermak's little army, and of those warriors who had come with Bolhovski. They were under command of Glúkhoff, who, fearing to remain in a hostile country with so small a force, decided to return west of the Ural. He left Sibir, and, not venturing to take the road by which Yermak had entered the country, sailed down the Irtish and Ob rivers, crossed the Ural Mountains well toward the north, came out in the region of Archangel, and went thence to Moscow.

Kuchum's son, Alei, entered Sibir, the capital, immediately after Glúkhoff's departure, but was soon driven out by Seidyak, a son of that Bekbúlat, whom Kuchum had killed when he seized the place originally.

In 1585 Tsar Fedor, son and successor of Ivan Grozney, knowing nothing of what had happened, sent Ivan Mansúroff to succeed Prince Bolhovski. When Mansúroff arrived in Sibir he found no Russians whatsoever. If a few were left in the country they had associated themselves with the natives, to escape destruction. It was impossible to return to Moscow for the cold season had come. Mansúroff was forced to remain in Siberia for the winter, hence with all expedition he raised a stockade and built houses on the right bank of the Ob, just opposite the mouth of the Irtish.

The Ostyaks made one attack, but were so frightened by the sound of the cannon that they fled. In the spring Mansúroff set out for home, going by the same road, through the Ural Mountains, which Glúkhoff had taken.

When Glúkhoff reached Moscow, and told his tale of defeat and disaster Tsar Fedor sent three hundred men to Sibir under two voevodas, Vassili Sukin and Ivan Myasnoi. Daniel Chulkóff, a secretary, was to follow. In July of that year, 1586, Sukin founded Tiumen on the Tura, and, not venturing to move farther on toward Sibir, he extended Moscow rule over tribes in the region around him. He was not too far from the Ural, hence safe. The position was good, geographically.

Early in 1587 five hundred men came from Moscow with Chulkóff, who brought to Sukin and Myasnoi a command, from the Tsar, to found a city on the right bank of the Irtish, near the mouth of the Toból—Tobólsk was founded.

Tiumen was the first Russian city built in Siberia. Tobólsk on the Toból followed quickly, but was soon transferred to the high bank of the Irtish. Chulkóff induced Seidyak, ruling then in Sibir, the town taken once by Yermak, to visit him at Tobólsk. Uzaz Makmen, Sultan of the Kaisak Horde, came also, and Karacha, who had slaughtered Koltsó and his Cossacks. Chulkóff seized all three of these men and sent them to Moscow. Then he attacked and captured Sibir, the capital. Its inhabitants fled, and the place was never reoccupied by any one.

In their advance toward the East the Russians did not meet with very serious resistance till near the Amoor River, generally the native tribes submitted to the Cossacks without a struggle and the Russian government gradually built forts which later on became towns.

In 1590, for the first time, colonists were sent to Siberia. Tobólsk was made the chief city and administrative center. New towns appeared, among others Pelym, which Prince Peter Gortchakoff founded. This place is notable as the first in Siberia to which exiles were sentenced. Many of the people of Uglitch, a place north of Moscow, were sent thither by Tsar Fedor because of the death in their town of his half-brother, the young son of Ivan the Terrible. Strangest exile of all was a church bell from Uglitch, sent to Tobólsk in 1591. The alarm had been sounded on that bell when the Tsar's son was killed. In Tobólsk it was hung in the tower of the church on the Market place, to strike the hours.

In this year Beriozoff was founded by Trahanistoff, a voevoda, and Surgut, on the river Ob by the Princes Lvoff and Volkonski.

From 1593 to 1598 there was immense activity in Siberia. Tara, Obdorsk, and many other towns were founded, and commerce began to flourish.

In 1598 Prince Masalski and Ivan Voyekoff set out with one thousand men to punish Kuchum for his pernicious activity, and for killing Koltsó. They met and crushed him. Kuchum lost his army and his family: five sons, eight wives, and eight daughters of his were sent to Moscow. The old man himself, though deaf and blind, did not yield to the Russians; he fled to the Nogai Tartars, who somewhat later killed him.

And now Russia established itself firmly in Siberia.

The first exiles of distinction to be sent into the country were sent to Pelym in 1599. They were Ivan and Vassili Románoff, who for acting against Boris Grodenof, now Tsar, were exiled from Russia. Their brother Fedor escaped exile by assuming the habit of a monk and the name Philaret, while his wife took the veil and the name Martha. From this monk and this nun sprang the founder of the Romanoff dynasty, Michael Romanoff.

The city of Tomsk was founded in 1604 by Gavrilo Pisemski and Vassili Tyrtoff. This city is now, in 1900, the educational center of northwestern Siberia. It has one of the largest Universities in the country, twenty-three Russian churches, two synagogues, and a large Catholic church. It is a wide-awake flourishing city in spite of a climate so cold that during winter the thermometer is about forty degrees below zero (Fahrenheit) for many days at a time, and the river Tom, on which the city is situated, is frozen quite half the year.

In 1620 it first became known to the world that in the far north, on the Lena River, lived a people who called themselves Yakuts. This information was given to officials in Tobólsk by the Mangazei Cossacks. In 1631 Martynoff sailed into the Lena by the Vilyno and discovered the Yakuts on whom he imposed tribute. The so-called Yakutsk Territory occupies the basin of the Lena River. Its climate is very severe, so severe in fact that agriculture is impossible, but the country is so rich in coal, iron, silver, and gold that within the past two centuries many and many thousands of convicts have been sent there to work in the mines, and because of this it has become known to the whole world.

In 1621 an event occurred of great importance for the future historians of Russia: Cyprian came as the first archbishop to Siberia. He was a scholar, and a man of remarkable foresight. His prescience has been of immense value to Russia. His earliest work was to find the few survivors of Yermak's forces and write down from their lips what they knew of that hero's expeditions and conquests. That information formed the basis of Siberian chronicles.

In 1622 the Russians first became acquainted with the Buriats. Yákov Hripunoff learned of their visiting the river Kan to get tribute, and he sent Kozloff, a Cossack, as an envoy to invite them to become Russian subjects. The result of this mission is unknown. We know, however, that in 1627 two expeditions were sent out, one under Bugór to explore the Lena River, the other under Perfilyeff, to force the Buriats to pay tribute.

Bugór reached the upper waters of the Lena, but Perfilyeff was unsuccessful; the Buriats would not surrender their independence.

In 1628 Piotr Beketoff, with a party of Cossacks, was sent against the Buriats on the Angara, but returned after reaching the mouth of the Oka River.

In 1632 Beketoff ascended the Angara and then the Ilim, crossed to the Lena, sailed down that river, and built a fort which he called Yakutsk. Later this fort was removed to the present Yakutsk, seventy versts higher up the river, and in 1638 Yakutsk was made the administrative center of northeastern Siberia. That same year Verhoyansk in the far North was founded, and in 1640 were discovered the rivers Indigirka and Alazli, both of which flow into the Frozen Ocean.

About this time an envoy, Vassili Starkoff, was sent to the Altyn Khan at Lake Ubsa. Among that khan's presents to Michael Romanoff was the first tea taken to Russia, two hundred packages, each weighing one pound and a quarter. Starkoff refused to take the tea, declaring that it was useless, and was difficult to carry, but the khan insisted and the envoy, not wishing to displease him, yielded. Tea taken thus to Moscow against the wishes of the envoy soon became a national drink among the Russians and has ever remained so.

Under the lead of Kurbat Ivanoff, a Cossack, the Russians appeared, in 1643, on the western shore of Lake Baikal, and also on Olkhon Island. In 1646 the Buriats besieged Verhoyensk, a place founded in 1641 by Martin Vassilieff. Ivanoff, the officer commanding there, was reinforced by Bedaroff and together they defeated the Buriats and ravaged their villages. Soon after this Ivan Pohalioff, sent to collect tribute from the Buriats on the Irkût, crossed Lake Baikal near its southern border, and then through the friendship of a petty prince, Turukai, reached Urga, the capital of Setsen Khan. As a result of this visit Setsen Khan, the year following, sent an embassy to Moscow.

In 1648 Bargúzin was founded near the eastern shore of Lake Baikal as a place to receive tribute from the Buriats. That same year an expedition was sent north under Dejneff, Ankudinoff, and Aleksaieff. Seven boats, each containing ten men, sailed eastward from the Kolyma, a river flowing into the Arctic Ocean. Four of the vessels disappeared during the voyage, and were never seen afterward. With those remaining the explorers doubled Shelag Point, which they named Svyatoi Nos (Holy Nose).

The vessel of Ankudinoff was wrecked there and he with his men were taken on to the other boats. After that they doubled Chukotchi, or Cape Chukchi, in which Dejneff describes beyond doubt the easternmost point of all Asia. In his report to the Yakutsk voevoda he explains how, in an encounter with the Chuchis, Aleksaiyeff was wounded and they put to sea at once. A frightful storm separated the vessels and they never met again. Dejneff was carried by the wind to the south of the Anadyr River. Thus he was the first man to show that there was a passage between the Arctic Ocean and the Pacific. To him in reality belongs the honor of discovering the straits which now bear the name of Bering, for they were seen by him eighty years earlier (in 1648) than by Bering. Cast upon the shore, near the mouth of the river Oliutora, Dejneff and his companions made their way to the Anadyr River. There they built a shelter for the winter, and soon after were rescued by traders.

Aleksaiyeff and Ankudinoff perished in Kamchatka. Though Dejneff's name is found in documents till 1654 his fate is unknown. He undoubtedly died during some expedition.

In 1650 there were several conflicts between Russians and Buriats, and only after much effort did the Russians assert their supremacy. During 1650 Yerofei Habaroff set out from Yakutsk with one hundred men, hunting for sable. He ascended the Olekma and the Tungar and reached the Amoor by the Ur and the Zeya. In two years he explored the whole river, and was the first man to launch a flotilla there. That year, 1650, the Buriats on the Oka withdrew up the Angara, and Nefedyeff, an official, was sent with his men to bring them back to the place they had deserted.

In 1652 Pohakoff established the post of Irkutsk on Irkut River near its junction with the Angara. In 1661 it was removed to the right bank of the Angara, the present site of the city of Irkutsk, and twenty-one years later it was made an administrative center.

The same year that the Irkutsk post was established Ivan Robroff was sent from the Lena in search of a northern continent, but this expedition disappeared and no word ever came from it. In 1653 Fort Balazansk was established in the Buriat country and sixty Russian families were settled there. Two years later the Buriats were preparing to withdraw to the East of Lake Baikal, but, listening to the counsel of their wise men, they resolved to remain in their home country and submit to Russian rule. There were uprisings, however, and it was not till near the end of the seventeenth century that the Buriats, completely subdued, became peaceful Russian subjects.

Seventy-five years after Yermak crossed the Urals into the almost unknown land of Yugra, Russia had swept across Asia; her boundaries touched the frozen ocean in the north, and China in the south; and in 1697 Kamchatka was added to her domains.

CHAPTER II. MY JOURNEY TO THE BURIATS

ON the morning of the 9th of July, 1900, the train on which I had traveled from Moscow came in sight of Irkutsk. I was greatly delighted with this capital of Eastern Siberia.

The city, as seen from the train which was nearing it swiftly, was extremely imposing, not only because of its size, and its many large churches, but also because the train approaches Irkutsk in such a direction that the front, and one side of the city, are presented together, as was the case with Grecian temples, the approaches to which were arranged toward the angle between the façade and one side of the structure.

Right in front of the city is the Angara, a deep, very clear and swift river which flows out of Lake Baikal, known as I have already stated, as the largest and by far the most beautiful body of fresh water in Asia. The Angara is the one outlet of Lake Baikal, which sends forth its waters through this river to the Yenissei, and thus they are borne on to the Arctic.

As the train nears Irkutsk the side view decreases, and the grade of the road is descending, hence the view becomes narrower and less striking each moment, and when the station is reached we are on the river bank.

Opposite the narrow front of Irkutsk, the façade, so to speak, the view is much reduced, very inferior to that seen from the train a little earlier. But, as a recompense, we have the Angara before us, that beautifully blue and mighty river gliding past irresistibly, smooth and silent.

It is said that the Angara never freezes till Christmas and freezes then in one night to the bottom. The great, blue current of Christmas eve has halted, and on Christmas morning stands motionless. That immense flow is chilled through and through

IRKUTSK, SIBERIA. *Page* 18

IRKUTSK, SIBERIA

to the river-bed to the point just above freezing, and then becomes ice in one night, as if by magic. The magnificent river is dead till its resurrection, when the sun will break its bonds and lead to life again.

There is no city on earth which has such a river in front of it as has Irkutsk—blue, very deep, and moving with a speed that gives the idea of resistless power.

Irkutsk seems new except in some of its churches and government buildings. Its streets are wide and unpaved. Its houses mainly of wood, and in large number unpainted.

The most interesting and remarkable monument of the city is the triumphal arch to commemorate the winning of a way to the great ocean. That is, the acquisition of the Amoor River by Muravieff, who received the title of count for his exploit in giving communication with the Pacific, and was known thereafter as Count Muravieff Amoorski.

We drove through the city and stopped at the hotel Metripole. No one came to take the baggage; the driver got it in as best he could. There was but one vacant room. The furniture was soiled and shabby, the bed hard, the blankets of the coarsest wool. And this was the best hotel in Irkutsk! In the untidy dining-room I discovered that prices were a third more than in St. Petersburg, that city celebrated for exorbitant prices.

In traveling through certain countries and among certain peoples the first requisite is to have letters and proper orders from those high in authority. The Russian Minister of Finance had given me a letter to each governor in Siberia. On delivering my letter to the governor of Irkutsk I was received not merely with much courtesy, but very cordially, and when I explained exactly what I wanted, namely, to study the Mongol language, customs, and religion among the Buriats in regions west and northwest of Lake Baikal, I was assured that every aid which the government could give would be given me. I was furnished with letters to district chiefs, and besides, though I did not know it till later, instructions were forwarded to officials along the road which I was to travel to help me in every way they could.

I considered Irkutsk as the starting-point of my investigations into the Mongol world, so far as the Buriat part of it was concerned. Hence I decided to spend a few days in studying the city and gathering what information I could concerning the people whom I was about to visit.

I had letters from friends in St. Petersburg to residents of Irkutsk, and at the house of one of these gentlemen, Mr. Popoff, editor of *The Eastern Review*, I spent many pleasant and profitable hours. Years ago Mr. Popoff was exiled to Siberia for political reasons. When free to return to Russia he preferred to remain in Irkutsk. His wife, the daughter of a rich merchant of Kiachta, is a pleasant and cultivated woman, the only person I met in Siberia with whom I could speak English. Mr. Popoff is well acquainted with the country and gave me much valuable information. During my stay in the city I met many people who came to Siberia as exiles, served out their sentence, and are now honored, and, in many cases, wealthy citizens of Irkutsk.

At the house of a friend I met Dmitri Petrovich Pershin, then acting Curator of the Irkutsk Museum who, when I told him that I wished to go among, and become acquainted with, the Buriats, said that he knew just the man who could best aid me, a Buriat, who would be in the city in a few days, and that he would introduce us to each other. I visited the Museum, and Dmitri Petrovich showed me its excellent collection with great care. It is mainly devoted to Siberian and Mongolian exhibits. Later in the season I photographed the Curator in one of the most valued articles of the collection, the ceremonial dress of a Buriat Shaman.

Two days after my visit to the Museum I called upon Dmitri Petrovich and found that Andrei Mihailovitch Mihailoff, the Buriat, had arrived. Pershin introduced us, and, with a good deal of emphasis, told the old man that I wanted to become acquainted with his people, and that he must aid me in every way he could.

Andrei Mihailovitch was friendly and promised co-operation. but it seemed to me that he was guarded. Though outwardly cordial I thought that he made internal reserves, and would try to satisfy the governor, and also me, without giving much real assistance.

I had explained previously to Pershin, and he now told Andrei Mihailovitch, that the authorities in St. Petersburg were anxious that I should have every aid possible in getting at the language, ancient beliefs, and customs of the Buriats, and hence would view with favor any exhibition of good-will shown me by his people.

A few days after this conversation Dmitri Petrovitch informed me that Andrei Mihailovitch would give me good lodgings at his summer place and bring me in contact with people who could tell much touching Buriat religion and folk-lore.

"It is a splendid beginning," said Pershin, who was very enthusiastic. "This man can make you acquainted with all the Buriats. His word is weighty among them. He still adheres to the ancient religion of his people, and can himself tell you much regarding it."

This is very well," thought I. "We shall see how he does it. I shall hope for the best, but keep my eyes open."

Dmitri Petrovitch assisted me in finding a good carriage for hire during the time of my journey—a couple of months or more, and in providing an outfit.

A suitable carriage is of the utmost importance to any man traveling in Siberia. It must have four qualities: it must be roomy and easy, rainproof, and strong beyond breaking. These Siberian carriages are made on the system of the American buckboard, but instead of planks or boards, as a spring under the body of the vehicle, poles are used. When rightly constructed the carriage is commodious, there is a cover which can be up or down, and leather aprons which can be attached to the sides to keep the sun or rain out. Sleep in it is easy, and no better vehicle in the daytime is needed for traveling in that country. It is not too heavy, but is strong, and easily repaired. It is made ready for the road in the following manner: First cover the bottom inside with a coarse Siberian-made carpet; on that carpet place a firm mattress, which should cover the bottom of the vehicle entirely. Spread on the mattress a thin blanket to protect it. A seat is made with a soft leather trunk, a specialty of Siberia. This trunk should be as long as the inside width of the carriage body. A good supply of pillows for the back and a couple of heavy blankets complete the outfit.

It should be stated that when hired the carriage is perfectly empty. The body is a kind of box somewhat lower on the sides than in the middle. It has no seat whatever, except that for the driver, which is in front of the body. There is room behind for a trunk to be strapped on; there is also some space with the driver.

Among the papers given me by the governor there was an order for private horses as well as post horses. Where there are no post stations the inhabitants are obliged to furnish beasts at the same rate as the post stations—three copecks (a cent and a half) a mile for each animal.

In due time I had made all preparations, purchased carpet, mattress, and provisions, and was ready to set out for the summer dwelling of Andrei Mihailovitch, which is about four versts nearer Irkutsk than the post station Usturdi, the latter being sixty versts distant.

At seven o'clock in the morning of July 23, after much effort, all things necessary were in the carriage and we were ready to move into the land of the Buriats. It was at least half an hour later than I had intended starting. The delay was caused by the Yamschik who came without the traces for the side horses of the troika, and had to go back for them. I learned then that tarnatasses are with and without traces, and that I ought to have mentioned the traces when ordering the horses.

The chief of the post station in Irkutsk had promised three good beasts, also an excellent driver, and he had kept his word faithfully.

The morning air was fresh, delicious, inspiriting. The horses moved at a gentle trot along the main street, "Great Street," out toward the rising and hilly country which surrounds the Siberian capital. Just beyond the city are broad low pastures where, near the banks of the Angara, immense herds were feeding.

From the rising road there are interesting views, one at least of these is very striking. The country is not grand, but is good looking.

I have commended the driver, whose name was Nikolai, and he deserves good mention. Had he lived in that age he would have been worthy to compete in a chariot race in the Circus Maximus at Rome. When a couple of miles outside Irkutsk he stopped to loosen the bell on the bow of the middle horse in the troika. That moment the driver of a carriage behind us urged his horses ahead suddenly at the foot of a long hill, and then drove at the pace he liked, which was somewhat slower than that of our carriage, hence annoying. He seemed to take pleasure in tormenting us.

Nikolai waited a few moments till the road widened sufficiently, then he turned and said in a low voice:

"I can go ahead of that scoundrel. Shall I do so?"

"I know you are a better man, but have you better horses?" I asked.

"I know my horses," answered Nikolai, and the next moment he had dashed toward the side of the equipage in advance of us; his horses' heads had reached beyond the hind wheels, when the enemy's horses were lashed, and sped up the hill at a great rate. Nikolai shouted to his horses and urged them forward.

It was the first race I had ever seen of the kind, a race up hill. Both equipages were drawn by three horses abreast, and the beasts gave a splendid example of exertion as they rose in great springs up that hill road.

Nikolai's horses were gaining gradually, but very surely, when the other man, at a point where the road was narrow a second time, guided his horses in such a way as to block the road to our animals. Nikolai was now angry. He made no secret of what he thought of that hostile driver, whose mother's family he declared to be of canine origin, beyond any doubt whatever.

He was resigned for the time since he had to be. He drove on and waited till we reached a wide place in the road and were on the hilltop. His horses then sprang forward fiercely. In one moment our carriage was half its length in advance of the other.

"Scoundrel!" shouted Nikolai, as he turned and looked back. "I'll show thee how to meet decent people!"

The enemy urged on his horses, lashed them, but he could not win now. Nikolai gained on him steadily till the end of the level land was reached, when he was perhaps two lengths ahead. At that point the road descended very gently for a mile or more, and then rose with another hill. No man could find, or construct a better race course. Nikolai turned for a moment to look at the other man, then with a series of shouts rising higher and higher, and with a deft use of his whip, he impelled those three horses down that road at full speed. The road was perfectly even so the carriage wheels went around like tops swiftly spinning. Down we went at the pace of wild runaways.

At last, and that last came very quickly, I looked around and saw our opponent about half way down the hill, and advancing at the usual pace of good traveling. I called to Nikolai to slacken speed, which he did, and then halted. I discovered at once that the king-bolt of the carriage was almost out; not more than one inch of it was left in the front axle. Had that inch slipped out in the race down the hill, the horses would have rushed away with the two front wheels and axle, what would have happened to us is unknown, nothing pleasant in any case.

A large stone was soon found to drive the king-bolt to its place, but it would not remain there till fastened, very clumsily, with ropes. The beaten man stopped his horses when down the hill, and seemed to be mending his harness. He did not approach us a second time.

At the first post station, which is called Homutooka, a blacksmith was found, who put a firm strip of iron through the lower end of the king-bolt and fixed it securely; for which he charged fifteen copecks (seven cents and a half).

Post stations are very interesting to the traveler and when well kept, which they are sometimes, are enjoyable places. There are usually a number of people waiting for horses to go in one direction or the other; some one is sure to be drinking tea, or lunching. The man in charge is obliged to furnish, at a fixed price, a samovar, that is a "self-boiler," an urn-shaped vessel with a tube running down through its center. At the lower end of this tube is a space with air holes. Charcoal is ignited in this space and the water in the urn is made to boil soon, since it is exposed to all sides of the tube, which is heated very quickly. Charcoal is added whenever the need comes, thus a good samovar gives boiling water for a long time. The excellency of tea in Russia comes in great part from the samovar,

Post Station at Elantsin. *Page 24*
Hitching in the horses

POST STATION AT ELANTSIN.

Hitching in the horses

OUR TRAVELING CARRIAGE WHILE MAKING THE BURIAT JOURNEY

My driver forgot to drop his arms. They always hold the reins in this way when driving rapidly

as most people assure me, and I believe. The chief place for making samovars is Túla, a city famed for this work throughout Russia.

We met at this first station an interesting woman, and found that the driver whom we had defeated was bringing her baggage from Irkutsk, where she had passed the preceding night. She was not more than thirty, and had set out on a journey which many an experienced traveler would hesitate to undertake. With five children, the eldest ten and the youngest a baby, and a nurse, she had started for the Yakuts country in the far north, where her husband was a government official. Weeks would pass before she could reach him. First a long journey with horses, then by boat up the Lena River, and again with horses. Not intending to return she was obliged to change carriages at each station, to unpack and pack all of her luggage—a great task. This she looked after, while the nurse was getting food for the children. Though physically frail she was wonderfully courageous, and love for husband and children seemed to give her strength to overcome all the difficulties of the journey.

While the horses were being harnessed and attached to my carriage I had a few moments' conversation with a political exile, a marvelously ragged beggar, who was loitering around the station. He told me that he was the son of a Russian priest, and had been in exile for several years. He was a bright and intelligent young man, but broken in health.

I was tempted to drink tea at Homutooka, but something, I know not what, seemed to urge me on, and as soon as the horses were ready they were put to their paces. I was anxious to see how Andrei Mihailovitch lived among summer pastures. Above all I was anxious to learn how he would welcome me.

The towns we passed through are straggling and dreary. In most cases the houses are surrounded by a high board enclosure, again one end of a house is visible, the fence meeting it on both sides. The blinds and outside casings of the windows are painted white, the body of the house has never been painted and in most cases looks to be a hundred years old. Some houses have sunk till the bottoms of the windows are on the ground. There is a huge gate in the board enclosure. The entrance to the house is inside the yard. Everywhere in Siberia, no matter how poor or small the house is, the window sills are crowded with plants, usually geraniums, and set into the threshold of the principal door is an iron horseshoe, to bring good luck.

At Jerdovski, the next station, we found a samovar boiling, so tea was drunk before fresh horses were ready. The second driver, taken at Homutooka, was not like Nikolai—he was slow, he needed urging. The third driver was a rare person. He had a harelip and was so deaf that it was difficult to talk with him. He heard only a part of what people said, and only a part of what he said could reach the mind of any man. The good thing about him was this: He was a firm driver, and sent his beasts over the road expeditiously. We were crossing a broad plain, dry and treeless. There was no cultivation whatever, but here and there were herds of cows and horses. In the distance were low hills.

After some time, an hour and a half perhaps, the driver stopped on a sudden, and said that we had just passed one road by which we might reach the house of Andrei Mihailovitch. There was another road farther on. The first led over a place little traveled, but more picturesque and more difficult. The second road was the usual and easier one. For me, who had halted on the highway and was looking eastward toward the lands of Andrei Mihailovitch, it was the left-hand road. How was I, who had gathered lore among so many peoples, to take a left-hand road when going to look for primitive stories among Mongols?

I turned back and took the right-hand road, of course, and did so with good fortune, as we shall find, hurrying on toward the unknown. By that road we came to the rear of Mihailoff's village, instead of the front, which we should have reached by, the other road, and met there more quickly and often frequently one of the great facts of life among Buriats; the chained dogs, which make such an uproar and which are quite unappeasable. No sop to Cerberus is possible among Buriats. If food be thrown to a chained dog at a Buriat house he will gulp down in a flash what is given and then would tear to pieces the stranger who gave it if he could get at him.

The carriage dashed through the village swiftly, dogs barking with fury, at one and another place. Each dog is chained to a fence or to a post driven into the earth very firmly. The beast is held to his place quite unsparingly. Whenever a team or some unknown person comes in sight, the dog rushes forward as if free; he springs furiously, reaches the end of his chain, and is jerked back with a force like that which he himself has expended. Each dog digs out, near his post, a great cavity with a ridge of fine earth all around it. He does this by his springing forward and being brought back, by the chain, toward his starting point. Dogs are always kept out of doors. When winter comes, some shelter is made over their posts, but this shelter is not very pleasant, or much protection from wind and storm. On the whole a stranger may justly infer that a dog's life among Buriats is by no means a sinecure.

After passing the ordeal of dogs we arrived at the front of my host's summer residence, composed of half a dozen houses enclosed by a high wooden wall, or board fence. After some effort the gate was swung open and we entered the enclosure. There was no one inside save the gate-keeper. So far as I could see the place was deserted. The gate-keeper informed me, however, that the master of the house was at home, and he pointed to the nearest building on the right, to which I went straightway. On the ground not far from the door was a man, whom I had not noted earlier. He was lying face downward, and, except by the stir of his sides, which showed breathing, made no motion whatever. He was, as I discovered later, intoxicated. I was astonished at the silence around us, since Andrei Mihailovotch had been informed that I would reach his summer dwelling on that day.

The gate-keeper announced me, and after waiting a few moments I entered. The master of the house was sitting at the edge of the central square space, in the middle of which the fire burns in every old-fashioned Buriat dwelling. On all the four sides of this space people were sitting and drinking arhi or tarasun. (The liquor is made of milk and distilled in each considerable house among Buriats.) They had the tarasun in a pail and passed it around in a large wooden cup or dipper. Some of the women were beyond the stage of being happy or sad. My host, who was very serious, seated me beside himself with honor, offered me tarasun, and soon inquired if I had received the letter despatched by him to the last post station. I replied that I had not. He told me then that his elder son had died suddenly; he had been ill only a few hours; this was the day of his funeral. He added that the house would be in mourning for some time. First, according to Buriat custom, there was a period of nine days during which the family stayed at home strictly, and saw no one outside its own circle. He had informed me in the letter of this sudden calamity, and declared in it that it would be impossible for him to receive me. In other words he had written me to stay away, and had forgotten, in his grief, to help me to another lodging place.

The virtue of my right-hand road was now evident. Had I taken the left-hand way I should have met the messenger, and have been forced to sleep at the next post station, and shift for myself the following day as best I might be able.

When I explained to Mihailoff that I had come in by the right-hand road, he saw at once how I had failed to receive the letter. His man had taken the other, the usual road, and thus missed me. The position was this: I was at a house not open on that day to visitors, but I was there unwittingly, in innocence; nay more, I was there by right, for I had been invited.

After thinking a moment or two my host rose and said, "You must come to my other house." We set out for the other house which stood on the opposite side of the broad enclosure. On the way he said: "First of all you must drink tea with me. I will order a samovar to be made ready."

We entered a neatly furnished house, built and furnished on the Russian plan, a samovar was brought in, and a table was soon covered with various small dainties.

"I wish you to eat some beef of my own rearing," said Mihailoff, who drank vodka freely and cheered up considerably.

In due time chopped steaks were placed on the table. My host drank more vodka, and we attacked the lunch cheerily. The steak finished, we had tea a second time; the beverage was excellent, deserving all the praise which I could give it.

By the time the lunch was over Mihailoff had become much more cordial, and at the end embraced and lifted me off the floor, expressing himself as greatly satisfied with my friendship. Then he said that I could go to his son's house at Usturdi, the next station, and make my headquarters there as long as convenience would lead me to do so. His second son, Vassili, was taking care of the place. Then, as the highest mark of favor, he took me to his yurta and showed me his "Ongons" and "Burkans" (household gods), hung up on a rafter in a dark corner of the room, and said that in his time he had entertained three Russian governors but had not shown them his "sanctuary." He showed it now because he felt such a deep affection for me.

As the hour was inclining rather closely to evening, and the distance to Usturdi was somewhat more than three miles, I thought it well to leave my host to his family at the earliest. So the carriage was summoned and drawn up outside the gate where we were to enter it. The harelipped and deaf driver had received a good share of food and drink since his coming,—especially drink, so that it was still more difficult to understand what he said and be understood by him.

When we were ready to continue our journey and had taken our seats in the carriage, the horses, instead of going forward, turned on their hind legs, stood as erect as if they had been men, then suddenly plunged toward the station from which they had come.

The driver, much roused by milk liquor, became very angry when told to turn and drive three miles farther, to Usturdi. He obeyed but spent his rage on the horses, urging them over the open country at a furious pace. The road was simply a wagon track, a mark along a level field. On they rushed for a time in the fashion of runaways. I shouted at the deaf, hare-lipped driver to slacken the speed of his horses, but without result in the least degree. There was no way to stop the man except to seize and hold him. He was in a state not uncommon with Buriats,—he was exultant, beside himself. His mind was excited while his body seemed sober. So on went the carriage almost as swiftly as during the race of that morning. Presently we approached a broad, rather shallow river. No decrease of speed was apparent. In we dashed furiously. The water reached to the knees of the horses and the front axle of the carriage. I was alarmed, for I thought there might be stones or deep places to avoid, but the dripping horses and carriage soon rose on the opposite bank, and the wild shouts of the driver urged the beasts forward again over a gray, dry, grassless plain. On and on they sped untiringly. To one who believed in metamorphosis those three beasts might have seemed men who had been changed into horses and who, hunted by the Furies sitting there on the carriage box behind them in the person of that harelipped mad driver, were rushing on with all their might, and in terror, to escape Divine vengeance. No one could tell whether the horses were running away or were driven to the utmost.

At last I saw near the roadside ahead of us the Russian—church outside Usturdi, the station to which we were hastening. Soon after the church was passed we thundered across a massive wooden bridge, and rushed into the main, and almost only street of the village. About two squares from the bridge stood the house in which Andrei Mihailovitch's late son had resided. Vassili, his only surviving son, was there in authority; in care of the place and the business. The father had given me a brief letter to Vassili, to insure a proper reception.

The house was two stories high, the best building in the village. Beyond, and belonging to it, was another house used for storage; behind the two was a deep courtyard entirely hidden by a very high fence and a gate with strong beams above it. A man, who stood near as we drove up, knocked at this gate for us, but we had to wait many minutes for an answer. Vassili, or Vassya, as he was called by every one, was occupied elsewhere, and had had no notice that guests were coming. It was necessary to wait till a servant inside could be found and the master informed that his presence was needed.

After a time Vassili came and opened the gate promptly. On hearing that I had come from his father with a letter he immediately put the upper part of the house at my disposal. It consisted of three rooms, and a glass enclosed balcony projecting over the street. From this balcony there were excellent views up and down the main road or street, and out over the broad fields, and beyond them to the range of mountains in front of us.

It was about seven o'clock and the samovar was made ready. That was all that we needed, for I had brought plenty of tea from Irkutsk, and a good supply of sukari, or rusks, which with tea are excellent. A couple of hours later we had supper and Vassili conversed with me until eleven o'clock.

This young Buriat proved to be a very interesting person. He was at that time a student at the Irkutsk gymnasium. He had passed six years there, and intended to work still another year. Besides studying he had read a good deal, and knew something of great problems in science and also in history. He could talk about Darwin, and the descent of man, and had some knowledge of chemistry. Above all, and for me that was the main point, he knew considerable about his own people, the Buriats. I congratulated him very heartily on being one of a people who had preserved their primeval religion, and who still held to the customs and beliefs of their remote ancestors. I told him that the Buriats were the only Eastern Mongols who had done this, an act which might be considered an exploit and a service to science.

After supper Vassili asked me about my experiences of that day. I described the first race, and then the terrible driving of the harelipped isvoschik, at the rate of what Hungarians call "horse death speed."

Wearied greatly after that afternoon of racing and movement and many surprises, I was glad to lie down and rest. I slept till some time after dawn. Rising, I went at once to the balcony. The morning was delightful, the air clear and invigorating. In the fields opposite, perhaps a mile away, were herds of cattle and many sheep pasturing with remarkable activity.

During the early forenoon I saw from that balcony, for the first time, a party of mounted Buriats. This party was twenty-five in number. The men had their feet in short stirrups, and sat leaning forward a little. The movement of Mongol horses is peculiar. Their steps, which seem short, are made quickly and the result is a more rapid advance than any one, not knowing those horses, could imagine.

There are two modes of movement made by man-serving beasts which are highly deceptive to the eye that is unpractised: the stride of a pacing camel, and the trotting step of a Mongol saddle horse. As I was riding once on a donkey through the quarries of Assuan, near the first Cataract of the Nile, several camels appeared on a sudden. I noticed that they were pacing. Being occupied, I dropped them out of sight for the moment, but looked again a little later. They had gone a great distance considering the interval, and though they did not seem to exert themselves much they were moving over that sand field very swiftly. The land now rose before them gently, but rose enough to form a hill which covered the horizon of the plain beyond in such wise as to hide any animal from a man standing where I was. I looked at the moving camels, a little while later they were on the flat, wide hilltop, and soon after their legs seemed to enter the earth. I turned my eyes from them purposely now and waited. I waited some minutes, then looked again. The camels had vanished. On the hill there was nothing save two or three old stone structures, like gravestones in the sand.

That morning the Buriat horses were remarkable for quick stepping, but when near by their speed was not evident. The more they receded the more noticeable it was. I stepped in from the balcony, walked across the front room a few times and went out again; the horses had advanced a long distance, they were far away, growing smaller and smaller very rapidly. I watched and saw them diminish. At last, when very small, they turned to the right and vanished behind a building.. I could not help thinking then and there of two wonderful animals, and the part which they have played in the history of mankind, namely, the Mongol horse and the Arabian camel.

What a mighty factor the Mongol horse has been! That horse which traversed all regions between the Amoor River and Burma, and all lands between the Yellow Sea and the Adriatic. No animal so enduring, no animal so easy to feed, has ever been in man's service. It found its own living. Mongol movement and conquest would have been impossible without Mongol horses.

It is not without reason that in Mongol mythology the horse in many junctures is more sagacious than the hero who rides him. In the myths of that country, the horse, in addition to his service, often gives wise directions and saving counsels.

Without camels not only would life in the Arabian desert be impossible, but the religion of Mohammed would not have been founded, or if founded could not have been extended.

I turned now to Vassya for information touching those horse-men. Why had so many assembled and whither were they going? He replied that on that day there was to be a wedding, or more correctly the fraction of a wedding, since among Buriats a wedding requires several days for its completion, and sometimes there are even many months between the first and the final ceremony.

"Would you like to go to-day?" asked he. I replied that it would give me much pleasure to see a Buriat wedding, or even a part of it.

Horses were ordered at the post station, and in half an hour we were ready for the journey. It was a little later than ten o'clock. Because of his recent bereavement Vassya himself did not go, but his place was taken by his brother-in-law, Lazareff, who lived in Shavarok, the village where the first instalment of the wedding was given on that bright day in July, 1900.

Lazareff is a cross-eyed widower; a shrewd, self-concentrated man whose mind is turned altogether toward material questions. His wife, Vassya's sister, had been dead only a few months.

Three horses were put to my carriage and we dashed off with all speed. Driving at this season of the year is very agreeable, especially in the morning. The speed of the horses is exhilarating and gives just the movement of air which is pleasant. The excitement and rush please me; there is nothing like it in America.

While on the way to the village of Shavarok, Lazareff explained many matters connected with marriage, and life among Buriats in general. That information, with more won from Vassya, I give later on in this volume.

The village is about four miles from Usturdi, and is very picturesque. Some distance up on a hillside is a level platform of land. On this platform stands Shavarok. Above is another slope extending to the top of the hill unbrokenly. From that point there is an extensive view. I counted fourteen villages.

Every one in Shavarok was rejoicing, the holiday was general. The people had but one object in view: to celebrate a part of the wedding, and spend the day in drinking and feasting. The houses, save that of the bride's father, were deserted. In his house there was a crowd of people. Just opposite the door sat the three matchmakers, old women, who looked as though they would have a good deal to say in affairs generally. An aged man stood in the center of the room. He was speaking, with face turned upward, imploring the gods to send happiness and prosperity to the bride and groom. After a time he threw tarasun up toward the central opening of the roof, spoke on, and then threw tarasun to the gods a second time.

Many people were sitting on the grassy slope above the village. The central space, devoted to hitching-posts for horses, had been turned into a temporary grove. Some dozens of young birch trees had been felled and thrust into the ground to give shade to the horses. The twenty-five which had passed Usturdi in the morning, and many others, were there.

After walking around for a time we went to the hillside and found there a multitude of people, not only from that village, but from many other villages in the region about. They were sitting on the ground in groups, disposed like three sides of a quadrangle, two sides of which lay up and down the hill, the third side connecting the other two at the top. The lower side was open and unoccupied. Through this open space people passed in and out, some bringing refreshments, which consisted mainly of tarasun (milk whiskey) and boiled mutton; others joined the feasters and sitting down on the hillside, talked, laughed, and amused themselves.

Meanwhile men bearing tarasun from group to group poured to each person who wished it. The people seemed to be tasting delight as they sat there. They were not noisy, or in any wise extravagant, but they talked and laughed as if that beautiful day and the event of it were giving them every good thing which they could wish for.

Gazing around, I saw on the ridge of the hill a flock of sheep followed by a man, who had a long white beard. I went up to look at the flock and found that the shepherd was a Russian. As usual when Russians are working for Buriats, he was an ex-convict, old, but strong. He was alone in the world, following those sheep for sustenance, living among strangers and waiting, there in Siberia, for his life to end.

When I had returned to the feasting people on the slope I was conducted again to the house of the bride's father, where in the upsodded yard we found a large company of young people dancing with might and main, dancing desperately, dancing as if the future happiness, not only of the young couple, but of all the Buriat people, depended on their energy. The air above and around them for some distance was filled with a cloud of dust, which was growing denser and denser. It seemed to me that if their strength should continue and their swiftness increase they would in time become invisible in that wonderful dust cloud.

After I had watched them a few moments Lazareff took me to his yurta, or house, at the opposite end of the village. This village fronted the south, hence the single door of each house in it opened on the south.

Every Buriat house which is built in the old way is eight-sided, the door is in the middle of that side which faces the south directly. This house has a wooden floor, which is raised above the ground somewhat. In the center is a rectangular space where there is no floor, and where the earth appears. In this space the fire is made on the ground, and directly above, in the roof, is an opening, or smoke hole. There are no partitions in the building. The only privacy obtained is by means of curtains. Trunks or boxes are used as wardrobes and storerooms. The central fire is the great point of assembly. Though many Buriats, especially those who are wealthy, build in the Russian style, particularly winter houses, even they find most delight in the old-fashioned octagonal house, with its central fire, around which they sit on the edge of the raised floor with their feet on the earth space. There they assemble in the evening, or whenever it suits them, gossip, transact business, and talk of whatever interests those present. From time to time a great open vessel, or pail, holding a gallon or more of tarasun is passed from one to another. In this pail is a wooden dipper and each person helps himself to the liquor.

Lazareff's house was thoroughly Buriat in structure and arrangement, but it was remarkably neat, quite a pattern of tidiness. I saw a good many yurtas after that, but none as clean as was Lazareff's. An old Russian woman cared for his little son and had charge of the house. This no doubt explained the unusual neatness of the place. Tea of good quality was brought now and cakes to go with it. While we were drinking tea a sandy-haired Russian, an exile, came in, a pleasant, good-looking man. He said that his home was in the Crimea but for political reasons he had been sent to live among the Buriats. At this time, however, he had only one year longer to remain. His eyes lighted up with happiness when he spoke of his approaching freedom.

In passing from Lazareff's yurta to the carriage there was a chance to finish my survey of the village. The earth was covered with dust which in the middle of the space occupied reached to the ankles as one walked through it. This stratum, thicker in some places, covered everything to the rim of the village, reaching to the outer houses and beyond them, growing thinner toward the open country till at last one could note it no longer. This dust is the dried and pulverized droppings of animals, such as sheep, horses, and horned cattle. In time of thaw and rain the droppings become a soft mud, in dry, warm weather they are turned into dust. When the days are calm the dust keeps its place and people wade through it; when the wind blows, it fills the air in all directions and is carried into each chink, cranny, and little crevice, into the smallest places. People breathe it, swallow it, drink it, eat it, live, move and have their being in it.

We returned now to Usturdi, leaving behind us that village on the hillside with its pursuits and its passions, which in the main are the same as those of man everywhere, namely: to call human life into existence, and when that new life is here to support it; or in some cases destroy it, in others live on it, in still others toil or even die for it. The motives are the same in all countries, only the details are different.

CHAPTER III. COLLECTING MYTHS

THE day following the wedding Andrei Mihailovitch came over from his summer place. He was supposed to remain at home for nine days, still he came. After a while he invited me to walk along the street with him. We went the whole length of the village. He met a number of people, who showed immense respect for him; he kissed one man, but there was much condescension in his kiss. The grandeur of the old Buriat as he led me, an American, on exhibition through the town, was truly fine.

We stood for a time on the long bridge across the Kudá, talked a little, and looked at the river, the country, and the Russian Mission Church.

"Bishops and priests," said Mihailovitch, "have asked me to be baptized, but I would not. I will stay with the beliefs into which I was born."

Just then a man appeared, racing on horseback at the highest speed. There seemed to be in the horse and man a peculiar impetus and internal force. Without decreasing the pace of the horse the man turned toward Andrei Mihailovitch, and, during the instant in which he was passing, saluted him with the highest respect. Soon the man was beyond the Mission Church, and next he was a speck on the horizon.

"Think," said I to my host as I watched the horseman, "of the time when Jinghis Khan had a cavalry of one hundred thousand men like that man and more than two hundred thousand horses swifter than that horse."

"Oh," replied he, "there was never on earth anything to equal the cavalry of Jinghis Khan. It swept everything down before it! What have we now?—Nothing. We were great once, we conquered many countries, we ruled many peoples. China and Russia overpowered us, but our turn will come again."

We went back to the balcony and talked long over the question of finding men who could tell the ancient myths and explain the customs and beliefs of the Buriats. A list was made, and that afternoon the search began. Messengers were sent to surrounding villages to look for wise men. Those who were able were to be brought to Usturdi, if possible. In case they were old and decrepit I could go to them. The first and most important step was to find persons who knew what I wanted and would tell it.

The number found was small. Some had gone on visits to distant places and were inaccessible, others had known much years before, but had forgotten almost everything. In the first attempt only two old men were discovered. These two promised to come the following day. They came, gave some information, told one story, good as far as it went, but told too briefly. The story was of Esege Malan, or Father Bald Head (Father Bald Head is the highest heaven itself), and Ehé Tazar, Mother Earth. It is given farther on in this volume, with other myths.

Other men were found after those two, but none came who were at all satisfactory till Manshut appeared. He told three stories: Gesir Bogdo, Ashir Bogdo, and The Iron Hero.

When Manshut had finished these three stories he declared that he was forced to go home. I was greatly disappointed, for I was convinced that he knew more myths. Though he promised earnestly to come again and tell me all that he could remember I was doubtful about his return, for he was a restless man and seemed to dislike anything that required concentrated attention. He was a great lover of the pipe and smoked continually, drew whiffs between sentences, even between words. As talking seemed to interrupt his smoking, at least to a certain extent, I felt that I should not see him again until he needed more money for tobacco.

Early in the morning of July 30th a procession of long-bodied one-horse wagons crowded with men and women passed through the main street of Usturdi. These men and women were convicts from Russia, and a stalwart soldier, carrying a rifle, walked by the side of each wagon.

A halt was called on the first open field beyond the village. The dusty wagons were at once abandoned, and the crowd of convicts, falling into groups, began to build fires and prepare tea. Meanwhile the soldiers formed a circle around the entire party and stood on guard.

There were two hundred and seventy-four of these men and women. They were on the way to the Lena River, and farther north to the frozen Yakuts country. They had received sentence before the ukas abolishing exile to Siberia had been issued, and were specially interesting as being, perhaps, the last group of prisoners to be sent into that country, which has so long been used as a place for exile and punishment. Following the convicts came a small party of political prisoners, but they were allowed to stop at the post station for rest and refreshment.

The crowd sitting on the ground ate brown bread and drank tea with great relish. The soldiers conducting the prisoners did not fare better than the prisoners, in fact they did not fare as well, for I saw them receive merely large pieces of rye bread; at this halt they were not given tea. It seemed to me that by united action the convicts with naked hands might overpower the soldiers, for though the soldiers were alert fellows with much presence of mind, they were few in number.

The impression produced by these people was peculiar. They were all strong and sturdy, mainly of the peasant class. They were by no means downcast, grieved, or troubled. Forty of them were manacled, and even those men seemed in no way affected. One could not think while looking at these convicts that they were an oppressed and punished people. I was very anxious to talk with some of them, but it was not permitted to go inside the line of soldiers.

After a rest of an hour or so command was given to "raise camp," and five minutes later fires had been stamped out, kettles packed, and the long-bodied wagons were again moving forward over the dusty road.

I then went to visit Andrei Mihailovitch at his summer place. When about a mile and a half from his house I met him riding

THE BAGGAGE OF THE CONVICTS AND PROVISIONS FOR THEM ARE CARRIED IN THIS WAY. *Page* 10

THE BAGGAGE OF THE CONVICTS AND PROVISIONS FOR THEM ARE CARRIED IN THIS WAY.

CONVICTS PASSING THROUGH THE VILLAGE OF USTURDI. *Page* 39

CONVICTS PASSING THROUGH THE VILLAGE OF USTURDI.

over to Usturdi in a little one-horse trap. He turned back, however, and drove forward rapidly, so as to reach home and be ready to welcome me. I wished greatly to photograph the "Ongons" or gods supposed to protect his house and property. I was doubtful about getting his consent, but he gave it with many pleasant words. I first photographed those that guard the home and are always hanging high up in one corner of the house. Then I went out to photograph the Ongons that guard the property. They were in a box having a door made of four small panes of window glass; this box was fastened to the top of a corner post of the carriage shed. With much difficulty it was unscrewed, and brought down and placed where I could photograph the gods which it contained. Andrei Mihailovitch could not carry these gods into a house nor could he take them out of the box, for that would bring misfortune to the family.

Inside the large box were two small boxes of home manufacture. In these were crude pictures of the gods, tiny men and women in outline, also the skin of a ground squirrel, and one or two other dried skins of very small animals. When these were photographed Andrei Mihailovitch invited me to visit his winter home, saying that on the way we would pass his field Ongons.

We drove over level pastures to the hill eastward, climbed rather slowly to the top and, after we had passed a gate, descended gradually to the brow of the hill, or rather to a point of the slope, whence there is a fine view of the country beyond: several villages, a narrow, winding river, and, somewhat to the left, the winter residence of my host. On the brow of the hill is a collection of twenty-five or thirty pillars, or hewn posts, with four fiat sides. Across the top of each post a small board is so fastened that it projects on the east side like half a roof. Under this roof, in a square aperture in the post, is a small box with handle and sliding cover. The aperture also has a sliding cover which protects and secures the box inside.

Andrei Mihailovitch took the box out of his own post, opened it and showed me the gods which were on pieces of silk or cloth. Fastened on a narrow strip of blue silk were several little metal images. On two small pieces of cloth were tiny painted figures. I photographed the pillars, and then tied the images around a pillar and photographed them as best I could. After I had finished Andrei Mihailovitch took the pieces of cloth from the pillar, folded them carefully, put them back in the box, and, placing the box on the ground near a small pile of dry juniper, which our driver had collected for him, lighted the herb. When it was burning well he put his foot on it three separate times to make it smoke and quench it. In the box, purified by the smoke, Andrei Mihailovitch placed a little bag of tobacco, which he had taken from it, then he closed the box, put it back in the pillar, and covered the aperture. Everything was done with the greatest care and reverence.

Each Buriat, as soon as he marries and has a home, must set up in the field one of these posts or pillars and place images of his gods in it. The Shaman assists him. When a man dies the box containing his Ongons is removed from the pillar, carried to the forest and hung high up on a tree, and there it remains till it rots away. The person carrying the Ongon from the pillar to the forest must not look back; should he do so it would bring great misfortune to the family of the dead man.

Andrei Mihailovitch's winter house is built on the Russian plan with large brick stoves in the partitions between the rooms. In the yard, however, are two or three eight-cornered Mongol houses where I think the family lives during winter unless some "governor" happens along.

Toward evening I started for Usturdi. The road was through a hilly or rolling country. We passed several rye fields, but with one or two exceptions the grain was very poor. After crossing an elevated ridge we came down into an opening in a forest of small timber—just such a weird opening as Sienkiewicz describes in "The Deluge "—and later on we reached another and larger opening, a remarkably lonely looking place in the dusk of approaching night, and there we came upon a Russian. He was uncouth, sturdy, and somehow uncanny. His horse was feeding near a cart, and the man himself was occupied in smoking, and in stirring something which he was boiling in a kettle over a small fire. He did not notice us or answer my greeting.

ONE GROUP OF CONVICTS RESTING AND LUNCHING. *Page* 40

ONE GROUP OF CONVICTS RESTING AND LUNCHING.

BURIAT WEDDING. *Page 42*
The first three women in the foreground are the matchmakers

BURIAT WEDDING.

The first three women in the foreground are the matchmakers

It was late in the evening when we reached Usturdi.

A few days passed now, during which I made no effort to get story-tellers but spent my time in studying the language. On the 2d of August the Horse Sacrifice was to be made and I needed to bring my work into order and prepare for this remarkable ceremony.

The Buriat country is one of two places in Asia where the Horse Sacrifice may still be seen. This ceremonial has existed among the Mongols from time immemorial and is a wonderfully interesting survival of a primitive religion.

Andrei Mihailovitch had finished his mourning now and he came over to be present at the great festival. With all his politeness I felt sure that he was not anxious that I should see the death of the horses,—on the contrary, that he was determined I should not see it.

He said to me the evening preceding the sacrifice and then again the following morning: "I will leave about nine o'clock; that is very early. If you start an hour later you will have plenty time." The evening before, however, I had made sure that horses would be waiting at the post station near by, and within ten minutes after the departure of my host I was driving rapidly across the country.

When we had gone a mile or so my driver wished to get a drink of milk at a house by the wayside. He was terribly thirsty, he said. He was as dilatory as might be in getting the milk, then drank a whole gallon, I should think. After that we drove on very slowly. I urged and urged, but still he would not hurry the horses.

Later, when more than halfway to the Hill of Sacrifice he was again about to stop before a house. I would not permit a halt this time, and commanded him to hasten forward. When at last we reached the Hill I found that seven out of nine horses had been sacrificed already. Two fine, white mares remained. I had come very near losing the ceremony. The two, however, were among the best animals, and as every detail was observed in their case, there was a chance to see the sacrifice. The death of the two was sufficiently painful.

CHAPTER IV. THE HORSE SACRIFICE

THE Tailgan, or Horse Sacrifice, takes place on a hill called Uhér, about seven miles from Usturdi. On this hill fifteen large stone altars have been built. The sacrifice is made by the first and second division of the clan Ashekhabat. In the mythological past the founder of this clan lived at Baganteng, perhaps two miles distant from Uhér. This first man, or clan founder, had seven sons. He and those sons sacrificed on the hill Uhér to the Burkans (masters or gods) of the hill, and to those of the mountain opposite, of whom the chief is Malan Noyon.

Of the seven sons five went beyond the Baikal, and there their descendants make sacrifice to this day, but they make it to Baganteng, where their clan originated,— where the tomta ı of the founder is. Long ago they forgot Uhér and its divinities.

The order of the Tailgan, or Horse Sacrifice, is as follows: About seven o'clock on the morning of the ceremony the various families of the clan send a sufficient number of men to Uhér with vessels, tarasun, milk, tea, twigs, trees, and bushes—in fact, with everything needed at the sacrifice.

The two liquids drunk are tarasun and that which is called "the white." Generally this is milk, sweet or sour as the case may be, but milk with tea in it is given also, since some persons prefer it.

The men sent in advance with supplies and utensils stop about halfway on the road to Uhér and sprinkle milk and tarasun to the Burkans of the hill and the mountain, and to all the Burkans that there may be in existence, asking that they give first of all a good Tailgan, and then success and prosperity to those who make the sacrifice. The reality, the essence, of the milk and the tarasun, goes to the Burkans, immensely increased and incomparably better in quality. Thus a single drop may become a whole barrelful when it reaches the home of the deities, when it goes to the mountain and the hill, in both of which there are beautiful dwellings, invisible to man.

On arriving at the Hill of Sacrifice the men sent in advance prepare places for the kettles, hang them on tripods over wood ready to be ignited, and dispose the vessels and other things used in the ceremony.

Each family has its place on the hill and not far from some one of the fifteen stone altars. Small birch branches are thrust into the earth at these places. Later, near these branches libations are made; that is, a few drops of milk are cast into the air to the Burkans, and when tarasun is passed around some of that is also cast into the air.

When the crowd assembles fires are lighted. First the horse is purified by being led between the fires (there must be either three, nine, or twenty-seven fires), then it is led up toward the officiating persons, who sprinkle milk on its face, and on the hair halter, and cast some in the air to the gods. After that there is a libation of tarasun, then a prayer or petition is made to all the Burkans. The horse, I should state here, has been led to the right side of a small birch tree which has been brought from a near-by forest; the lower part of the trunk of the tree is on the ground, the upper part and branches rest on a crosspiece. The tree is called "The foot of the place of sacrifice."

The officiating men then turn, as they say, "with knee bending," first to the ninety western Burkans, then to the four eastern Tuget—Tuget means "complete." These are deities who have come down from the sky and are in the east, but their place is not known exactly. They turn next to the Undir Sagan Tengerin (the lofty clear heaven); sprinkling to each deity or group of deities as they name them. Then they implore Uligin Sagan Deda (the revered pure earth). Next in order is Buga Noyon Babai (bull prince father), then comes Budung Yihé Ibi (blessed mother mist), and Zayahung Yihé Zayasha (the creating great one, who has created). This is at present the hedgehog, and in Buriat religion he is the wisest of all the deities, though greatly supplanted by other gods. Next in order is Zayang Sagan Tengeri (creator, pure heaven). Then Esege Malan Babai (Grand-father Bald Head); next Ehé Ureng Ibi, and then Adaha Zayang (creator of cattle); and Uha Soldong (the golden Sorrel), which means the light of the sun, the dawn of the morning. The dawn of the morning is creator of horses. Then Hotogov Mailgan (Crooked Back), the goddess of the night heavens and creator of people.

All these divinities are addressed by name and in turn, addressed very much as saints are in a Christian litany. Those who are officiating appeal to the divinities, and the people follow them, either aloud or mentally. Each man prays usually for what he likes best, or most desires. When this prayer was ended long ropes were tied securely around the fetlocks of the horse, each rope was held by four men, then the eight men in front pulled the forelegs forward and somewhat apart, while the other eight pulled the hindlegs back and apart. The horse fell on its side, and then turned on its back. The sixteen men held the ropes firmly and the beast was utterly helpless. A man, his right arm bare to the shoulder, now came with a long sharp knife and with one blow made a deep incision just behind the breast bone. He thrust his hand into the opening, seized the heart of the horse, and wrenched it free from its connections. The poor beast tried to struggle, but could not, and died very quickly. With the other horse it was somewhat different. The man must have done his work unskilfully, or his hand was weaker, for after he had withdrawn his arm and finished, as he thought, the beast regained its position to the extent of being able to bite the ground in agony. The sight was distressing. Its teeth were bared in a ghastly grin; the eyes became green and blue, much like the color of certain beetles. A more striking expression of piercing and helpless agony I have never seen. It groaned once with a sound of unspeakable anguish, kept its mouth for a moment in the earth and then dropped over lifeless.

When the horses were dead men hurried to skin the bodies, quarter them, and remove the flesh from the bones. The bones were then placed on the fifteen stone altars where fires were not merely burning, but roaring. The flesh was put

PEOPLE ASSEMBLED FOR THE HORSE SACRIFICE. *Page 45*

PEOPLE ASSEMBLED FOR THE HORSE SACRIFICE

into the iron kettles under which fires at that time were blazing briskly.

There was much animation on all sides; men were sitting in groups along the entire hillslope, beginning at the highest altar and extending down to the fifteenth, near the foot of the eminence.

Meanwhile a good number of groups were seated near vessels of tarasun from which they drank freely. As the flesh was cut into small pieces the cooking did not require a long time. The flesh of the horses killed first was cooked before that of the last two was placed in the kettles.

Small bits of the cooked meat were thrown on to the blazing fire of the altars, where the bones were burning; soup from the kettles was also thrown from small cups on to the fire of the altars.

When all the meat was cooked and the flesh of the nine horses was ready the whole company of people stood in groups before the fifteen altars. At times they moved toward the altars, at times they receded, throwing small quantities of soup and little bits of meat on the fires, as they uttered the following invocation to the deities already mentioned:

"We pray that we may receive from you a blessing. From among fat cattle we have chosen out meat for you. We have made strong tarasun for you. Let our ulus (villages) be one verst longer. Create cattle in our enclosures; under our blankets create a son; send down rain from high heaven to us; cause much grass to grow; create so much grain that sickle cannot raise it, and so much grass that scythe cannot cut it. Let no wolves out unless wolves that are toothless; and no stones unless stones without sharp corners or edges. Hover above our foreheads. Hover behind our heads. Look on us without anger. Help those of us who forget what we know. Rouse those of us who are sleeping (in spirit). In a harsh year (a year of trouble) be Compassion. In a difficult year (a year of want) be Kindness (in sense of help). Black spirits lead farther away from us; bright spirits lead hither, nearer; gray spirits lead farther away from us. Burkans lead hither to us. Green grass give in the mouths (of cattle). Let me walk over the first snow. If I am timid, be my courage. If I am ashamed, be a proper face to me. Above be as a coverlid, below be as a felt bed to me."

When the people stood before the fifteen stone altars and uttered their petitions the ceremony seemed very solemn and had a real character of worship. The invocation which I have given is repeated by all, then each adds what seems good to him. The prayer over, the company seated themselves by families, ate of the horse flesh, and drank tarasun till the end came.

During the throwing of the meat on to the altars vultures, of which there were many, flew back and forth over the hill and at times swooped down very near to us. During one of these times I took a piece of meat from Vassya and threw it toward a vulture. The bird caught it with the utmost dexterity, and darted away.

Vassya then threw a piece to another vulture which seized it in like manner. They hit a boy's cup, and caught the meat from it. I asked Vassya afterward if the people did not look on these birds as perhaps divine. He said not in the full sense, but that vultures were represented in some narratives as rushing in front of the Burkans when they were passing from one place to another, and in that way they might be supposed to indicate that the masters of the opposite mountain were present, or on the hill where we were standing.

When the people had finished eating and drinking, boys pulled up and threw on the fire the twigs, or little branches which had been planted by the designated place of each family. This indicated that the sacrifice was ended. Any soup or meat left is taken home. If not all used it is carefully burned, for none of it must be eaten by cats or dogs; that would be desecration and misfortune would follow in its wake.

The Horse Sacrifice is a ceremony of immense interest, a remarkable relic of religious and social antiquity, the value of which we can hardly overestimate. A number of things become clear after one has looked on this sacrifice carefully. The first of these beyond doubt is this: that there is and must be a correspondence between a society and the faith professed by it—a sufficient harmony between the religion and the people.

As I walked up and down among those Buriats, talking with some and observing others, I saw that they enjoyed that sacrifice heartily. For men in their position there was reason for enjoyment;

STONE ALTARS ON THE HILL OF SACRIFICE. Page 45

STONE ALTARS ON THE HILL OF SACRIFICE.

there was cause to be satisfied during that day in every case. They were seated on a pleasant hill possessed and inhabited by Burkans, or divinities, who had descended from the sky and occupied in the hill a magnificent dwelling. In fact they were sitting on the great roof of a divine house, and were feasting delightfully, in company with friends and relatives.

Out in front of them and near by were mountains in which lived other Burkans. Opposite dwelt, in homes of indescribable beauty and wealth, Burkans, who were kindly and liberal to persons who remembered them. They had power to give every good thing in abundance.

Feasting there on that roof the Buriats ate, drank, and made merry with profit. They sent a share of the flesh and soup from their horses to the gods, who received that flesh and broth multiplied enormously. Each drop of broth when it reached the gods' mansions sufficed a hundred persons, each bit of flesh was increased in like manner, and so with tarasun, a few drops of which would cheer thousands.

The gods ate and drank of these multiplied offerings, while they, the faithful worshipers, sent up requests and prayers to gain every profit and good for which their hearts hoped. The feasting worshipers then filled their stomachs with unmultiplied food, which they had in abundance.

There were pleasure, sociability, eating and drinking with gods, those world forces who are able to grant prayers and listen to the petitions of all men who please them.

The social part is very instructive, showing clearly in this Buriat survival a strong and prominent trait of primitive religion: the intimate relation of gods and men, the nearness of the gods and their friendliness. Most interesting of all is that strange philosophy, at least strange for us, by which gods are pleased and profited by a small material outlay on the part of mankind.

While a society and its religion correspond the society is greatly attached to the religion, and if a society is simple and well-nigh stationary, as pastoral societies are, if environment will permit it, the society and its religion may live on in harmony for ages. Religion once it is established changes little comparatively, and not in its essence. Its forms and ceremonies are sacred. Its statements are myths taken literally. To modify, change, or abolish forms, ceremonies, or statements of a religion is to destroy that religion; for the spirit of religion is not what men have in view generally, but forms, its outward seeming, its mythology, its connections with popular life, with the customs and history of the people professing it. A pastoral life is almost immovable, especially in a country where grass is abundant and agriculture unknown, or if known little cared for. Were it not for the influence of Russia and China the Buriats might live on for ages without changing their religion or customs.

Of course nothing in the world is or may be immovable. An inner motive or an outward shock is sure in time to stir every object or being in existence. No planet in space, though immensely remote from all others, and moving by itself in a loneliness which is appalling, is secure from collision. No man or group of men, tribe, nation, republic, or empire has ever been or ever will be left to his, their, or its own will save for a comparatively short period. The groups of men under various designations, from small primitive societies to great republics or empires, have their will for a season. This is the time during which the character of a group is made manifest, and during which it conquers. This character is always special to each. A group comes in collision inevitably with other groups which also are special. The result is the destruction or absorption of some groups, the modification and enlargement of others. The whole course of history may be represented as an endless succession of these collisions.

With reference to preserving their religion the position of the western Buriats was specially favorable, and continues to be so. Their fellow tribemen, who live east of Lake Baikal, and touch on the great world of Buddhism, became Buddhists. The western Buriats are secluded considerably, and little troubled by neighbors. They prefer their own primitive religion thus far. The Russians have no objection to offer, and would rather that they retain Shamanism than become Buddhists. If they have no wish to become Christian they may remain Pagan.

For a people in primitive conditions to accept a new religion which condemns the chief part of their life and the main customs

I. HORSE SACRIFICE. *Page 45*

I. HORSE SACRIFICE.

II. Horse Sacrifice.   *Page 46*

II. HORSE SACRIFICE.

of their country is a great step indeed. To introduce Christianity would involve a complete revolution among Buriats. For Mongols the transition from their Shamanism to Buddhism after the latter has passed through Thibet is less difficult. The western Buriats are satisfied with Shamanism. If there is any propaganda among them, Buddhistic or Christian, it is very slight, and touches only an odd individual.

After the sacrifice came wrestling at the southeastern or valley foot of the hill. This is a very popular amusement among the Buriats. There is always wrestling after the Horse Sacrifice and after the making of Shamans.

The whole company deserted the hill-top. Some went to the place of wrestling, others remained on the brow of the eminence, not far from where the horses were sacrificed.

In wrestling there are two parts: the first is the manœuvring for advantage in the hold; this requires time, perhaps fifteen or twenty minutes are occupied before the opponents grapple and close in the conflict. Very often the wrestling itself does not last as long as the preliminary manœuvring for advantage.

After the Tailgan I decided to make a trip northeastward and northward through the Buriat country. I wished above all to visit Olkhon, the "sacred" island of Lake Baikal. On this island live perhaps seven hundred people, who are more primitive than other Buriats. I was anxious to see these islanders and get their folk-tales, if possible.

I laid in all the provisions that I could find either in Usturdi or at the next post station, and made arrangements for Vassya and Lazareff, the Cross-eyed, to go with me and assist in every way. Andrei Mihailovitch gave them a light, convenient carriage, and I was to furnish provisions and pay their traveling expenses. One or the other was to translate for me from Mongol into Russian. I always preferred Vassya, for he was far more intelligent, and acted more willingly, as he was himself interested in the mythology of his people. He was an excellent translator as well, having an equal command of both Buriat and Russian.

I do not think that I have ever found a better case of what development means than that presented by those three Buriats,—Vassya, his father, and Lazareff. Vassya during six years at the Irkutsk gymnasium had not only learned what is taught in the regular course there, but he had acquired a real love for good reading. He knew what science means, and found pleasure in mental development. Vassya's father was a man who believed that knowledge is power, but simply power to win wealth, to make money, acquire land, herds, and cattle—and importance. This was the power which he valued. Hence he was what is usually called practical.

Lazareff would esteem that knowledge which would make three blades of grass grow where two grew before, if they would come by magic, intrigue, or some other man's labor, given because he was outwitted.

Mutual benefit was looked for in the journey. I hoped that the two men would help me in many ways. They spoke Russian fluently, so I could talk with every Buriat. They were well known in most places, and with them the journey would be successful in some degree. They were glad to go, moreover, for I paid their expenses. The weather was fine, the country as a whole very interesting, and parts of it beautiful. They also, as I learned afterward, had errands to perform and business to transact for Vassya's father.

III. Horse Sacrifice. *Page 46*

III. HORSE SACRIFICE.

IV. Horse Sacrifice. *Page 46*

IV. HORSE SACRIFICE.

Footnotes

44:1 See ceremonies after the birth of a child, page 96.

CHAPTER V. JOURNEY TO THE ISLAND OF OLKHON

AFTER annoying delays the day for starting on the journey came at last (August 6); but only at one o'clock were we ready for the road. A few moments before leaving I witnessed an interesting ceremony. Eight men with Vassya seated themselves in a circle on the ground, then one of the eight rose and with a glass of vodka in his extended hand implored the gods, as he sprinkled the vodka on the ground, to grant Vassya a prosperous journey.

From Usturdi I drove directly to Lazareff's house, whence we were to set out on the journey together. The two men had proposed to start alone at two o'clock, but I preferred to have them with me, if possible.

On arrival I found that Lazareff was "not quite ready"; he needed an hour at least, and he and Vassya wished to stop a short time at a near-by village where there was a wedding in progress,—a friend of theirs was celebrating a part of his marriage. Lazareff promised faithfully to overtake me on the road, or at Olzoni, the next station.

I drove on, and at the first village, which was a short distance from the highway, I saw a large assembly of people. The inhabitants had no work on that day, nothing to think of but the marriage. The young people were dancing most vigorously; the old men and women were sitting around in groups, laughing and talking, taking refreshments, solid and fluid.

That afternoon in the first half of August was delightful, sunny and bright, but not too warm. The road was excellent, being the highway between the capital of eastern Siberia, Irkutsk, and Yakutsk, which has been for so many years the city of exile. Along the road on the left there are many good winter houses.

The places chosen for these buildings are in most cases well sheltered by high hills from winds of the north and northwest.

There is nothing in which Russian influence on the Buriats is shown more emphatically than in the matter of winter homes. Before Russian times the Buriat house was always an eight-sided log structure, with a hole in the middle of its earth-covered roof to let smoke out. A fire of sticks was made on the ground under this smoke-hole. How cold those places were in such a climate we can imagine very easily. The winter house now, with its great stove made of brick, is in use among the better class, and often it has double windows.

Though there were many dwellings along the way, people were living elsewhere for the summer months. There was perfect quiet, no man or woman was to be seen, no horses or cattle were grazing in the pastures.

Twenty-four hours before there had been rain, hence the road was clean, with no trace of dust on it. Rarely have I traveled with such pleasure as on that clear sunny day in August. There was no racing of horses this time, the carriage moved on at an easy, good pace, very comfortably. Only once did we meet an equipage. It seemed as though the whole world was at home sleeping.

About seven o'clock we rolled into Olzoni, a pleasant-looking village in a narrow valley. Along the middle of the village runs the single street, which is also the highway.

On the left hand, at the entrance to the village and just out-side the first buildings, is an ostrog, or palisaded prison enclosure, which has a suggestive and sinister look, mainly because we know why it is there and what it is used for. It was the first of the kind I had ever seen.

At the other end of Olzoni the valley turns to the right quite abruptly, and the street seems to end in a hill. On this hill is a small wooden church, beyond which there are no houses. The church at one end, the prison at the other; narrow fields at the right as we enter, and wooded hills beyond them. On the left green fields and a rolling country, perhaps fifty feet above the highway.

At Olzoni there is an excellent post station. Tea was in order,

V. Horse Sacrifice.   *Page 46*

V. HORSE SACRIFICE.

VI. HORSE SACRIFICE. *Page 46*

VI. HORSE SACRIFICE.

and then preparations were made for a supper, which came about two hours later. On the street there was considerable activity. I met two children who were playing horse, and I discovered that the horse was Timofei and the driver Andrei. I had to remonstrate with Andrei for using his whip too freely, though Timofei explained that he was whipped because he was a horse and did not want to work. A man sitting on an ox and going for water with his cart and barrel furnished a good picture of domestic life. The ox was well trained and walked off briskly.

To add to my stock of provisions, and to find out something of possible interest regarding the inhabitants of the village, I went into the principal shop, where I made the acquaintance of the merchant Pan Tembovski, a Pole, who told me very interesting things touching the Buriats. He was exiled many years ago for political reasons; after serving out his sentence he went back to Russia, but returned soon, because "there is more money and life in Siberia." To me it seemed that all the powers of a financier would be needed to make even a meagre living in Olzoni.

At ten o'clock Lazareff and Vassya made their appearance. They had not left the wedding till six in the evening. There had been an immense consumption of food and drink, and the merry-making, they assured me, "was great."

Fresh horses were brought, and I set out at eleven o'clock. Olzoni is a place of some interest, and for a post station really very pleasant. When returning from the island I remained four days in the village.

About three o'clock in the morning I arrived at Baiandai (pronounced Buy-and-die), the next station, but saw nothing of that broad, straggling village with which later on I became quite familiar. There was no delay for horses, and soon the carriage was moving toward the, station, Hogotskaya, where I arrived at five o'clock in the morning, and slept on a hard bed till seven. The night ride had been very pleasant, for the weather was perfect. Lazareff and Vassya came an hour later, in time for a short sleep.

About nine o'clock we set out for a visit to the brothers Alexandroff, who are numbered among the wealthiest and most influential of the Buriats; their estate is about five miles from Hogotskaya. It was warmer that morning than the day before— it was hot, in fact.

The country about Hogotskaya is a fine rolling region of good grass-land and black soil of sufficient depth. Hay and grain are abundant, with culture. Between ten and eleven o'clock we were at the Alexandroffs'. The three brothers live in one neighborhood; their houses are near one another, and form a whole town, if considered together.

As these brothers are good friends of Andrei Mihailoff, they received us very cordially. We were conducted to a pleasant sitting-room fitted up in Russian fashion, and while we were conversing there with one brother another set servants to work in the kitchen and elsewhere. In half an hour they had ready in the dining-room a zakuska, or "bite," the collection of preliminary tidbits which, in all parts of Russia, precedes each considerable meal, and are taken to rouse appetite and also to nourish. In great houses these "bites" are elaborate and enticing.

Invited to the dining-room we found there two tables; on one of these stood bottles containing vodka and two kinds of wine, sherry and claret. On the other were things to be eaten,—boiled eggs, brown bread, smoked fish, pickled herrings, sardines, cheese, fish, eggs, and other rich "appetite rousers."

The zakuska is always taken standing. The first thing is a small glass of vodka, kummel, or some other liquid of similar quality, "to increase appetite and induce cheerfulness." Then comes the eating, which bears somewhat the relation to dinner that a skirmish does to a murderous battle.

After the zakuska, as our mid-day meal was not ready yet, we went again to the sitting-room and talked for a time.

We spoke of the country, the Buriat methods of managing land, of rearing cattle and horses, of moving from one place to another in summer, and back to the first one in winter.

While the brothers were explaining these customs to me carefully a servant declared that the "guest meal" was ready and waiting. There were two tables, at one of these, which was square, sat the master of the house, with my wife, Vassya, and me; at the second table was his brother, with Lazareff and persons of the family,—a dozen at least in the company.

One cause of the delay in the dinner was that a lamb had been slaughtered and cooked for our nourishment. The great dish of honor at our table was the boiled head of that lamb, with the wool on. There was also a species of soup made of blood and kidneys, which seemed much like diluted blood pudding. It was relished by the Buriats, but strive as I might I could only make a very scant trial of its qualities. There was an abundance of other food, however, hence I could let these Mongol dainties pass.

The Alexandroffs are the most Russianized of Buriats in their style of living, and manners; though they, too, live a double life in some measure. They are of the rich and small class which builds at least three houses. The winter house is like that in use throughout Russia; it has brick stoves and chimneys. The old-fashioned Buriat house is modelled on a tent. In summer these houses are cool and agreeable, but in winter it is impossible, in a cold country, to heat them sufficiently for modern comfort. When well improved they are delightful from May to October. Should a chilly hour happen at any time, or a cool evening come at the beginning or at the end of the season, a fire is made quickly, and people sit around it to enjoy the warmth and to talk. To rouse conviviality tarasun is drunk; it is brought in a jug holding one or two gallons. This jug, which always has a wooden cup in it, is moved around the circle, and when emptied of liquor is filled again straightway.

All Buriats, without any exception, prefer the style of house used by their forefathers, and are attached to it greatly. Pagan Buriats must have this house, if they are to be married according to the rites of their people, since the last act in the ceremony of marriage is performed at the central quadrangle of bare earth, where the fire is made, when the new wife takes her place at the milk barrel which stands there, and becomes house mistress. Her special office is to make the tarasun, always distilled at this fireplace. Beside its good qualities, the old house is strong through its hold on the ancient religion, the needs of the people, and their habits and customs.

The Alexandroff dinner, as to food, was peculiar only by the sudden slaughter of the lamb, to show honor to strangers, and the special preparation of its head for the table. Otherwise the dinner might have been given by a Russian. The flesh of the poor little victim was cooked in the ordinary fashion, by boiling.

When the meal was ended the masculine part of the company retired to the summer house, and sat smoking and conversing for an hour or so.

This summer house was very well built. The floor was higher than usual above the bare earth in the center, and thus afforded a more comfortable seat for the company; chairs also were in use, so that whoso preferred one might sit on one. The smoke-escape was better constructed,—wider at the roof than in other houses.

The Alexandroffs' summer and winter establishments are different from any among Buriats in this that they are adjoining; only a road lies between the two places. The houses stand almost opposite each other and not more than half a mile apart. The difference between the two places is remarkable, however. The summer land is level or slightly rolling, and is exposed at every point of the compass, open to winds from north, south, east, and west, so that whenever the air moves men and animals feel it. On the right of the road, where the winter place lies, all is changed. The land slopes away toward the east and the south; on the north is a large and dense forest, which wards off the north wind effectively.

Some distance from the highway there are well-watered meadows and splendid pastures. A great deal of hay is produced on this land; I counted fourteen immense ricks in one part of the meadow. The wealth of the Alexandroffs comes chiefly from the breeding of cattle and horses, and from lending money at a high rate of interest.

Since we had planned to continue our journey that same day we soon bade good-bye to our host, who strove to persuade us to remain at his house till the morrow in every case.

An easy life is that of those three brothers. Every year they sell many horses and cattle. Whether the price falls or rises they have a good income. Thus far they are free of political problems. They have had their own way under Russia up to this time. At present, however, they fear that their land supply is about to be lessened.

At Hogotskaya there is a "narodni dom," or people's house, in which travelers may find a room and a samovar. That room we had made our headquarters. Near this narodni dom is the home of the chief of the district. We returned at four o'clock, sent for post horses, drank tea, and were soon ready to start for the island. In the morning, before going to the Alexandroffs', I had called on the district chief, and now he came to wish me a prosperous journey. Though I did not know it at that time, he had sent forward word to officials to help me in every way needed. I thanked him heartily for his kind wishes, and promised to explain my success, if I had any, and tell him all my adventures when I came back from Olkhon and Lake Baikal.

I was off at exactly five o'clock, Vassya and Lazareff a few minutes later. Each carriage was drawn by three horses. We intended to travel all night. The weather was perfect, the road dry and in fairly good condition. I thought we might reach the third station about daybreak, or at least very early in the morning.

After leaving Hogotskaya, which was our last station on the Yakuts road, we passed a mile of level road, and then traveled over land gently rising till we came to the base of a ridge. This ridge was perhaps eight hundred feet high where the road lay, and much higher on either side. On reaching the highest point of the road it was seen that the ridge, which was wooded for the greater part, turned more and more from the highway till its direction was at a right angle, then it turned backward gradually and formed a great ellipse. Into the picturesque valley formed by this elliptical ridge we now descended, and through it, and a valley adjoining, we traveled till midnight.

The whole region around was either woodland or meadow. People were cutting hay and making stacks as we passed along through it that evening. Places like this are very frequent in Siberia. Warded well against winds and surrounded in great part with dense forests, they are sheltered marvelously from cold, and cattle are driven to them for the winter.

At nine o'clock we reached the first station; at midnight we arrived at the second, where, after some waiting, a samovar was set up, and we ate a bountiful lunch which I had brought with me. The station furnished hot water for the tea and boiled eggs; I had sweet bread, brown bread, and ham of good quality ready cooked.

Roughing it on the road is delightful at times, and at times very dreary. Good health, good weather, wholesome food, and pleasant people make traveling a holiday, and joyous. Bad weather, vile food, hostile people, take away the best charm even from scenery, since they weaken power and mental vision in the traveler.

If one is working for a purpose, however, all hardships grow easy, they become even pleasant if devotion be strong enough in the mind of the worker.

Of all hardships in traveling, and there are many, the greatest and most bitter, in fact the only serious ones are those caused by people. The deceit, opposition, and active harmfulness of mankind create the only troubles worth mentioning as we move on examining the crust of this earth ball, striving to discover what is on it, and under it, and above it. If men were as good as they are evil,—and they are evil through ignorance and weakness,—it would be easier and much pleasanter to travel than it now is. It would also be easier to do those good deeds of which each man is capable. I thought thus as I supped at that station, which was poor and not very clean, but the people in it were obliging and courteous.

When supper was eaten three horses were attached to my carriage, but Vassya and Lazareff had to wait for horses which were out in the pasture. Men had gone to search for them, hence my companions might have to remain long at the station or only some minutes. I resolved to set out at once, promising to wait at Kosaya.

It was one o'clock when I started. No moon was visible; the night was one of stars only, the most impressive of all nights, and that means the most impressive sight possible to man during earthly existence.

The majestic and marvelous dark night of stars, that face of infinity looking down at us in silence, affects every serious man deeply by its presence. In days past that presence, though the same in its features as to-day, was not the same in meaning. It was looked on variously by different people in different ages. To all men the sky seemed in old times dome-shaped and solid, the greatest single thing visible to any one. By some it was revered as a deity, and is so revered even to the present; by others it was esteemed to be a dwelling-place. Whether a deity or a dwelling-place, it was closely connected with the earth, to which it was in great part subservient. I was thinking of this as I looked on that beautiful night from the swiftly moving carriage, when it occurred to me on a sudden that if I were to credit my own eyesight I should believe myself to be just in the center of all things. The horizon in front, behind, and on both sides was equidistant; the highest point in the sky was directly above me; I held the center, apparently. Eye-sight, the first simple witness, uncorrected by examination and afterthought, formed the basis of current belief and philosophy touching everything in existence till Copernican teaching destroyed it.

How self-satisfied were men in the old time, how contented and happy. They believed that this earth was the center of the universe, that it was fixed and immovable, that the sun went around it, that all things existent came and vanished because of it. The sun rose and set just to serve man.

All that belief and philosophy has gone from us. That which seemed to be the great fact was found non-existent and illusive, that which *is* has proved so stupendous that no one is able to grasp it. Man's home in the sky, the heavenly house just above, has been rent from him. His yearning remains, or at least in most cases, and he is like the poet who never had a home, but who sang of home, that sweet home, as no man ever sang of it before him or afterward.

As the carriage rolled on I recalled how a man in London, three months earlier, had spoken to me very earnestly as follows: "This earth is no longer the center of the universe. People now do not think that in the sky straight above them is a heavenly city, where they will live through endless ages in happiness. Science, which is encroaching on ancient beliefs, and destroying old systems, is taking away every basis of earnest conviction, and so far has given nothing in the sense of assuring a future existence, by showing where or how that existence could be realized. My father died," continued my acquaintance, "with the firmest conviction that he would live soul and body hereafter. I believe in nothing. I should be glad to believe, but I cannot. Some scientists tell me that at death I shall die altogether, that my conscious I, which is talking this moment, will vanish forever. Others tell me that if for individuals there be a hereafter, no man can prove it. The majority of men hope and wish for a life in the future, hope and wish for that which the old beliefs promised. I should like wonderfully to have such a belief, but how am I to get it? Who can help me? This is for me the great question."

The horses had passed half the road, perhaps, when I dropped asleep while pondering over the words of my London friend. I woke soon, for we had come to rough places and the harsh jolting roused me. After that we were in an open region. The whole sky was visible, and the carriage moved smoothly. Again I fell to thinking, and my friend's words came back to me:

"Can Science find eternal life possible in the same human being? Science finds eternal life everywhere, but not in the same form.

"To be permanent and undying a material body must either not change, or must receive the equivalent exactly of that which goes from it, and, besides, it must retain all its life vigor. There must be no loss to it in exchanging.

"Given the immortal body, where is its home to be? The heaven is gone, that solid region, that firmament, as men once considered it. There is nothing now overhead save expanse. Where shall we look for the home of undying individual existence? Not on this earth, since on earth there is no place for an endless and happy hereafter. Is there in infinite space out beyond us a place where immortal existence might have a fit dwelling? If there is, how can we find it? From the various groups of men who ponder over the mystery of existence three may be chosen to illustrate the problem before us, and how men relate themselves to it.

"The first group is made up of persons who declare that there is no spirit whatever save what is inseparable from and connected with matter, and which inheres in it. There is in this way a spirit in everything various in each case; from that in the atom, which is, perhaps, the most restricted, to that in man, which on earth is the most comprehensive and intricate.

"Whenever an organism, such as man, comes to dissolution, or death, the spirit which inheres in it must vanish; and when that organism is resolved finally into elements or atoms, there is simply a myriad of atomic spirits, but no spirit of a man to consider, because there is no man in existence, and so with all other living creatures and organized existences.

"There is nothing immortal save the atom in any place. From atoms all things are aggregated, and from atomic spirit is built up all the mind in the universe. Since the organisms are transient, the spirit is transient.

"For thinkers of this group the question just raised has no interest whatever.

"The second group is formed of all Christian believers, and also of those who, though they may not be Christians, believe in a spirit, or soul, as distinct from each body. For this group the question cannot be without interest.

"The first and the second group have no common ground of agreement.

"The third group ascribes enormous, nay, unbounded, importance to the atom, but only in conjunction with that all-pervading substance which men for the moment call ether, but which in reality is spirit.

"What is the atom, and what is ether? The atom is deathless; no one can seize it, no one can injure it, fire cannot burn it. In the raging heat of the sun or on Sirius the dog-star, in the maximum of cold where life would cease suddenly, in a dew-drop, in a tempest, in a blizzard, or in Niagara the atom is there. Invincible, eternal, equally contented in the highest heaven and the pit of the inferno, infinitely obedient; inconceivably flexible it enters into beauty as readily as into the vilest deformity. Equally at home in the diamond and the dung-heap, the atom is everywhere present and constitutes all things material. There is no existence possible without it.

"What may we say of the ether? The atom is everywhere, but the atom is always embraced by the ether, always upheld and kept down by it. Wherever the atom, which constitutes all things, has an office, and it has one in every place, the ether is present.

"In the scheme of the first set of thinkers among the three to which I have referred, the atom alone is important; in fact, there is nothing to begin with, the atom which is so small that no human eye can behold it is the first unit, the starting-point. By an infinite accretion of atoms effected through impulse or love which atoms have for one another, all the forms in the universe are constituted gradually; all the beauty and intellect in existence are thus evolved; all the millions of suns, stars, and other heavenly bodies, as well as the various kinds of living creatures, man, and everything that has life on our planet.

"By this scheme all physical forms and all degrees of mentality come from the association of atoms, which, increasing in certain lines, always growing in number, cause with each increase a higher mentality and a more varied physical development.

"The statement of the third group is this substantially: When an accretion of atoms has happened, an inflow or pressure of ether takes place with this growth, simultaneously, and at every phase of it. For instance, if two atoms unite, a mind to grasp this situation is needed; the ether is present, and the mind is immediately. The association of atoms increases to a hundred for example, the association is vastly more complex with that number than it was with two atoms. The great point being that from an aggregation of atomic mind it is quite possible to reach a cosmic mind, or one even that embraces a solar system, and finally the universe.

"With change effected by new atomic accretions there was always an inflowing of ether and an increase of mentality sufficient to dominate the situation. If there was not, the new association failed and went to pieces, fell back into atoms, to begin anew and continue till success came at that or another time.

"The impulse to accretion is indestructible in the atom, and is active unceasingly. The ether is everywhere present, going through each accretion, embracing and testing it. The ether finds every joint, seam, or line of union between atoms, inserts itself and breaks up the union, unless it be suitable and strong enough. If it be suitable, the ether stays with it, gives the mentality needed in the new combination while it is fit to continue. When not fit, its mentality withdraws and it perishes, that is, drops apart and reverts to its atoms. In this way from the beginning of ages, from the time when atoms began first to seek one another, that is, as soon as atoms were divided from ether, from the time that one became two and the Son was sent forth from the bosom or personality of the Father, creation began and continues to the present, and will continue while existence endures, or, in other words, while there is force in the universe, or still in other words, while there are atoms and ether in existence.

"We have now this point. From the time of the first dissolution of atomic aggregation to this moment there is a continuous going out and returning of ether, each return bringing with it a life history beginning with the first failure of two atoms to associate beyond a certain period, and ending with the latest dissolution of some structure in the universe. Each one of these returns has its memory, and each one of them is deathless.

Each temporary aggregation reverts to its atoms, which begin new adventures, while the ether returns to the source whence it started.

"According to the thought inherent in the scheme of this third group of thinkers there was a period when ether and atoms were indifferentiated, merged in one. At the end of a period, beyond calculation in length, a period which might be called an eternity without a beginning, one became two, atoms and ether became segregated and each was indestructible for opposite reasons. The atom because it stands alone, the ether because it is infinitely yielding, no power can separate it, and it pervades all things no matter how closely their particles are compacted. Out of atoms all forms may be created. *Ether* knows everything, because it is in all places, and is never separated or interrupted. The *Great Ether* knows all that the small parts experience, but the small parts know only by observation, reasoning, and inference anything of the Great Ether.

"We have thus two forms of immortality at present, existent in all places, the ether and the atom. The aggregation of atoms is perishable, and an individual made up of atoms and ether would be immortal and safe only in a place secure from invasion, safe from every external shock and collision, and from chemical action which would destroy the adhesive force of its atoms. Is there such a safe dwelling, and where is it?"

The reasoning of my friend which I give here was in my mind, unexpressed, as I dropped asleep thinking: Is there a real heaven in existence instead of that one up there which is lost to us? I had been looking straight into the wonderful night sky, my mind filled with that awful reality before me; my eyes closed now, and I was dreaming,

I seemed still to see everything around me, and all grew in size, gradually; next I saw nothing, and rested, I know not how long, and then again I was dreaming. I opened my eyes, as I thought, and found myself standing near a telescope enormous in size and far better than any I had ever used or seen thus far. "Will you look in?" asked a person, as I stood there in wonder. "If you look you will see the great center of all things, the place of repose amidst all the action in existence. You will see clearly through this telescope the storm center of the universe, where there is a perfect balance of forces, and where there is peace kept by infinite power and knowledge. There is no decay there, and there will never be. It is the great result of all the toil, suffering, death, and anguish in every other place, and only beings who are perfect can ever reach it."

"But will the balance not be lost?" I asked. "Will not trouble come to it, as to all other places?"

"As long as force and matter last this region which I show you will be as calm and happy as it now is." He moved to go before me, but that moment something happened; I was pushed and jolted, my driver shouted and whipped his horses, and I woke and asked:

"Where are we, what 's the matter?"

"Kosaya Steppe!" (Crooked Prairie) called out the driver.

And he rushed into the village, Crooked Prairie, made half a turn in front of a church, so as to face a large gate before which he stopped, slipped down from his seat, rang a bell, and then waited. The gate was opened after some minutes and we drove into the yard of the "People's House." The woman, who had charge of the building and all that pertained to it, appeared at a porch, and the gate-keeper came out and took from the carriage some things for my use.

The house, which was of good size, had apparently not been occupied much in recent days. The windows had not been opened, the air was close and unpleasant in odor. The first thing was to open the windows, and then, pure air secured, to have breakfast made ready.

A boiling samovar was brought about half an hour later. In Russia tea is the greatest, the best drink of the country. So far as my experience goes Russian tea is the most refreshing drink in the world and when there are suhari (rusks) to go with it food and drink are at hand for a good meal in the morning.

After drinking tea I slept till seven, that is one hour, then I went to the courtyard and there in the middle of the open space was a carriage and in it Vassya and Lazareff sleeping soundly. I had engaged my horses for half past seven, hoping thus to have them in season. A little before eight the two men woke, and the horses were brought in. Vassya wished to remain two or three hours at Crooked Prairie, so I went on to Elantsin, the next station, where I arrived only at two o'clock after some delay on the road and slow traveling.

At Elantsin I was informed that it would be impossible to get horses that day; I must wait till the morrow in every case. No help for it. This station, which is about a verst from the town, is one of the best on the road. It is a large building with fairly clean rooms and an immense kitchen. Just across the road is a small house, and near by a small church with dome and bell tower. Behind the church is a high mountain. The place reminded us of Ragats, Switzerland.

The station master, a young married man, had provisions in plenty, and treated us well. Toward evening Vassya appeared and we had the promise of horses for an early hour on the morrow. But in spite of every exertion it was almost noon when we started. The road was rough and dusty. As one approaches the lake there are low, unwooded hills with stony summits that look in places as if altars had been set up, or as though covered with the ruins of ancient fortresses.

When within a few versts of the Kutul Vassya and Lazareff turned off to go to a village where a man lived to whom, as they said, Andrei Mihailovitch had sent a letter asking him for assistance in our work. I never saw the man, however, and later I discovered that the letter was about private business, and had nothing whatever to do with my work.

We reached Kutul in the evening. This station is well kept and spacious. There is a large room in it where the Buriats hold their public meetings and discuss questions touching interests in the district. The mistress of the house, a Russian, was not at home, having gone to a town a hundred versts away to send a telegram to her husband, who was in the army.

The journey from Kutul to Olkhon, though a short one, required considerable exertion and patience. To all appearances there was much difficulty in obtaining horses. There was delay for other reasons also. When I was in the greatest doubt as to what to do the chief of the district arrived at the station, to be present at a Buriat meeting, and he gave me willing assistance; without his aid I should have had a good deal of trouble. He advised me to hire an additional man, one who knew the Olkhon people, and also informed me that the road to the lake was so rough as to necessitate leaving my carriage at Kutul and taking wagons.

The master of post horses at Kutul is a stripling named Muravieff. This man, half Russian, half Buriat, is tremendously bent on making money, and in his dealings is quite as crooked as the world-renowned ram's horn. His father was a full-blooded Buriat. When Count Muravieff Amoorski was

CONVICT PRISON AT A POST STATION. *Page* 54
What looks in this photograph to be a board fence is a square enclosure
at least twelve feet high

CONVICT PRISON AT A POST STATION.

What looks in this photograph to be a board fence is a square enclosure at least twelve feet high

BURIAT WOMEN IN FULL DRESS. *Page* 67

BURIAT WOMEN IN FULL DRESS.

governor of Eastern Siberia he took a fancy to this Buriat. Through his influence the young man became a Christian, and at baptism received the name Muravieff; in this way bettering his condition in a worldly sense. Some time after that a Russian girl, deceived by a man, who in due time deserted her, was alone, without a friend or money, and not far from childbirth; the Buriat Muravieff married her; the child, which was a son, he adopted. Later she had a son by Muravieff; this is the half-Buriat stripling whom I have mentioned as being so fond of money.

On the island of Olkhon there is only one store; this store is owned by Muravieff, the Russian, the half brother of the half-blooded Buriat; both are sons of the erstwhile deceived Madame Muravieff.

After annoying delays I obtained four horses and two small springless wagons for the continuation of our journey to the island. My extra man was Protopotoff, "the official inoculator for small-pox." Starting about ten o'clock in the forenoon, we had a most interesting day. Between Kutul and Lake Baikal there are two villages, Kuchulga and Togot; the first contains about fifty houses, the other is much smaller.

The region from Kutul to the lake is in the main rugged and rocky. From the brow of the last elevation to the edge of the water, a distance of two miles, the road we went over is remarkable; it is not the one taken generally; the road for laden wagons is at least a third longer. By this shorter route we crossed a broad stretch of smooth grassland which slopes toward the lake; the descent is not abrupt enough to be dangerous, but is sufficient for swift driving. When well started we went along at a pace like that of tobogganing in Canada. It seemed like coasting on wheels in summer time. The land is so even, its surface yielding the least trifle under the wheels, that the sensation which comes of swift motion was wonderfully pleasant, almost equal to sliding down hill in those days which are now in eternity.

We halted at a house near the water, but still half a mile from the Olkhon Island ferry. At the house, or rather directly in front of it, was a Shaman; around him were five or six bark and iron dishes containing sour milk, sweet milk, and tarasun. He was performing some function of his office. Just before we stopped he made a libation, throwing tarasun up, and chanting a prayer.

The Shaman was a very strange person in visage and action. To a dark, sweating face and bright eyes he added a large round lump or knob on his nose just under and halfway between his eyebrows. He swayed gently from side to side as he chanted and then made a few steps which were short and spasmodic, a kind of twitching. Soon he halted, made another libation, chanted again, sprinkled with tarasun and milk the bushes growing near the house, took a few more spasmodic steps, and finished.

All I could learn was that these offerings had been made to drive sickness away.

The Shaman sprinkled my men with tarasun, muttering a prayer meanwhile, and then he treated them to the liquor with such liberality that it was only after much delay and great urging that I at last got them started again.

The passage to the island, which is rather more than a mile, should be made in good weather, since the lake is very rough at times, and the boats are far from reliable. Our chance for safety was good, as in August the weather is excellent, usually. Two boats, all there are in service, were needed for our company, as we had four horses and two wagons. One of the boats was at the mainland, the other was returning from the island, and we waited for it, wishing to set out together.

The wagons were lifted into the boats. The horses sprang on board very nimbly, showing that they were accustomed to this way of traveling. Each boat carried two horses and one wagon. On my boat there were six rowers, men, women, and children; on the other boat there were four. It took thirty-five minutes to cross.

I felt very curious on approaching the island which the Buriats call "sacred." On one side of the small bay toward which we were sailing a lofty cliff juts out boldly. On the front of that cliff are two immense faces, so distinct that all people note them. One of these looks at the mountains on the mainland; the other on the water in front of it. One as if watching the great world outside to see who might come from it to examine the island and its secrets, the other as if watching the visitors whom the men ferry across.

I drew attention to the faces and learned that they are called "The Watchers." There they gaze, watching night and day, never sleeping; looking, waiting, as waits the great sphynx near the pyramid of Ghizeh.

We landed without any trouble or adventure, and now I was on the sacred island of the Baikal. There are no houses near the landing. The first village is about three miles from the lake. At that place, which bears the name Nur, young Muravieff showed his high qualities and quite a comedy was presented.

I had supposed when we started from Kutul that we should be taken to Sem Sosen (Seven Pines), the chief village of the island, and the only one where there is a store and a possible stopping place. Muravieff, knowing that we were all going there, and that we expected him to take us, made his own plans, but he hid them from us carefully, until we reached Nur. There to our surprise he demanded a change of horses, though we were only a few miles from Seven Pines, our destination. He drove into the village and stopped in front of the house of the elder, the official who is obliged to furnish horses if they are demanded by travelers. The elder's wife, who was quick enough to see what was wanted, declared that her husband was off fishing some twenty versts away and that she did not know when he would return. At that moment he came from an out-house, where he had evidently been sleeping, and thus unwittingly gave a lie to her words, but she was not embarrassed in the least.

As soon as he appeared Muravieff demanded a relay of horses. The elder had no horses to give. All beasts trained to draw wagons were far from the village at pasture.

It was the bounden duty of the elder to find us four horses—they were not to be had, and he could not create them. There were only two or three miles to the end of the journey, and the horses we had were well able to make it, but Muravieff very bluntly refused to drive them farther.

At last, through his friends, he informed the elder that he would take us to Sevens Pines for ten rubles. The elder's claim was less than a ruble; government allowed him to receive but three copecks a verst for each horse. He paid the money, however, and Muravieff drove on.

I told Muravieff what I thought of him, but he only smiled with satisfaction. He had gained his point and saw no reason to be ashamed. To him success in any form was a thing to be proud of.

We arrived at Seven Pines about nightfall. The evening was warm and pleasant. The first move, of course, was to find lodgings. There was only one row of buildings in that part of Seven Pines where the store was. The first of these buildings was the storekeeper's dwelling, a house with but one large room; the second building was his store. This proved to be very small, and closely packed with groceries and dry-goods. The third was a shed and could be of no use to me. The fourth belonged to a Russian who was absent. I went to the fifth house, but the woman who lived there told me that there were billions of fleas in her house, and she could not with a clear conscience let any one try to pass a night in it. She felt obliged to refuse me. My search for a place in which to spend the night proving fruitless, I went back to the storekeeper and asked him what I could do. He suggested that I might sleep in the church, or *Molitvenny dom* (the prayer house). I agreed to this, and my things were transferred to the little prayer house.

Vassya and Lazareff were to sleep under the shed, in their wagon.

HOUSE WHERE WE BOARDED ON OLKHON ISLAND. *Page 72*
The building with the white sign is the Russian store

HOUSE WHERE WE BOARDED ON OLKHON ISLAND.

The building with the white sign is the Russian store

THE ONLY RUSSIAN CHURCH IN OLKHON. *Page 73*
The author spent three nights in the building

THE ONLY RUSSIAN CHURCH IN OLKHON.

The author spent three nights in the building

CHAPTER VI. SOJOURN ON THE "SACRED" ISLAND

THE morning following my arrival on Olkhon the golovar of Kutul, who had accompanied me to the island, returned to the mainland, after sending for a man whom he said could tell me much about the religion and customs of the people, and I was left to the devices of the islanders and others.

The messenger came back alone—the story-teller had gone to the Angara to fish, and would be away for some weeks. We were discussing the position when we saw two men riding in from the direction of the lake, and all called out, "There comes the story-teller." But instead of the story-teller it was Ilbik Urbashkin, the starosta of the second division of the Abazai clan. All the Buriats of Olkhon belong to this clan, but it has two divisions.

I now sent in various directions for men supposed to know stories, but when they came they could give me no information of value.

I had slept two nights on the floor of the little prayer house when the Russian in charge returned from fishing, and immediately deprived me of a shelter. He was an ignorant, self-sufficient peasant whom neither kind words, money, nor documents showing government protection influenced in the least. He was angry that the building had been opened to me during his absence and without his consent. He was in authority, and his authority had been ignored. It was impossible to reason with him. He strove to hide the real cause of his anger by repeating continually, "God's church has been desecrated by being used as a lodging." I was forced to move out.

I had become acquainted with the people of Seven Pines, and a young Buriat, who had recently built a one-roomed house, said that I could occupy it as long as I remained on the island. A stove, a couple of chairs, a pine table, and a bedstead were all the furniture that the room contained. He and his wife were exceedingly kind people. The woman cleaned the room with great care, and the man came several times each day to light the samovar and do what he could to make us comfortable. When not serving us they were busy in a meadow near by, cutting and raking grass. It was pleasant to witness their pleasure and gratitude when at parting I rewarded them for their kindness.

Meanwhile the search for knowledge continued. At last the starosta of Olkhon assembled a crowd near my cottage and questioned each man; but no information was to be obtained. "My father knew much about the old time." "My grandfather was a very wise man, and could have told you a great deal." "I had to work when a child, I had no chance to learn the lore of my people." Such were the answers given.

After a few days of very unsatisfactory work I decided that it was useless to remain longer on the island. Lazareff was uneasy, and anxious to go. He had relatives on the mainland, he said, "who knew all about the Buriats of the old time. They were more intelligent than the islanders, and would give me much valuable information." I was aware that Lazareff had his own interests in view, not mine, but I consented to visit those wise relatives as I wished to meet as many of the Buriats as possible. And on August 13 we left Seven Pines.

When we reached the Baikal a sturdy young girl, wearing pants, boots, a dark shirt and very short skirt, assisted the men in getting the wagons on to the boat, and was afterward one of the rowers. Two men and two small boys managed my boat.

When I turned and looked back at the rock faces, I thought that they had a satisfied expression, as though down in their rock hearts they were glad that we were leaving their sacred island.

It was evening when, greatly wearied, we reached the first post station, which after our experience on Olkhon seemed a very clean and hospitable place. The mistress of the house had returned and we found her an intelligent, kindly woman. At noon the following day we were at the "Ragatz" station, where we were forced to remain the rest of the day and the night. In the morning, after traveling a few versts the carriage gave out, and we stopped at the little village of Kuntin for repairs. The blacksmith, a good-looking old man, with bushy gray hair, was an Italian from Udine near Rome. When he heard his mother tongue once more his eyes lighted with pleasure, and he could not express his delight at meeting some one who knew his language and his country. While he was mending the carriage we took shelter in the house of a certain Petrof, a Russian who owned the vodka shop of the village. The old man boiled eggs and heated the samovar for us, and provided tarasun so liberally that I was afraid that we should have to leave Lazareff in Kuntin. When we returned to the blacksmith shop I snapped a photograph of our outfit, " *en memorium,*" as the old Italian said.

We had a splendid run out of Kuntin; dozens of dogs flew after us, like the wolves after Mazeppa. The horses went at full speed. It was splendid! glorious!

At five o'clock that afternoon, during a heavy rain storm, we reached Kosostép. Seven versts farther on lived Lazareff's relatives. He urged me to continue the journey that evening, but I was weary of bad roads and rain. The station was untidy and miserable. Our supper consisted of bacon and eggs, which for the sake of cleanliness we cooked for ourselves. Lazareff, like most of the Buriats, did not eat "pig meat," so bacon was cut out of his menu. Education had freed Vassya from this prejudice and had roused in him the desire to live as Russians live, hence he shared our supper with pleasure.

The Buriats, even those who are rich, live much like American Indians. There are no regular hours for meals, or any apparent forethought regarding them. Rye bread and mutton are the staples. When guests come, or a family gets hungry, a sheep is killed, skinned, cut up and boiled, and the tough meat is eaten with great relish. Occasionally a cow or a horse is slaughtered for food. If all of the meat is not disposed of immediately, it is dried for future use. Ice, one of the luxuries of modern life, is unknown, except as the covering of lakes and rivers during winter months. If an official or some person whom they wish to show more than usual respect arrives, hidden-away "Russian dainties" are brought forward, and a "lunch before dinner" is served. But this is the reception meal, and will not be repeated.

I was glad to get away from Kosostép early in the morning. The ride, after the rain of the evening before, was delightful.

On each side of the road were meadows where Russians and Buriats, both men and women, were busy mowing and turning grass. The dress of the Buriat woman—pants, boots and a short loose sacque—is convenient for field work, but it is not picturesque. A Russian woman of the laboring class wears a short dark skirt and a bright colored waist, and usually ties a red or red and yellow kerchief around her head. The hay fields that clear cool August morning were animated and dotted here and there with brilliant colors,—a beautiful harvest picture.

With a different climate the rich, black soil of this district would be exceedingly fertile, but as it is wheat will not grow; oats, though they ripen, are not good and the only reasonably sure crop is rye. Grass, however, grows wonderfully well, and at this season of the year nearly all of the men and women were busy in the hay-fields. There is no fruit in any part of Siberia which I have visited. The only berries I have seen were blue-berries, and those were cultivated.

On my arrival at Alaguersk-rod, a beautifully situated little village surrounded by meadows, I found that I was expected. The Uprava, a building used for government purposes, had been made ready, and a samovar was boiling. The "writer," or official translator, and twelve or fifteen Buriats were there to meet me.

The writer, a Russian exiled for life, is an educated and interesting man. Though only forty-five years of age his face is deeply lined and he looks worn and sad, for he has suffered much; fifteen years of his life exile have already past. Later, from an official at Irkutsk, I learned that the man had been in the army, and had been exiled for striking a superior officer.

After drinking tea the work of obtaining information and stories began. The hay-makers, glad of an excuse to leave the field, crowded into the uprava, and soon the place was dark with the smoke and vile with the odor of bad tobacco. An old man commenced well, but was interrupted by a young man, who said that he was not telling the story as he (the young man) had learned it. Then he tried to tell it himself, but could not; the old man was angry and the story was left unfinished.

A man from the Trans-Baikal gave me much important material, but after an hour or so a Buriat from the village, who had been drinking heavily, interfered, and tried to prevent his giving a foreigner information regarding the religion of the country. Only after much uproar and talk and a wearisome answering of questions, asked to establish my position, was the enemy silenced by his neighbors and the officials. In the evening when the crowd had dispersed and the room had been cleared the man in charge of refreshments brought us a dish of beef cut into small bits and boiled—not tempting, but we ate it, for we were hungry. The next day work went on well for a couple of hours, then the story-teller informed me that Irkutsk merchants had sent him to Alaguevsk-rod to hire men to go to the mouth of the Angara to fish. As he had contracted to have the men at the river within a week he could not stay with me longer. I was unable to find another man who could tell me anything of importance.

Lazareff, tired of his relatives if relatives they were, went back to Kosostép at once. I remained for the night, for accommodations, though poor, were better than at the post station. The crowd disappeared, only the exile remained. The man was poor, and his life was one of hardship and anxiety. Later I went with him to his home and met his wife, a frail woman whom trials and poverty have greatly disheartened. I promised to speak a good word for her husband and a few weeks afterward was able to fulfil my promise in such a way as to make his position somewhat easier.

The following morning was so chilly that a fire was needful. There was delay in starting, and it was noon before we reached Kosostép, where I found horses waiting, and we were off at once. At the first station beyond Kosostép we were treated to Siberian fruit—blueberries—which we ate greedily, though they were hard and sour. From this station a sturdy young Russian was our driver. He whirled us over twenty-nine versts rapidly, rushing through Hogotskaya to the post station as fast as the horses could run. Priestoff, the stanovoi of the town, called immediately and invited us to dine with him that evening. This made a pleasant break in the monotony of our return journey.

From Hogotskaya to Baiandai the horses were miserable; one side horse especially was contrary, and would not pull. The driver unharnessed him at last, and hitched him between the thills, where he was forced to work.

Upon our arrival at Baiandai Lazareff and Vassya learned of the death of a relative's child, and, though the child was only a few days old, they made the death an excuse for hastening to Usturdi. Lazareff had been of little help to me, he had caused me much vexation and expense, and I was glad to say: "God speed you."

Baiandai is a curious place. It is a collection of Buriat villages with one Russian settlement. In this settlement nearly every man and woman is either an ex-convict or a person exiled for life. I could have easily gathered many stories there, life tragedies, vastly interesting for a man who wishes to study all phases of life, but I was in Siberia to obtain Mongol material, and did not wander from my task.

Baiandai houses, like most of the houses in Siberia, are unpainted, except the casings and blinds, which are painted white; they get black and old quickly. Many of the buildings have shattered roofs and look uninhabitable, still they are occupied. Though a large place, there was but little to eat; no butter, white bread, or meat of any kind could be obtained. My bed in this village, or collection of villages, was made by putting two doors on two boxes and placing my carriage mattress on those doors.

The Russian secretary of the village was away, but the assist-ant secretary was very kind, and made every effort possible to find "wise men" for me. He was an exile from Little Russia, where he had held a government position. Losing in some way a thousand rubles of government money, he was sent to Siberia for twelve years, leaving at home a son and a daughter, and a position which gave him more than a hundred rubles a month. He had already lived through eleven years of this exile. What he will do when the term ends he does not know. His health is broken; evidently exile has been a frightful experience for him. It is doubtful if work in a mine is worse for an educated and refined man than the monotony and associations of such a place as Baiandai.

After a time a story-teller came. I paid him and sent him away, for he knew only fragments of folk-lore; another came who was not much better, and still others. I remained three days in Baiandai searching diligently for folk-lore, but I could find nothing of value.

The man detailed to care for me during my stay was Danilo of Moscow, a rogue. He was sent to Siberia when nineteen years of age, under sentence to work in the mines, in chains, for fifteen years. Seventeen years ago, when he had served out twelve years of that sentence, he was pardoned. He came to Baiandai, married, and nine children have been born to him. His own account of the crime he committed was that at a festival, when intoxicated, he, with three associates, beat and killed a man whom they had long hated. He has the appearance of being a quiet, inoffensive person, but I found him tricky and wholly unreliable.

Now a great excitement rose in Baiandai: fifteen hundred soldiers were on their way from the Yakuts country to join, at Irkutsk, forces which had been ordered to China. It was reported that they were unruly, destroyed property, and did as they pleased in the villages they passed through. Two hundred were expected in Baiandai; they must be fed, supplied with bread, and the population must furnish carts and horses to carry them to the next station. Officials assembled to keep order. Five hundred rubles were raised to pay for bread, and every competent housekeeper was ordered to bake a certain number of loaves. In this time of unrest I made the acquaintance of Arkokoff, a rich Buriat, who invited me to visit him, and promised to find men familiar with the folk-lore of the country.

August 23, very early in the morning, there was a wonderful commotion and turmoil. The two hundred soldiers had arrived. The uproar was made principally by cart-drivers, those who had brought the men, and those who were to carry them away; by Buriats disputing and quarreling, and by dissatisfied soldiers, who had received mouldy bread when fresh had been paid for. Some exhibited this bread. I heard one soldier declare that it was not fit to feed to hens, another said that pigs would refuse to eat it. The breadmakers defended themselves, and there was a noisy battle of words. But at last the soldiers were off, and when the squeaking of the rickety carts had died away in the distance Baiandai sank back into its usual apathy.

A few hours later I started for the summer home of the Arkokoffs, fifteen versts distant. As the road was smooth and level and the horses were good, we were soon there. Within one immense enclosure are three houses built on the Buriat plan, and one on the Russian, together with sheds and storehouses. The gate of the high board enclosure was open and we halted in front of the Russian house out of which came a very old and very dirty woman and two of the dirtiest men I have ever seen. Arkokoff himself came from one of the Buriat houses. He invited us into the Russian house, and ordered a samovar. While that was preparing he spoke of his wealth and position. He had several thousand head of cattle, four hundred splendid horses, five hundred sheep, and goats as well; a hundred and thirty thousand rubles in the Irkutsk bank, many houses, and a great deal of valuable land. He was a man of influence, for he had money to loan.

When the samovar was brought the steam from it had such a terrible odor that it made us ill at once. Upon asking what caused this peculiar odor Arkokoff said that the water they used was from stored snow, and asked me to go with him and see how well he had it protected.

Back of the houses was a small building, with a door loosely hung and always open. Inside of this building was a hole twenty-five feet deep with steps going down to the bottom. This hole, or reservoir, was filled in cold weather by shoveling in snow, stamping it down and packing it as solid as possible. Men in the reservoir trampled the snow as others threw it in. The well at this time was about one quarter full. The snow had turned to ice,

ARKOKOFF, HIS WIFE, SON, AND SON'S WIFE. *Page* 81

In background a Buriat official

ARKOKOFF, HIS WIFE, SON, AND SON'S WIFE.

In background a Buriat official

LAZAREFF AND HIS RELATIVES. *Page* 60

Lazareff stands at the end dressed in white. Vassya stands in the centre

LAZAREFF AND HIS RELATIVES.

Lazareff stands at the end dressed in white. Vassya stands in the centre

and there was water over the surface. This water was of the color of tea and was full of dirt. A man brought up a bucketful for my inspection. The odor was nearly as bad as from the steam of the samovar.

On looking around outside I saw that the houses and the cattle-yards were on higher ground than the reservoir, and in such a position that the well was to a certain degree a drain.

I decided to leave at once if this was the only water supply. But when I said that I had never used snow water, and thought that undoubtedly it would make me ill, Arkokoff sent men to a small river, quite a distance away, to bring water for my tea.

I now made the acquaintance of Mrs. Arkokoff, a short, fleshy, determined-looking woman about sixty-five years of age. She wore a double-breasted Canton silk coat, blue pants tucked into the tops of long-legged boots, and a pair of new, heavy rubbers—Buriat women think that the gloss of new rubbers gives a dressed-up appearance, and they wear them over their boots in the driest and hottest weather—On her head was a round felt cap, and over her shoulders a bright kerchief, knotted in front. She could speak only Buriat, hence my conversation with her was somewhat limited, but I saw that she ruled every one, with the possible exception of her husband. Later on, in Usturdi, I learned that a few years earlier Arkokoff had married a young woman and taken her to his home. Though among the Buriats it is not unusual to have two wives at the same time, Mrs. Arkokoff No. 1 was very angry, and young Mrs. Arkokoff did not live long.

The old man had a curious collection of people around him. In the kitchen of the house in which I was given a room was a queer-looking woman, a Russian, the widow of an exile. Her sole occupation was making rye bread, and though she complained bitterly of Arkokoff as a miser, who would not pay his help, and when they revolted would say: "Go and sue me; I have money, you have none. See how you will come out," she had labored for him twenty-four years, for three rubles (about a dollar and a half) a month. Near the oven in her untidy kitchen stood a tub of rye flour and a tub of yeast. On a bench, not far from the flour tub, slept, during the day, the night-watch, a man who had served out a sentence for murder. He was tall, lank, and always barefooted; his face unwashed and beard and hair unkempt, a wretched specimen of mankind, mentally unbalanced. He had been a servant in the Arkokoff family for twenty years.

I was invited to visit the Buriat houses in the enclosure, three in number. In the first lived the old man and his wife; in the second their son and his wife; in the third the widow of their elder son, and her four children, one boy and three girls, whose dress—pants, loose shirts, long-legged boots, and caps with visors—made them look precisely like boys. Near the widow's house was a long wagon shed in which were ten or twelve large barrels, each three-fourths full of curd left after distilling tarasun. This curd is given as food to the shepherds, herders, and other laborers. Arkokoff said that it was excellent. The barrels are never covered. When the curd dries and hardens it cracks, as does mud under the heat of the sun. Dust fills the cracks and covers the top. Fresh curd is put in each time that tarasun is made. Curd dried in this way lasts for years. When needed a chunk of the vile stuff is chopped out and cooked with rye flour. Tarasun is distilled almost daily, but fresh curd is seldom eaten. For economy's sake they use the dried. The dust comes from the horse, cattle, and sheep yards near by.

In the Buriat country nearly all the milk from horses and cows is made into tarasun. The Arkokoffs make a great quantity of this liquor, but they also make butter of which the master of the place is very proud. A large panful was brought for my inspection. I noticed that it was covered with specks. I asked to have a section cut out; this was done, and I found that the butter was permeated with fine dust.

A dish of soup, a piece of roast mutton, and some rye bread were brought for our supper, but I did not enjoy it, for the mutton was very tough, and I had seen the breadmaker.

The only possible place for us to sleep in this rich man's house was on the floor of the room which had been given me in the Russian house. The family slept on benches in the Buriat houses. My mattress was brought from the carriage and spread on the floor. The door into the kitchen where the old Russian woman slept, and where the night-watch, the ex-convict, came and went while on duty, could not be locked. Of course I had money with me sufficient to meet traveling expenses and pay men. But I was too weary to borrow trouble, and slept in spite of everything.

Next day story-tellers came and went. Many men crowded into the room to listen, and were a great drawback and annoyance. I got one fine folk-tale, and sent twenty versts for a man who had the reputation of knowing a good deal. He came, but declared that he knew nothing about the old time. Arkokoff insisted that he did, but neither urging nor money availed. I paid him for his lost time and he went home. Another man came; as it was late in the evening he said he would stay and begin work in the morning. In the morning, although I was up at daylight, he had disappeared. At noon an old man arrived, who told one good folk-tale, then his memory failed, and another man took his place. During these hours of waiting and annoyance tea acted as a wonderful sedative. It was fortunate that I had plenty of Russian tea with me, and also rusks, for in Arkokoff's house the only meal during the day is a dish of mutton and a loaf of rye bread, some time between four o'clock in the afternoon and nine in the evening. The family lives mainly on rye bread and tarasun. I had seen the rye bread made and could not eat it, but I derived great pleasure from feeding it to an old, lame, sore-backed dog. My translator was a Russian in the employ of Arkokoff. I paid Arkokoff more each day for the loss of the man's labor than he paid him for a week's work. I also paid the man in the same proportion.

The third day I had no better luck with story-tellers than the second day. My rusks were gone, and at four o'clock I ordered the horses, which a tall Buriat had had in waiting for two days, and in half an hour we were on the road to Olzoni.

Though I was weary and hungry and had paid exorbitantly for my experience, I was well satisfied, for I had spent three days in a typical Mongol family. Arkokoff professes to be greatly devoted to the old religion; perhaps he is. One thing is certain, he is tremendously devoted to making and hoarding money and drinking tarasun.

The Olzoni station was commodious and clean. I should have spent several days there had it been possible to find folk-tales. Trembovski, the Polish merchant, came to welcome me and assist me in getting stories. I had brought Arkokoff's man to aid me, having paid Arkokoff in advance for the time I expected to keep him. But as soon as we reached the village he began drinking and after that I was not sure of him for even half an hour at a time.

In spite of worry and vexation, I remained four days in Olzoni. Then, taking my drunken servant, for fear that I should not get a better one, I started for Upper Kudinsk.

The country we passed through was uncultivated though the soil was rich. I have noticed that there are many wild flowers in Siberia and that they are usually of a purple tint. Daisies of a lavender shade grow everywhere.

At Upper Kudinsk the "People's Quarters" is in an open field half a mile from the village. The house is surrounded by a very high fence. The guest room is small, the bed simply a wooden bench upon which one is expected to put his carriage mattress. The window-sills were packed with tall plants which kept the light out and made the air bad. The official in charge, a Buriat, was very obliging and sent off immediately for "wise men."

Next morning my translator was wonderfully and fearfully drunk. Fortunately I now understood the language so well that I could dispense with his services. A man came who knew folk-tales, and he gave me much valuable information. In the after-noon a middle-aged, blue-spectacled man appeared, and stated that he would tell me "all about the Buriat religion." With him was the son of a Shaman, a bright, intelligent fellow. The middle-aged man, whose name was Kongoroff, was the son-in-law of Arkokoff. He had turned away from the religion of his. forefathers, and was perfectly willing to show me his abandoned gods and tell me about them. I was glad to meet such a man.

That evening there was a good supper, the first enjoyable meal I had had for more than two months: beefsteak and baked potatoes, such potatoes as I had not seen since leaving London, and they were grown in a garden near the house, there in the Buriat country, where I had frequently heard it stated that no vegetable would grow.

But if we had a good supper we had a miserable bed, and a wonderful experience with cockroaches. The moment daylight

KONGOROFF AND HIS WIFE. *Page 85*
The other persons of the group are neighbors who crowded around to listen to Kongoroff. K. sits at the end of the picture near his wife, who is standing

KONGOROFF AND HIS WIFE.

The other persons of the group are neighbors who crowded around to listen to Kongoroff. K. sits at the end of the picture near his wife, who is standing

ANDREI MIHAILOVITCH, MIKILOFF AND HIS YOUNG WIFE
AT RIGHT, VASSYA. *Page 28*

ANDREI MIHAILOVITCH, MIKILOFF AND HIS YOUNG WIFE

AT RIGHT, VASSYA.

disappeared they came from their hiding-places and raced everywhere, up the walls, down the walls, on the table, floor, stove, bed, and baskets. Only once before in my life had I seen so many. That was in Guatemala, where in my sleeping-room they ate everything available; ate even the films off photographic plates which I had set up on a shelf to dry. These Buriat cock-roaches were very aggressive, when I tried to sleep I found it beyond the possible. Toward morning I surrendered, dressed, and went out on to the porch. There I found a Jew tailor whose home was in Lodz, Poland. He had been exiled for eleven years, for smuggling, but at that time had only one year longer to serve. He was a peculiar-looking man with curly hair, white, except at the back of the neck, where it was jet black, which gave him a remarkably odd appearance. He had no friendship for the Buriats, whom he said the excessive use of tarasun was destroying as a people. As he spoke German he could converse freely without fear of being overheard, and we had a long talk, mainly about the country and the Buriats.

In the morning, as soon as I could get horses, I started for Kongoroff's. The ride of fifteen versts would have been pleasant but for the horses and the driver. The first were wretched, pitiful; the second was inhuman. The land was rolling and the road heavy, the horses lean and underfed. I was afraid they would give out, but urge or threaten as I might I could not make the heartless driver rest them.

Kongoroff's place was disappointing. The house was so badly kept as to make tea and lunch undesirable. A German from Riga, as he himself declared, came in and began talking rather rapidly. Kongoroff had him turned out soon, and quite rudely, I thought, excusing the act by saying that the man had been drinking. Later he appeared a second time, but was sent off promptly. It seemed much as though Kongoroff, who did not understand German, feared that the man might make some complaint. When I was going the exile came to the carriage, shook hands with me, and said in German, "God sees everything."

Kongoroff brought his Ongons, took them from the boxes, and nailed them to the side of the house to be photographed. They were much like those shown to me by Andrei Mihailovitch. Kongoroff told me their names and attributes. The visit was not very pleasant, and though I obtained a few important facts, I was glad to get away from the place.

Another night-conflict with cockroaches and I was off for Usturdi, accompanied by Zabailenski, the translator, who had made good promises. The trip was delightful. There was just the right temperature and the proper breeze. It was a beautiful day! I had been away one month.

I was anxious to go to Irkutsk, but was determined to get the rest of Manshut's folk-tales before going. I sent for him immediately. My messenger soon returned with word that Manshut was sick. I did not credit this, so I got an order from the chief of the village for the old man to come to the uprava. The man who carried the order was gone an entire day. When at last he came he brought the same message as the first man: Manshut was sick. I did not know what to do. There had been a festival, and nearly all the men in the village were intoxicated. I tried hard to keep Zabailenski from bad company, but toward evening of the first day he disappeared. Andrei Mihailovitch was also drinking heavily. Vassya was about the only man in Usturdi who was not to some degree intoxicated.

CHAPTER VII. A BIRTHDAY IN SIBERIA

ON September 6, my birthday, I hired a troika for four rubles and a half and set out to bring in Manshut, dead or alive. The day was beautiful, the air clear, sweet; the sun shone brightly, and there was a breeze just strong enough to give tone to the atmosphere.

The troika moved not too quickly, but still briskly over the country, which was slightly rolling. The road was excellent, and soon we were abreast of the Hill of Sacrifice, then beyond it. Manshut's village was said to be twenty versts from Usturdi, but it was a short twenty versts. At last we came in sight of several villages, one not far from the other. At the first I inquired for the house of Manshut's employer, and found it by driving through what seemed to me a series of unfenced cattle-yards. In front of the house were half a dozen stolid, stupid women, one of whom was the employer's wife. She gave no information except that her husband was away, and Manshut, who was not at work, was somewhere with friends. Just at that juncture the worst-looking man I have ever seen ran up from somewhere around a corner. His red face was decorated with a nose which was an immense lumpy knob, red as blood. He was terribly repulsive, ragged and dirty beyond description, a man who had drunk barrels and barrels of tarasun.

"I will show you where Manshut's house is," said he. The driver made room for him, and we went, at his direction, toward the end of the village where there were several tumble down houses.

My guide said that Manshut lived with his mother in the second house, but we found that he lived in the first house, not with his mother, but with an old, weird, witch-like creature, who was at the second house sitting on the ground outside with three other very old women. When I asked where Manshut was she did not answer, but got up and going to her own house sat down by the door. Then an unsatisfactory conversation began; one story was that Manshut was visiting somewhere in the neighborhood, another, that he was off cutting grass. I thought that he might be hiding, so I gave the woman some money and she let me go into the house and look around. He was not there.

Meanwhile, the knob-nosed man, with fifty copecks in hand and a promise of more, had gone off to hunt Manshut up. Seeing the man start away the old woman laughed, and said, "Red-nose is a terrible drunkard; you will not see him again."

I decided to go back to the employer's house. On the way I met a Russian-Buriat, who had seen me with Andrei Mihailovitch at the Horse Sacrifice. He was drunk, but gave me more information than I had been able to get hitherto. He said that Manshut's employer had a great deal of grass to cut, and would not let the old man go to Usturdi. He offered to go to the hayfield with me, if I wished. The driver objected to this. He said that the place was across the river, and more than a verst away; his horses were too tired for the trip. I sent for other horses. Then he did not want his wagon to cross the river. At last, very reluctantly, with an increase of pay, he decided to go to the hayfield. The drunken man took his seat by the driver, and we were off.

After driving about half a mile we halted in front of a small house built on the Russian plan. I inquired why we were stopping. "To get a drink," answered my guide. "It is hot; I am terribly dry."

The small house was a dram shop; fortunately it was closed. When he rapped heavily on the door two children came to a broken window, but they refused to let him in; their mother, who was at work in a field quite a distance away, had told them "not to unfasten the door for any one." The man insisted, offered them money, scolded, but they would not disobey. I told him that I was in a hurry and could not wait; that it was almost night. At last, when my patience was nearly gone, he took his seat and we started.

Just at that moment some one who was running across the

MANSHUT. *Page 87*

MANSHUT

BURIAT YOUNG LADY, ISLAND OF OLKHON.

field hailed us. It was our knob-nosed friend, who when near enough called out,

"I have found Manshut!"

We turned back at once. The man had somewhere pro-cured a bottle of tarasun. A Shaman came up and a drinking bout began. The bottle was emptied quickly and with great gusto. I was afraid that the driver would get intoxicated; but accustomed to tarasun it had no visible effect.

The knob-nosed man and the Shaman stood up on the back of the wagon and we drove on. Just outside the old witch's house we came upon Manshut. He was ragged and dirty, and had an old handkerchief tied around his head.

Without waiting for words I greeted him, and said: "Get up by the driver. It will be night soon, we must be off immediately!" He took his seat, not hesitating for a moment, and we started.

Usturdi seemed far away that September evening, for the horses were tired, and the air was chilly. It was nine o'clock when we reached the village. It had been a holiday and of course the Buriats had feasted on tarasun; the effects of it were evident everywhere. With great effort we succeeded in getting a samovar and a few pieces of rye bread. It had been a strange birthday; but I was content. I had fought a battle and won a victory.

Manshut told folk-tales for four days, and his work was very satisfactory; nevertheless they were hard days, for my provisions were gone, except tea. No matter how large a Buriat village may be there is never a meat market. Occasionally at the little grocery shops one can buy bacon, kept for Russian customers, but it is of a very poor quality. At this time Usturdi lacked even bacon.

In a Buriat house, as I have stated, there is but one meal in twenty-four hours; tough mutton, rye bread, and tarasun. This meal is eaten without ceremony. Plates and knives and forks are placed on a table which usually has an oilcloth cover, a dish of mutton and a plate of rye bread are brought, and each person serves himself. Tea is used in the morning. The poorer classes drink what is called "block tea," the odor of which is very disagreeable. The well-to-do drink ordinary Russian tea. I am sure that the constant use of tobacco destroys their desire for food, for the rich live as badly as do the poor.

Buriats smoke almost continually, using a pipe with a large bowl and long stem. I have seen children five years of age smoking. Young girls seem more addicted to smoking than boys are, if possible. They are dissipated in every way. It is only after marriage that morality is expected, and then it is strictly enforced.

To the large majority of Buriats Russian is an unknown language. It is difficult to find a man able to carry on an ordinary conversation. Buriat women make no effort whatever to learn Russian. There are no Buriat schools.

I was rejoiced when I had on paper all that Manshut could tell me, for he was so unkempt as to be exceedingly repulsive. I recompensed him well for his time, and his knowledge of ancient tales, and he went away satisfied. Zabailenski was happy also, for I did not count out the days that he had been so intoxicated as to be useless.

We left Usturdi September 13. I was glad to go from the Buriat country, where, though I had gained considerable knowledge, we had endured many hardships.

Seven versts beyond the first station I passed through Iyók, a town of about four thousand ex-convicts, Poles, Jews, Russians, and Tartars, mainly peasants. It is a town with one immensely long street of unpainted houses and fences, all in a more or less tumbled down condition. When we reached Kudà (Where), it was already dusk and we remained for the night, not only because it was difficult to get horses, but because I thought it unsafe to travel in the night time, as within two or three years there had been several murders at this end of the route.

At the Zemski quarters I found the ispravnik ₁ of Vernolensk, an uncultured, stupid man. He was on his way to Irkutsk. His wife and aunt had met him at Kudà, and he and they occupied the guest room with trunks and bags which should have been left outside. This was vexatious, but I had an opportunity to study the real character of the man. He would have been officious and guarded had he known that I was traveling under government protection.

The woman in charge of the house gave me a small room where I tried to sleep on a huge box which occupied a good part of the chamber. But at midnight a party of young officers arrived with the governor-general's order for horses. When horses were not to be had there were high words and disputes. They had been ordered to Iyók to make arrangements for quartering a regiment of soldiers there for the winter. As they would not wait for station horses private horses were found, and they continued their journey, much to my satisfaction.

Next morning we were on the road at an early hour, carrying with us the house mistress' blessing, who said, as we parted, "If you never pass this way again I hope to meet you in that other world."

It was a cold and rainy day, and our driver informed us that thereafter there would be "little heat and much cold."

That evening I dined with the governor of Irkutsk, and went with him to the opera. In this quick change from life among the Buriats to the refinements of civilized life in the capital of Siberia, I experienced the striking results of some centuries of social evolution,—an evolution which through its effects upon humanity enables the man of cities to step back in a moment and with no mental effort from the wild, free life of fancy to the prescribed surroundings of material facts.

. . . .

Thus did I leave the heroes of the past, who fought so bravely with the many-headed Mangathais, and return to the no less valiant men of the present who, struggling with the evil forces of indifference and ignorance, are bringing to Siberia the prosperity that country so well deserves to call her own.

Footnotes

CHAPTER VIII. CUSTOMS OF THE BURIATS

THE MAKING OF TARASUN

THE most important work in a Buriat house and of a Buriat woman is to keep the milk barrels full, and to distil the milk into tarasun, a liquor looking like alcohol or pure water. When the milk is sour enough for the watery part to separate from the curd it is ready to distil. As much milk as is desired is taken out of the barrel and put in a large iron pot, then the pot is sealed up with a heavy paste made of mud and cow manure, and is placed over a slow fire burning on the ground in the center of the Buriat house.

From the pot a pipe runs into a tub which stands four feet or so away. From the end of this pipe drips out the tarasun.

If strong tarasun is desired the first is redistilled. The strongest is made by distilling the liquor three times.

I should judge that the milk barrels in a Buriat house are never empty, for they look as if they had not been washed for years.

In some of the houses two or three barrels of sour milk stand in the room where the family lives. But, when there is a large herd of cows, and many people to be supplied with tarasun, the barrels are kept under a shed near the house. f These barrels are left uncovered, consequently the milk is permeated with dust.

The "arsá," or substance left in the pot after the liquor is distilled, is stored in barrels. It hardens and is mixed with rye flour and cooked for laborers. Arsá becomes so solid that an axe is used in getting it out of the barrel. These barrels are also left uncovered in a shed or outhouse.

Buriats keep many cows, but nearly all the milk is made into tarasun; there is no cheese made, and very little butter. What butter is made is wholly unfit for use.

MARRIAGE CEREMONIES

When a young boy and girl take a fancy to each other their parents, if in favor of the marriage, begin the regular negotiations through matchmakers, or one father may say to the other, "You have a daughter and I have a son, let us become relatives." This agreement made, the matchmakers' work begins.

The matchmakers, usually, if not always, elderly women, go to the father of the girl with the proposal from the father of the boy. The girl's father will entertain this formal proposal, or, if he has changed his mind, will definitely refuse it. In the former case he will receive another visit. This time five or six persons come. They enter the eight-sided yurta, and the two matchmakers sit down opposite the door; with them are men whose business it is to decide upon the sum to be paid. The father must always get "kalym"—the price of the girl. Now begins bargaining, one side asking a big price, and the other offering little. This is often a mere formality, for many times the question has been decided in advance. The girl's father reduces the price somewhat, the boy's father offers a trifle more, until finally they reach an agreement as to the amount.

This kalym is almost always paid in horses, cows, sheep, grain—anything of value among the Buriats; the amount varies from three to seven hundred rubles, according to the wealth of the two families. A day is appointed for the next visit, and the matchmakers and their assistants go home.

On the day appointed a large company goes to the girl's home. They sit on the ground, talk, and drink tarasun. Then dancing begins in front of the house. Sheep are killed, and if the father is rich he kills a horse also. The meat is cooked, and the crowd feasts. Only friends, relatives, and neighbors are present; neither the girl nor boy attends the ceremonies of this first day.

The second day of the marriage ceremony, which may be some weeks later, the bridegroom comes early in the morning to the bride's father, bringing provisions. If he is wealthy he has a horse killed and gives the head of the beast to his father-in-law. The ribs are cut out and given to those of the wedding guests who are most distinguished. All of the meat is cooked, then the best parts are distributed among the people present. Tarasun is dealt out in abundance. There is dancing and feasting. This entertainment takes place in the open air. Chairs and tables are unnecessary; every one sits on the ground to eat.

The third day the groom is at his father's. The house where the young couple are to live is made ready. In the room is a bed, and near the bed is fixed a place where the bride is to sit. Meanwhile she is at home. All at once a small party on horse-back is seen in the distance approaching on the keen run. They halt in front of the door, enter, seize the girl, put her on a horse, and race away to the new home. There. she is swept off the horse, taken into the house, and seated by the bed, where she remains with a handkerchief over her face. The groom is around everywhere, but does not approach to greet her. A table is placed near the bride and the Ongons or household divinities are put on it. Four of the bride's friends now inform the groom that the bride is there. He approaches, she rises and takes his hand, then three old men, of family and importance, appear. The bride and groom bow to the Ongons and are then led around the table three times by the three old men, who ask of the Ongons that the newly married may be prosperous, gain much wealth, and have many children to begin a new line. After this ceremony the bride returns to her father's house.

On the fourth day of the marriage ceremony the bride again goes to the new house (or yurta), puts on a mask and bows before the Ongons. There is a fire made on the ground in the center of the yurta; she bows to this fire, and throws a piece of butter into it; then she takes a piece of fat mutton, perhaps a pound or two pounds, cuts it into bits, rolls it into a lump and throws it into the hands of her father-in-law; in this way she assures him that she will be bountiful and kind to him. The ceremony over, the bride sits down near the milk barrel, which always stands at the northwest corner of the fire. Taking her place at the milk barrel concludes the marriage ceremony, for this denotes that she takes formal possession of the milk of the house. Thereafter she is mistress of the milk, and everybody must go to her for it. It is her business to make, or to cause to be made, the tarasun.

In Balagausk, where another branch of the Buriats lives, the marriage ceremony differs slightly. On the day that the bride is first taken to the home of the groom, a man, taking with him a large arrow, goes ahead of the party having the bride in charge. When he arrives at the new home he sticks the arrow into a pillar in front of the house, and calls out that the bride's party is coming. When they are within a short distance of the house a man appointed for the purpose throws the meat of the second joint of an animal—a cow, sheep, or horse—to the boys of the village who are waiting to catch it. The bride leaves her father's house either on horseback or in a wagon, but always approaches her new home on horseback. She rides up at full gallop, is swept from the horse, and conducted with covered head and face to the bed, where she sits down on the chair placed there for her. The more speed with which this is accomplished the greater the good luck of the bride will be. The horse she rides is ornamented with a bell. The bell is removed, rung, and hung on the western post near the door.

The day following the last day of the ceremony the women of the ulus, or village, come to visit the bride. She must meet them with cap and handkerchief on. She must not call certain persons by their names, but always by the relationship. When they come to the house they cough outside the door; this is done simply for fun and to confuse the bride.

On the second day of the marriage ceremony the bride sits in the house and begins to cry, and some of her girl friends come and cry with her. Then she lies down on the bed with her most intimate friend. They take each a tress of their hair and sew it to the other's shoulder. Then they clasp each other firmly, friends come in, girls and boys, and try to pull them apart, to tear one from the other; there is laughter and screaming. This ceremony is to show that after marriage the young woman will be true to the friends of her girlhood. If a bride is enceinte she is not permitted to bow down to the Ongons. Such an act would bring misfortune to the whole community.

CEREMONIES AFTER THE BIRTH OF A CHILD

Just before the birth of a child a "receiving mother," or mid-wife, is summoned. As soon as the child comes into the world the father takes a broad arrow-head and cuts the umbilical cord. The infant is then washed in warm water, wrapped in a lamb skin, and put into its father's fur coat. The friends and neighbors assemble, and an animal, either a cow or sheep, is killed and the meat cooked. Then a man accustomed to perform such ceremonies makes libations of the meat and of tarasun, in this way sending it greatly multiplied to the gods, asking, meanwhile, that the master of the house may be blessed with many children and an increase of flocks.

From the animal they have killed is reserved the leg bone below the knee; this they boil. On the second day the meat is cut from the bone, and the bone is tied to the outside of the child's cradle, on the right-hand side. If the baby is a boy, a boy stands by the cradle ready to answer questions and to give the child a name. If it is a girl, a girl stands by the cradle.

We will suppose the child to be a boy. The receiving mother holds the infant in her arms in front of the cradle and asks, "Which are we to rock, the child or the bone?" She asks the question three times, then the boy answers, "The child!" Then she asks three times, "Shall we rock up or down?" the boy answers, "Up!"

The baby is put into the cradle and tied in, then the receiving mother asks, "What is the name of the child?" and the boy repeats the name which the parents have selected.

The third day, if the father is well-to-do, a second animal is killed; this one is divided among the most distinguished people of the village, those who have not been present at the ceremonies attending the birth and the naming of the child.

On the third day the tomta (placenta) is buried. Two planks are removed from the floor near the mother's bed, a hole is dug in the ground, and dry juniper is burned near it. The tomta is put into the hole, covered up, and the planks are replaced. Then the mother is purified. Only women are present during this ceremony.

The tomta has a sacred significance among the Buriats. If you ask a Buriat where he was born, he will answer, "My tomta is buried in that house;" or will say, in such or such a village "is the house where my tomta is buried."

The Buriats beyond the Baikal, when questioned about the origin of their people, will answer, "Our tomta is on the western side of the Baikal." They make libations to it. In this case the tomta is that of the recognized ancestor of all the Buriats. When they are making libations they sprinkle tarasun to the gods, naming them all, then to their ancestors, and finally to their tomta.

ORIGIN OF THE BURIATS

An account of the origin of the childbirth ceremonies as told me at Usturdi by two very old men.

Buhan Khan lived at Haugin Dalai, not far from the sea. He was a bull in the daytime, but always turned himself into a man at night. Not very far off, but on the west of the sea, lived Khunshai Khan, who had a beautiful daughter. One night Buhan Khan saw Khunshai's daughter and fell in love with her. After a time a son was born to them. When the child was placed in its cradle Buhan Khan stole it away, tied it firmly to the cradle, carried it to the edge of the sea, and with his hoofs dug a hole in the earth, and there buried the child and the cradle.

A Shaman named Usihun and his wife Asihan lived by the sea. They saw Buhan Khan digging the hole, and when he had gone they went immediately to find out what he had buried there. They found the cradle and took it home, but so tightly had Buhan Khan hooped it around that work as they might they could not open it. Then Usihun began "to shaman" and to ask how the cradle was to be opened. He was answered by Buga Noyon Babai, the god to whom he made libations. "Fasten the right leg bone (below the knee) of a two-year-old bull on the right side of the cradle," said the god, "and place a sharp knife by the cradle, then ask, 'How is it, shall we rock the bone or the infant?' A child must answer, 'The infant.' 'Shall it be head down or up?' 'Up.'" When the Shaman did as Buga Noyon directed, the hoops snapped and the cords untied, and there in the cradle was a beautiful child. Usihun and his wife reared the boy and named him Bulugat. When four or five years old Bulugat became very fond of playing by the sea. After a while he began to get up and slip away in the night-time. The Shaman's wife wondered where the child went; then she followed, and saw that two children, a boy and a girl, came out of the sea and played with him.

The Shaman and his wife were very curious to know what kind of children they were, so one evening they set out milk and tarasun and told Bulugat to give it to his playmates. The boy and girl came out of the sea, played till tired, then they drank the milk and the tarasun, and straightway fell asleep. The Shaman came from the reeds where he had been hiding and caught the boy, but the girl slipped away, turned to a seal, and sprang into the sea.

The Shaman named the boy from the sea Uhurut, and he and Bulugat, son of the bull, grew up together. All the Buriats west of the Baikal are descended from Bulugat, and all the Vepholensk Buriats are descended from Uhurut.

ANOTHER VERSION OF THE ORIGIN OF THE TRANS-BAIKAL BURIATS

A hunter one day when out shooting birds saw three beautiful swans flying toward a lake not far distant. He followed the swans, saw them come down by the water, take off their feathers, become women, and swim out from shore.

These three swans were the three daughters of Esege Malan. The hunter stole the feathers of one of the swans, and when she came from the water she could not fly away with her sisters. He caught the maiden, took her home, and made her his wife. Six children had been born to them when one day the daughter of Esege Malan distilled strong tarasun, and after her husband had drank much she asked for her feathers, and he gave them to her. That moment she turned to a swan and flew up through the smoke-hole. One of her daughters, who was mending the tarasun still, tried to catch her and keep her from flying away, but only caught at her legs, which the girl's dirty hands made black. That is why swans, a sacred bird among the Buriats, have black legs.

The mother circled around, came back within speaking distance of her daughter, and said, "Alway at the time of the new moon you will pour out to me mare's milk and tea, and scatter red tobacco."

From this swan, the daughter of Esege Malan, came all the Trans-Baikal Buriats.

SICKNESS

In case of sickness a Shaman is sent for at once. To discover the cause of the illness he burns the shoulder-blade of a sheep until it is white, then by the cracks in the bone he learns what the sick person has done to anger this or that Burkan. When he has thus found out which Burkan has caused the sickness he knows by experience what sacrifice must be made to appease him. If the illness is slight, an offering of tarasun may be sufficient; but in case of serious sickness, besides the offering of tarasun, an animal must be sacrificed.

Many of the Burkans are very exacting about what is offered to them, others are indifferent. To some the offering must be a black ram, to others a white ram; to some a white goat, to others a black goat; and there are Burkans who cannot be appeased without the sacrifice of a bull or a horse.

The Shaman kills the animal by making an incision in the breast and pulling out the heart. The body of the animal is disjointed at the neck and at the knees, the skin removed, except from the legs and head, and the body carried away to be boiled. Then a long pole is driven into the ground and the skin of the animal is fastened to the top of it, the head facing the mountain, hill, or place where the Burkan who has caused the sickness is supposed to have his home. The pole leans slightly toward that same mountain.

The flesh of the animal is cut up and cooked, and bits of it offered to the Burkan, either thrown into the air or burned, the rest is eaten by the family and those who assist at the sacrifice. Tarasun is used freely at such times. During the ceremony the Shaman mumbles mysterious words and prayers.

There is a second way of offering the sacrifice. The liver, gall, and intestines are burned, the bones of the animal are broken into small pieces, and together with the pleura put into a bag and placed on a pole, where the bag remains until it rots and falls.

If the patient has pain in any particular part of his body the Shaman puts spittle on it and prays to the Burkan who has caused the pain; sometimes he touches the man's tongue with a red-hot iron, or he pours hot water over his body, and though the water is very hot it feels cold.

If after the first sacrifice the sick person does not recover, a second is made, and perhaps a third. The Shaman does not get discouraged, but continues his efforts until his patient recovers or dies. In former times he was paid very little for his labor,—whatever the family thought proper,—but at present the reward is sufficiently large.

The light Burkans, as well as the dark, can cause sickness. Sickness sent by a light Burkan is usually in punishment for the taking of an oath (to swear by the name of a Burkan is an oath); or for the killing of a sacred bird, which is a great sin, and if the man is not punished for the sin his children will be.

Berkut, the white-headed eagle, is a sacred bird. Ejin, the god of Olkhon, the sacred island of Lake Baikal, had no children; so he created the white-headed eagle and called him his son, adopted him. Ejin himself is the son of the Fiery Heaven, and is called Utá Sagan Noyón (High White Prince). He is counted a brother of Dalai Lama, who is also a son of the Fiery Heaven (Galta Tengeri Xubun) (Fiery Heaven son). The swan is a sacred bird. Vultures are not sacred, but they are often sent by the Burkans to locate persons whom they are about to punish.

THE OWNER OF THE LAND IS SICK; A RAM
HAS BEEN SACRIFICED WITH DUE
CEREMONY. *Page* 99

THE OWNER OF THE LAND IS SICK; A RAM HAS BEEN SACRIFICED WITH DUE CEREMONY.

BONES OF THE RAM. *Page* 100
They will remain until the bundles rot and fall

No one is permitted to kill a white-headed eagle. If an eagle alights on a sheep or lamb and scratches it, the owner kills the animal immediately.

The Buriats do not sacrifice to the eagle, but to its ancestors "the ancients of eagles." In some cases those ancestors are represented as people, in others as birds.

RITES ATTENDING THE BURNING OF THE DEAD

The Buriats usually burn their dead; occasionally, however, there is what they call a "Russian burial," that is, the body is placed in a coffin and the coffin is put in the ground.

But generally if a man dies in the autumn or the winter his body is placed on a sled and drawn by the horse which he valued most to some secluded place in the forest. There a sort of house is built of fallen trees and boughs, the body is placed inside the house, and the building is then surrounded with two or three walls of logs so that no wolf or other animal can get into it.

The horse which drew the body to the forest is led away a short distance and killed by being struck on the head with an axe, then it is left for wolves to devour.

If the man was so poor as not to have a horse, but had a cow, the cow is sold and a horse bought to take the body to the forest. If so poor that a horse cannot be purchased, the body is carried on a stretcher.

If other persons die during the winter their bodies are carried to the same house. In this lonely, silent place in the forest they rest through the days and nights until the first cuckoo calls, about the ninth of May. Then relatives and friends assemble, and without opening the house burn it to the ground. Persons who die afterward and during the summer months are carried to the forest, placed on a funeral pile, and burned immediately. The horse is killed, just as in the first instance.

Often the ornaments and the most valued trinkets of the dead are burned with them, as well as their best garments. Ordinary garments are left for their heirs.

A Shaman does not officiate at this cremating ceremony, which is conducted in the most quiet manner possible.

BURIAT BURIAL OF THE DEAD

As soon as a Buriat dies he is dressed in his best garments and his face is covered with a white cloth. On that day no neighbor or friend begins any work; to do so would bring misfortune. They call the day "mu udir," bad day.

It is customary to keep a body three days, but often it is buried or burned on the second day. In the coffin a small sum of money is placed, each friend contributing. A sheep or cow is killed and bits of the meat put in the coffin, together with a small bottle of tarasun. "The spirit of the dead man will meet the spirits of friends and relatives who have died earlier, and he will wish to entertain them." Every necessary article, such as his coat, cap, pillow, and blanket, is put into the coffin, as well as his pipe and tobacco, even his whip for his horse, if he has owned one in his earth life, goes with him.

The family and friends eat the meat of the animal they have killed and drink tarasun. As they drink they pour out some to the dead man, pouring it on the ground and mentioning his name. For three days and nights refreshments of every kind are served in the house—the man's spirit is there among his friends and relatives and it partakes of the food.

The spirit has the form of the body but is invisible, except to persons having "second sight." The spirit is often sorry to go from among the living, and tries to prove to itself that it is still alive; that is, in the visible form. "It goes to the fire, steps on the ashes, and when it sees no track fears that it is no longer in a material body. It goes close to the chained dog to see if the dog will bark. If the dog barks it is a proof that he sees something, and the spirit hopes that it is visible. When the man's friends breakfast, dine, or drink tea, the spirit waits anxiously to see if any one will offer it food or drink. If four or five are drinking tea, the spirit takes a cup and wonders that they do not notice it; but the five cups are there, it has taken only the spirit of the cup. The man is there in spirit among his friends, he moans and weeps, hopes and tests the position; no one sees him, no one pays any attention to him. Poor man, he is sad indeed."

When the corpse is taken from the house for burial it is carried out head first. During this ceremony, if a button or any small article drops it is lucky, and each person is anxious to pick it up, for the man who does so will have a child added to his family, or some other good fortune will come to him.

Sometimes the dead man is taken from the coffin and placed on the back of his favorite horse; a friend sits up behind to hold him on, and thus he rides to his own burial. But more frequently the body is left in the coffin and the coffin is carried on a sleigh or a wagon. Women and children take farewell of the dead at the house, only men attend the burial.

When they reach the spot where the body is to be buried they sprinkle the earth with tarasun, and then dig the grave. The saddle is taken from the dead man's horse, broken into small pieces, and put in the bottom of the grave, and if the body has been brought on a wagon the wagon is broken up also. This done, the coffin is placed in the grave so that the body lies facing the southeast. The horse is led aside and killed, either by the blow of a sledge hammer on the forehead or by a knife being driven into the spinal marrow; the latter is the nobler form of death. The skin on the horse's back is cut away to represent a saddle, and on his head and face a bridle is outlined in the same way; then he is either burned, or left for wild beasts to devour. The horse has gone to its master and is ready for use. The friends now return to the grave and fill it with earth.

Nine days of remembrance are incumbent on the nearest relatives; they must remain in their houses and think only of the dead. If a near relative lives far away he will come when he hears of the death, even if it is not for a month; he will bring food and drink and "make remembrance."

Where the dead are buried or burned, there are large settlements, houses, and buildings of every kind; but all this is invisible, except to persons with second sight.

The spirits of the dead wear not only the garments in which their bodies have been buried, but also their old garments, those they wore many years before their death, for they wear "the ghost" of the clothes.

When spirits take the form of living people, as they can if they wish, the effect is the same as if they were clothed in real garments. The spirit of a woman sometimes takes the form of a bird and flies around its old home, but this is considered unlucky and the bird is shot at, not to kill it, but to drive it away.

The Buriats believe that sometimes a person dies because the spirit or soul gets tired and sad, and wants to leave the body. In such a case the Shaman and friends talk to the spirit, tell it to come back, and it shall eat well, drink well, and have a good time. This effort to persuade the soul to return to the body is called "the invitation." "You shall sleep well. Come back to your natural ashes. Take pity on your friends. It is necessary to live a real life. Do not wander along the mountains. Do not be like bad spirits. Return to your peaceful home." (They think that the spirits of the dead wander about the mountains, returning to their homes from time to time.) "Come back and work for your children. How can you leave these little ones?" And the Shaman names the children. If it is a woman these words have great effect; sometimes the spirit moans and sobs, and there have been instances of its returning to the body.

CHAPTER IX. THE ORIGIN OF SHAMANS

FROM Baronyé Tabin Tabung Tengeri, the first spirit to emerge from the Highest Existence in the Universe, Delquen Sagán Burkan, World White god, often called Esege Malan, came the fifty-five Tengeris. One day the spirit of one of the fifty-five, it is unknown which, entered into a hailstone, fell to the earth, and was swallowed by a girl thirteen years of age, whose name was Mélûk Shin. Soon after swallowing the stone Mélûk Shin became a mother. The son she bore—Qolongoto Ubugun, or, as he was also called, Mindiú Qúbun Iryil Noyon Tunkói—lived three hundred years. He established the Buriat religion, gave the Buriats all their prayers, and told them of their gods. (My translator, a Christian, states that Mindiú is the same for the Buriats that Christ is for Christians).

Mindiú chose and consecrated the first one hundred and seventy-six Shamans, ninety-nine males and seventy-seven females. In a sense he was himself the first Shaman. He commanded to pray to Delquen Sagan, to Tabin Tabung, to the fifty-five Tengeri, and the forty-four Tengeri,—to heavenly spirits only. But in later times Shamans have forgotten or do not follow his command, and pray sometimes to the spirits of dead Shamans, male and female, and to the Bumal (descended) Burkans.

Mindiú's portrait is always made of skunk skin.

There are two kinds of Shamans,—those made directly by Burkans, and those who have inherited from either the male or female branch of their family their right to be Shamans.

A man whose father or mother, grandfather or grandmother, has been a Shaman has the inherited right; he must, however, have this right confirmed by the Burkans. A child or young person is supposed to be acceptable to the Burkans when the spirit of a dead relative, a Shaman, comes while he is sleeping and takes his spirit to the residences of the Earthly and Heavenly Burkans, who conduct him through their mansions, show him their possessions, power, and wealth, and instruct him in all things.

To one selected directly by the Burkans the spirit of a Shaman, who has died within four or five years, comes at night while he is sleeping and conducts his spirit to the Burkans. In the morning the spirit returns to the body. This Shaman guide may select two or three, or perhaps four, children or young people and educate their spirits while their bodies sleep.

It happens sometimes that a person who seems foolish in this world becomes wise in the mansions of the Burkans, and one who seems wise to us may be found by the Burkans to be foolish and incapable.

When this education, which may require several years, is finished, the spirit of the Shaman, in the form of a flame, strikes the student a heavy blow on the forehead. He falls to the ground, and is raised to his feet by those who chance to be near him. If this happens away from his home, he is taken home, and an offering of tarasun is made by sprinkling tarasun to the young man's Shaman ancestors, and to those Burkans who gave rights of Shamanship to those ancestors. Or if he has been chosen directly, they offer a libation of tarasun to the Burkan who has chosen him. A person who has inherited the right to be a Shaman is educated exactly the same as one who is chosen directly.

Even after his education is finished it is a long time before a young Shaman can offer sacrifice; often there are years of trial. The Burkans may leave him at any time as unfit or incapable, and then he is no better than an ordinary man. His first libations and offerings are made to Bumal Burkans (those who have their homes in sacred groves) and to the spirits of Shamans. He officiates by request of the people.

The spirit of his ancestor strikes him again on the forehead. He falls, the people raise him and cut birch sticks for him an inch or so thick. He takes these sticks and sways them behind his back, then in front. Then he holds them in one hand, sways

TEA FROM CHINA, COMING FROM KIAKHTA TO THE RAILROAD IN IRKUTSK. *Page 20*

TEA FROM CHINA, COMING FROM KIAKHTA TO THE RAILROAD IN IRKUTSK.

BURIAT WATCH DOG. *Page 27*

BURIAT WATCH DOG.

them, pats his forehead with his palm, and begins to speak of the life and work of his ancestor. It is not the young Shaman who speaks, but the flame or spirit which struck his forehead, and which speaks through him.

Another flame strikes him. He falls, throws away the sticks, is raised, and the second flame speaks just as the first did. This may continue till all his Shaman ancestors have spoken. While speaking for a dead Shaman the live Shaman often approaches some person present and says such and such a Burkan wishes of you an offering and libation. If it is not given, you will suffer from sickness or misfortune.

When the young Shaman is ready to become a Shaman in full a day is appointed by the people. They invite an experienced Shaman to conduct the ceremony, and he makes libations and offerings to a number of Burkans, asking for their assistance.

Fifty-four birch trees are cut from a sacred grove, by the permission of the Burkan of that grove. Three of these trees are large, the others are small. The small ones are planted in a row called "dry"; a large tree is placed on the right side of the row and is called sergé, "pillar "; beyond this is the second large tree, called turga. The third large tree is placed in the middle of the yurta, the top coming out at the smoke-hole; to this top are fastened silk strings representing the colors of the rainbow; the strings are carried to the tree called the pillar and tied to its highest branch.

From the young Shaman's village nine men are selected to assist in the ceremony. They represent the nine Heavenly assistants of Xoxode Mergen (one of the Burkans). Then the old Shaman and the young one enter the yurta and stand at the right-hand side of the door; each holds in his right hand as many one-branched twigs as he has friendly Burkans. The old man sets fire to his twigs and summons by name the Burkans which the twigs represent; when he has finished his invocation, the young one begins. As soon as they have summoned the Burkans they leave the yurta and go to the great birch tree, "the turga."

The people of the village and of surrounding villages have brought milk, tarasun, sheep, and horses, all things necessary for a great sacrifice.

There can never be less than nine animals offered on such an occasion, if there are more than nine there must be eighteen or twenty-seven (it is not necessary, however, to have nine of a kind, there can be eight sheep and one horse, or any combination which will make up the nine).

Again the two Shamans summon the Burkans. Milk and tarasun are sprinkled as a libation on each of the nine animals, and they are then sacrificed. The old Shaman calls on the Burkans. Three of his assistants stand at his side, the first man sprinkles milk en the ground, the second tea, and the third tarasun. This, immensely multiplied, goes to the Burkans supposed to be present, or, if not present, in their dwellings where they can partake of all that is offered them.

During this ceremony the young Shaman removes his outer garments, leaving only his shirt, and approaches the row of small birches; when he reaches the birches he takes off his shirt, and is entirely naked. Then the nine young men, representing the Heavenly assistants of Xoxode Mergen, bring up in front of him a white goat and stab the goat in the breast in such a way that the blood spirts over the naked body of the new Shaman. This ceremony is called ugälga, purification. When it is over, the goat, still alive, is thrown far off to where women are waiting; they seize it, give it the finishing blow, then cook and eat the meat.

Before the sacrifice begins, if any of the animals are impure the Shaman knows it, and has them purified by being led through the smoke of burning juniper.

The flesh of the animals sacrificed is boiled, parts of it offered to the gods, and the rest eaten. When this ceremony is ended the young man is declared to be a full-fledged Shaman. If there are a number of Shamans present they begin now to tell about their family of Shamans, and there is much talk and uproar. The feasting lasts for three days and nights. Some of the Shamans go to the tops of the trees and make offerings to the gods from there.

In old times there were such mighty Shamans that they could walk on the silk strings connecting the top of the tree which comes up through the smoke-hole of the yurta with the great birch tree outside; this was called "walking on the rainbow."

The Buriats have many traditions regarding the power of their Shamans.

Once two Shamans went to heaven on the real rainbow; when coming back in the same way the Heavenly Burkans saw them and were very angry. "How did those black beetles of the earth dare to come up here on the rainbow, and think of going back on it?" asked they, and immediately they cut the rainbow. The Shamans were falling to the earth when the stronger of the two, a very powerful Shaman, seeing that they would surely be killed, turned himself into a yellow, spotted eagle, seized his companion in his claws, and brought him down to the earth gently and safely.

Once a Lama came from beyond the Baikal to visit a family at Usturdi. A Shaman by the name of Badai, who did not like to have a Lama among his people, turned himself into a gray wolf and went to the house in the night-time. The Lama, who saw the wolf and was terribly frightened, called out: "There is a wizard here in the form of a wolf! He has come to kill me! Build a fire quickly!"

The master of the house did not see the wolf; it was invisible to every one save the Lama, who was so terrified that his eyes burned, and he was as pale as a dead man. All night the beast stood in front of the Lama, apparently ready to spring at him; not till daylight did it disappear.

The Lama left Usturdi that very day.

They tell of Shamans who cut open their stomachs, take out their livers, roast and eat them, then close their stomachs and are as well as ever. Others take a sharp shaman stick called "haribo," thrust it in over one of their eyes to the depth of several inches, and ask some one to pull it out. To do so requires all the strength of a strong man, still the stick leaves no visible wound.

There are Shamans who cut a man's head off. He walks around without it, they put it on again, and he is the same as ever. Some Shamans can stab the central pillar of a yurta and a stream of tarasun will flow out, for the Shaman has power to summon tarasun from a distance, and command it to be in the pillar.

Another can call the birds of heaven, and they will come and sit on his shoulders. Then he will put the back of his hands to his head and spread out his fingers, and immediately his hands and fingers will be covered with worms for the birds to eat.

Almost any Shaman can dance on fire. A large fire is built on the ground, the Shaman strips naked and dances on the live coals until they die out; not even the soles of his feet are burned. Once a half-drunk Buriat, seeing a Shaman dancing in this manner, said, "I am as good a man as you are, I can dance on fire!" Pulling off his shoes he danced on the live coals for one moment and was so badly burned that he could not step for three months.

The seven Heavenly Blacksmiths have given a Shaman living in Usturdi the power to handle red-hot iron. He can heat a bar of iron until it is red, take it in one hand, draw the other hand over it and make sparks fly. He can lick it with his tongue and it does not burn him. This same Shaman if locked in a room whispers a few words, spits, and the door flies open.

There are Shamans who can ride on horseback through the two walls of a yurta, and leave no opening.

In Irkutsk, a long time ago, the Russians, who did not believe in Shamans, said, "We will see what power those people have."

They built a great fire and put a Shaman into it. The Burkans turned the fire into water and the Shaman danced in what seemed fire to others, but was water for him. The Russians shot at the Shamans; they caught the bullets in their hands, held them out and said, "Here are your balls." Every effort against them was useless.

A Shaman has nothing to do with marriages; with deaths he has nothing to do after it is certain that the spirit has left the body and cannot be persuaded to return. His field of action is soothsaying with the shoulder-blade of a sheep; sacrificing, preparing Ongons, tying a ribbon on the cradle of each infant when a few days old, and conducting. the great feast made when the child is one year old.

A SHAMAN STORY

In Olzoni, where this story was told, there lived three hundred years ago an old Shaman who could raise the dead. One day when he was in his seventy-fifth year he went on a visit to a neighboring village. The people there were so glad to see him that they killed a number of sheep, roasted them, and all feasted for three days.

On his way home he came to a large gate opening into a field, and there he met three hundred horned cattle. He thought that a butcher was driving them, but soon discovered that they were driven by a woman who was riding on a red ox. The woman was holding an infant in her arms. After the red ox had passed him he met a man whose head was as big as a cock of hay, he was riding on a gray stallion of enormous size.

"From where do you come, flesh merchant?" asked the Shaman.

"I am not a flesh merchant," replied the man, "I am Minga Nudite Milá (Thousand Eyes), and I have just destroyed all the cattle in the country around here."

The Shaman hurried home and found that his cattle were gone, not a cow, sheep, or horse was left. He was very angry, and going to his five brothers, who were all Shamans, he said: "Let us take counsel. Shall we not go in pursuit of Minga Nudite Milá?"

"Of what use?" asked they. "He would not yield to us, for he is subject to no one."

When he saw that his brothers were unwilling to help him, and he must do all with his own magic, the old Shaman went home, made tarasun and drank it; then he went to the corner of the room, got his axe and put it under the pillow on his bed, tied his horse to a post in the yurta and lay down, saying to his wife,

"Do not let my horse out, and do not waken me." Soon he and his horse were sound asleep. But they were not asleep, it was only their bodies which were so quiet. In reality the Shaman was riding swiftly toward the Angara.

Before reaching Irkutsk there is a mountain, Torkoi Tonkoi. From the top of this mountain the Shaman saw that Minga

Milá had made a bridge across the river and was beginning to drive his cattle over it. Half of the bridge was silver and half of it was gold.

The Shaman turned himself into a bee, made his axe equally small, and, taking it with him, flew under the bridge and hewed the pillars so that the bridge broke in two. All the cattle fell into the Angara, as well as the woman on the red ox. Minga Milá fell, but he saved himself—at least he did not sink, though he and his gray stallion remained in the water.

The old Shaman threw his gold ring of a Shaman toward heaven, and a dreadful wind sprang up which lasted for three days. Minga Milá sat on the water and was driven back and forth by the wind. After the three days of wind came three days of strong rain. By the end of those six days the hoofs of Minga Milá's horse fell off. When the storm was over Minga Milá came out of the river; his horse followed him, and they began to dry themselves. The horse's hoofs came from the river and went on to his feet.

Enraged by the loss of the cattle and the woman on the red ox, but frightened by the terrible storm, Minga Milá swore a great oath that henceforth he would not go to the Olzoni country. "Should I go there may my one thousand eyes jump out of my head, and my body be cut in three pieces. I will neither kill people hereafter nor destroy cattle," declared he. Hearing this oath the Shaman was greatly pleased, and at once started for home.

On the road he went to his five brothers and told them how he had punished Thousand Eyes. "I have freed myself and you of this monster," said he; "we can now live in peace." When he reached his yurta he rose from the bed, where his wife thought he was sleeping, untied his horse and drove it out to pasture. And all was as if it had not been. But the cattle of Olzoni were never stolen again.

The Shaman began to drink tarasun and visit his friends. In the spring, about a year after his return from the Angara, he was on his way to see friends in Olzonski-Rod when he came upon three men who were burying a dead child. "What are you doing?" asked the Shaman.

"Go thy way, grandfather," answered the men. "Stand not there, for the child is dead. No one is free from death."

They let down the body and began to cover it with earth.

"Take away that earth," commanded the Shaman; "give me the child and do you kill a goat and bury it in this grave." He carried the child to its home, had six stones heated red hot, took off his leggings, danced with bare feet on the red hot stones, and "shamaned" till morning, stepping over the dead child from time to time, until the first cock crowed. That made the blood move in the child's body, and he opened his eyes, but could not talk.

The next night the Shaman had the boy's father and mother tied to a post in the yurta, and again he danced and shamaned until the first cock crowed. All this time the child lay without moving. At sunrise the Shaman blew on the child's head and feet. He sprang up and asked, "What are you doing, father?"

Then the Shaman unbound the father and mother. "Your child is alive and well," said he; "now I will go home."

"No," said the father, "I must reward you; I am rich. I will give you half my money and half my cattle for what you have done."

"I do not need your money or your cattle," replied the Shaman. But the father was too happy over the recovery of his child to let the Shaman go without a reward. "Well," said the Shaman, "all I need is one cock of hay, an arkan rope (skin rope, hide), and nine copecks in money."

The father gave him the money, the rope, and the hay, and loaned him an ox to draw the hay home. The Shaman fed the hay to his cattle, hung up the rope, and kept the nine copecks in memory of the father's gratitude.

The raising of the boy from the dead was the last great act of the Shaman's life, for he died soon after.

BURIAT GHOST STORY

There was once a Shaman named Gaqui Guldief. One day he was returning from Irkutsk to his home, when night overtook him on the Kanjirevsk steppes. Soon after dusk he saw dead men dancing, "for he was second-sighted." He heard them say, "Be careful, Gaqui Guldief is coming!" They had known him when they were living, and knew that he understood the dead and could see them.

Among the dancers was one who danced better than any of the others, and his friends were urging him to dance his very best. He was about to do so, when Gaqui shot at him, hit him, and he fell to the ground a skull. Then a terrible disturbance arose among the dancers, and turning to one of their number, a tall strong man, they said, "You must punish him for this!" Guldief hurried away, for he heard what they said. When he got home he led into the house the savage dog he usually kept chained in the yard. He was not disturbed that night, but early the next night the tall, strong dead man came into the room followed by a great crowd of people of all ages.

There were food and drink on the table. The strong man began to eat; then the crowd ate and drank, and passed food to the living man. When they had finished eating, one of the number, looking at Gaqui, who was watching them, carefully, said, "Let us play tricks on him, and punish him." "No," cried others; "he is a good man at heart. We have eaten of his food; we will not harm him."

They remained a long time, then silently disappeared. When the watcher was alone in the room he saw that the food and drink which he had placed on the table was all there; there was not one bite of food or one drop of drink less, though all the dead had eaten.

SECOND SIGHT

Once a man having second sight was passing through a large field about dusk, when he saw three men, whom he knew to be dead, coming toward him. One of them was carrying a small box.

"What are you carrying?" asked the live man.

"We are carrying the soul of an infant," answered the dead.

The man knew that the son of a rich Buriat was very sick, and he made up his mind that the child had died, and the dead were carrying its soul away. "The dead are sometimes very shrewd and sometimes very stupid," said he to himself. "I will try and get that soul away from them."

"How queerly you walk!" called out one of the dead men. "Your feet make a dust, and you shake the earth when you step."

"I have been dead only a little while," answered the live man, "and have not yet learned to walk like the dead." Then he asked cunningly, "Are you afraid of anything?"

"We are afraid of the shipovnik bush (a shrub which has long thorns). What are you afraid of?" "I am afraid of fat meat," replied the man. He walked on with the dead until they came to a large clump of shipovnik bushes; then he seized the box in which they were carrying the child's soul and sprang into the bushes. They dared not approach, but ran off to get fat meat; they were back in a flash and began to pelt him with it. He ate the meat, and kept firm hold of the box.

After a time the dead went away, and the live man took the soul back to the house where the body of the dead child was. The soul went into the body; the child came to life and began to sneeze.

SACRED GROVES OF SHAMANS

When a Shaman dies his spirit, in the form of fire, goes to a Shaman who has been his friend during life, and strikes him such a strong blow on the forehead that he falls to the ground (the spirit or flame is invisible to bystanders). They raise the Shaman, and when he has recovered somewhat he says: "The spirit of my friend has come to me for assistance. It wishes to settle in a grove, and tells me where the grove is."

No one doubts that this is the request of the spirit of the dead Shaman. Friends go to the place mentioned, and, selecting one of the largest and best trees, cut a small box-like aperture in it. The body of the dead Shaman is burned, the ashes placed in the aperture in the tree, and a slab fastened across it. Ever afterward the grove is sacred. Later on, if the spirit of a Shaman of the same family asks that the ashes of his dead body be deposited in this grove, the request is granted. Hence often in such a grove there are several trees which contain ashes of the dead.

There are many of these sacred groves in the Buriat country. When a Buriat is passing a grove where the ashes of a Shaman or of several Shamans are deposited, he sprinkles vodka or tarasun to their spirits. If he has no vodka or tarasun he sprinkles tobacco, thinking they may like to smoke. He mentions such and such Shamans of the grove, and sends the tobacco to them specially. It is supposed to reach the spirits multiplied immensely in quantity and improved in quality.

No tree can be cut down, grass mown, or sod turned in a sacred grove. A man would come to great grief if he were to injure a tree, even by breaking off a branch or twig. The punishment would be inflicted by the spirits of the dead Shamans.

No woman can enter a sacred Shaman grove.

THE SACRED GROVES OF THE BURKANS OR BURIAT GODS

There are Burkans who are called Bumal Burkans. They are so called because instead of residing always in lofty places their homes are in certain groves. No tree can be felled, twig broken, or grass cut in such a grove. In passing the grove offerings are made of tarasun or tobacco.

Not far from the village of Usturdi, where I spent several weeks, there is a sacred grove of a Bumal Burkan. Some years ago three or four Buriats who had lost faith in their ancient religion decided to measure the land and cut the grass around the grove. Shamans warned them that not only the grove, but the land to the extent of some acres around it, belonged to the Burkan. Paying no heed to the warning, the men began to cut the grass.

The Burkan was very angry, and to punish them for trying to take his grass and curtail his domain, he sent an epidemic upon the village. People began to die off rapidly. The land around the grove was immediately abandoned, and sacrifices were made to the god, who after a time was appeased, and the epidemic died out.

One or two of the Bumal Burkans allow women to pass through their groves, but others are very strict in this regard;

women not only are forbidden to enter their groves, but are punished if they step on the land.

Sometimes there is a mountain or high hill between villages, and on the summit of the hill, not very far from the road, is a sacred grove belonging to a Bumal Burkan. If a man dies in one of the villages no person is allowed to pass the grove for three days. At the end of that time the first man to pass must purify himself before leaving home. This is done by gathering dry juniper, placing it in a pile on the ground, setting fire to it, and, when it smokes well, walking through it repeatedly, inhaling the smoke. The horse the person is to ride must be purified in the same way.

SACRED TREES AND GROVES

It has happened at times during past centuries that a Shaman seeing a beautiful tree or a fine clump of trees has thought that a Burkan or the spirit of a dead Shaman if passing by there would surely like to stop and have a smoke; hence he has declared that tree or clump of trees to be sacred, and no man would be so foolhardy as to meddle with trees which they know have been given to the Burkans and spirits.

Buriats dislike to cut down a beautiful tree which has grown up on a clean place. They are inclined to believe that the tree belongs to a Burkan; for there are cases where a man engaged in felling such a tree has been taken suddenly ill, and the Shamans have discovered that the illness was caused by the Burkan to whom the tree belonged. Sometimes the name of the Burkan is unknown; then, although an offering is made, the man may die.

A beautiful pine tree growing near Usturdi was cut down by one of the Buriats, who almost immediately fell ill. A Shaman was sent for, and by reading the cracks in the charred shoulder bone of a sheep he found that the tree belonged to a Burkan—was a sacred tree. But he did not know which Burkan; consequently, though several offerings were made, the man died.

CHAPTER X. THE GODS OF THE BURIATS

DELQUEN Sagán Burkan, World White God, is the highest existence in the Universe. He is also called Esege Malan. In him are three spirits: Baronyé Tabin Tabung Tengeri, Zúm Dishín Dirlún Tengeri, and Sagadé U!gu!gun.

From the first spirit came the fifty-five Tengeris, from the second the forty-four Tengeris; the third has seven sons and seven daughters. Of the seven sons the eldest is Golói Qûn Shara Qúbun. The eldest daughter is Golói Qûn Shara Basagán.

Prayers are offered and sacrifices made to all the Heavenly Burkans as well as to the Highest Existence. People ask the World White Burkan for cattle, for grass, and for health. They ask the three other spirits, especially Sagadé U!gu!gun, far rain, good crops, and children.

When they ask the gods for children they offer Sagadé U!gu!gun twenty pots of tarasun; they pray in the yurta, tie a hair rope around the four posts, and hang wooden rattles (playthings) on them. These playthings are to persuade the child to come. They bring from the forest and place in the middle of the yurta a tall birch tree, the top of which comes out through the smoke hole. At the roots of the tree they put three sods of earth taken from a swamp. Up this birch tree prayers are supposed to go to the Heavenly Burkans. After the offering and prayers a cradle is made, and all its belongings prepared for the coming of the new child.

No pictures are ever made of the Highest Being, or of the first and second spirit. Pictures are made of the third spirit, Sagadé U!gu!gun, of his wife, Sanqali`n Qatĕ`n, of their eldest son, Golói Qûn Shara Qúbun, and of their eldest daughter, Goloi Qûn Shara Basagán.

To the fifty-five Tengeris a sacrifice should be made three times in his life by every man who has the means. These sacrifices are as follows: the first sacrifice is fifty-five pots of tarasun, and five beasts,—one virgin mare, three virgin ewes, and one goat; the second sacrifice, fifty-five pots of tarasun, one virgin mare, five virgin ewes, and one goat; the third, fifty-five pots of tarasun, one virgin mare, seven virgin ewes, and one goat.

To Qoqodai Mĕgûn Qubi`n, the eldest of the fifty-five Tengeris, sacrifices are made frequently; the other fifty-four are simply mentioned with him.

Qoqodai Mĕgûn Qubi`n has nine sons and nine daughters. His eldest son is Qurĕndé Buqú Qubûn; the second, Qugén Mergĭn; the third, Qorsa!gái Mergĭn, the fourth, Boroldái Buqú. The eighteen sons and daughters have eighteen gray steeds. On these gray steeds they race and gallop over the sky, and make the awful thunder which we hear.

Of the forty-four Tengeris who are from Zúni Dishi`n, the second spirit of Delquen Sagan Burkan, the Highest Existence, seven are very important. These are Gutár Bai`n Tengeri, the eldest; Qap Sagán Tengeri; Togóto Bain Tengeri; Qásan Burún Qui Tengeri; Galta Ulan Tengeri; Qûng Germa Tengeri; Qair Qur Tengeri.

To the third spirit, Sagadé U!gu!gun, his wife, Sanqali`n Qatĕ`n, and their eldest son and eldest daughter, the sacrifice of a "fat, harmless ram" is made, and prayers are offered with libations of tarasun.

Buriats worship a heavenly spirit, a son of Bulage Iji`n, one of the fifty-five Tengeris. His name is Búir Sagán U!gu!gun. To this spirit and his wife, Qwir Sagán Qamagan, they make an offering of twenty-seven pots of tarasun, and two, or sometimes three, virgin ewes.

To the forty-four Tengeris offerings are made of tarasun, and thirty skins of various small animals,—three rabbit skins, five skunk skins, three ermine skins, seven squirrel skins, six small kid skins, and the skins of six small he-goats.

Irlik Namun Qûn, a descendant of the forty-four Tengeris, had three sons, Uqûr Qara Bisheshi, Selmendé Saga Bisheshi, and Shandá Bukqû Bisheshi; each of these sons came to earth, and each has his dwelling-place in a mountain of the Buriat country.

At springs Buriats worship a heavenly power, a son of one of the fifty-five Tengeris, Bulage Iji`n, Buir Sagán U!gu!gun, and his wife, Qwir Sagan Hamagan. They make sacrifices at such springs,—twenty-seven pots of tarasun, two virgin ewes, and sometimes three.

HOUSE ONGONS

First. The wheel, with an image inside representing Tumúr Shi`n Qulain Seji`n Bará, who was a holy Shaman of ancient times. People boil meat for him and in important cases sacrifice a goat. At marriage the bridegroom sacrifices a he-goat to this divinity, and a small pot of meal pudding as well as eight pots of tarasun, asking for health, happiness, prosperity, and children. The wheel is made of birch; from the bottom hangs a bunch of hair taken from under the belly of a he-goat. The figure is metallic and represents the sacred Shaman himself. The garment he wears is of red cloth, and is supposed to be a shuba or mantle. Two coral beads answer for eyes.

Second. On a square piece of black felt are represented the third spirit of the World White God, Sagadé U!gu!gun, his wife, Sanqali`n Qatĕ`n, and their eldest son and eldest daughter, as well as a tiny infant which represents the infant that people ask for in their prayers. In the pockets below the little tin pieces which portray these spirits meat is placed as an offering.

Third. A long piece of felt containing three virgin sisters (little tin figures on blue cloth), Munqugshin Basagán, Munqoden Basagán, and Boryúntēn Basagán. When these are consecrated the ceremony is performed by a Shaman. Three virgin ewes are offered, thirty pots of tarasun, and one big pot of meal pudding. Through these sisters the people ask of the World White God, or Esege Malan, land, cattle, and all that is necessary for prosperity.

OUTSIDE ONGONS

In the first bag is the skin of an ermine. The skin is so dried and shrivelled as to be unrecognizable, and two little tin images

ANDREI MIHAILOVITCH'S FIELD ONGONS TAKEN OUT OF THE BOX AND TIED AROUND THE PILLAR. *Page* 41

ANDREI MIHAILOVITCH'S FIELD ONGONS TAKEN OUT OF THE BOX AND TIED AROUND THE PILLAR.

represent Ugin Xubun and his wife. They were Shamans. People turn to them as to gods, begging for anything they wish for,—good crops, rain, etc.

In the second bag are two figures representing Qulebo and his wife. Both were Shamans. They are petitioned to intercede in all affairs pertaining to cattle-raising, buying and selling, etc.

In the largest gray bag are seven figures on two pieces of cloth; on one piece are five, on the other two. These represent Yûn Yiqé Qóta and his wife, Qazagar, and their two sons and one daughter. On the second piece of cloth are the son-in-law and one daughter-in-law. These have about the same attributes as those in the other bags, and are petitioned for similar things.

The long skin is that of a skunk, and represents the god who came down in the form of hail and entering a girl of thirteen was born and named Mindiú Qubun Iryil (see Origin of Shamans). All things are asked of him. He is very kindly and grants many prayers.

The two little beasts are ermines—two sisters who are represented in little metallic figures. The names of these sisters are Búlai and Budraganá; to them must be offered horse meat and two salmon as well as nine pots of tarasun. They are invoked in sickness, especially in cases of scrofula.

THE CREATION—ESEGE MALAN

In the beginning there were Esege Malan, the highest god, and his wife, Ehé Ureng Ibi.

At first it was dark and silent; there was nothing to be heard or seen. Esege took up a handful of earth, squeezed moisture out of it, and made the sun of the water; he made the moon in the same way.

Next he made all living things and plants. He divided the world into East and West, and gave it to the highest order of gods. These gods are very strict, and people must sacrifice horses and rams to them. If angered, they punish by bringing sickness, especially to children. Some of the higher gods punish with disease or misfortune people who offend local gods. For instance, if a man calls to witness or swears by a local god, either he is punished by that local god, or judgment is rendered by one of the superior gods, for it is a great sin to swear by any Burkan, whether the man swears truly or falsely.

Among these principal gods are the bird gods of the South-west. Many of them take the form of swans. They are very kind to good people. To these bird gods offerings are made twice each year. In the autumn a wether is offered, and in the spring mare's milk, tea, millet, and tobacco. Between these two higher orders and the Ongon gods there is a secondary order of Burkans of both sexes. Some of these descended from the higher Burkans, and others were in the old, old time people who by the favor of the divinities were made Shamans.

ESEGE MALAN AND GESIR BOGDO

(TOLD BY ARHOKOFF)

Our great story is from the sky,—the story of Gesir Bogdo. There are, as you know, people in the sky as well as here. They existed long before we did—no one knows how long. The oldest and chief of those people is Esege Malan.

Esege Malan had nine sons. The four elder sons said: "We will succeed our father." The four younger said: "No, we will succeed him." The fifth, or middle, son, a hero and very powerful, was on the side of the four younger brothers. His name was Mahai Danjin.

The four older brothers and the four younger began a dispute, and nobody knows how long it might have lasted had not Mahai Danjin interfered and sent the four older brothers down to the earth, to some place beyond the Frozen Ocean (Arctic), where they created wicked creatures, Mangathais, and vile serpents, some of which could fly around and swallow people. They also made immense and savage dogs to destroy things. This they did to spite their brothers who were ruling in the sky. They would allow no one to approach them, and to this day no man has been able to reach their dwelling-place.

As a result of the action of these four brothers, the earth became full of evil and great disorder, and continued so for many thousands of years—no man knows how long.

Meanwhile Esege Malan, having ceased to rule, had built for himself a great, splendid fortress around the sky. One day while walking about and looking at the fortress he found a place broken. He immediately called a meeting to discover who was trying to destroy his work.

In the heavens there are ninety-nine Tengeri provinces, and this meeting was formed of one Tengeri from each province. They debated long, but were unable to find out who or what had made the breach in the wall of the fortress. At last Esege Malan sent for Zarya Azergesha, "Esh," who was a very wise man, but he was footless. He refused to come to the meeting because, having no feet, he was afraid of being laughed at. Then Esege Malan sent two Shalmos (invisible spirits), to hear what Zarya Azergesha (hedgehog) might say to himself.

They found him sitting at home, and he was talking, thinking that no one could overhear him.

"That Esege Malan," said he, "does not understand. He has ninety-nine Tengeris, and still he could not control his four sons, and they went down to the earth and are making so much trouble there that the tears of people have risen to the sky and are weakening the walls of the fortress. The people have prayed and made libations, have sprinkled their own blood toward heaven, and when that did no good they sprinkled their tears. How is it that Esege Malan does not know this? Why send for me to give him information? All this trouble comes from his four sons. They are to blame for the tears and the broken battlements."

When the Shalmos heard this they waited no longer, but went quickly to Esege Malan and told him what Zarya Azergesha had said. Then Esege sent down to the earth his grand-son, Gesir Bogdo, the son of Mahai Danjin the hero, sent him as a bird, and he flew over the earth three years, unable to alight, because of the dreadful odor from dead bodies of every kind.

At last Esege Malan sent flies which created maggots, and the maggots ate the dead flesh and purified the earth, and it was sweet and clean. Then the bird alighted on a broad steppe called Urundashéi, turned itself into a blue bull, and bellowed loudly in challenge. The four brothers in their home beyond the Frozen Sea heard the voice and said, "That is the voice of one of our relatives, one of our own people!"

Then one of the four turned himself into a pied bull and went to the steppe. The two bulls fought until the pied bull threw the blue bull, caught him on his horns and tossed him through the air so furiously that he fell to the earth on the other side of the Altai mountains. Then the pied bull raced after the blue bull to kill him, but the blue bull turned himself into stone and stood in his road. The pied bull rushed at the stone bull, but broke one of his own horns. Then, finding he could do the blue bull no further harm, he roared:

"Thou hast deceived me! Hereafter I shall be the enemy of all horned cattle!" And, defeated, he went back to his brothers.

Beyond the Altai that stone bull stands to this day. But Gesir Bogdo, its spirit, went back to Esege Malan and created heroes to fight the Mangathais, the evil animals, and the serpents of the North. He had a son named Buqû Noyon. Buqû Noyon had seven sons and one daughter, whose name was Irgí Súban. Irgí Súban married Shandu Buqú Besbesh, the grand-son of Irlik Nomun, the eldest of the four brothers of the North, and thus the family of Esege Malan was at last pacified.

Solobung Yubún, the Morning Star, is a great personage. He is the favorite son of Esege Malan. If Buriats want many cattle they sacrifice a ram at dawn of day, pray to Solobung Yubún, and for three successive nights dance till daybreak.

ESEGE MALAN AND MOTHER EARTH

After Esege Malan had straightened out all things, Ehé Tazar, Mother Earth, went to visit him, and they spent several days very pleasantly. When Ehé Tazar's visit was ended and she was ready to go, she asked Esege Malan to give her the sun and the moon, and he gave them gladly; but he soon found that it was very difficult to get them for her. He called a thousand Burkans together and asked how he was to accomplish the feat, and though they studied long and seriously over it they could not tell him. Then Esege Malan sent for Esh (the hedgehog),

Field Ongons. Page 11

FIELD ONGONS.

and Esh went up to the sky to the dwelling of Esege Malan.

Esege Malan had three daughters who often came down to the earth, removed their clothing, turned themselves into swans, and sported in the sea. It happened that the three were at home when Esh came.

Esege had told his daughters that Esh was a queer fellow, that he was lame and hairy, but he was very wise, and they must not laugh at him. Notwithstanding this, when Esh walked in Esege's daughters looked sidewise and laughed; they could not help it, he was so droll. He saw them laugh and said to himself, "Esege Malan has called me up here for his daughters to laugh at and ridicule!" He was terribly angry, and left so quickly that Esege had not time to say a word. Esh knew, however, what Esege wanted, for the messenger had told him. He came down from the sky very quickly, but two Shalmos (invisible spirits) followed, sent by Esege Malan to listen and hear what Esh said as he traveled. For Esege knew that Esh was raging, and he thought that he might say something about the sun and the moon.

The first thing Esh saw as he came to earth was a herd of cows and bulls. When they caught sight of him they were frightened, put up their tails and ran. Esh, angry that they should be frightened at him, cursed them, saying:

"May the hair rope never leave your nostrils, and the yoke never leave your necks!" And so it has been.

He went farther and came to a herd of horses. They were frightened also, raised their tails, and ran away. Zarya, terribly angry, cursed them, saying:

"May the bit never leave your mouths and the saddle never leave your backs!" And so it has been.

The Shalmos followed him always, listening to what he said. After a time Esh began to talk to himself and abuse Esege Malan. "What sort of a ruler is that Esege Malan?" asked he. "What sort of a master of the world? He manages everything, fixes everything. He has given away the sun and the moon, but does not know how to get them! If he is so wise, why does he not come to visit Mother Earth, and when the visit is ended and he is ready to go, ask her for the hot dancing air of summer and the echo, habra yirligin and darbon. She would give them to him gladly, but how could she get them for him?"

When the Shalmos heard this they followed no farther, but went to the sky very quickly and told Esege Malan all that Esh had said.

Esege waited until a sufficient time had passed; then he came to return Mother Earth's visit, and while they were walking around he said: "When you came to visit me I gave you the sun and the moon, now I ask for a present. Give me the hot dancing air of summer and echo." She gave them, but try as she would she could not get them for him.

When she found that it was impossible to get them, and no one could tell her how to do it, Esege said:

"Let the sun and the moon remain where they are and the hot dancing air of summer and echo stay here!" And so it is that though the sun and the moon belong to the earth, they are in the sky, and the hot dancing air and the echo, though they belong to Esege Malan, remain with Mother Earth.

CHAPTER XI. MYTHS CONNECTED WITH MONGOL RELIGION

GESIR BOGDO. No. I

(TOLD BY SCKRETARYOFF)

AT first—in the beginning of the world—there was confusion here below, and great disorder. There were also various vile creatures, especially Mangathais. Then a council was held in the sky at which Qurmus Tengeri, one of the forty-four Eastern gods, said, "A middle son can pacify and set aside all this evil."

Esege Malan had nine sons. He called the middle one, whose son, Gesir Bogdo, said: "If I get what I need I will go to the earth and destroy the evil creatures there. But the ninety-nine Tengeris must give me all their tricks."

The Tengeris delivered their tricks, one hundred thousand in number, and Gesir Bogdo swallowed them. Then, turning to Esege Malan, he said:

"Now it is thy turn. Give me thy black steed and a hero's outfit." Esege gave the black steed and the outfit. "Give me thy lasso and thy dart." Esege gave the lasso and dart. Then Gesir asked for a wife and got her. He said to his wife, "Thou hast three daughters, give those three daughters to me." At first the woman refused. "It is bad down there," said she, "they cannot stay there. I will not give them."

"If I cannot get all that I need I shall not go," declared Gesir Bogdo.

Then Esege Malan commanded Otqon Tengeri to soothsay and find out what to do, to give or not to give. Otqon obeyed and said: "They will be of use to Gesir Bogdo. It is necessary to give them."

The mother gave her three daughters, and Gesir Bogdo swallowed them, as he had swallowed all that Esege Malan gave him. Then he took farewell, but he did not come down to earth at once; he traveled around in heaven for three years, looking down always. And during those three years he saw all the evil-doers everywhere,—all the bad spirits and vile creatures. Then he said, "I cannot go down as I am, I must be born in that country." He saw a woman sixty years of age; her name was Tumún Yarigûl, and her husband's name was Sindlei U!gu!gun. And he said, "I wish to enter that woman's head."

That year Sindlei U!gu!gun was very prosperous, his herds increased, and his grass grew wonderfully well. One day Tumún said: "I feel that I am to be the mother of many. I hear children talking."

Many children were soon born to her, each in a different way, but all flew to the sky. At last one was born who said, "As I am born all people will be born hereafter." And so it has been. This infant was thin, and very ugly to look at; but it changed quickly and at once grew to a man's stature. This man, who was Gesir Bogdo, cleaned away all vile things, destroyed evil spirits and bad people. Lusugúi Mangathai was the last evil spirit he killed, and when Gesir Bogdo had him by the legs he scratched the earth with his fingers and ten streams gushed out. They form the river Aqa, which falls into the Angara on the left side. Then Gesir said:

"Now I will lie down and sleep. Let no one waken me. I will sleep till again there will be many harmful things, evil spirits, and bad people in the world; then I will waken and destroy them."

Gesir Bogdo had three sons and six grandsons before he came down from the sky. Of each of his nine descendants there were in the old time nine tales, in all eighty-one. They had to be told in groups of nine, and the relator could neither eat, drink, nor sleep while telling them, and when each group of nine was told an unseen person said, "Thou hast forgotten where thou placed thy Pfu!"

Gesir Bogdo was born in Qonyin Qotoí. He sleeps at the

FIELD ONGONS, CHURCH IN WHICH THE AUTHOR SPENT THREE DAYS, AND THE GROUP OF HOUSES MENTIONED ON PAGE 72. *Page* 11

FIELD ONGONS.

CHURCH IN WHICH THE AUTHOR SPENT THREE DAYS, AND THE GROUP OF HOUSES MENTIONED ON PAGE 72.

Rising of the Sun (Qúlaganá Qóli). He lies under an immense flat rock; all around it is a great taigà (a marshy forest of Siberia). When, to rest easy, he turns from one side to the other, the earth trembles. The Russians call this trembling an "earthquake," but the Buriats know that it is Gesir Bogdo turning over.

GESIR BOGDO. No. II

A VERSION OF THE PRECEDING STORY

IN a time unknown, but very, very long ago, in a world preceding this world there were people called Marat; there were also Mangathais, who were ruled over by Shalmo Khan (Invisible Khan).

Once Delquen Sagan, the Highest Being, said: "Let Shalmo Khan and his people be destroyed. Let a people be created who will be peaceful." Then he sent his grandson, Gesir Bogdo, to the earth to be Khan.

In the South, in a land called Altai Deda, lived an old man and an old woman. He was seventy years old and she was sixty. His name was Sundlei U!gu!gun, and hers was Sundlei Hamiagan (U!gu!gun means old man, and Hamiagan, old woman). They were of the Marat people.

One day Sundlei Hamiagan said, "I feel that I am to be the mother of many children, I hear them discussing as to how they will come into the world."

Soon many sons were born to Sundlei Hamiagan, each in a different way, and each immediately went to the sky. After ten days a child was born, who said:

"In the way that I am born all people will be born hereafter." And so it has been.

This child was Gesir Bogdo. No knife could cut the umbilical cord. At last the boy said to his father:

"On the west side of the yurta roof is a plant, the khan of plants. Get that plant, wave it three times in the sun over the cord, and I shall be free." This was done; the cord withered and dropped. When they had swaddled the boy and placed him near his mother, he said to his father:

"Go to the forest and cut nine birch trees. In your herd is a strong black stallion. On the lintel of the yurta door is a yellow flint given me by Esege Malan; that flint has magic power. In a box on the west side of the yurta is a saddle, sweat cloth, and all the outfit of a hero." Sundlei U!gu!gun did not know of these things; they had come with Gesir Bogdo.

When the old man brought the nine birch trees and placed them, as Gesir told him, against the hitching-post, they became nine blue horses. That moment nine Shalmos came riding nine horses just like those at the hitching-post. As they rode up, the boy rose and went to the door of the yurta.

"Have you not horses to run against ours?" asked the Shalmos.

"I am young, just born. I do not know how to ride yet. Mount my horses and try them. When I grow up I will ride with you."

The nine sprang on to the horses, and the horses rushed away to the Yellow Sea. They did not stop at the shore, but raced on till they reached the navel of the sea; there, turning into nine trees again, they sank in the waves, and the nine Shalmos were drowned.

When three years old Gesir Bogdo was full grown; then changing the strong black stallion and his hero's outfit into a flint, he put the flint in his pocket and went away on foot.

It is unknown how long he traveled, but at last he came to a place where three roads met. There he became a small, deformed boy; one arm and hand grew out of his back, one leg was drawn up to his hip, his eyes were sunk in his head. He was ugly, terrible to look at.

From the southwest came ninety-nine Shalmos on ninety-nine blue horses. They approached the deformed child and wondered what he could be, but said nothing and rode on. The boy sat awhile longer; then by his magic he went around the ninety-nine Shalmos, was at the Yellow Sea before them. There he made with his flint, from the bark of a tamarack tree, ninety-nine little boats, and commanded them to be large and strong; then he made a shed by the sea, turned himself into an old man, and was sitting there in the shade of the shed. The ninety-nine Shalmos rode up on the ninety-nine blue horses. Seeing the old man and his boats, they said:

"We are going to the Northwest Tengerin (heavens). We cannot cross the sea on horseback. Take our ninety-nine horses and give us thy ninety-nine boats."

The old man consented. As he untied the boats, he said to each one, "When thou reachest the navel of the sea turn into a chip of tamarack bark, and let the Shalmos drown in the abyss of the sea."

When the Shalmos were in the boats, the boats shot away of themselves and could not be stopped or guided. They reached the navel of the sea, turned into tamarack chips, and the ninety-nine Shalmos were drowned.

Then Gesir Bogdo went back to the old man's yurta, saddled his strong black stallion, put on his armor of a hero, and went to the Northwest, where lived three hundred and sixty Mangathais. Of those the greatest, Danjin Shara Mangathai, had seventy-three heads.

Gesir Bogdo turned his horse and armor into a flint, put the flint into his pocket, became a weak old man, and went to the yurta of the Mangathais.

"A splendid dinner has come of itself," said the chief Mangathai. "I was without a dinner, now I have one."

"What dinner am I for you? I am an old man," said Gesir Bogdo. "I paint. Have you no work for me to do?"

"Paint the inside of my yurta," said the Mangathai.

The old man began painting, and as he painted he said, "Let the Black Colt people increase, let the Mangathais perish!"

"What are you saying?" asked the Mangathais, and Gesir Bogdo answered, "I say, let the three hundred and sixty Mangathais increase, let the Black Colt people perish."

Instead of painting, Gesir Bogdo was making the yurta iron inside. When he had finished inside he went outside, and painted until the outside of the yurta was iron also. Then, going to the smoke hole, he said:

"Let thirteen enchantments lie on this yurta. Let twenty-three iron hoops surround it. Let the three hundred and sixty Mangathais perish, and the Black Colt people increase."

"What art thou muttering up there?" asked the chief Mangathai. "I was saying, 'Let thirteen enchantments settle down on this yurta, let twenty-three iron hoops surround it, let the three hundred and sixty Mangathais perish inside it!"

The Mangathais could not escape from the iron house, though they felt that the weight of enchantment was sucking them into the earth.

The whole yurta was sinking. Soon the smoke hole was level with the ground. The chief Mangathai stuck one of his heads through the opening. Gesir crushed it with a mighty blow from a seventy pood hammer sent him by his grandfather, Esege Malan. Then he asked the Burkans for an iron hero to watch at the yurta and crush with the hammer any Mangathai who should try to escape. Thus perished the Mangathais, "evil creatures who lived in a world preceding this."

GESIR BOGDO. No. III

BETWEEN two sky-dwellers, Khan Tyurmas Tengeri and Atai Ulan Tengeri, a dispute arose as to which of them should be master of Segel Sebdik Tenger, the cold ice sky. At last they agreed that in three days they would meet and decide the question by battle; and they arranged that both should lead their forces to Sebdik Tenger, and the one who reached there first should wait for the other.

When Atai Ulan arrived with his forces Khan Tyurmas was not at the place appointed. He was not there because he had gone to his grandmother, who lived in the West, at Yoldá Molyán Qurmé Tudi. He went to ask her advice. While at Yoldá Molyán he got drunk on tarasun, spent six days in his grand-mother's company, and forgot his contest altogether.

Atai Ulan waited one day, waited two days. After three days had passed he took possession of Segel Sebdik, and turned homeward, thinking that Khan Tyurmas was frightened and did not dare to fight, hence the case was won by him.

Then the youngest son of Khan Tyurmas, Gesir Bogdo, a boy four years of age, caught his father's horse, saddled him, put on his father's clothes, took his weapons, and with a long spear in his hand rode out to war against Atai Ulan. He overtook Atai when he was in the middle of his own dominions, and half-way home. He thrust this spear into Atai's right side, unhorsed him, and cast him down from the sky to the earth.

When Atai Ulan fell to the earth he turned into Mangathais, and evil Shalmos, spirits who sow dissensions and disputes, and destroy people.

The thousand Burkans, who live above the many skies, assembled on Dolon Odun (Great Bear, the seven stars) and counseled what to do to stop the activity of all the evil spirits that come from Atai Ulan, that is, to set aside evil. They decided to send to the earth Dashin Shuher, the eldest son of Khan Tyurmas, and said that he might be able to conquer the Mangathais. But Dashin Shuher would not go.

"I will not go," said he. "Let him go, who overthrew and hurled down Atai Ulan. Let Gesir Bogdo go."

Then the thousand Burkans summoned Gesir Bogdo. When he appeared all asked: "Why didst thou hurl Atai Ulan down to the earth? If it was thy wish to crush, why not crush him in the sky? If to kill, why not kill him in the sky? Go to the earth now and destroy all the Mangathais and Shalmos that came from him."

Gesir Bogdo said that he could not go to the earth in that form which he had, and asked that they send Uhul Khan (Death) to him, and directed that when Death had his body they should prepare a place for the body, and put it there. The place was to be so made that the body would not decay in summer, or freeze in winter. It was to be sitting on a throne, before it was to be a table, and on its left hand a paper. When his body was thus cared for his spirit would enter the body of a woman on earth, and be born again.

Gesir Bogdo's three sisters were to go down to the earth with him.

When Death came, and his body was cared for, Gesir's spirit turned into a raven, his sisters turned into cuckoos, and all four flew down. They flew around the whole world below, made the circuit of the world. At last they saw, at the upper end of a valley called Orhé Yalga, Entering Valley, a poor yurta. In that yurta was a man seventy years old, who had a wife who was sixty years old. The spirits of Gesir Bogdo and his sisters entered that woman. When they had lived there six months Gesir said to his earthly mother:

"O mother, take off thy cap."

The woman was terrified, took off her cap and threw it aside from fear. Then Gesir flew out through her head, rose to the sky, and higher up to the thousand Heavenly Burkans.

"I have found a yurta, a father and a mother," said he to the Burkans. "When I am born send me, I pray, thirty-three strong champions, three thousand warriors, and cattle of all sorts; besides, give me all that I may ask for to carry out what I wish. Leave me not on earth without protection."

After this he went to earth again and entered his mother a second time. The woman was greatly alarmed at this second visit, and counseled with the old man, her husband. "Do not take off thy cap again, for any reason," said he. They thought that evil Shalmos were trifling with them, and they were terrified.

About ten months after the first visitation, the woman knew that she was about to become a mother, and she said to her husband:

"Stay at home to-day, do not leave me."

"Nothing will happen," said the old man. "I will go and come back again quickly." So he went to hunt rabbits, but was not gone long when the woman gave birth to three daughters, all very beautiful. But they turned to ravens, flew out through the smoke hole, and went up to the sky.

A son was born next. He was very ugly; his feet were crooked, his arms were behind his back, and twisted. He looked more like a frog than a boy.

When the old man came home the mother scolded: "You would not stay, our beautiful daughters have flown away, now take this ugly, deformed creature. He is just like a frog. Do what you like with him."

The old man cared for the child, and in three days the boy spoke: "To-morrow," said he, "before sunrise you must put me in a cradle. I will cry, cry all the time. You must sway the cradle, and the more you sway it the more I will cry. At sunrise two men will come, they will hear me cry, and ask: 'What have you here in this cradle?' You will say: 'We know not, whether it is a child, or some ugly creature; its legs are bent upward, its hands are twisted behind its back. Can you free the hands and feet, and straighten the arms and legs for us?' They will come to the cradle and look at me. That moment I will strike out with hands and feet and kill those two strangers."

Next morning before sunrise the boy began to cry fiercely. His father put him in the cradle, rocked him, talked to him, soothed him, but all to no purpose, he only cried the louder. Then, just at sunrise, as he had said, two young men entered the yurta and asked:

"What have you here in the cradle? Why does it not keep its tongue in its mouth?"

"We know not if it is a child, we know not what it is or what it will be. Do ye know how to cure it, or straighten its arms and legs?"

"Yes, we know," said they. The old man and woman gave the child to them. The boy stretched, struck out his hands and feet with such force that it hurled down the strangers, crushed them, killed them both.

Then the child said to the old man and its mother: "To-morrow I will cry and do you try to hush me, rock me, sing to me, talk to me. Two young men will come in and ask the same questions as those asked to-day, and I will kill them, just as I killed those two."

Next day two men came in the same way, asked the same questions, and were killed in like manner. After that the child said: "Six Shalmos will come to-morrow. I will cry, you will rock me, soothe me, talk to me. I will cry and cry. When they come in they will ask: 'What is the trouble with that child of yours.' Ye will answer: 'Oh, we do not know. Something is the matter with its tongue, there are pimples on it. Can ye not cure the poor child?' They will say: 'Oh, yes, only give the child here, we will cure it.' Ye will give me into their arms."

The Shalmos came in the form of young men, asked questions, and were ready to cure the crying infant. The mother gave the child to the foremost of the Shalmos. The little boy opened his mouth, the stranger put out his tongue, the child caught it, drew it in hard, then sucked it out roots and all, and swallowed it. The Shalmo could not say one word, he could only groan, and give the child to the second Shalmo. The same thing happened to the second, and to the third Shalmo, and so on to the sixth. All six lost their tongues and could not say a word, could not tell what had happened. They went away speechless, and the woman put the child in its cradle.

Next evening the boy said to his mother: "Fill my sucking bottle with milk and put it in the cradle at sunrise, carry the cradle to the roadside, and leave me there till sunset. If not I shall not be thy son."

Next morning they put him, as he wished, near the roadside. At midday came two mighty ravens, with iron beaks and iron claws. They alighted one at one side of the cradle and one at the other. Just before alighting they said to each other: "If we let this boy alone he will grow to great strength and destroy us; we will pick his eyes out to-day."

"Ah!" thought the boy, and he said to them as they came down to the cradle. "With those beaks ye would soon devour everything. I will take them from you, and give you bone beaks." With that he plucked the iron beaks from their heads and wished for them to have bone beaks, then he said: "With those iron claws ye would tear and rend everything, I will give you bone claws in place of those." With that he tore their claws off, and gave them such beaks and claws as ravens have in our time. The ravens flew away small, insignificant, and weak.

At sunset the old man and woman came and took the child home. He gave directions to be carried out a second time, in just the same way. The second day they left him by the roadside. Three valleys distant was a mighty mosquito as big as any bullock; it had a great bone sting, sharp as a war spear. It had bone legs as hard as horse legs, and it had tremendous strength in its bulky body.

"Oh," said the mosquito, "if that old man's son grows up he will destroy me. This day I will suck his blood out and kill him."

The mosquito flew over the three valleys, stood at the cradle, and thrust its sharp, enormous sting at the infant. The boy seized the sting, broke the mosquito into bits, made it as small, puny, and tiny as a mosquito is in our time, gave it slim legs and a miserable little sting, and it flew away with a voice as weak and low as it is to-day.

The next morning the boy said: "At Sazgai Bain Khan's there is a wedding. He is giving his daughter, Sangha Gohun, in marriage to the son of Shurik Taiji Hubun. I will go to that wedding."

"How couldst thou go; thou art a little fellow, thou canst not walk yet," said the father and mother. "Some person there would crush thee to death."

"The khan's daughter is to take me as bridegroom, and I must go," answered the boy.

He made them gird his goat skin on, and then he toddled off. When out of sight he called on the thousand Burkans to send his steed, with outfit for beast and rider. The steed was there immediately. It was ninety fathoms long, and other parts accordingly. The saddle was of smooth silver, the saddle cloth of silk, the bridle of silver. The trousers of the rider were of elk skin, the cap of sable, boots of fish skin, coat of silk and belt of silver.

Gesir Bogdo put on his dress, mounted, and rode to the house of Sazgai Bain Khan.

In the evening at the wedding he danced in the circle, and no one there was as graceful or as beautiful as he. All admired him. The first night he danced splendidly, the second night he danced so that no one equalled him; and then he began to pay attention to the bride. The third night the bride was in love with him, and he urged her to go with him. At midnight he stole Sangha Gohun, put her on his steed and shot away homeward. When he came to the rock where he had hidden his goat skin he dismounted, took Sangha Gohun down, pointed out the yurta where his father and mother were, and said:—

"That is my yurta, go on ahead, I will follow quickly." She did as he asked. He let his steed loose, put on his old goat skin, became a stumbling little boy again, and toddled on toward the yurta.

When Sangha Gohun reached the yurta and saw the wretched place she lamented. "Why did I come to this dreadful yurta?" cried she, "why did I, the daughter of a khan, desert a khan's son, and come to this misery?" And she resolved to go back to her father. So the next morning she started and traveled; traveled all day till the sun had gone down, and then what did she see when the sun had set, but this, that she was right there by the old man's yurta.

She was held to the yurta by magic. She had to stay there all that night. She knew not what had become of her new husband, but when she went out of the yurta to escape she saw a boy tumbling in through the doorway, and thought him some ugly, dirty, unknown little urchin.

The next morning she again tried to escape, but after traveling all day at sunset she was back near the same wretched yurta, back to the place from which she had started.

The third day she tried, and the fourth, but each evening she was at the yurta: she could do nothing, could not get away. Then she lay down to sleep by the boy, concluding that he was her husband in another form.

The fifth night she went down on her knees before the boy: "Turn back to thy own form, become thy real self," implored she. "Why torment me? Turn back and be as thou wert when I saw thee first." She begged for two days.

On the morning of the ninth day, after going to sleep in the poor, wretched old yurta Sangha Gohun woke up in a white stone yurta three stories high. She was lying on a golden couch. Everything there was in wonderful plenty and splendor, the boy was there too, and, though in a palace in place of a wretched yurta, he was no handsomer or cleaner than before.

When Sangha Gohun woke there were thirty-three strong champions outside, three thousand warriors, and a great many people standing or moving about. She wondered where that ugly, nasty, little creature got such magnificence.

The twelfth evening, when going to bed, she tied, unknown to him, a silk string around his ankle. At midnight she woke; he was gone. She was astonished when she saw that the silk string which she had tied around his ankle had stretched from the bed to the ceiling. She went to the top of the yurta and saw that from the roof to the sky there was a beautiful rainbow. He had gone to the sky on that rainbow, and she followed him.

He had gone to Esege Malan to beg for more power and riches. Esege Malan looked down and asked angrily: "Who is that following thee?"

The boy looked, and saw Sangha Gohun. When she reached the sky he gave her a push, and she went sliding down on the rainbow till she came to the roof of the white stone yurta, and then he followed her. Esege Malan was so angry that he pulled in the rainbow and put it down on the earth where it has remained, and there has never been a rainbow in heaven since that morning.

The boy too was angry, and he fell to beating his bride; he beat her three days and nights, calling out as he struck: "If thou hadst not followed I might have got all I wanted; Esege Malan would have given it."

He commanded the thirty-three strong champions to lead his cattle and horses to water. When they reached the seashore, they found an aspen tree growing there; they pulled it up by the roots, and from the hole came a Mangathai with ten heads, and as he came out he cried:

"I will eat you up! I will eat up every one of you."

"Thou wilt gain nothing by eating us. If thou eat us our master will come and kill thee."

"What weapons has your master?" asked the Mangathai.

"Ninety-nine arrows, and a great yellow bow. There are ninety-five knobs on the bow to protect it from the string, and the arrow is of that kind that it will cut off not only thy head, but any head in the world. The arrow head is three sided."

"Destroy those weapons," said the Mangathai, "and I will take you into my service and treat you like Burkans. Ye will live in the same way that I do. With your present master ye will always be cattle herders."

"We will work for thee," said the men, and they went home to cut and break the bows and arrows. They tried the string and the knobs, but could not injure them in any way, could not do the least harm to them, but they returned to the Mangathai and told him that they had destroyed the weapons.

The Mangathai now went to fight with Gesir Bogdo, thinking that if his weapons were destroyed he could be killed easily. About midnight the dogs at Gesir Bogdo's yurta began to bark, and Sangha Gohun said:

"Perhaps some one will shut you in, and kill you."

"I am not afraid," said Gesir; "no one can injure my weapons, no one can destroy me." He knew that his strong champions had tried and had failed in the trial. He went out to defend his yurta. The Mangathai appeared at a distance, riding on an immense stallion, but when he saw Gesir Bogdo ready and brandishing his weapons be turned quickly to flee from him. Gesir sent his arrow. "Go," said he to the arrow, "and cut off the right arm of that Mangathai, and then cut off all his heads."

The arrow did as commanded. Then Gesir burned the Mangathai's body and scattered the ashes.

Three days later the thirty-three mighty champions came to him. Gesir Bogdo was angry and reproached them. They told him that Gal Nurman Khan (fire ashes and fire) was at war and they begged him to go with them to the war. He was unwilling, and said that they must not go to war in a year of bad grass and great accidents.

"Take us! Take us even for three days!" urged they. When Gesir refused, they took skin straps and hair ropes and declared that as it was better to die than to be deprived of such pleasure, they were going to hang themselves. Then Gesir Bogdo promised to go with them. He sent them to collect all weapons that were of use in war; and in three days the thirty-three champions and three thousand men were armed properly.

Gesir Bogdo mounted his wonderful steed and went in his dress of a hero, which he always wore now. The thirty-three mighty champions were afraid of Gal Nurman, with whom they were going to fight, for he never slept save for a few moments just before daybreak, hence they decided to climb a high mountain and watch from there.

They climbed the mountain and waited, watched to see if Gal Nurman would come out as fire, or in his own shape. He was off in the southeast, but he saw them and stood up immediately; drank tarasun, mounted his golden bay steed and started, without armor or attendants; rode out against them, rode straight to where Gesir Bogdo was, and asked:

"Hast thou come to fight with me? If so let us fight man to man."

Gesir Bogdo threw his armor off, sprang from his horse, and they began to wrestle. They wrestled three days and three nights, and fought with such fierceness that they tore off all the flesh from each other's backs with their hands, and from each other's breasts with their teeth.

VASSYA, HIS FATHER, AND MR. CURTIN. *Page 33*

VASSYA, HIS FATHER, AND MR. CURTIN.

At last Gal Nurman began to overpower Gesir Bogdo, then two of Gesir's mighty champions sprang forward; one of them seized Gal Nurman's right leg. Gal kicked him and sent him rolling, turning over and over down the hill. Then the other champion seized Gal's left leg. Gal kicked, and sent him rolling and turning in the same way. Then Gesir Bogdo called on the Burkans to help him, but they would not; they were angry because Sangha Gohun, his wife, had followed him up the rainbow to the sky. Then Gesir called on his brother Dashin Shuher. He came immediately, and the two killed Gal, put his body in an iron cask, and rolled it into the sea; then they went to Gal's yurta.

Gal Nurman had two wives. Gesir Bogdo let an arrow fly at the yurta, struck the younger woman and out of her body sprang an infant. "I am born three days before my time!" cried the child. "If I live nine days longer I shall conquer Gesir Bogdo and Dashin, his brother!" and he began to sway his head.

"Why kill that woman?" asked Dashin of Gesir Bogdo. "I should have taken her for a wife." And Dashin, angry at his brother, left him, and went up to the sky.

Gesir Bogdo put the elder wife into an iron barrel and rolled the barrel into the sea; then he built a furnace, made a fire in it, and put the child in the fire. Next morning when he went to the furnace the boy was playing with live coals. "Ah, father," cried he, "into what a nice warm place thou didst put me!"

The second night Gesir made a still greater fire, and put the child into it. The second morning he again found the boy playing with the live coals. The third night Gesir watched the child and saw that a red and green tube came down from the sky to his navel. It raised the child up, and a stream of water fell on him. Bogdo took an arrow, shot at the tube and cut it. Then he made a great fire, and burned the child to ashes.

Bogdo took all the cattle, all the people, and all the treasures; ruined Gal Nurman's place. When he brought the people to his domain he told them where to live, fixed homes for them. Then he went into his white stone yurta and lay down to sleep, but first he said to Sangha Gohun: "In case of danger if you cannot rouse me take my sword and stab me in the right heel. If that does not rouse me stab me in the right thigh. If that fails to waken me let cold spring water drop into my right ear."

He went to sleep, and soon a seventeen-headed Mangathai appeared, a brother of the ten-headed one whom Gesir had killed. The dogs began to bark; the watchmen and the thirty-three champions raised a great outcry. Sangha Gohun was frightened, and tried to waken her husband. She was going to stab him in the heel, but said to herself: "If I do that it will injure him and how can he fight? If I stab him in the thigh blood will flow, and what strength will he have to fight? If I pour water into his ear it will run into his head and make him foolish; he will have no sense; how could he carry on a war then?"

And she did neither of the three things, but began to cry. She cried all day, cried bitterly. At night when she put up her hand to wipe the tears away one chanced to fall in Gesir's ear; it woke him at once. He was frightened, sprang up, and before he was well awake he snatched his weapons and hurried into the courtyard. The Mangathai was there, and cried to Gesir:

"Go to that mountain on the northwest, and I will go to the one on the southeast, and we will hurl axes at each other."

Gesir agreed. The Mangathai said: "I will hurl my axe first."

"No," said Gesir Bogdo, "I was born here; I should have the first throw."

"No, thou hast killed my brother; I should have the first throw!" And the Mangathai whirled his axe and let it fly to the opposite mountain.

The axe was coming straight toward Gesir's head and would have cut it off surely, but that instant he turned himself into stone. The axe hit the stone, but made no hole or dint in it. Gesir took his own form, seized his best arrow, and said:

"Fly, fly, O my arrow, and break the spinal column beneath the Mangathai's neck, break his right forearm, fall then upon his breast and whirl through his heart and lungs, cut them into small pieces, and come back to me."

He whispered with such force to the arrow, that, from magic, red fire appeared on the bow where the arrow touched it, and little blue flames ran along the whole bowstring. He drew the arrow to the very head, drew it back until the bow was like half a circle, then let the arrow fly. It went straight to the Mangathai, struck his spinal column below the neck, broke his right arm, went into his left side and cut his heart and lungs into small pieces, killed him; then returned to Gesir Bogdo with a whistle, and went of itself into the quiver.

Now the Mangathai's horse cried out to Gesir: "Thou hast killed my master, but thou wilt never kill me. May my body break into bits if I yield to thee!" Then he rushed away south-west to the great barren steppe.

"Where art thou, my blue steed, ninety-nine fathoms long?" called Gesir.

That moment the horse appeared. Gesir Bogdo sprang on to him without a saddle. The horse said: "I will not let the Mangathai's horse run across five valleys till I have bitten the strong muscle in the back of his leg, and he will not run across six valleys till I have him by the bridle bit."

Then he ran with all his strength, and at the fifth valley so nearly overtook the Mangathai's horse that he bit the strong sinew of his leg. In the sixth valley he caught him by the bridle bit. Then Gesir Bogdo said:

"I have killed a great hero in killing the Mangathai, now I will send him his horse, so that he will have a good beast to ride in that other world."

He took the horse back to where the Mangathai was killed, and there he killed the beast. He plucked up the mountain then and planted it on the body of the Mangathai and the horse. After that he went home.

"If I fall asleep," said he to his wife, "waken me as before." "There are many Mangathais," said he to the thirty-three mighty champions and the three thousand men, "and they will come; do ye defend well my property. Walk around and keep watch, but go not one at a time. Let two or three go in company, so that if one is eaten others will defend themselves, and still others come to assist them."

Again he fell asleep. But his men, instead of watching, began to play games. Meanwhile a Mangathai with twenty-seven heads came upon them. Gesir with his magic knew of this; woke up of himself, and, without saying a word to his wife, stole out to a mountain in the southeast, and from there watched the Mangathai, saw that he went to the seashore, where they had pulled up the silver-leafed aspen tree, and went into the hole there.

Gesir watched and waited all night. At daybreak the Mangathai thrust his heads up through the hole to look around. At that moment Gesir sent his arrow and cut off the twenty-seven heads of the Mangathai. This Mangathai's horse called out in the manner of the first horse, and was treated in the same way: overtaken, killed and buried under the mountain together with his master. Gesir rode home, and said to Sangha Gohun, his wife, "My champions and men do not watch carefully; they forget, but do thou watch for me."

After three days a Mangathai came into the courtyard. Gesir's wife looked out, saw him, and said to herself: "If my husband goes out to fight and is beaten the dogs will cower. If he beats, the dogs will have their tails up, and be full of courage." But again she cried and was afraid to waken Gesir Bogdo; at last a tear drop fell into his right ear and wakened him.

The horse knew that the Mangathai was there and ran in from the open country. Gesir sprang on to his back, rushed off to a hill and called to the Mangathai:

"How shall we fight, hand to hand, or with weapons?"

"Let us wrestle," said the Mangathai, and he rode out to meet Gesir.

Each man sprang from his horse and approached the other. They held their heads like two bulls. They clinched and fought so fiercely that each tore the flesh from the back of the other with his hands, and from his breast with his teeth. They fought two days. The Mangathai had lost all the flesh from his back and his breast. Gesir squeezed him when he was nothing but bones; what was inside the Mangathai squealed like a goat, whined like a kid, and he died.

Gesir was dreadfully wearied after killing this fifty-three headed Mangathai. "I must sleep now," said he to Sangha Gohun. "I must sleep for nine days and nine nights. Watch, sleep not, waken me as before." ₁

Gesir had slept three days and three nights when a seventy-seven headed Mangathai came. He was more cautious at first than any of the others, for his brothers had been killed. He watched from a distance, standing on a mountain.

When Sangha Gohun saw this new Mangathai she was terribly frightened and pushed her husband, but did not waken him. Gesir was dreaming that a Mangathai had come, and was on his land.

Sangha Gohun tried again, tried to prick him in the heel, but had not the courage to do it, so she waited two days. After five days she pulled Gesir's arm and woke him. He woke more easily because he was dreaming.

"What is the matter?" cried Gesir, springing up. He looked out and saw the Mangathai on a mountain. "Once he has come I may not leave him on my land," said Gesir. So he took his horse and weapons and went out to meet the Mangathai. When he reached the mountain top, he asked:

"How shall we fight? Shall it be with the strength of arms, or the swiftness of arrows?" They agreed to run to the opposite mountains, Gesir to the southeastern, and the Mangathai to the northwestern one, and the one who reached his mountain first should send the first arrow. Gesir was on his mountain top when the Mangathai was within a few steps of his. He pointed his arrow. It flew straight to the Mangathai, entered his side, tore out his heart, broke his arm and his spinal column, and killed him.

Gesir burned the body of the Mangathai, burned the horse, and went home. This time he had no need of sleep; he was not weary.

Barely had he reached his white stone yurta when a Mangathai rushed straight into the courtyard: "Thou hast killed my elder brothers!" cried he. "Come out at once and meet me!"

"Go into the open steppe, where the fifty pine trees are growing; I will meet thee in that place."

The Mangathai went to the fifty pine trees, killed two splendid deer, male and female, put them on spits, and was roasting them in front of a big fire when Gesir Bogdo rode up suddenly, seized one of the spits, sat down on the ground, and fell to eating. The Mangathai rushed at him with his axe; Gesir turned himself into rock. The Mangathai struck till he was tired, but made no impression on the hard, white rock; he only broke his axe on it. When the axe was broken Gesir took his own form and said to the Mangathai:

"Who art thou who strikes and tries to kill people when they are lying down?" and he hit him such a blow that the blood gushed from his nostrils. "Thou and thy brothers," roared Gesir with a shout that was heard in the fifty-fifth sky, "are always coming with war, and never with peace. Ye are great fools!"

Not only was the blow which followed the roar heard in the fifty-fifth sky, but Hohodai Mergen (Thunder) heard it and asked:

"Why does our heaven child roar so? He must be in trouble." And he sent down his nine sons to help him. When they came the nine sons hurled lightning at the Mangathai and his steed, and tore them into small fragments.

Gesir ate the two deer, burned the bits of the Mangathai and his horse, and went back to his yurta. When he got home he said:

"There is a young Mangathai; I hope he will come soon." Gesir drank tarasun, and went around and gave directions to his people. While doing this he saw, coming on a fiery, red horse, a young man with a neck like a bull; he had a white face, enormous eyes, and ears with big rings in them. When he saw Gesir Bogdo he shouted: "Be greeted!

"Be greeted!" said Gesir in reply.

"I have heard," said the young man, "that in this place lives Gesir Bogdo, of great vigor; I have come to try strength with him. Shall we wrestle?"

Bogdo agreed, but said: "It is not convenient to wrestle here, let us go out on that broad, barren steppe, where the fifty pine trees are growing." And taking his weapons, he mounted his steed and went to the place where he had fought with the Mangathai.

They began to wrestle and wrestled for three days. Wherever they pressed their feet they knocked out a piece of earth as big as a calf one year old, but neither could conquer the other. Then they agreed to use arrows. In the night each tried to learn where the life of the other was.

Gesir Bogdo had two lives. One of them was in his stone yurta, the other was in the heaven next above the sky. This second life was in a vial, and the Burkan, Hulgin Sagán Namo, kept the vial between his knees, and his hand was always closed on the mouth of the vial.

The life of the Mangathai was on a mountain in the south-west. On that mountain, in the top branches of a golden-trunked, silver-leafed aspen, at the foot of which flowed the Water of Youth and Life, sat the king of birds, Khan Herdik Shubùn. In the outside feathers of the right wing of that bird was a life; Gesir thought it was the life of this Mangathai. But he had a second life, and Gesir by his magic learned where it was: On the bottom of the Milk Sea lived the old grandmother of the Mangathai and she had a box; in that box were thirteen woodcocks, and in those woodcocks was the second life of the Mangathai.

Each learned by magic where the life of the other was, but it was of no advantage to the Mangathai to learn that Gesir's life was in the heaven above the sky, for Burkans would not let him go there.

The mountain where the Mangathai's life was, was so far away, and its top was so high that no horse could run to it, even a bird could not fly to it, so Gesir Bogdo took an arrow from his quiver, and said to it:

"Go to the top of the golden-trunked aspen tree where the king of birds is sitting; go when he is sleeping, pluck the out-side feather from his right wing, and bring it hither."

Gesir was not sure that it was the life that he wanted, but it proved to be. The next morning Gesir said to the Mangathai: "As master of this land I will shoot first."

"No," said the Mangathai, "I come from afar; I am a guest, the first shot is mine."

After much disputing Gesir Bogdo shot first. His arrow went into the Mangathai, but the Mangathai had such power that the arrow could not tear him. He pulled it out, took grass and stopped the blood flow, then sprang up, and cried:

"Now I will shoot my arrow!" He stretched his bow and the arrow flew straight to Gesir, went in under one of his armpits and out under the other. Gesir caught the arrow as it came out, planted it in his saddle, put stones against the wound to stop the blood, and screamed to the Mangathai:

"What kind of archer art thou, that can only hit my saddle-bow?"

Gesir kept the stones against his wounds, and in two days he had recovered. The Mangathai grew well also; then he mounted and rode to Gesir Bogdo, who showed him a feather as big as a small tree, and said:

"See what a beautiful feather I have." It was the feather which the arrow had brought back from the mountain.

"Oh, that is the feather of a sacred bird," said the Mangathai. "It would be an awful sin for you to write with it; thou art too young. Let me have it; I am not so young as thou art."

Gesir would not give it; he twisted the feather and put it away.

"I have a terrible pain in my head," said the Mangathai. "I must rest two days or three." And he went to his yurta.

Gesir knew now that one of the Mangathai's lives was in the feather, and he set out for the Milk Sea to find the Mangathai's grandmother and get the second life. By magic he made himself exactly like the Mangathai.

When Gesir reached the Milk Sea, not knowing the way into it, he began to weep and call, "Oh, grandmother, grand-mother come out. Come up to me. I have been fighting three years with Gesir Bogdo, and have worn out my strength. Inside me there is no power, outside I have nothing."

The old grandmother came from the sea, and was wonderfully glad to look at her grandson. She took him on her knees and to strengthen him gave him her breast. "Oh," said she, "I am astonished, my children do not draw as they used to."

"I have been fighting three years, of course I cannot draw as I used to," said Gesir. Then he drew the breast so hard that he drew the lungs out of the old woman and she died, crying: "A deceiver has killed me!"

Then Gesir went to the bottom of the Milk Sea, where he found the box and kicked it open. The thirteen woodcocks flew out, but Gesir could catch only one, the others flew up to the sky. He killed the one, turned himself into a falcon and flew after the twelve woodcocks; caught eleven and killed them; the twelfth fell to the earth, turned into millet, and covered seven acres and a half with small grains, and each grain had the second life of the Mangathai within it.

Gesir turned himself into ninety-nine hens and fell to eating the millet. The hens ate till only three grains were left, then those three turned into three wild goats and ran off to the forest. That instant the ninety-nine hens turned themselves into three gray, hungry wolves. They caught two of the wild goats, but the third got away, escaped to the edge of the sea, turned into hundreds of small fish and sprang into the water. From three wolves Gesir turned into a great many hungry pikes and began to swallow the small fish.

The pikes ate till only two of the small fish were left. Those darted to the edge of the sea, sprang out and became two wild goats. The pikes turned into wolves and ran after the goats. They caught one goat, the other changed into seven skylarks, and rose through the air swiftly.

Gesir Bogdo now called on Hohodai Mergen (Thunder) to make stone hail and let it fall on the skylarks and kill them.

Hohodai listened, was favorable to Gesir, and helped him. The hailstorm came, but wherever there was a ray of sunlight the larks darted into it, and thus were saved from the hailstones.

Gesir saw the larks hanging in the sunshine; he turned into a raven, darted at them, and caught them. He went back then to where the Mangathai was and found him very feeble.

"Thou art not able to fight yet, thou art sick it seems," said Gesir, as he put his hands in his pockets and took out the skylarks.

"Hast thou ever seen such beautiful birds?" asked he.

The Mangathai was dreadfully frightened, and cried:

"Oh, it is a terrible sin for a young man to take hold of those birds. I am older than thou art, give them to me."

Gesir Bogdo squeezed the birds, then gave them to his horse to bite. The horse bit them, killed them; the Mangathai died, and Gesir covered him and his horse with a mountain.

When Gesir reached home he said to his wife: "The father of the Mangathais is left yet, but it is better for me to go to him," and he went.

This father had ninety-nine heads. The old man came out with a club in his hands and shouted: "Oh, thou dog! thou hast killed all my strong sons, and now thou art here to kill me, but thou wilt not do it!"

Bogdo laughed and said: "Thy flesh is tender, thy bones are weak!" And he spoke as if the Mangathai were a young boy. The old man became terribly angry and sprang at Gesir. Gesir seized him, raised him up, and struck him against the earth. Right there was a larch tree of such bulk that ten men could hardly reach around it. There was a split in the tree, Gesir pushed the old Mangathai into the split, pressed it together firmly, put ninety-nine hoops around the tree trunk, and said: "Now stay there forever!"

Gesir went home then, and Sangha Gohun said to him: "In five months I shall give birth to a child, go not out during that time." He waited five months. She was ill, very ill, and Gesir prayed to the thousand heavenly Burkans that she might be delivered the more quickly, and in two days a son was born; an old midwife received the child. All the people were called and Gesir put out kegs of tarasun and killed many cattle, so that there was a sea of drink and a mountain of meat for every one present. Then they asked the old men and women, "What name is the child to have?"

Gesir took the right shoulder bone of a bull, held it, and said: "Whoso is able to give a name to my son and will give it, let him do so now."

. An old man from the North stepped out of the crowd and said: "I can give a name. The eldest son of Gesir Bogdo will be called Ashir Bogdo."

Gesir accepted the name, gave the old man the bone of the bull and three gallons of tarasun, and when the time came sent a man with three horses to take him home with honor.

"Till five months are passed," said the mother to Gesir, "thou wilt not leave the yurta."

When five months old the boy walked. "I will ride around the whole world now," said Gesir, "and see what is happening." He started and during twelve years he went everywhere; went to the yurta of Gal Tulan Tengeri (Fiery Red Sky) and fell in love with Gal's beautiful daughter. When parting from her, he said: "I will return soon and take thee home as my second wife."

"Who art thou?" asked Ashir Bogdo when his father came home. "Art thou good or bad? Hast thou come with good or evil wishes?" Then Sangha Gohun came, recognized Gesir, and said: "This is thy father, who has come back to us after wandering twelve years around the world." When Ashir heard her words he embraced his father and led him into the yurta. Sangha Gohun gave all there was to eat and to drink; meat and tarasun in plenty, and the three ate together.

In the evening Gesir lay down to sleep on a beaver skin and under a sable cover. Then he told Sangha Gohun how he had seen the daughter of Gal Tulan and that he wanted her for his second wife. "She will not trouble thee," added he, "and I wish to have as many sons as possible."

"Thinkst thou that I am old? I am not old. Why take the other woman? We have a son. I beg thee not to take her."

"I took thee when I was young," said Gesir. "I deceived thee and brought thee home, therefore I married thee. But when I took my present form it was commanded me to have two wives, first thee, then this other one."

Three days and nights he argued with Sangha Gohun, but she would not consent, would not yield to him. Then he said: "I will ask thee no further. I will go and bring her. If I do not I shall die to-morrow or the day which comes after."

"I am sorry for thee," said Sangha Gohun. "Bring her, bring her not. Do what pleases thee."

He made ready, mounted his steed in full outfit as at first, and rode away to Gal Tulan Tengeri's kingdom. He traveled night and day at a gallop. At last he came to a bronze and silver square where man had never sat. In that square was a spring dark as liver and from that spring horse had never drunk. Gesir watered his steed there, then sat down, took his silver pipe, filled it with tobacco, named the thousand Heavenly Burkans, made fire with a flint, and smoked. When he blew out smoke it went with a roar like rushing wind; when he opened his mouth and let it come out of itself it came in silence. He smoked these two ways.

After Gesir had finished smoking he put away his pipe and went toward the northeast. When he jerked the reins the bridle bit cut the horse's mouth so that blood flowed; when he struck with his whip it cut to the bone. The horse raced on with fierce pace till at last they reached the mountain called Tiphin Ündir Hada.

"Well," asked Gesir of his steed, "what skill hast thou?"

"What skill have I? I can spring to the top of this high mountain. If I go back one day's journey, with the force of my run I can rise to the summit. If I fail in the spring and fall, we shall perish, both of us."

Gesir went to the foot of the mountain and saw piles of bones there, immense piles, bones of men and of horses. He took the thigh bone of a man, measured it against his own; it reached the whole length of his leg. Then he took the thigh bone of a horse and measured it against his steed; it was long as his whole leg. "Oh," said Gesir, "since they, who were so mighty, have perished we are sure to fail. Let us weep."

They wept during three days and three nights, steed and rider. After that Gesir Bogdo turned back the journey of one day and rested. Then the horse rushed furiously toward the mountain, rose with one immense spring, but did not quite reach the summit, he only got his front feet over the highest edge, and hung there, holding on first with hoofs and then with hoofs and teeth.

"Now master," cried he, "save me if thou canst, or kill me if it is thy wish." Bogdo sprang from the saddle-tree over the horse's head and was on the summit. That done he drew the horse up by the strong bridle and they lay there, both of them, on the top of the mountain for twenty-four hours without moving. When they came to their senses and looked around they saw a spring near them. In this spring was the Water of Life and Youth which gushed forth at the foot of a golden-trunked, silver-leafed aspen tree; on a branch of the tree a cup was hanging.

Gesir took one of the silver leaves of the golden tree, ate it and gave another silver leaf to his stallion. Then he drank a cup of the water and gave one to his horse. He took the saddle from his steed with great difficulty, so firmly had it clung to the saddle-cloth; the saddle-cloth itself had so clung to the horse that it had almost grown to him.

Gesir fettered his steed and led him out to graze. At that moment a stag and hind passed. He took his black bow and strong arrow and killed them both. He dressed them, spitted the female on a whole pine tree and the male on the trunk of a great larch tree; then he lay down and slept three days and three nights.

When Gesir woke he saw that his steed had grown fat and was far handsomer than he had ever been. He himself had improved wonderfully. This change was from the silver leaf of the aspen tree and the Water of Life.

Gesir sat down and ate the two deer; chewed the meat, bones, and all. He cleared in his mouth the flesh from the bones and cast the bones out through his nostrils. When he had finished eating he turned his steed into a flint, put the flint into his pocket, changed himself into Khan Herdik Shubùn (Eagle) and flew to Gal Tulan Tengeri's kingdom, where he saw the khan's yurta hanging between the cloudy sky and the first heaven.

When Gesir came to the yurta he found that it had no doors, so he prayed three days and three nights, going around on the sun's road (in the same direction as the sun).

In front of Gal Tulan's yurta was a tree of such size that a man on the swiftest horse could hardly ride around it in a day. On its boughs thousands of heavenly birds were singing; on its branches hung all the written wisdom in existence. The religions of all peoples were recorded and hanging there.

After Gesir had gone around on the sun's road for three days, praying to the Burkans, the doors of the yurta opened of themselves on the west and he entered.

The rooms inside were without doors, apparently, as well as the outer walls of the yurta. Gesir prayed one day and one night, two doors opened, and out came Gal Tulan Tengeri.

They greeted each other and Gal invited Gesir Bogdo to sit down and then he gave orders to bring milk to him. When he wished to drink Gal said, "Whence hast thou come, black, earthly mouse?"

"I am no black, earthly mouse," replied Gesir. "I was created by the thousand Heavenly Burkans. I am the youngest son of Khan Tyurmas, the eldest of the fifty-five Tengeris. I have come because my father and thy father poured to each other wine into a red goblet and exchanged the second joint of the right leg of a bullock in agreement that the son of one and the daughter of the other were to marry."

"Soft meat needs no knife and a true word needs no road," said Gal. "Show me thy book and I will see if it is recorded in it that our fathers exchanged cups of red wine and the leg joint of a bullock and made this agreement."

Gesir gave the book and Gal Tulan read three days in it; he found everything as Gesir had said.

"Now I have entertained you," said Gal, "and have looked through the book. It is as you have said, and I will give my daughter, but first go and see her; she is in the seventy-seventh chamber. If she consents all will be well."

Just before sunset Gesir Bogdo turned to go to Gal's daughter; soon he was in the seventy-seventh chamber, and he saluted her quickly. She brought various dishes to him, sweet milk, curds, and the film of boiled milk. They ate heartily, then ceased to eat.

That night the pillows of his bed were of otter, the bed itself was of otter, the quilt of sable was as soft as if all the fur were in a lump without the skin; it was as soft as the lungs of an animal. The next morning when one half of the round of the sun was above the earth Gesir sprang up at the call of Gal Tulan, who shouted: "Art thou sorry to leave a soft bed?"

"Soft meat needs no knife, a true word needs no road. My bride had so much to say that time passed without notice till the sun was half up. When our fathers made the agreement what were the conditions?"

"Your father was to give a cart-load of gold and the arms and armor of a warrior."

Gesir went west that day and up to the region of the fifty-five Tengeris. He went first to the seven smiths of the sky; they were to make for him the arms and armor of a warrior. He told them that he had promised the arms and armor to Gal within three days. It took him one day and one night to go to the sky-smiths.

Then Gesir went to his father, and told him that Khan Tulan had given him but three days, and he asked for the gold. Khan Tyurmas got the gold, and gave it to Gesir, for the time was short, and great haste was requisite.

Gesir pulled a tree out by the roots, tied the roots to his horse's tail, and said to the man with the gold: "Follow the trail that this tree makes and you will know the way by which I go."

Bogdo was late with the weapons. The time for delivering the gold had not been mentioned. "Why art thou late?" asked Gal.

"Because the sky-smiths were late; there was much work in making the weapons."

Gal Tulan received the armor and weapons. "Where is the gold?" asked he. "Thou wilt deceive me, perhaps, if I give the wedding."

"The wedding will last more than one day," answered Gesir; "the gold will be here before the wedding is ended."

Gal Tulan invited the thousand Burkans. All the Burkans and people danced and ate and drank for nine days. There were mountains of meat and lakes of tarasun; whoever wanted to dance danced, whoever got drunk fell down, and lay where he fell. At last the load of gold came, and the father-in-law received it.

"It is time to go home," said Gesir Bogdo, on the ninth day. Gal Tulan assented, Gesir's horse was saddled, and a horse for the bride was brought; its body was ninety fathoms long and its ears nine ells high; he was a bay, with a star on the forehead.

The bride asked then what her mother would give, and the mother gave her a pair of golden scissors. Then she asked her brother, and he gave her a silver magic cup. The cup had such power, that if she held it in her right hand and made a sweep with it toward herself everything within thirty versts followed her.

They mounted their steeds. "Now," said Gesir Bogdo, "let all the guests follow me." He pulled up a young tree, tied it to his horse's tail and said: "Follow the trail!" The bride held the magic cup in her right hand, made a sweep with it, and said:

"Everything that is here follow us!" So her father and mother, the yurta, and everything had to go with them. She and Gesir Bogdo rode forward, and she did not look back till her father called:

"Daughter, look around and see what is happening!"

She feigned not to hear and rode on. The father called a second and a third time. "But look around, daughter!"

She looked half over her shoulder. That moment one third of all that was following remained behind. The father soon called, "Daughter, everything is burning up! Is it possible that thou wilt let thy father and mother be burned?" The bride was so frightened by what he said that she looked over her shoulder. That moment another third remained behind, and only the last third was following.

They traveled in the sky till above the mountain where the Water of Youth and Life was, and the golden-trunked, silver-leafed aspen tree.

Gesir's father-in-law had given him a silver stairway. On this stairway they came down from the sky to the mountain; the stairway looked like a ray of sunlight. All came down on it,—people, cattle, and herds. Then they went to Bogdo's great white stone yurta. His wife and son were waiting there. Ashir Bogdo was now old enough to marry, and he asked his father: "Is this a bride whom thou hast brought for me?"

"No, she is for myself; thou art young, for thee there is time enough."

Three days later the people came. When they appeared Gesir

DRYING FUEL—COW DROPPINGS—ISLAND OF OLKHON. *Page* 74

DRYING FUEL—COW DROPPINGS—ISLAND OF OLKHON.

CHURCH NEAR A POST STATION ON THE ROAD TO LAKE BAIKAL. *Page* 68
The place which I called "Ragats"

CHURCH NEAR A POST STATION ON THE ROAD TO LAKE BAIKAL.

The place which I called "Ragats" had another wedding feast which lasted for nine days and nights, with a mountain of meat, and a sea of drink. On the tenth day he sent back the guests, but the cattle remained with him.

Gesir and his young wife had a pleasant life for the first day and first night. The second evening the old wife scolded, and quarrelled with her husband and his bride.

The next morning the young wife said: "I cannot live thus, I would rather be with the hundred and nine headed Mangathai than with thee in this yurta. Remain with thy old wife, I will go to the Mangathai."

Gesir begged her to stay. "I ought to have married thee first," said he, "since that was the agreement between our fathers. But I was young. Bow down to my old wife, and stay with me."

"I will promise to stay and be thy wife if thou wilt turn into a six-year-old horse, and for one day eat grass in the field out there."

Gesir consented, for he was greatly in love; he turned himself into a horse and went to graze outside in the field. Then the bride began her magic, and chanted. She chanted that Gesir must be a horse and draw a plow as long as the hundred and nine headed Mangathai lived. She chanted "Gesir is in my hands; come hither thou hundred and nine headed Mangathai," and her voice reached the Mangathai.

The Mangathai appeared that same night, rode in on his terrible black stallion. Gesir was then out in the field eating grass like any other horse, one of his fore feet tied to a stake while he pastured. Gesir's young wife, whose name was Apha, sprang up, opened the door and let in the Mangathai. All that he asked for she gave,—food, drink, and everything. "Where is thy husband?" asked the Mangathai while he was eating.

"He is out in the field gnawing grass; each day thou wilt plow with him, and each night put him in an iron stable without windows or opening other than the door, so that he may never escape from thee."

The next morning the Mangathai rose and began to plow. He plowed all day with Gesir Bogdo, then tied him firmly in the iron stable, and closed the door securely.

Sangha Gohun with her son left the yurta and went southwest to Red Mountain. There the son made a box of bark, put his mother inside, raised up the mountain and placed the box under it; then he turned himself into a falcon, and flew away to Khan Tyurmas, his grandfather. When he had told him all his trouble Khan Tyurmas said: "I will summon the thousand Heavenly Burkans to assemble on Dolon Odun" (The Great Bear).

From the time when the Mangathai came to Gesir's yurta till all the Heavenly Burkans assembled nine months had passed, and every day Gesir had drawn a plow and been driven by the hundred and nine headed Mangathai, who had settled in his yurta and was living with Apha, Gesir's young wife.

Ashir said to the thousand Burkans, "Ye created a hero; did ye create him to plow for a Mangathai?"

The Burkans looked down, and saw the hundred and nine headed Mangathai plowing with Gesir Bogdo as a horse. The Mangathai had a strong club in his hand, and was beating the hero to make him work faster.

Nine days did the Burkans take counsel on Dolon Odun; at last they decided to make an iron hero. The smiths of the sky made this hero; they were forging him during nine days, and while at work they chanted these words: "May man with thumb never crush thee; may man with shoulder never kill thee; may no weapon or sharp steel ever harm thee!"

After the sky-smiths had finished the body Ashir Bogdo went to the seven heavenly smiths to have armor made,—bow, arrows, and quiver. He returned then to the thousand Burkans, and said, "Ye have created a hero, now give him a steed." In the sky were nine blue stallions. The Burkans gave the Iron Hero the youngest of these. This stallion heard all that happened on earth, and all that was done in the sky, or above it. One ear he pointed upward to hear what was done higher up, the other downward to hear all the sounds on the earth beneath him. Ashir took this steed to his grandfather's yurta; and just as he reached there, with the stallion and all his trappings, the Iron Hero came, for the thousand Burkans had breathed into him and given him life. When this hero walked seven acres of earth groaned around him; when he came to the yurta Khan Tyurmas, who was very anxious about his son, said:

"Thou hast no time to wait here, mount thy steed, and hasten to free Gesir Bogdo."

Ashir started and with him went the Iron Hero mounted on the all-hearing steed, which traveled lower than the clouds, and higher than the trees, till over Red Mountain, where Ashir Bogdo had hidden his mother; there they came down and Ashir went to his mother and asked: "Where are the weapons and the armor which my father used?"

"I put them aside," said she, "where no one could ever find them." Then she told him what storehouse they were in, and gave him the key.

"We will go now," said Ashir, "to that Mangathai who is plowing with my father."

"Go," said Sangha Gohun, "but go not to the yurta, for Apha would kill thee."

The Iron Hero went then to free his brother, Gesir Bogdo, from the power of the Mangathai, and Ashir went to find the armor and arms of his father.

The Iron Hero found the Mangathai plowing with a terribly lean and wretched horse, and he shouted to him:

"Why plow with such a poor, miserable beast. Take my good sturdy steed for a little while; let thine rest and get breath again."

"I will not use thy horse," said the Mangathai; "mine is good enough." But he changed his mind soon, and said, "I will try the fresh horse."

The Mangathai let out Gesir, and put in the blue stallion. Gesir saw that the Iron Hero was his brother, created by the Burkans, and he began to weep, but in such a way that the Mangathai might not see him.

The Mangathai fastened the reins round his own neck, and put the plow in the ground. The blue sky stallion had awful strength; no one knew what his strength was. He began slowly, then went faster and faster till at last he broke the plow, and then he dragged the Mangathai in great circles around the Iron Hero. The Iron Hero sent arrow after arrow into the Mangathai's body, and killed him. Then the blue stallion came up to him with the body of the Mangathai.

Ashir Bogdo brought water from nine springs; he went to a forest and brought juniper leaves from it and dried them. He washed Gesir with the water, and incensed him with the smoke of the dry juniper leaves, and restored him perfectly.

After that they took a barrel, with ninety-five iron hoops, put the body of the Mangathai into the barrel, and rolled it into the Gazada Sea (Lateral Sea).

Gesir Bogdo went toward his yurta. Apha, who had seen all that had taken place, ran out, and put her arms around him.

"Since thou hast magic and power, why didst thou let the Mangathai torment me so long?" asked Gesir. "Now I will make thee work like a three-year-old bullock, and have you milked as a three-year-old cow."

"Thou wilt never do that!" screamed Apha, and she closed with him. They wrestled for three days and three nights; she was gaining. They fought for nine days and nights, and then she was winning the victory surely.

"Where is thy aid?" cried Gesir to the Iron Hero. The Iron Hero approached Apha then, saying, "I will take thee now; my brother brought thee here by deceit, thou shouldst be my wife."

"Was I brought here to be the wife of one after another? Am I to be the wife of one of you when another is tired of me?" asked Apha, and she hurled herself at the Iron Hero, screaming, "May Gal Tulan and Dul Tulan Tengeri crush thee into fragments!"

Ashir Bogdo helped now, and it was as much as the three could do to conquer Apha, and confine her in a barrel, with ninety-nine iron hoops around it. When they had put her into that barrel they rolled it into the Lateral Sea; then all went into Gesir's yurta.

"Well," asked Sangha Gohun, "didst thou have much happiness with thy young wife? If I had not borne thee a son and sent him to the sky the Mangathai would be plowing with thee yet, and beating thy lean body."

"Now," said the Iron Hero to Gesir, "thou art my elder brother, and I am ready to help thee, but I am old enough to look for a bride."

"Thou art old enough," said Gesir Bogdo, "thou mayst go to find her."

Footnotes

147:1 Here the storyteller said: "The story of Gesir Bogdo is the father of the world of stories. It is not as beautiful as some, but it is the greatest of all, and is true."

THE IRON HERO

THE Iron Hero cut open his side, and found a book in his liver. He read this book three days and nights, without stopping; at one time he laughed, at another he cried, at a third he sang songs.

In this book it was written that there were seven noble Dongins, that the eldest of the seven had a beautiful daughter whom the Iron Hero was to marry; the other six brothers were childless.

Before he set out to find this bride the Iron Hero turned his horse into flint, and placed him inside his own midriff. Then he boiled the flesh of ten sheep in one kettle, and made it as small as the flesh of one sheep. He distilled ten pots of tarasun and redistilled it till one kettle held all, and the liquor had ten strengths. After that he put the meat and drink into an iron car, and set out on his journey. When going up hill he gave the car a push and it went to the top. When going down he mounted the car, and rode in it pleasantly.

The Iron Hero hurried directly southwest. He reached the boundary of a new country, crossed it, and traveled on till he came to a bronze and silver square on which man had never stepped. In that square there was a spring as dark as liver, a spring from which horse had never drank. When the Iron Hero had drunk water and smoked, he said: "Thou art such a land that when the mountain wind blows downward thou art waving like a beaver fur, and when the valley wind blows against the mountain side thou art like a sable fur. When I return with my bride I will settle here; this will be my place."

After that he descended all the time. It was a sloping region, and he went swiftly. He heard ahead the panting, as it were, of ten men, and the tramp, as it were, of ten horses. He knew not what to do, he was frightened, but he said to himself: "If a wolf hunts a deer two days he will die of hunger. If a man does not carry out what he plans he would better perish. If a woman does not sew what she has cut, better that she cut off her fingers." Then he made his breathing as great as the breathing of ten men, and the noise of his car as loud as the noise of ten carts.

Soon he met a twenty-five headed Mangathai. When he saw him in front he added to the speed of his car, and went so fast that he carried off the bottom of the Mangathai's stirrup and twisted up what was left of it. He cut off a part of the Mangathai's right cheek, and went forward a while, then turned his car around toward the Mangathai, saluted, and asked him:

"What place dost thou wish now to ravage and ruin?"

"I am going far to the northeast," said the Mangathai; "I have heard that Gesir Bogdo has a brother called the Iron Hero; I want to test his strength. While he is young, while his voice is thin, and his bones are soft, I wish greatly to kill him."

"Oh, thou wilt not let people come to their age, and gain strength. Thou wilt kill and ravage!" cried the Iron Hero, and springing from the car he gave the Mangathai a blow on the forehead.

"Oh, it is thou, then, thou art the Iron Hero, going to look for a bride!" cried the Mangathai, mocking him, and he sprang down from his stallion.

The two approached looking sidewise at each other, like two bulls going to battle. They were as dark as two gloomy clouds; both were raging. They rushed at each other to wrestle, and soon the ground under them became hills and valleys.

The Iron Hero tore all the flesh from the Mangathai's back with his fingers, and all of it from his breast with his teeth. At mid-forenoon of the next day he killed the Mangathai, put his head toward the northwest, his feet toward the east, put a mountain on his head and his breast, and another across his feet and legs, leaving a road between by which people might travel.

Now the Iron Hero went farther, saw an iron yurta, the top of which touched the sky. He was frightened; he turned the car into a flint, himself into a skunk, and went toward that iron yurta underground. He ate a hole through the floors, and peeping up, saw a hundred and eight headed Mangathai, his feet against one wall, his head against another. This Mangathai was breathing very heavily. Out of one corner of his mouth a blue flame was quivering, out of the other corner a red flame gushed forth.

Seeing that the Mangathai was sleeping soundly, the Iron Hero crept up and stole his axe, which hung there, made it small, took it away underground, came back and gnawed through the Mangathai's throat quickly. The Mangathai sprang up, and cried: "Cunning people have robbed me! Sharp arrows have hit me!"

He stumbled around through the place, could do nothing, lost his senses, blood flowed from his nostrils, his breath failed, and life left him.

The Hero turned the great iron building bottom side upward. He made small trees for elks to eat, for deer he made brush. He made black ravens to croak on the place, and a yellow fox to race around it. He commanded that on fallen snow there should never be tracks in winter, and that grass should not be broken or crushed in the summer, so that everything might be secret; all things lone and deserted.

He made a fire from flint, and began to smoke. The highest flame from his flint rose through every heaven to the ninth, and the lowest flame went down through all regions of the earth to the seventh. He invoked the thousand Burkans. He sent out his smoke first with a roaring whistle, and then he let it go of itself in deep silence.

When his smoke was finished he set out again with his car, going southwestward continually. When he came to a hill he gave the car a great push and it went to the summit. When going down he mounted the car and rode along swiftly and in comfort. At last he saw a fifty headed Mangathai riding on a horse black as the earth. The Mangathai wore a mantle of goat skin, and he shouted from his horse to the Iron Hero: "Thou hast killed my father and my younger brother, and now thou hast happened into my hands very luckily!"

He sprang from his horse, the Iron Hero leaped from his car, and the two went toward each other like two bulls, or like two black threatening clouds, and they closed in a desperate struggle. Each tore the flesh from the back of the other with his fingers, and bit it away from his breast with his teeth. Three days and nights did they fight. They made hills and valleys. Where there had been a hill there was a valley and where the valley had been there was a hill. But neither could conquer the other. They agreed then to hurl weapons from opposite mountains. The Mangathai from a mountain on the western border of the sky, the Iron Hero from one on the eastern border.

They disputed long, and with hot words, as to who should shoot first. The Mangathai demanded the first shot because he lived there. The Iron Hero claimed it because he was a stranger. He insisted, but yielded at last to the Mangathai, and took his place on the eastern mountain, where he turned into a jade stone before the Mangathai's axe could reach him.

The Mangathai hurled his axe, hit the stone but could not harm it. The Iron Hero took his own form again, seized the axe, struck it into his car, and shouted: "Thou hast a fine aim, to hit my car. How now am I to travel? Stand up in thy own size, and let me shoot at thee."

The Iron Hero took his bow, bent it to a half circle, and spoke to the arrow, as he drew the string to the arrow head:

"Go thou, my arrow, into the side of my enemy, tear around through his heart, lungs, and liver. Come out then, break his forearm, and crack his spinal column at the neck, then come back to me."

The arrow did all this, and came back to the quiver.

The Mangathai's black steed called to the Iron Hero: "My mother is in the Milk Sea, my father is on a high mountain. I have no fear of thee. I will go to them!" and he sped away.

The Iron Hero took out the flint, and turned it into his blue stallion of the sky. The blue stallion rushed after the black steed of the Mangathai, calling out as he started:

"When thy two hind feet are in the second valley my fore feet will be there; when thy four feet are in the third valley my three feet will be there, when all thy feet are in the fourth valley my four feet will be in the same valley, and in the fifth valley I will bite the great muscle of thy leg, catch thee by the bridle bit, and bring thee back here."

The blue stallion did this. He brought the black steed of the Mangathai to the Iron Hero. The Iron Hero killed the steed with the Mangathai's axe, put a hill on the dead Mangathai, another one on his steed; then he put his blue stallion into his breast as a flint, and pushing his car went into a cold place, a land so cold that horse droppings froze solid and were as ice when they touched the ground.

"Pfu! pfu! how hot!" cried the Hero, and he opened his bosom; he was sweating. Then he went into a country so hot that horse droppings dried up, and scattered into dust before they touched the earth. "Pfu! pfu! what a cold place this is!" cried the Hero, as he drew his cap down and buttoned his shirt very closely. "Oh, how cold; I am almost frozen!"

After he had driven out of the hot land he came to a forest so dense that the thinnest snake in the world could not squeeze through between the trees, and so vast that no eye could see side or end to it. He begged the thousand Burkans to give him an axe with a blade one ell wide. He got the axe and began to hew and cut, but all that he cut in the day time grew up again during night hours. He cut three days and each night all the trees grew up again, and were there in the morning. Seeing no good in the axe he took his arrow from the quiver and spoke to it, saying: "Cut thou the trees level with the earth; cut a road so wide that a laden camel might go through this forest easily, and a pied ox with a sleigh might pass without trouble. When all is done come back to the quiver."

The arrow did as commanded. The trees thus cut never grew again, and the Iron Hero passed through the forest without difficulty. Then he went to a high place and looking down saw a broad valley, and he thought, "To spring over this valley—no hero could do that; to pass through will be difficult; there are so many serpents here."

The serpents saw the Iron Hero, and said, "We must not let that man pass under us, or over us, or through us!"

There was nothing to be accomplished by pushing ahead, so the Iron Hero turned his car into a flint and put it into his pocket, then turned himself into a yellow, spotted serpent, and went into that valley. He passed up and down, passed three times through the valley so as not to be suspected, then slipped out on the opposite side, took the flint from his pocket, made it into a car again, and became himself,—was the Iron Hero again.

When the serpents saw this they fell to asking each of some other one, "What didst thou see?" The other answering, "What didst thou see?" "We promised not to let this man go over us, or under us, or through us, and now he has gone through us." They grew so angry that they bit one another, and fell to fighting savagely. There was a terrible uproar, some bit others to death, and were themselves bitten to death.

After that the Iron Hero traveled on till he came to a lake. Beyond the lake was a narrow strip of land, and beyond that a second lake, a lake of poison. He took out his horse, and asked: "What are we to do? How are we to cross these lakes?"

"Go back one day's journey," said the horse, "and I will spring over the lakes. Hold fast to me."

They did so. The blue stallion sprang over both lakes; the end of his tail and the tips of his hind hoofs touched the poison water of the second lake, and fell off immediately.

The Iron Hero whipped his horse, and pulled the bridle till blood came. "Why not spring through clean? Thou mightst have fallen into the poison lake, then both of us would have perished!" cried he.

"Till this day thou art a fool," answered the stallion, "and knowest not that it would have been a sin not to touch the water. We are living people, and must touch things as we pass them."

"True, I did not know this till now," replied the Iron Hero.

Then he made the stallion into flint again, and journeyed on, pushing his car before him. He approached Red Mountain and saw there a hill of men's bones, a hill of beasts' bones, a hill of flesh, and a stream of blood. He saw a multitude of blind, a multitude of lame, people without hands, people without feet, and all, great and small, rich and poor, striving to climb the mountain. The great and the rich went on horseback, they rode up some distance and then fell back, with their horses. The poor and maimed climbed up on foot, or crawled up as best they were able. They wore all the flesh from the front part of their bodies in climbing up, and tore all the flesh off their backs in falling down. All who climbed fell, and every one who fell perished.

The Iron Hero went near. He looked at the hills of bones and the multitude of people, and wept for three days and three nights. He took out the flint, changed it to his steed, and the steed wept. Then the Iron Hero made his steed flint, put him in his bosom; made the car flint, put it in his pocket; turned himself into a skunk, and went one third of the way up the mountain, climbed till his claws were gone; then he became a squirrel, and went from the limb of one tree to the limb of another; went from place to place. He was dreadfully tired, but he climbed till his claws were gone. At last he became a falcon, and with great effort flew to the top, fell there, and lay for three days and three nights without moving.

At the end of the third day he revived, took the horse and the car out, gave his horse water, and let him graze. Two deer passed there; these he killed, roasted on spits, and ate.

After he and the stallion had eaten he took an immense iron barrel, with ninety-nine hoops, which he found there, filled it with the Water of Life and of Youth, and rolled it down the mountain.

The barrel broke; the water ran out in a broad stream, and the people and horses at the foot of the mountain came to life. One old man begged all the Burkans to prosper the Iron Hero. "May he live," said that old man, "till a stone as large as a bull turns of itself into ashes, and a stone as big as a stallion drops out of a solid mountain."

From Red Mountain the Iron Hero saw on the edge of the horizon an enormous white yurta which touched the sky, that was the yurta of his father-in-law. From the mountain he came down to a brass and iron hill which no foot of man had ever touched, and he sat down on that hill. Then by his magic he made big boils on his neck and on his back, and on his hands and feet sores disgusting to look at. He made himself old, sick, and wretched, made his car worn and battered, and then pushed it ahead toward the yurta till he entered the courtyard.

In the middle of that courtyard was a pillar with branches, and on those branches were ninety-six hitching rings. Seven splendid horses were tied to seven of those hitching rings. Each horse was of a different color; on the saddle of each were the arms of its rider. The riders of those seven horses were suitors for the maiden whom the Iron Hero wished to be his wife.

The Iron Hero pushed in his car, put it between two of the horses; then going over silver stairs and through golden doors he entered the yurta as a nasty, malodorous old man covered with sores. When inside the yurta he saw the seven splendid young suitors sitting at a table, and with them sat the bride's father.

"A greeting to thee, O my father-in-law," said the old man, tottering in and approaching the khan.

"What father-in-law am I to thee? May thou drop into pieces! The one of the seven who throws thee out will get my daughter."

One of the suitors sprang up to seize the old man and throw him out, but he could not raise him from the floor; the old man was as if fastened down, no one could lift him.

"If all of you seize him you can throw him out!" cried the father-in-law. "Some demon has come to me!"

All seven took hold of the old man. One grasped a leg, another an arm; but the seven could not stir him. He pushed them away, hurled them in different directions. One fell in a corner, another under a table, a third into a third place, and soon all seven of the suitors ran out to the courtyard in fright and confusion, untied their horses and rode off at a gallop.

The old man dragged himself through the chambers. Sitting down here and there in each chamber, he soiled all the floors and the seats. The khan could do nothing,— could not frighten, entice, or drive him out, so he sent for two heroes who lived in the southwest. It was necessary to ride three days to get to those heroes. When the messenger reached them they said: "We must make ready our weapons and armor. Go home; we will follow and overtake thee."

Five days the old man was left to himself, and during that time he soiled all the chambers of the yurta. Then he crawled into the courtyard, took his car and went to the Iron and Silver Square on the hilltop; there he made a fire and lay down to sleep quietly.

The day that the old man left the yurta the two heroes came. They shouted at the entrance, and the khan went out to meet them. "Where is he who is troubling thee?" asked the heroes.

"He left here just before ye came. Fifteen women are washing the rooms which he soiled. He went away when he heard that I had sent for two great heroes. The seven suitors could not drive off the wretched old man, but he has fled now to the north-east, with his car."

Straightway the heroes followed in the direction which the khan pointed out to them. They came to the Iron and Silver Square on the hilltop and found the old man there sleeping soundly and snoring loudly. They shouted at him. He stopped snoring, opened his eyes, and sat up. The heroes came down from their horses, and asked:

"What wounds and sores are those on thy hands and body? Why lie there? What art thou doing?"

"If ye had been bitten by a venomous, yellow serpent as I have, ye would be as sore as I am," said the old man. "Why are there boils on thy neck and back?"

"If Hohodai Mergen (thunder) had struck you, ye would have boils."

"Thy life is hanging on a red silk thread," said the heroes, "and thou art speaking to us insolently. We will break thy back for thee and pull off thy head!"

They sprang then to finish the old man. He rose. They rushed at him, and wrestling began. He did not give way. He limped and struggled. Nine days and nights did the conflict last. Wherever a foot pressed a hole was made, wherever a hole was made a pillar of dust rose. A hill of flesh was formed from the pieces which the two heroes tore from the old man, and which the old man tore from them. Crows came in clouds from afar to seize the flesh; they came from all sides. "May ye fight on for years!" croaked the crows. "It is pleasant to look at you."

On the tenth day the old man began to grow weak, and toward evening he fell to the earth, powerless. The two heroes put him in an iron barrel with ninety-five hoops on it, and rolled him into the Black Misty Sea. But before he fell into the water the old man said:

"In the place from which I started there is a promontory, on that promontory is a white cuckoo as big as a horse's head. Between the Bronze and Silver Square and that promontory are seventy mountain ranges. Along those seventy ranges ninety mad wolves are prowling. That cuckoo will come with the ninety mad wolves to save me;" then he fainted. Those were his last words.

The white cuckoo heard those words and set out at once, and the ninety mad wolves followed her.

Only when three days and nights had passed did the cuckoo and the ninety mad wolves appear on the shore of the Black Misty Sea. The cuckoo flew three times along the shore singing loudly; and the whole Black Misty Sea vanished, went into the earth before the power of the cuckoo, and the grass which grew around on every side of that sea dried up and withered at sight of her.

When the sea was almost dry the iron cask was seen on the bottom. The ninety mad wolves rushed at the cask and gnawed its ninety-five hoops off. When the hoops were gone the cask fell apart, and they found the skeleton of the Iron Hero. The wolves took the skeleton up carefully and carried it to the cuckoo at the seashore. The cuckoo began to sing, began at the Iron Hero's feet. When she reached his head the first time flesh began to come on his bones; the second time he almost breathed. When she reached his head the third time he sprang up. "How long have I slept?" cried he. Then he remembered what had happened. He washed, and thanked the cuckoo and the ninety mad wolves. He was in the same form as before, a wretched old man with sores on his body.

"Why art thou so foolish?" asked the cuckoo. "Why not go to the khan in thy real form?"

"If I went in youth, as I am, the khan would give me hard tasks to do,—tasks which might kill me. It is better to act in this way. My bride knows all that I am doing." Then he said to the wolves and the cuckoo: "Ye have served me well; good thanks to you, go home now, in peace." The wolves dragged the car from the bottom of the sea. The sea took its old form and grass appeared again along the shore.

The Iron Hero went a second time to the khan for his beautiful daughter, but in a worse form than before.

There was a wedding that day at the yurta. The khan was giving his daughter in marriage to the younger of the two strong heroes who had put the old man in the iron barrel and rolled him into the Black Misty Sea to stay there.

When the two heroes saw the old man coming rolling his car on in front of him they rushed out, mounted their steeds, and rode away swiftly. They had thought never to see that old man again, now they felt sure that they would never get rid of him.

The old man walked into the chamber which he had soiled on the first day, and said, "A greeting from me to thee, father-in-law!"

The khan was terrified. "What does this mean?" cried he. "The thirteen khans have all become wizards, the seventy-nine languages are all used for sorcery! I am frightened! I know not why any one comes to me, whether for good or evil reasons."

"Give me entertainment though I am poor and wretched," said the old man. "It is due me."

"Give entertainment to this old man," commanded the khan.

They brought him milk, but in a trough from which dogs drank. He took the trough, raised it as if to drink, and let the milk run down all over him. The milk reached the floor and soiled the chamber.

What was to be done? The khan sent five days' journey for Milén Buhé, an immensely strong hero; wrote to him to come quickly, that some terrible wizard in the form of an old man was tormenting him greatly, that no one yet had been able to conquer him. "If thou conquer him," wrote the khan, "thou wilt have my daughter. The old wizard soils my yurta, and thirty-three women are all the time cleaning chambers after him."

In nine days and a half the strong hero came, half a day before his time. When the old man heard of the hero's coming he went away with his car to the Bronze and Silver Square on the hilltop and fell asleep as before.

When Milén Buhé reached the khan's yurta he shouted and the khan went out. "Is that demon here now?" asked the hero.

"No, he has just gone from here," said the khan, "but come in for entertainment."

Milén Buhé followed the khan, but when he saw the vile remnants the old man had left at the entrance he halted. "I will not go in!" said he. "Come through other doors," said the khan, and they went in elsewhere. "I know not who it is that has come to me," said the khan, "an old man with good intent, or with evil. I know that if thou kill him I will give thee my daughter."

The hero ate and drank quickly, then hurried off. He came to the hilltop, saw the old man, dismounted, woke him up, and asked, "Why hast thou such vile hands and feet?"

"If poisonous yellow serpents had bitten thy hands and feet they would be as mine are."

"Why are those boils on thy neck and back?"

"If Hohodai Mergen had struck thee thou wouldst have boils also."

"Thou art on the sharp edge of death, and answer me rudely in this style! I will tear thee to pieces!"

They rushed at each other like two bulls, and were as fierce and gloomy as two clouds filled with thunder. They closed and wrestled,—wrestled two days so desperately that the third morning their lowest ribs were bare. Each seized the other by the last rib, each threw the other, and each pulled out a rib in the struggle, but remained in his senses. They lay on the ground, each holding a rib in his hand.

The thousand Heavenly Burkans called together a wise assembly. "These two are brothers," said they. "We made them both, why do they fight?"

The Burkans threw down a written message. It fell between the two wrestlers, and it said: "Ye are brothers. The Iron Hero is the younger." Milén Buhé took the message and read it, then the Iron Hero read it, read that they were brothers created by the thousand Burkans. The two were reconciled at once. Each gave the other his rib, put it in place, and both were well again.

The Iron Hero took out his steed and was ready to ride back to the khan's yurta, when his brother asked:

"Why didst thou make thyself old? Why not go in thy real form? Let us both go to the khan."

They set out together.

"That old man was a terrible sorcerer," said Milén Buhé to the khan. "He had immense magic power. I was not able to conquer him alone, so I summoned from northern regions my brother, this Iron Hero. He helped me, we conquered the sorcerer, and finished him. Thou wilt never see that old man again. I am married, so give thy daughter to my younger brother, this Iron Hero here."

The khan consented. He sent men to kill rams, and held the feast which is given at the asking in marriage. "Go now to see thy bride," said the khan when the feast was over.

The bride was in the seventieth chamber, and was such a beauty that her neck had the brightness of sunrays. When she looked toward the west her right cheek shone so that all western people said, "The sun is rising!" When she looked toward the east, all eastern people said, "The moon is rising!"

When the Iron Hero entered the seventieth chamber the maid met him, and said: "I know all that has happened since you left the home of Gesir Bogdo to come to me. Many of the difficulties were made by me. I raised them to test thee, to learn if thou wert able to overcome them. You came as an old man, and ridiculed my father."

"If I had not come as an old man your father would have killed me. Had I come as a young man he would have given tasks that are impossible. I had to conquer him, and that was the only way."

The Iron Hero rose just at sunrise and hurried to the khan. The khan, Milén Buhé, and he drank together." I have been delayed so long," said the Iron Hero, "that we should have the wedding immediately."

OUR BURIAT FRIENDS IN THE SACRED ISLAND OF OLKHON
IN LAKE BAIKAL, SIBERIA. *Page 74*
The man and woman who gave up their house to us

OUR BURIAT FRIENDS IN THE SACRED ISLAND OF OLKHON IN LAKE BAIKAL, SIBERIA

The man and woman who gave up their house to us

The khan invited all his people to the wedding feast. There were mountains of meat and a sea of drink; amusements of all kinds and dances. Nine days and nights did the feast last. When it was over the bridegroom mounted his steed and the bride mounted hers, a golden bay of great beauty. The bride begged a gift of her mother. The mother gave her golden scissors, which had the power to multiply cloth. When the owner of the scissors began to cut, she could cut all day without using up the cloth.

The khan had six brothers; he himself was the eldest of seven. "What will my six uncles give me?" asked the bride, as she turned to them.

The eldest uncle gave her a red kerchief, which had the power to make a dead man alive. The second uncle gave a silver cup. "When thou hast a son thou wilt drink soup with bits of meat from this cup, and be strong," said he. "Here is a golden horn," said the third uncle. "When thou hast a son he will suck milk from this and never suffer from thirst." "Here is a silver bracelet," said the fourth uncle. "It will protect thee against all weapons and attacks of every kind." The fifth uncle gave a ring, which had the power to make a poor man rich. The sixth gave good wishes for health and wealth, nothing more.

Milén Buhé wished his brother health and great prosperity. The Iron Hero invited all the people to a feast at his own house. "When the road is straight," said he, "you will travel on; when you see a circle, that is your camping place, spend the night there."

He took a larch tree, tied it to his horse's tail, and rode away in front of his guests. The Iron Hero came to the mountain which he had climbed with such difficulty, that Red Mountain on which was the Water of Life and Youth, and there he waited for the company. The bride knew another road down. All drank of the water, and then went down by an easy road, which no person in the world but the bride knew of.

ASHIR BOGDO

AFTER Gesir Bogdo had been saved and cured by the Iron Hero, and Ashir had gone westward to take as bride Nalhan Taiji, the daughter of Gasir Baiyin, Gesir Bogdo began to live with his old wife, and lived in peace for a while, then eleven Mangathais came at one time. They were strong and terrible. The eleven had four hundred and seven heads.

"Why have ye come?" asked Gesir Bogdo.

"We have come to find work. Give us tasks to do, if not we will kill thee."

"I have work enough, why not give it," said Gesir.

He sent his thirty-three strong champions, mighty heroes, to dig a very deep ditch. When the ditch was finished Gesir said to the Mangathais, "Come, Mangathais, I will show you where the work is." He started, and with him went the Mangathais, followed by the thirty-three strong heroes. When the Mangathais came to the edge of the ditch, and stood in a row looking into it, the thirty-three strong heroes pushed them from behind into the ditch, and then threw down one great long stone and covered them.

The Mangathais struggled, were lifting the stone by main force, but the thirty-three kept it down. The eleven Mangathais died in that ditch; the great stone settled on them, and then other stones were piled up on that one. Gesir built a splendid yurta above the ditch. On a wall of the yurta Gesir had his image in full armor sitting on horseback, with his bow drawn. Then he went back to his own yurta and found that the Iron Hero had come with his bride and many attendants. All the guests had not arrived, but when all were there Gesir Bogdo assembled his own people, and made a feast which lasted nine days and nights. After that the Iron Hero went to live in the Iron and Silver Square as he had intended.

Ashir Bogdo, who had gone to get Gasir Baiyin Khan's daughter, reached at last the boundary. of that khan's dominion. When he came the time was autumn; the leaves had turned yellow, and were falling on his side, but beyond the boundary, in the khan's country, it was springtime,—the leaves were just opening and grass was beginning to grow.

Ashir sat there on the boundary between the two countries. "I have traveled all summer," said he to himself, "and have reached the boundary, what will happen to me now?" And he began to weep. He wept for a time, then smoked, and rode forward.

On the road he met a youth riding a horse as red as blood. In the ears of this youth were rings as big as a cart-wheel; his eyes were as large as plates, his face red, and his teeth were each the size of a spade. They greeted, and each said to the other that he was going to seek a bride.

Ashir rode farther till he met a Mangathai with seventy-seven heads.

"Where art thou going?" asked the Mangathai.

"How does that concern thee? I am traveling on my own affair," replied Ashir. "Thy road is open before thee. I am Ashir Bogdo; what is thy name?"

"I am Huhshin Ahai; I live in the southwest. I heard of thy birth, but did not think that thou hadst grown to such size." "Hast thou killed many like me?" inquired Ashir.

"I have met many stronger men, and have killed every one of them."

"Would it take thee long to kill me?"

The Mangathai sprang from his saddle; Ashir slipped down from his horse and looked at the Mangathai. They approached each other cautiously, and closed in struggle.

Three days and nights they fought furiously. Each bit away all the flesh from the front of the other's body, and with his ten fingers tore off all that was behind.

On the third evening Ashir killed the Mangathai. He tore his body into two parts. The first part he put under a hill on the west of the road, and the second under a hill on the east of the road; then he killed the horse and buried him under a third hill.

Now Ashir rode farther, rode on till he came to a meadow so broad that he could see neither side nor end to it. Far off in front of him on the horizon was a black house a verst and a half long, and so high that the sky seemed to touch it. It was roofed with brass. On each of fifty-seven stakes before this house was a horse skull and on fifty-seven other stakes outfits of arms and armor.

"My father told me," thought Ashir, "that he had killed all the Mangathais. I have killed one and still I find more of them." When he reached the yurta he turned himself into a woodchuck and dug a hole under the floor; but the floor was iron, and he could not cut through it. On the west side of the yurta was a small hole, left by accident. Ashir crept through that hole. Inside the yurta was a Mangathai with seven hundred heads, the father of a great many Mangathais. His wife was there also. It was dangerous to attack both, so Ashir crept out very quietly. He made his horse one hundred and ninety fathoms long, and himself so large that his head and the sky seemed to touch each other. His neck was immense; he was terrible to look at.

When Ashir was thus changed he shouted to the Mangathai to come out and meet him.

"Who has dared to rouse me? Who has dared to call me?" cried the Mangathai, going out. When he saw Ashir he asked: "Who is this, who can it be? Is this a Burkan?"

"What kind of person art thou with fifty-seven skulls impaled here before thy dark house?" asked Ashir. "I am here to give thee battle; I have come on purpose to fight thee."

"Thou art Ashir Bogdo. I know thy father and mother; I will not fight with thee; thy father has never harmed me."

"If thou wilt not fight, dig a deep pit for me," said Ashir. And he made the Mangathai dig a pit. He dug for seventeen days, then he wished to come out, to be drawn up with a rope. "I do not think," said Ashir, "that the pit is deep enough." He called the wife of the Mangathai and said: "Go down and see if thy husband has done the work well."

"Why should I go down, my husband is there; he can do the work alone."

"He is not able to dig fast enough," said Ashir; "he cannot dig the pit alone and fill buckets fast enough. Let him dig and do thou fill the buckets."

She hesitated. "Get into the bucket," ordered Ashir. "Get in I tell thee!" She stepped in reluctantly. "The pit must be sixty feet in depth," said Ashir, as he let her down. She measured as the bucket was lowered. "Sixty-one feet deep!" cried the Mangathai. "I have measured carefully." "That is enough," replied Ashir, "send up all the tools down there." They sent up the tools. Ashir let the bucket down to them. The Mangathai got in first. Ashir drew him up to the top almost; then cut the rope quickly and the bucket fell. The Mangathai was crushed and killed.

"Oh," cried the wife of the Mangathai, "I knew that thou hadst such a plan. Thou art cunning; thou wert wheedling and kind to me. Thou hast killed my husband. I yielded to thy persuasive words and am ruined. I might have fought with thee. I could have conquered if I had stayed up there."

Ashir Bogdo filled the hole with immense stones, then he turned the iron yurta bottom upward, took all of the Mangathai's property and sent it to his father's yurta.

Ashir traveled farther; traveled till he met a Mangathai with three hundred heads and thirty horns in them, who called out, "Thou thinkest thyself a hero! thou hast killed my father and brother, but I will repay thee! Thou wilt not deceive or overcome or trick me!"

They sprang down from their horses and rushed at each other. The struggle was long and dreadful. They wrestled twelve days and nights. All the flesh was torn from their bones; ravens flew in from the east and the north and the south, crying: "Fight on, fight on! Give us flesh forever!"

"Let us try arrows," said the Mangathai. They went to the tops of opposite mountains. In the evening Ashir saw two wild goats; he killed both at one shot, spitted the two, put them in front of the fire to roast, then lay down and slept. The next morning he was eating the goats when the Mangathai called to him.

"Thou hast killed my father, mother, and brother; do not dare to shoot thy arrow before I shoot mine!"

The Mangathai had no arrow, he wanted to deceive Ashir. His only weapon was an axe eighty fathoms broad. Ile threw the axe. It went but halfway. Ashir's magic power stopped it. "What is this!" thought the Mangathai. "Am I tired? Have I grown weak after fighting twelve days? This is the first time I ever failed to hit. What has happened?" He started for his axe.

"Stop! I will shoot!" cried Ashir.

"Wait till to-morrow," said the Mangathai; "why art thou in such a hurry?"

"Very well," replied Ashir, "my arrow might not reach thee. Let us see which of us has most magic."

"Agreed," said the Mangathai.

Ashir read in his book and discovered that the Mangathai had been made by Galta Ulan Tengeri. That far away in the southeastern sky the Mangathai had an aunt, and that aunt kept his life. Ashir made his horse into a flint, put the flint in his pocket, turned himself into a falcon, and flew away toward the southeast. He flew nine days and nine nights, flew till at last he came to the aunt's house.

Ashir now made himself exactly like the Mangathai, and as he went along he began to cry bitterly. The aunt lived in a white yurta; she had only one tooth and one eye. She heard her nephew crying, and came out of the yurta. "Why cry?" asked she. "Come here." And she gave him her breast to draw.

"Ashir Bogdo has appeared on earth," said the false Mangathai. "My strength is not enough to overcome him. Give me strength enough, give me power."

"How strangely you draw my breast," said she. "You took only a little milk in the old time, now you take much."

"I told you that I had lost strength in fighting so long with Ashir Bogdo." He drew fiercely, drew all the life from her and she fell senseless to the earth. Ashir trampled and killed her; then he found a golden box. He kicked the box till it broke. Inside were thirteen woodcocks. He caught them all, put them in his pockets and hurried away. In nine days he was back to the place of combat. The Mangathai was not there; he had gone for Ashir's life. He made himself just like Ashir, went up to Esege Malan and said:

"Why didst thou make me? The Mangathai is fighting, and I cannot conquer him. Give me more power; give me strength enough; give me my life."

Esege Malan did not recognize the Mangathai, thought him Ashir and gave Ashir's life to him. Just then Ehé Ureng Ibi came to Esege and said:

"Thou wert deceived. That is a Mangathai."

"How deceived?"

"Deceived. Those were not Ashir's eyes, his eyes are quite different. Take thy spy glass and look at the Mangathai."

Esege took the rosy glass and saw the Mangathai flying as a raven. He watched him long. Saw the raven reach the earth and turn into a Mangathai. That moment Esege summoned Hohodai. "I have been deceived by a Mangathai," said he, "I want your help."

"I will help you," answered Hohodai. And that instant he sent bloody rain and hail and hurled jagged lightning at the Mangathai, tore him and his horse into fragments, smashed them into small bits.

Ashir's life was on earth, and Esege Malan sent two Shalmos (Invisible Spirits) to bring it back. The two turned into ravens, went down, found the life, brought it with them, and gave it back to Esege Malan.

After waiting some days on the mountain, Ashir would wait no longer; he crushed the thirteen woodcocks and went farther. Soon he met another Mangathai, the largest he had ever seen. He had a thousand heads. The lower jaw of the main head reached the earth when the Mangathai was standing and the upper jaw touched the sky. He moved forward with open jaws and began by his breath to draw Ashir into his mouth.

Horse and rider went racing toward that immense mouth, they had no power to resist the current of breath.

All at once Ashir made his horse into a flint chip and himself into a black stone as big as a large stallion. The stone rolled along, swifter and swifter, rolled into the Mangathai's mouth, straight on to his tongue. Ashir's hands and arms were stone; they stuck in the Mangathai's throat, and resisted swallowing. The Mangathai could not get the huge stone down, could not spit it out. He struggled, groaned, ran around in great agony; ran seven days and seven nights.

"This is Ashir Bogdo, surely," thought he. "He is the only one who can beat me. Kill me if thou wilt," cried he to the stone, "if not let me go!"

No prayer could move the stone; on the tenth day it had worn through the tongue. Ashir now asked Esege Malan for weapons; they appeared and he cut up the lungs of the Mangathai. The Mangathai fell dead on the earth. Ashir came out, took the Mangathai's axe, which was fifty feet wide, and cut off all his heads, cut out his ribs. Something was moving through his interior. A terrible serpent came out. Ashir cut the serpent open and found three hundred and seventy-five people alive in the body. They had fires and were cooking food. "What is thy name?" asked those people of Ashir Bogdo. "We have lived here a long time. There is no change of season in this place, no spring, no summer, no autumn, no winter. What a good hero thou art to rescue us. May thou accomplish all thy wishes and all that thou hast set out to do."

"Go all of you people to the places whence ye came," said Ashir. "Go to the lands where ye lived before. I have fought many years with this Mangathai and his father and brother. I set out to find my bride, now I will go to her."

He killed the Mangathai's horse, mounted his own steed and rode till at last he reached the house of his father-in-law, one of the great Tengeri.

"Why hast thou come hither, earth creature?" asked the Tengeri.

"I have come for thy daughter."

"Wait, I will read thy book," said the Tengeri. Ashir gave his book. The Tengeri read and discovered how Ashir had warred with the Mangathais; read all of his exploits. He read for three days and finished. "Read thou my book," said the Tengeri. Ashir read for fifteen days, read all. "Thou art a master at reading," said the Tengeri, "I can hardly read it myself in fifteen days. Now thou mayst see thy bride." And he opened the door to Ashir with respect.

"Be greeted! Whence hast thou come?" asked the bride.

"I have come for thee. There are many maidens down on the earth," said Ashir, "but I heard of thy wonderful beauty, and came."

"There is a bad odor on earth," said the maiden. "Such a bad odor that I could not live there."

"There are houses down there just as good as those here," answered Ashir. "If the air were bad all the people would die, but they live and are well. Burkans come down to visit us and eat in our houses."

"Let me see thy book," said the maiden. She read Ashir's book and embraced him. "Forgive me," said she, "I was not sure that it was thee."

"We must have the wedding to-morrow," said Ashir. "How much time have I spent in struggling? How many terrible journeys have I made in coming?"

"I knew of thy journey and thy struggles," said she. "I knew that thou wert coming."

Next day the Tengeri assembled all the people of the sky, and they feasted nine days and nights in great splendor. When ready to start the bride received from her father a gray steed ninety fathoms long, and a silver goblet of such kind that it would neither sink nor move with the current when thrown into a river.

Before starting Ashir and his bride turned their horses into pieces of flint, made the presents small and put everything in their pockets. They became ravens then and flew down to Gesir Bogdo's yurta, where they took their own shapes again and restored their horses and presents. Gesir Bogdo then assembled all his people, and they feasted for nine days and nine nights as they had never feasted before.

CHAPTER XII. MONGOL MYTHS AND FOLK-TALES

BURULDAI BOGDO, No. I

ONCE there was a khan named Buruldai Bogdo. He was seventy years old and his wife was sixty, and they had no children.

One day the khan took a book out of his head and read in it. In that book it was written that he had not counted his cattle for fifteen years. So he set out to find and count them.

In one place he discovered that the cattle had not increased, that they were thin and hungry, and had but little water to drink. He went farther and came to a mare that had a colt. This colt seemed to the khan to be as big as a mountain, and looking at it he began to weep, for in his mind he was saying:

"This colt will be a wonderful steed, but I have neither son nor daughter to ride him." Then he said to the colt: "I am seventy years old, and when thou art fitted for the saddle there will be no one to conquer and ride thee; I am too old and I have neither son nor daughter."

When he reached home the khan was still crying bitterly. "Why art thou weeping?" asked his wife. When he refused to tell her she went out, got a hair rope and declared she would hang herself if he did not tell. Then he said: "I am crying because I am an old man, and thou too art old. I saw a wonderful colt to-day, but when it is fit for the saddle there will be no one to ride it, for we have neither son nor daughter."

"Cry no more," said his wife; "though I am old, I am not without hope of having a son or a daughter; but go thou beyond the mountain to the house of the seven Lamas and beg them to soothsay for us."

Buruldai Bogdo went beyond the mountain, and came to a great square yurta, but could find no door. He walked around the yurta; there was no door to be seen. Then he said to himself, "What a fool thou art; go back ten yards, run, kick the wall with all thy strength." This he did and seventy doors flew open before him. Inside were seven Lamas, but they were silent. The khan begged them to soothsay for him, begged the first day, begged the second and the third day. Then the youngest of the Lamas asked without looking at him:

"Why make so much foolish noise? It is thy wish to have children; there is a child at thy yurta already."

Buruldai Bogdo went home. A son had been born to him, but neither knife nor axe could ciit the umbilical cord. The father took a hair rope, tied one end to the child and the other to his horse, but the rope broke; he cried then, and begged his good steed to tell him what to do, and the horse said:

"Take a hair from the tail of the wonderful colt, tie one end of it around the child, and give me the other end."

The khan rode out to the field where the colt was at pasture, but the colt would not let him come near. At last he found a long hair that had caught on a thorn bush. This he took home, tied one end of it around the child's body and gave the other to the horse. The horse pulled, and the child stood up.

In seven days the skin of a sheep seven years old could not cover the boy. When he was ten months old he minded sheep, and was everywhere. One day he saw a wolf, and he asked his father what it was.

"It is a brave fellow, kill it!" answered the father. The boy asked for an arrow and bow, got them, and killed the wolf. "See what a son we have!" said the old father and mother to each other.

One day the boy came upon a fine open meadow, and he decided to build a yurta there. After it was built he was tired and lay down to rest. He wished to sleep seven months, but in the fourth month his mother strove in every way to waken him; when at last she stuck a file in the sole of his foot he sprang up quickly.

"Whilst thou wert sleeping a sister was born to thee," said the mother, "but some one came in through the smoke hole and stole her."

"Write a petition to Esege Malan for a horse. What can I do without a wise horse," said the boy to his father. The petition was written, and Esege Malan answered, "Horse and arms are on the flat top of Red Mountain.'

The boy took three casks of tarasun and three sheep, made libations, ate and drank, then went to Red Mountain.

Off at the edge of the sky he saw a horse; it came near, ran around him, but he could not catch it. At last the horse called: "If thou art my right master shoot me in the heart, the arrow will go through without drawing blood; if it draws blood thou art not my master but an evil enemy."

The boy shot and drew no blood.

"Sit on me," said the horse, "thou art my master."

When the boy was on his back the horse ran for thirty days trying to throw him, but he could not. "Art thou fooling with me, thy rightful master? I will kill thee!" cried the boy at last, very angry.

"I had to test thee and thy strength," replied the horse; "now I will serve thee faithfully."

Straightway they set out to look for the sister. They traveled on and on till they came to another kingdom. The boy saw a trail and thought it was his sister's; after following it for many days it came to an end at the foot of a rock. He stopped, took tobacco, threw some to the gods, and then smoked. While he was smoking a young man on a black horse galloped up from the west. He was the son of Khan Zuduk Shin Mergín Xubún Zud. He greeted the boy, and said he was in search of his sister, an infant.

Now a young man from the East came up on a gray horse. He was the son of Gazar Xara Khan. Then from the south-west came a third young man, Nadur Gai Mergín, on a bay horse. Each was in search of an infant sister, each had followed a trail which led to the rock. The four held a council, and decided that their sisters must be somewhere under that great rock.

"Raise the rock," said the first young man to the second. He raised it until he sank into the ground to his knees. The third man raised it until he went into the ground to his waist. The fourth raised it until he went into the ground to his shoulders. Then the first one became angry and said: "Of what use to come so far, if we can do nothing?" And he seized the rock of ninety-nine poods in weight, hurled it beyond seven valleys, and found that it had covered a deep hole.

"Now," said the young men, "one of us must go and order the nine heavenly blacksmiths to make a chain long enough to reach to the bottom of this hole."

No one of them was willing to go. At last Buruldai Bugdo's son went himself and begged for a chain nine hundred sachens long, so long that it took the nine blacksmiths nine days to make it.

He brought the chain to the opening and said "Whoever goes down shall be drawn up as soon as he shakes the chain," then he asked Zuduk to go first.

The young man went down two hundred sachens, then became frightened, and shook the chain. The second young man went down four hundred sachens, then shook the chain. The third young man went down six hundred sachens, shook the chain, and they pulled him up.

"I went to the bottom," said he; "there was no opening there save one little hole as big as the eye of a needle."

Altun, the old khan's son, was angry now, and said to the three young men, "If you have so little power in you why did you come to look for your sisters?" Then he turned his horse loose and said, "Stand at freedom, and wait me, for a time. If I stay very long run home. In every case be watchful of these three men, they may want to kill thee."

He went down the whole length of the chain; it was a hundred sachens short. He thought and thought. At last he said to himself, "To rise is inconvenient. Once I have undertaken I will finish," so he dropped, fell on his side, broke all his ribs, and sank one half into the earth. He had plenty of room, but no one came to him, and he lay there nine years. At last a mouse crept up and made her nest in his clothes. When he saw that he thought, "I am only half alive, if I were altogether alive the mouse would not build her nest on me." With that he struck at the mouse, and crushed one of her sides. She crawled away, found an herb, ate it, and was as well as before.

Altun crawled along on the ground for three days and three nights, crawled until he found the same kind of herb. He ate of it, and was as well as ever. He walked then till he came to an open place and farther on to a great meadow, and there he saw an old eagle that could not rise. "What troubles thee?" asked Altun of the eagle. "I am so covered with sores," said the eagle, "that I cannot move. Go thou and bring me living water from nine springs."

Altun brought the water, the old eagle drank of it, and rose up in the air. "When thou hast need of a friend," said he, "call me, and I will come."

Altun went on through the meadow, and farther, till he came to a flat-topped mountain; he climbed the mountain, and saw people standing as thickly as planted trees. He went nearer and saw a hundred kettles over fires scattered here and there. In the kettles flesh of both men and beasts was boiling. He turned himself into an old withered man, went up to one of the kettles, and asked of the men standing near, "For whom is all this meat in the hundred kettles?"

"For the Mangathai of a hundred heads," replied they.

Not far away was the yurta of the Mangathai, and behind seventy curtains he was sleeping. On the right were seven curtains, and behind them were the four wives of the Mangathai.

"Whence hast thou come, old man?" asked one of the wives, when he went to the yurta.

"I am Xapmyam Yama's herdsman; some of his cows and horses have strayed away. I am in search of them."

"They have not been seen here," said the woman, but just then she looked into his eyes, and thought: "Though that man is old he might be my brother." As Altun turned away she hurried after him, and said: "I am your sister, but do not worry about me; I am happy here. Do not fight with the Mangathai, for he is a great wizard."

"I am the son of Khan Buruldai Bogdo, I must gain glory, I will fight the Mangathai and free thee," replied Altun. She could not dissuade him so she said: "I will tell thee a secret. On the right of the door the Mangathai has Water of Life, on the left he has poison water. If thou even catch the odor of the poison water thou wilt die."

"I have magic too," said the brother. "I can change Water of Life to poison water and poison water to the Water of Life, so that when one drinks of the Water of Life it will be as though he had drunk the poison water, and when one drinks of the poison water it will be as though he had drunk of the Water of Life."

On a pillar near the yurta was this inscription: "If any one wishes to fight with me, let him go to the top of the mountain opposite, and wait until I come."

Altun drank of the Water of Life, and went to the mountain. Two goats happened before him, he caught them, twisted their necks, skinned them and put them to roast on spits before the fire. He saw many bones of animals and of people; this frightened him, but he said to himself: "I drank of the Water of Life, the Mangathai will drink of the poison water, I shall conquer him," and he lay down to sleep.

Soon the Mangathai rode up. He had an axe, seventy wedges, and a hammer of ninety poods. "What sort of a hero art thou," cried he, "lying here on my land, and roasting my goats? With one blow I will kill thee!"

He struck at Altun with the axe, but the axe made no impression. Then he chopped at his right side, made a slight gash, and took the wedges to drive them in, but the wedges sprang back, flew up to the sky, and floated away toward the ocean. He struck at him with the hammer; it broke in the middle and flew off to the sea. So the Mangathai was without weapons. "What man art thou on another man's land?" shouted he in a rage.

Altun woke up, shook himself, and said: "How long I have slept! Fleas have been biting me," and he rubbed his side. Then he saw the Mangathai, and at once they began to wrestle. For three days they fenced for a hold, and then fought for thirty days, but neither could overcome the other. At last the Mangathai said: "I am thirsty, let us go down to the yurta and get a drink of strengthening water." They went down, and Altun drank of the Water of Life, and the Mangathai drank of the poison water, for Altun by his magic had changed them.

They went back to the mountain, then fought for another thirty days; the Mangathai was getting a little weaker.

Again they rested; Altun drank of the Water of Life and the Mangathai drank of the poison. During the third thirty days Altun knocked the Mangathai against one tree after another until the trunks of all the trees on the top of that mountain were bloody. Then in a rage he killed the Mangathai and tore his heads off.

Altun made a mill, ground up the Mangathai's body and his heads, burned the mass into ashes, threw the ashes into the air, and the wind carried them off to the ocean. He went down the mountain then, collected the people, and told them that their master was dead, and they were free. "But he has a son seven sachens under this floor and under a gold cover," said Altun's sister.

Altun raised the floor, raised the gold cover, and brought up the young Mangathai. He made a fire and threw him into it; but the fire did not burn him.

"If he lives ten days he will be able to kill ten thousand people, and in twenty days a hundred thousand could not overcome him. Kill him quickly!" said Agui na Gun, Altun's sister.

Altun built a great furnace and put the young Mangathai into it. It took nine days and nine nights to burn him; then Altun carried the ashes to the mother of the boy, who was herself a Mangathai, and asked, "Which would you rather have, seventy horse tails, or seventy tree-tops?"

"Out of the horse tails I could make ropes, out of the tree-tops I could make wood," said she,

Altun brought seventy horses and tied her to their tails. This frightened the horses; they ran in all directions and tore her to pieces. He collected the pieces and brought the woman to life. Then he impaled her on seventy tree-tops, and she died.

He overturned the house and took whatever pleased him. He drove the cattle ahead, and with him went the four women to the hole where the chain was. He sent up everything by the chain, and then told the four women to go.

"Go first," urged his sister; "there may be enemies up there."

"I had no enemy but the Mangathai, and he is dead," replied Altun.

They went up then and he followed; but just as he was getting to the top the chain was cut, he fell to the bottom, and went into the earth up to his chin.

Altun remembered the eagle; he called him and he came. "Thou art in deep trouble," said the eagle, "but I will go for living water."

When Altun had drunk of the Water of Life he came up out of the earth and was as well as ever. "I saved thee once," said Altun, "and thou hast repaid me, but canst thou get me out of this underground kingdom?"

"I will take thee out on my back," replied the eagle, "but first get me meat to eat, that I may grow strong."

In the open country Altun found a goat, killed it, and gave it to the eagle. After he had eaten he took Altun on his back and flew up, but when within a few sachens of the top the eagle grew weak, was failing.

Altun cut a piece of flesh from his own thigh and fed the bird, but the moment the eagle ate of the flesh he fell to the bottom.

"I am sick; I may die," said the eagle.

Altun hurried to bring the Water of Life and revive the bird.

"Why didst thou give me thy flesh?" asked the eagle; "I should have exerted my last strength and carried thee out; now thou canst get out of this place as may please thee."

The young man grew very sad; he put his hands behind his back and walked away, saying, "I came down here to save, not to offend. Why am I thus punished?" He went on and on until he came to a shed made of hay. An old man and an old woman were inside the shed counting silver coin. They were disputing.

"I have much," said one. "I have more," said the other. When they saw Altun they called out to him, "Come and divide evenly between us. As thou sayest we will do."

He divided the coin equally, and the old man asked what he wanted for his trouble. "I wish to go to my home, which is in a country above this," said Altun.

"Follow my advice, do what I say, and thou wilt go. Take dudkí (a kind of cane), bite it, thou wilt be at the hole; bite it a second time, thou wilt be a skunk and climb till tired; bite a third time, thou wilt be a magpie and fly high; bite the fourth time, thou wilt be a raven and fly to the top."

Altun did this, and when he reached the top he took his own form, put the dudkí in his pocket and traveled on. He soon found his horse lying on the ground, its hind quarters terribly gnawed by wolves.

The three young men had tried to kill the steed; he got away from them, and, though they followed on horseback, they could not overtake him. Then they got nine wolves from Esege Malan Babai. The nine wolves chased the horse, sprang at him, gnawed him; but he escaped, and made his way back to wait for his master, or die near the hole.

Altun went to the top of Red Mountain, brought back some of the Water of Life, sprinkled his steed with it and healed him; he was as strong and well as ever. Then Altun mounted and rode toward the west, rode to the home of Zudu, he of the black horse. When near the yurta he made his horse into a flint and put the flint into his pocket. Then he turned himself into a fly and sat on the edge of the smoke-hole. He listened and heard Zudu's sister ask, "Why didst thou throw that good man down into the hole?" and the young man answered, "If thou art sorry, why dost thou not go down after him?" and he scolded his sister.

Then Altun flew away, took his own form, turned the flint into a horse and rode up to the yurta. When the brother and sister saw him they were frightened. One ran one way and one the other.

"Why are ye afraid?" asked Altun. "Who will be above ground, and who below?" and taking the dudkí from his pocket he called Zudu and forced him to bite it. As soon as he bit it he turned into a fox and ran away into the woods.

Altun took possession of Zudu's yurta and people, and sent Zudu's sister to his own home. Then he went to the yurta of

THE RUSSIAN EXILE AND TWO BURIAT SHAMANS, ONE STANDING ON EACH SIDE OF HIM. *Page* 76

THE RUSSIAN EXILE AND TWO BURIAT SHAMANS, ONE STANDING ON EACH SIDE OF HIM.

MY CARRIAGE READY. THE ITALIAN BLACKSMITH.

the man of the gray horse, turned his steed into a flint, himself into a fly, sat on the edge of the smoke-hole, and listened. Soon he heard the young man's sister ask, "Why didst thou treat that good man so cruelly? He saved me from the Mangathai."

"If thou art so sorry thou canst go down into the hole and die with him," said the brother.

Altun turned himself back to his own form, went into the yurta, and said:

"While I was in the underground kingdom I found a present for you." They were greatly surprised to see him, but the brother was glad to receive a present. Altun made the dudkí look very attractive, held it out, and told the young man to bite it; as soon as he bit it he became a skunk and ran off into the woods. Altun took possession of everything and sent the sister to his own yurta.

He went to the third man's house, turned himself into a fly, listened, and heard the sister say, "Why didst thou cut the chain and kill that good man?"

"If thou art so fond of him," answered the brother, "why not go back to him?"

Just then, much to the surprise of the man and the delight of the sister, Altun walked into the yurta. He asked the brother to bite the stick of dudkí, and the young man did so out of curiosity. That moment he turned into a magpie and flew away. Altun took all of this man's possessions and his sister, and went home to his own yurta. There he found the other sisters as well as his own sister.

All the place around had fallen into bad condition, for his father and mother were very old. His parents did not know him, but the sister did, and there was great rejoicing.

He married the three sisters of the three young men. The people assembled, and there was feasting for nine days and nine nights.

BURULDAI BOGDO KHAN. No. II.

BURULDAI BOGDO was the eldest of thirteen khans and was master of seventy-three tongues. He was seventy years old, and his wife was sixty. For many years they had no children. Finally, behind seventy-three curtains twin boys were born to them.

One night while all in the yurta were sleeping the father and mother were stolen away; it was unknown by whom. When the children opened their eyes in the morning they could see no one. Immediately one of the boys became as a child of three and the other as a child of four years of age. They went into the forest, turned themselves into squirrels, and began to eat nuts.

The next day seven hundred men came through the forest looking for the boys, but they could not find them.

When the men had gone the boys took their own forms and walked eastward till they came to a yurta so immense that it had seven hundred doors. The elder brother sent the younger brother in to see what kind of a place it was. He went through thirteen doors, and came to a sixty-three headed, six-horned Mangathai, sleeping soundly. The boy was frightened and started to go back quietly, but when he had reached the third door the Mangathai woke, opened the eyes in all his heads, and called out:

"Whoever thou art, if pure, greet me; if impure, leave me." Then seeing the boy he asked:

"Whence comest thou?"

"I am the son of Buruldai Bogdo Khan."

"Thy father has injured me, has done me great harm; now thou hast come to torment me!" cried the Mangathai, in a rage. He seized the boy, bound him, and said, "To-morrow I will eat thee."

The brother, who was waiting outside, grew tired, turned himself into a squirrel and went back to the forest.

The Mangathai went to the woods for spits on which to roast the boy. While there he met a merchant returning with goods from various countries. The Mangathai invited the merchant to his yurta and entertained him. The merchant heard a child crying. "Who is that?" asked he.

"The son of a man who has done me much harm. I am going to eat him to-morrow," answered the Mangathai.

The merchant gave the Mangathai seven kegs of strong wine. The Mangathai drank the wine and grew merry; then some of his heads talked about war, some went to sleep, some cried, and others laughed.

"Give me the boy," said the merchant, "I will put him on the spit for thee." The Mangathai gave up the boy, but the merchant did not kill him or put him on the spit. He took him home and made him his own son.

The boy cried and cried. "He is afraid of the Mangathai," said the merchant's wife. "Go to the seven Lamas and let them soothsay; perhaps the child is sick." But the boy said:

"I am not sick; I am crying for my brother."

The merchant sent seven hundred men to look for that brother; but he was still a squirrel, and the men searched nine days without finding him. Then the boy went with the men to look for his brother. He turned himself into a squirrel, and instead of finding the brother the seven hundred lost the boy they had brought with them.

The two squirrels met, but the elder did not recognize the younger. "Is this an enemy," thought he; and he went straight up to Esege Malan.

The younger brother followed him to the door of Esege Malan's yurta, but did not go in. "Let my brother come out!" cried he. "If not I will choke myself." But the elder brother did not believe that the other squirrel was his brother, and he would not go out.

"I have a birth-mark as big as ten finger-tips under my left shoulder; so has my brother," said the elder boy to Esege Malan. "If this squirrel has the same, he is my brother; if not, he is an enemy."

The mark was found, and the two brothers embraced. Then they went to the merchant, who was flogging the seven hundred men, first for failing to find the one boy, and then for losing the other.

The merchant was glad to have two boys in place of one, and set them to herding cattle; but they neglected their work, and the calves took all the milk from the cows. The merchant was going to flog the boys, but his wife would not let him. He asked where they had been and why they were gone so long.

"We have been wrestling with the son of Khan Laraja Miná," answered the boys.

The second day they drove the cows home very late, and the calves had taken all the milk. "Where have you been?" asked the merchant. "You have not been watching the herd."

"We went up to the sky to order bows and arrows of the ninety Heavenly Blacksmiths. Our bows and arrows will be ready in seven days."

At the end of the seven days the blacksmiths had the bows ready and a quiver of arrows for each boy. The brothers took their bows and arrows home, and the merchant gave a great feast.

"I found these brothers in an open field," said he to the people. "I ask you to give them names."

He put out a piece of butter as big as a cup, and a piece of meat as big as a plate. An old man ate the butter and the meat, and said:

"The elder boy I name Altin Gorye; the younger, Mūngun Gorye."

The people gave each boy a horse; the elder a red stallion ninety sachens long, with ears nine sachens in length. The horse had forty teeth, four big ones and thirty-six smaller ones. They gave the younger boy a bay stallion eighty sachens long, with ears eight sachens in length. He had forty teeth,—four big ones and thirty-six smaller ones. The brothers had now all that was needed for warriors, and they made ready to travel until they found their father and mother.

"When you were young I took you and have cared for you always. Why do you leave us in our old age?" asked the merchant.

"We are going in search of our own father and mother, but we will come back; for though we live a thousand years we will not forget thee."

They went then to the place where they were born; but everything had dropped away, except a hitching-post that had stood near the yurta. On that hitching-post the father had written: "If my sons live, let them read this: 'We are taken by Bugú Curté Zulut, and are in his power. If ye are able, rescue us! In the yard of the sheep house is sheep's flesh, and an iron vessel full of arsá [solid sour, sour milk].'"

The brothers opened a granary, and found oats for their horses. They found the sheep's flesh and the arsá; they ate and drank, and were about to leave the place when they saw that it was written on the hitching-post that they must travel eighty versts a day for eight days.

They had traveled for three days when they met the two sons of a khan. Those two, by their magic, knew of the coming of the brothers, and preferred to meet them with war. They had an army, and weapons, and all things needed.

The four advanced, but could not decide who should shoot first; finally Altin Gorye, the elder of the brothers, said that the khan's sons might shoot first.

By magic the brothers caught the arrows and put them in their saddles, then they laughed and said, "You cannot shoot, and still you go to war. Now it is our turn. Yield not to any magic," said they to their arrows, "but go and scatter the enemy like sand before the wind." The arrows flew away from the bows, and both the sons of a khan were killed. The two brothers burned the two men and burned their horses as well. Then they went to the yurtas of the dead men, found their wives and children there, and said:

"We have come to see your husbands. When we came into the world some one stole our father and mother. Have you seen them?"

"We are but women; we are not wise, like men. We know nothing," they replied, but among themselves they laughed. "Short hair, short sense," said they, when the brothers had left.

The two traveled toward the west till they saw a beautiful yurta, closed and guarded; but it opened at their command. They entered and found there their father and mother; their right eyes, hands, and feet were gone. They did not recognize their children.

"Where was your home?" asked the brothers.

"In the opposite land," said the man. "I was once the eldest of thirteen khans and I knew many languages. Two sons were born to me. Have ye not seen them?"

"We are thy sons; while we were asleep behind seventy-three curtains thou with our mother and all thy property were carried away. Though you are our parents, a merchant reared us. We are going for the Water of Life, and will make ye well again."

They brought a vial of the Water of Life, restored the eyes, hands, feet, and strength of their parents. Then they took father, mother, and all the property and families of the khan's sons and went home to their father's ruined yurta, which by magic they made large and beautiful.

"Now," said the younger brother, "we must go to the merchant."

"Go thou," said the elder; "I will remain here to guard our father and mother."

They argued and disputed, and at last both went. The merchant was glad when he saw them, and he made a great feast which lasted seven days and seven nights.

"We rescued you from death," said the merchant. "When one brother was lost we sent seven hundred to hunt for him. All this cost much time and treasure. Now you should not leave us. If you wish we will go to your father's yurta, but in any case we must not part."

"Come with us," said the brothers.

The merchant made all things ready, filled wagons with gold and treasures, and he and his wife went with the brothers to their father's home.

In time the two young men became great khans, but they lived always with their two fathers and two mothers.

SHARAU

ONCE there was a young man by the name of Sharau. He became restless, and one day told his mother that if he had a small sum of money he would go out into the world and make a great deal more. His mother gave him what he asked for, and he started out to begin life. On the road he met an old man with a cat under his arm.

"Where are you going with that cat?" asked the young man. "I am taking it away to kill it," replied the man; "for it fights my dog and scratches him."

"Don't kill the cat; sell him to me," said Sharau.

"Very well, but what will you give me for him?"

"Will you take a hundred rubles?"

The man could hardly hide his joy, but said, "Yes," very grudgingly, and gave the foolish young man the cat.

Then, as he had no money, Sharau started toward home, but he had not gone far when the cat sprang out of his arms and ran away.

When he reached home his mother asked, "What have you done with your money?"

"I have bought a fine storehouse full of grain," replied the young man. "If I had a hundred rubles more I could do as well again."

His mother gave him the hundred rubles, and he started out with the intention of being very wise this time. When only a short distance from his mother's yurta he met a man with a dog. "Where are you taking that dog?" asked the young man.

"I am taking him out to kill him," replied the man. "He fights my cat, and takes her food from her; I have no peace."

"Do not kill the dog; sell him to me. I will give you all the money I have." He was afraid that the hundred rubles would not be enough to buy the dog, for he had paid that much for a cat.

"I will give you a hundred rubles for him."

The man was glad to part with the worthless hound for such a big sum of money, and the young man started toward home; but the dog bit and jumped, and pulled so badly at the leash that at last Sharau lost patience and turned him loose. The dog ran away at once.

When the young man got home his mother asked what he had done with his money.

"I bought much fine grain," replied he; "now I wish to marry. In a kingdom not far away lives Sazrai Khan (Magpie Khan); he has a daughter Sarung-gohung (another kind of bird). I would like to marry her."

The mother went to Sazrai Khan and said: "I have a fine young son; you have a beautiful daughter. Let us become relatives."

"How can that be?" asked Sazrai. "The father of your son was a merchant, and I am a khan. If your son will build a silver bridge from my yurta to yours I will give him my daughter. If he does not build the bridge I will have his head."

The mother went home crying. "What are you crying about?" asked Sharau.

"You must find some one else for your bride," sobbed the mother. "Sazrai Khan says you are a merchant's son and cannot marry his daughter till you build a silver bridge from his yurta to ours, and if you do not build this bridge he will cut your head off."

"Then I had better run away and keep my head," said the young man, and he started off at once. He went far, went until he came to a dense forest. In this forest he met the dog whose life he had saved.

"Oh, dog!" cried Sharau, "I saved your life; now do you help me. I must build a bridge of silver for Sazrai Khan, and I know not how to do it, for I am a poor man."

"Take this ring," said the dog. "Go home, look at the sun, make three circles with your hand, and say while turning around, 'Let a bridge of silver be built to-night from my yurta to that of Sazrai Khan.'"

This the young man did, and when he woke the next morning there was the silver bridge. He went to it, took an axe and began to work, as though he were just finishing a difficult task. The khan came to look at the bridge, was much surprised, but only said, "Why are you so long at the work; were not all the hours of the night sufficient?"

"I have built it in one night," said Sharau. "If any man can build it in a shorter time he may have my claim to your daughter."

"We will have the wedding in seven days," said the khan.

After the wedding the khan's daughter went to live with her husband, but she grew dissatisfied, and complained bitterly.

"How is this?" asked she. "You can build a bridge of silver, and yet you live in this wretched old yurta."

The young man said nothing about the ring, hid it very carefully. At night he slept with it in his mouth. One night he coughed and the ring blew out and fell to the floor, but he grasped it quickly.

"What is that? What do you keep in your mouth?" asked his wife; and when he refused to tell she teased him both day and night until, weary of her teasing, he told her that it was a ring with such magic power that if he looked at the sun and made three circles with his hand while turning around he would get his wish, whatever it might be.

"Let me keep the ring for you," begged Sarung-gohung; "you may lose it." She teased him a whole week, teased until he gave it to her.

Now Sarung-gohung had a lover in a kingdom beyond the sea, and that very night while her husband was sleeping she determined not to wait, but to rise with the sun, and try the power of the ring. So at sunrise she made the circles, wished, and that moment she was with her lover.

When Sharau woke and found his wife gone he went to the khan and said, "See what a wife I have. She has gone away and left me."

"I gave you my daughter," said the khan; "if you haven't her now you have killed her."

Straightway he seized Sharau, bound him, and threw him into a dungeon. Then he said to him, "I will wait seven days. If my daughter does not return by that time she is dead, and I shall have your head cut off."

The young man sat in the dungeon a day and a night. He had nothing to eat, and wondered what he could do to save his life. The second day he heard a noise, and saw a cat coming toward him. "You are a fool," said the cat. "You should not have told about the ring. Your wife is in another kingdom, and has married her lover. The dog and I have counseled, but can think of no way to help you. How long are you to sit in this dungeon?"

"Seven days," answered the young man. "On the eighth day I shall be killed."

"If the dog and I cannot get the ring back within the seven days you are lost," said the cat. "But be of good courage; you saved our lives, we will try to save yours."

The cat went to the dog and they counseled again. At last the dog said, "Get on my back, we will go to that kingdom beyond the sea."

When they came to the place where the wife was the cat caught a mouse that lived in the yurta. "If you do as I tell you," said the cat to the mouse, "I will let you go; otherwise I will crush and eat you."

"I am without offence," replied the mouse. "Why destroy me? Do not crush or eat me; whatever you wish I will do."

"This is what you must do. In the mouth of the woman in whose yurta you live is a gold ring; get it for me."

The mouse worked all night at making a hole into the room where the woman was sleeping, and was there just at daybreak. He sprang on to the bed, crept up to her face, and tickled her nose. The woman sneezed once, and a second time, and the ring fell from her mouth. The mouse snatched the ring and was out through the hole that minute.

The cat went back to the dog, sat on his back, and they started for their own kingdom. The dog wanted to carry the ring, but the cat said:

"No, you have a large mouth, and always keep it open. Whoever saw a dog running with his mouth closed? My mouth is small. I will carry the ring." The cat wished; there was a boat. They were halfway across the sea when the cat sneezed, and the ring dropped into the water.

"The man is as good as dead," said the dog; "for we can never get the ring from the bottom of the sea."

They came to land, caught fish, and were eating them when the cat found the ring in a fish she was gnawing.

"We must hurry!" said the dog. "Hold as tight as you can!" And he ran as never dog ran before. When daylight came the dog looked at the sun, wished, and they were at the dungeon. The cat went to the young man.

It was the afternoon of the seventh day, and Sharau had lost hope of rescue.

"Take the ring," said the cat, "make the circles toward the west, and, though the sun is not shining in this dungeon, you will get your wish."

Sharau wished himself out of the dungeon and in the khan's palace. He was there, and said to his father-in-law, "My wife is living with a man in a kingdom across the sea. I want you to get her back."

"You have killed your wife," replied the khan. "If not, bring her here yourself and I will spare your life."

The young man looked at the sun, made three circles with his hand, and wished his wife and her lover to be there before him. They appeared immediately. "Now," said the young man to his father-in-law, "what are you going to do?"

"I will do to them what I was going to do to you to-day," said the khan; and he had their heads cut off.

HÚNKUVAI AND THE HORSE WITH ROUND HEAD

AFTER this world had become a world, and this earth had become earth, and water had become water, there lived near the northern side of the Altai mountains, on the ridge called Huhúi, a khan so rich that he could not grow poor, and so healthy that he could not die.

This khan had a wife named Deri Sisin (Steel File). She held every place where she was with her dignity and filled her own yurta with her presence. The thoughts of Deri Sisin were as clear as the sunlight.

The khan had a gray steed with round head, and this steed was kept at pasture on the Altai mountains, where thirteen elks pastured with him.

When the khan began to rule, his herds had not been counted for a long time, so he determined to count them. He went first to Arin, his white uncle in the northwest, collected all his people, every clan there, ordered the elders to assemble, and began to count on the northwest side. When he had counted all on that side he went to the southwest, and counted every animal in that place.

The khan found that his people and his cattle had increased very greatly, and he was much pleased; but he failed to find his gray steed with round head. He saw tracks of a man and of an immense horse, and knew that some one had come to the Altai And stolen his wonderful steed. Because of this he went home in great sadness.

Deri Sisin placed food and drink of all kinds before him. "Why art thou sad?" asked she. "What evil has happened?"

"Some one has stolen my gray steed with round head," said the khan, and he told of the tracks he had seen.

"Thou hadst a book given thee at birth, look in that and learn what has happened. The book is under thy midriff."

The khan opened his midriff, took out the book, read, and found that the son of Timur Shi Bain Khan had stolen the gray steed with round head. In the book it was written also that Timur's kingdom was distant a journey of fifty-five years, that the khan himself had not power to go so far, but there was a great hero, a certain Húnkuvai, who could do it.

To find this Húnkuvai, the khan summoned all subject people. All appeared except one young man.

"Why did all come and not that man?" asked the khan.

The young man's uncle spoke up and said: "Húnkuvai, my nephew, is the only son of his father; he is not here because he has much wealth. He is so rich and powerful that he did not regard thy call."

The khan was enraged, and sent three heroes to bring Húnkuvai.

When the three heroes reached Húnkuvai's yurta they saw that it was richer than even the khan's yurta.

"We are here from our khan!" proclaimed the three messengers to the servants of Húnkuvai.

Shik Shuri Nogon, Húnkuvai's wife, appeared before the yurta.

"Why have ye come?" asked the woman.

"We have come at command of the khan to tell thy husband that he is summoned."

"For the last three days my husband has had a headache. He sees no man, goes nowhere," answered Shik Shuri. Then she seized a club and drove away those three messengers.

"Húnkuvai's yurta is better than thine, O Khan," said the three on returning. "It is so bright from gold and silver that we could not look at it with open eyes."

"Who came? Why did the dogs bark?" asked Húnkuvai of his wife when she went into the yurta after beating the messengers.

"People were passing and the dogs barked at them," was her answer.

When he heard what his men said the khan fell into a terrible rage.

"What!" screamed he, "ye three heroes beaten, driven away by a woman!"

He sent nine heroes now to summon Húnkuvai. When they appeared in the distance the man at the yurta whose duty it was to watch for people, told Shik Shuri that nine men were coming. She went out to meet them.

"Why do ye come?" screamed she. "I have told all that no man is received here!" And seizing a great club she beat away the nine heroes as she had the first three, but beat them more savagely.

"What is the trouble? Why do the dogs bark?" asked Húnkuvai when Shik Shuri went into the yurta.

"A she elk ran by with her little one; the dogs barked at her."

"We could do nothing," said the nine heroes when they stood before the khan. "The woman clubbed us savagely and drove us away."

Confined by the khan in an iron prison was a very strong hero. The khan raged at the nine beaten men and let out the strong hero, whose iron cap weighed forty poods. He seated this hero in a car drawn by nine stallions and sent him to conquer Shik Shuri. When he was near her husband's yurta Shik Shuri came out to meet him. She seized her heaviest club and began at the hero. She clubbed him, and he fought with her till at last both had to stop for breath. The woman tottered into the yurta, panting heavily.

"With whom art thou fighting?" asked Húnkuvai.

"I have seen no one," replied she; "I am not well to-day."

"She must be doing something," thought Húnkuvai. "The dogs have barked three times. She is keeping some secret from me." And he went outside to see what was taking place; at that moment the great hero was starting off in his car drawn by nine powerful stallions.

"Why art thou here?" shouted Húnkuvai.

"The khan has sent men three times for thee," answered the hero, "but thy wife has let no one come near thy threshold."

"If that is true I will obey the khan's orders." So saying Húnkuvai made ready and went with the hero.

"Why not come at first?" asked the khan. "I wish thee to find and bring back my gray steed with round head. It has been stolen. Thou mayst be khan after me."

"I am willing to go, but I must have the right steed and good fighting weapons. In three weeks I might start," said Húnkuvai. "Ask all the people to pray to the Burkans; thou thyself pray, and I will pray too, that weapons be given me, and a steed on which I may ride such a distance."

When Húnkuvai went back to his yurta he had become more active; he was full of resolve and venom and was twice as strong as before.

One day during those three weeks a stallion appeared in the courtyard, and on his saddle was a hero's full outfit.

When the time came to go for the steed with round head the khan himself and all the people came to Húnkuvai's yurta. They prayed to the Burkans and asked for success. People said that no one could go with the young hero, since the road was so long that if a boy of five years were to start he would be sixty years old at the end of his journey, and if a man of full age were to go he would die while still traveling.

With each step which Húnkuvai's stallion made he covered sixty paces, and went on increasing the length of his steps. He threw out behind lumps of earth each as big as a calf a year old, and his speed was of that sort that in one day he made the whole journey.

Húnkuvai was at Timur Shi's yurta on the following evening, and shouted for some one to come out and meet him. Timur Shi sent a man to say that the hour was late; the guest must sleep in some other place and he would meet him on the morrow.

Húnkuvai turned his stallion into a flint chip, went to the neighboring forest, and passed the night there.

He met Timur Shi next day, and they went out together to wrestle on a high place. When they had gone the distance of a promontory Timur Shi and Húnkuvai began the trial of strength. Each seized the other, and they wrestled for three weeks. They tore away all the flesh from the backs of their bodies, and bit away all that was in front of them.

At the end of the three weeks they were so feeble that when a slight wind blew they bent before it. The sun and moon had grown red from the awful dust which they raised in that country and from the blood which they shed there. They could not stop fighting, for neither could free himself from the other.

The thousand Burkans looked down from the sky and were frightened. They called an assembly and decided to separate the two champions; so they sent Timur Buqú (Iron Bull), a great hero, to part them. When Iron Bull came down from the sky and touched the two, they broke one of his legs. That strong hero went up to the sky again, and declared to the Burkans that neither Timur Shi nor Húnkuvai would stop till one had killed the other. Then the thousand Burkans asked Hohodai (Thunder) to strike and kill both with a thunderbolt.

Hohodai tried, but could not kill them; they did not yield to his thunderbolt, though it separated them.

They rested for a time, greeted each other, and smoked. Then they decided to shoot at each other with arrows. One went to the top of the southwest mountain, the other to the top of the northeast mountain.

"I am master in this place and ought to send the first arrow," shouted Timur Shi, when they were on the two mountains.

"I came from afar, I am a guest, I should send the first arrow," answered Húnkuvai.

After much disputing it was decided at last that Timur, as the master of the place, should have the first shot. He took from his quiver an arrow having three edges, drew his bow, and said to the arrow:

"Cut my enemy into seven pieces, and cover the seven pieces with seven mountains, so that they may never grow into one."

The arrow flew straight at Húnkuvai, cut him into seven pieces, and covered each piece with a mountain. Barely were they under the mountains, when the seven pieces turned into seven huge, raging wild bulls, broke their way out with their horns, freed themselves, and became Húnkuvai. The hero, now in his own form, called to Timur Shi from the northeast mountain and said: "Now it is thy turn to stand and my turn to shoot!" Then he stretched his bowstring and said to the arrow: "Strike him in his right arm above the elbow, break his spinal column below the neck, and kill him!"

The arrow broke the right forearm of Timur Shi and then his spinal column. The hero fell to the earth, but had barely touched it, when he rose well and strong again, just as if nothing had happened.

The two came down from the mountains and met in the valley, greeted each other like friends, smoked, and talked.

"There is nothing left for us to do but to find where our lives are," said Húnkuvai.

"Thy life," said Timur Shi, "is beyond the third valley. On the fourth mountain lives a black bear in whose body, thy life is. I will take that bear by the ears and tear him in two; that will be the end of thee."

Húnkuvai knew not where Timur Shi's life was, and he asked his stallion to tell him.

"On the top of Sehir Mai, the white mountain," said the steed, "is a great, flat round stone; under that stone are thirteen skylarks; the life of Timur Shi is in those skylarks."

Húnkuvai sat on his horse, rode away, and never stopped till he came to Sehir Mai. At the foot of the mountain were bones, immense piles of them; they were the bones of men who had tried to go to the top of that mountain and had perished,—had fallen and been killed, for no man could reach the top of Sehir Mai.

"How are we to climb to that high summit?" inquired Húnkuvai.

"We must go back one day's journey," said the stallion, "then turn and rush to the mountain. With the force of the running I may spring so high as to hang at the top. At that moment do thou cut a strip from each front hoof of mine. I shall succeed then; otherwise I shall fail."

All was done as the steed directed. Húnkuvai rode back a day's journey; the stallion rushed with mighty force, rose with one leap to the highest edge of Sehir Mai, and clung to it. Húnkuvai took his knife and cut strips from the front hoofs of the horse, and he sprang to the summit. Right there on the top of the mountain was the Water of Life, and Húnkuvai and his horse drank deeply.

Húnkuvai's whip handle was hollow, and he filled it with water. This water he scattered down on the bones which he had seen at the foot of the mountain, and all those men were alive again.

"A great hero has brought us to life," cried out thousands of people. "May he go to whatever object he wishes."

Húnkuvai went farther, went to the great, flat round stone, but struggle as he might he could not raise it; so he collected wood, lighted a fire on the stone, and heated it red hot; then he begged the thousand Burkans to make rain fall. The rain came, and the stone split into four pieces. Húnkuvai raised one of those pieces, caught the thirteen skylarks, killed ten of them, put three in his pocket, refilled his whip handle with the

Water of Life, and went down the mountain. He went toward the fourth mountain, where his own life was in the black bear. He knew that Timur Shi was going there. When near the mountain he saw a light, rode up to it, and there lay Timur Shi with his back toward a fire.

"I am sick," said Timur Shi, "I have a terrible headache, I am warming my spine. Where hast thou been? What hast thou seen, or what hast thou heard? What hast thou been doing?"

"I have just traveled around here and there, I have seen nothing of value, but I caught three little skylarks."

"Show them to me!" cried Timur Shi.

Húnkuvai showed the three skylarks.

"Oh," said Timur Shi, "those birds are sacred; a young person should not touch them. Give those birds to me. I am master of this place, I will let them fly away."

"Here they are," said Húnkuvai, and he stretched out his hand as he strangled the three skylarks. That moment Timur Shi put his palm on his mouth and dropped dead. His head fell toward the north mountain, his feet stretched out south-westward.

Húnkuvai gathered wood, made a pile, and burned Timur Shi Bain Khan, broke his larger bones fine, and scattered to the winds all that was left. Then he went to Timur's yurta and searched for the gray steed with round head. At first he could not find him anywhere. But he looked and looked, and at last he found him in a stable of three iron walls, one wall inside the other.

The steed could hardly stand, was barely living. Húnkuvai gave him the Water of Life from his whip handle and led him out of the iron stable.

Timur Shi had much silver and gold, flocks and cattle. He had thirty-three heroes to serve him, and a great many people. Húnkuvai took away everything, took the thirty-three heroes and all the people. He told them the way to his yurta, and went home himself by magic as quickly as possible, leading the gray steed with round head and riding his own stallion. After he had ridden a part of the way and was on his own land, he came to a great Shaman place, Huhai Hubshi, and stopped a short time to rest there.

When going from home Húnkuvai had left his uncle, Hara Zaton (Black Zaton), to manage in place of himself. While Húnkuvai was returning Shik Shuri gave birth to twins and named them Huragin and Isbegin.

The uncle had hoped that his nephew would never come back and that he himself would manage all and possess it. When he knew that his nephew had conquered and was coming, he decided to meet him on the road at some distance, and he made ready.

He distilled tarasun of ten strengths and mixed strong poison with it. From ten pots of this poisoned tarasun he made one pot, from twenty pots of pure tarasun he made one pot. Next he killed ten sheep and made the flesh of those ten into the bulk of one sheep. After that twenty sheep were cooked and made into the size of one sheep. Then he put all into saddlebags, went to the yurta, and called to his nephew's wife, Shik Shuri:

"Come out! I thought that my nephew had conquered, but it seems that he was beaten, and his own stallion trampled and killed him. War is near us. Three hundred and thirty-three heroes are coming to drive away my nephew's cattle and take all he valued most. Give me the two little boys, I will hide them away in a place of safety."

"They are in the cradle," said Shik Shuri. "They are but three days old; let me keep them till to-morrow. Let them grow up a little. The next day take them whithersoever thou wishest."

As she would not give up the boys willingly and Hara Zaton could not wait, he mounted quickly. "While I am gone," said he," if thou feed the boys badly or hide them in any place, I will kill thee."

Hara Zaton rode away to the Shaman Mountain, and there they met,—the uncle and the nephew.

"I greet thee, and am glad that thou hast gained a great victory," said Zaton; and he stretched out his hand.

Húnkuvai would not take it.

"While thou wert gone two sons were born to thee. They were born only four days ago."

Húnkuvai never stopped, or gave his hand, but rode away toward his yurta.

"Nephew!" cried Zaton, "what is the matter? Why dost thou scorn me?"

Húnkuvai would not stop, would not listen.

"Oh, nephew, of what art thou thinking? Thou hast gained a great victory, but thou art passing a holy mountain without pouring out a libation. This is a sin, and, think, thy sons are only four days old!"

Húnkuvai stopped. He stopped because of his sons. When they dismounted Hara Zaton embraced his nephew and kissed him. He seemed very glad, the deceiver. They poured a libation of good tarasun, sat down, ate, and drank. Zaton drank very little; he just feigned to drink. Soon they had drunk all the pure tarasun and eaten the good meat.

"Well, uncle," said Húnkuvai, "since we have begun let us finish. Hast thou more tarasun?"

The three horses were tied to trees near them. Hara Zaton now brought the poisoned meat and drink. The nephew ate and drank and soon dropped down without life or motion. From his right nostril a green and a blue flame quivered, from his left came a red flame. The uncle sat down at some distance, with a drawn bow, ready to send an arrow should his nephew revive. He sat there day and night and waited. On the third

VILLAGE OF ALAGUERSK-ROD IN SIBERIA. *Page 76*

VILLAGE OF ALAGUERSK-ROD IN SIBERIA.

A GROUP OF UNMARRIED MONGOL WOMEN OR YOUNG LADIES
IN USTURDI. *Page 82*

A GROUP OF UNMARRIED MONGOL WOMEN OR YOUNG LADIES IN USTURDI

day Húnkuvai raised his head somewhat, and saw that Hara Zaton was sitting with bow drawn ready to send an arrow.

"Uncle, it is thy wish to kill me! Well, kill, but spare my children."

Zaton let the arrow go and killed his nephew. When the arrow struck Húnkuvai his stallion and the gray steed with round head tore themselves free and called out to Zaton:

"While we have hoofs thou wilt not possess us, we will fly to him who made us!" And they went to the sky.

The widow of Húnkuvai knew by her magic of all that had happened. "The murderer will come to-night," thought she; "I must save my two sons."

She put one boy under her right armpit, the second under the left one, and hurried on toward that same Shaman mountain. By a turn to the northwest she came to a spot where two immense pine trees stood close together. She made two small pits under those two pine trees and put her little boys into them.

Shik Shuri wished to hurry home and be there before the evil uncle. When she had left her sons behind and had gone some distance, she looked back. The children had crawled out of the pits and were sucking each other's fingers. This sight made the mother cry. She turned back, and gave them her breasts; then she put the boys down in the holes and vanished.

Near the yurta Shik Shuri saw a ewe with two little lambs. She killed the lambs, heated an oven and put them into it, and when both were well burned she placed the bones in a bag, took the bag to a lake, tied a stone to it, and sank it at a place which she marked carefully. Now it was daylight, and she went back to the yurta and waited. Hara Zaton was not long in appearing.

"Come out," called he to Shik Shuri.

She went out to him.

"I saw my nephew's body lying dead," said he. "Give me the little boys. I will put them in a place where no enemy can find them; I will feed and bring them up carefully."

"Thou didst say," replied Shik Shuri, "that warriors were coming to kill us. I thought that we should all have to die; so I burned the boys, put their bones in a bag, and hid them."

"Show me where they are hidden. I must know the place," said the false uncle.

She led him to the place, raised the bag, and showed it to him. He took the bag from her and carried it to the yurta. Whether from fear that the bones might come to life, or thinking that they would strengthen him, for the boys would have been great heroes, he ground the bones into very fine dust, mixed the dust with fat, cooked the mixture, and ate it.

Hara Zaton moved now into his nephew's yurta and took possession of all his wealth and utensils. He put Shik Shuri's left eye out, broke her left arm and left leg, and set her then, as a serving woman, to feed the dogs of his courtyard.

The two boys, Huragin and Isbegin, grew up under the two pine trees very quickly. They made bows for themselves, and then arrows. In two days they killed birds as well as rabbits; they ate them raw. On the third day they killed nothing, though they hunted till midday. After midday they met in a small valley of a great forest Dainjin Sharaman, a Mangathai of seventy-three heads.

"I have traveled the forest all day and found nothing till now," said Dainjin Sharaman; "here I find splendid eating!" And seizing the two boys by the feet, he strode on, holding them like sticks. At his yurta he tied each boy to a pillar, cut two slices of flesh from their thighs and spitted them for his supper. While the pieces were roasting he fell asleep. The two boys, from pain and fear, cried bitterly.

At just this time a man who was as rich as any khan but was childless was passing with eighty packs of merchandise. He heard the boys crying, and stopped all his train. He went into the yurta and roused the sleeping Mangathai. "Why dost thou eat the flesh of these boys?" asked he.

"I hunted all day and found nothing till I met them. Their flesh is good, and I am glad to eat it."

"Well," said Turgubai, the rich merchant, "eat what is on the spit, but sell me the boys. I will give thee eighty horses for them." "Take them!" said the Mangathai.

The merchant took the boys to his home, cured them, and called them his sons.

Huragin and Isbegin lived a whole year with the merchant. They grew large, and became skilful hunters, filled their father's storehouses with game and with fine fur of all sorts.

"Hunt no more, I have no place for game," said the merchant, at last.

"Let us herd cattle then," said the brothers.

Near by was Tomtoy mountain. They drove out the merchant's flocks and herds to pasture on that mountain. While the cattle were eating, the boys exercised, tried their strength; hurled stones, as big as a sheep, so far that a man would need two days to go to the place where the stones fell. Then they threw great rocks, as big as a bullock, and those fell one day's journey distant. Near by was a fallen cliff covering two acres; they carried this cliff home in turn,—one brother carrying it a short distance, then the other. They placed the cliff near the gate, and carved on it the history of their lives since they hunted the first time. They told how they had searched for game, how the Mangathai treated them, how the merchant had bought them. They told all the present as well, and added: "If any man harms our new father we will take dreadful vengeance on that man and then slay him."

They went into the yurta, ate and slept, and afterward went to the high mountain where they had found the fallen cliff. The boys had never been to the top of Tomtoy. As they climbed they heard cattle roar and men cry. The cattle roared much, and the men cried as if suffering terribly, and these sounds seemed to come from a distance. When the boys reached the top of the mountain they saw a long narrow valley. From the beginning to the end of that valley was a row of pots; in each pot were ten bullocks, and at the side of each pot was a huge spit with ten men impaled on it.

The two brothers sat down on the mountain-top and looked. "Who is doing all this?" asked they. Then by magic they learned that those were the people and cattle of Todai Bain Khan. This khan had warred for three years with Shara Nagóy (Yellow Dog), mad master of the Land of Peace, and had been conquered.

Todai Bain Khan had two daughters, Altan Hurubshe and Mūngun Hurubshe. When he had beaten Todai, Yellow Dog demanded those two daughters.

Huragin and Isbegin, the two brothers, now planned on the mountain-top how to conquer Yellow Dog and assist Todai Khan. "How much harm Yellow Dog is doing!" thought they. "He boils one thousand bullocks each day and spits one thousand people."

Now the two brothers took two huge round stones, which were like two great wheels, heated them as red as red cloth, and one said to the other:

"Yellow Dog has such jaws that when he travels the upper one touches the clouds and the lower one grazes the earth. At sunrise he rushes up the valley toward the spot where we are now sitting, and goes toward the sun with open mouth. At that time we will roll these two red-hot stones into his mouth. If we are lucky he will swallow the two, and they will burn out the heart in his body."

The next day, as the sun was rising, Shara Nagóy rushed toward it with open mouth. The two brothers rolled down the hot stones. They bounded into his mouth. He sprang high, howled dreadfully, and fell backward. His head struck the northwest mountain, and his feet stretched to the southeast mountain.

When the mad master of the Land of Peace was dead the two brothers went along the valley, threw the bullocks from the pots, and drew the men from the spits. Some were half roasted, and some half alive. They brought all to sound health, the bullocks from the pots as well as the men from the spits, and then went toward Todai Bain Khan's yurta.

When they were in sight of the yurta the largest and oldest blue mare, the largest and oldest red cow, the most aged and decrepit old woman, came out and addressed the two brothers:

"In vain have ye come to relieve us. Go not against Yellow Dog; he will kill you, and we shall be lost, whatever else happens."

When Todai Bain Khan heard that Yellow Dog was dead he harnessed eight blue horses and hurried forward to meet the two brothers. After the greeting they went with him to his splendid yurta. Nine days they spent there, and Todai Bain Khan made great feasts of all kinds to please them. "You have done such a deed," said he, "that it could not be greater. I will give whatever reward may seem good to you."

"We live far from here, no reward is needed; only give us your two daughters."

"I will do that," said Todai Khan; and he went to prepare the wedding. A sea of drink and a mountain of meat were made ready. Nine days and nights did the wedding last. When the time came, and the brothers were ready to go back to their father's yurta, Todai Khan gave orders to harness eight bay stallions and send with them a low chariot and eight heroes. The mother went half-way home with her daughters. On the road they stopped at the yurta of Dainjin the Mangathai, who had cut flesh from the two brothers and spitted it. The brothers seized him, put chains on his wrists and ankles, chains weighing forty poods. They laid a strong beam across the smoke-hole and hung him face downward over the fire, where he died, and they continued their journey, rejoicing.

At last they reached the yurta where Huragin and Isbegin were born and where their false uncle was master. Near the yurta they met a woman with one eye, one hand, and one foot; she was carrying meat to the dogs of the place, and lamenting.

"What khan's children are ye?" inquired she of the brothers. "Have ye ever known my Huregin and Isbegin? Have ye ever heard of them? Are they still living in any place?"

"We have beard that Dainjin the Mangathai caught them in Hapgata valley, that he spitted their flesh, and then ate it."

"Oh," cried the mother, "I had hoped till this day that they were living, and that hope held me up in my misery." Then she fell back and died there before her two sons.

The brothers went in and seized the false uncle. They carried him and his family northward to the foot of a mountain where three roads met; there they nailed them to seven pines, put an empty cask near each pine, with a dull knife and a pair of blunt scissors fastened to each cask. Above each person was nailed these words: "If a man passes this place he is to cut off with a knife a small piece of flesh from each person hanging here. If a woman passes by she is to cut with the scissors a small piece of flesh from each person. The one who fails to do this will be beheaded."

The two steeds which had gone to the sky rushed in from the west and stopped at the hitching-posts near the yurta. On them was everything necessary for the outfit of horse and rider. The two brothers took the horses and removed the outfits; then they prayed long in thanks, prayed three days and nights to the Heavenly Burkans; after that they mounted the steeds and rode away beyond thirteen lands to the northwest, where stands a high mountain, Sehir Mai, the White mountain. On that mountain were the healing Water of Life and the red restoring larch tree. They went to the top of the mountain and took bark from the tree and water from the spring.

Khan Herdik Shubun (eagle) had gone up three fourths of the way; three years was he flying. He could go no higher and lay there exhausted, barely living, holding on by his wings and his beak to the mountain side.

The brothers took some of the water from the spring and some of the bark from the red restoring larch tree, and sprinkled the eagle with the water mixed with the bark. He revived, circled three times about, then flew to the mountain-top and still higher.

"Thanks to you," said Khan Herdik. "If war or any peril threatens call me, I will fly to you; we should help one another." Then he vanished in the clouds.

The two brothers hurried home. They put some of the bark in Shik Shuri's mouth, poured in the Water of Life, cured her. She grew young; regained hand, foot, and eye. When she came to her senses she knew her two sons, embraced and kissed them, led them into the yurta. There were five of them now.

"Was there a father of ours?" asked the brothers.

"There was, but he was beaten in battle and killed when ye were infants."

"Thou art hiding something from us, thou art afraid to tell us. We will dig out and discover the ashes and bones of our father, wherever they may be."

Shik Shuri took their father's book out of a box, brought it to her sons, and they read all that was in the book. They read how their father went to find the gray steed with round head, how their uncle had killed him. All was described there. They saddled their two stallions and rode away. Shik Shuri had no power to stop them. They went to Huhai Hubshi Barsam, the Shaman mountain, and there found their father's bones, over which moss had grown.

Huragin and Isbegin gathered the bones; all were there save the great toe of the right foot. They searched everywhere, and at last found the trail of Ungin (fox); she had stolen the toe. They followed the trail, followed till they discovered that Ungin had been eaten by Shono (wolf). Going farther, they saw that Shono had been devoured by Hara Grojung (black bear); yet farther on they found that Hara Grojung had been eaten by Bara (tiger), and then that Bara had been eaten by Irbit (lion). They hunted till they came upon Irbit. They killed him and found in his stomach the great toe of their father; then they returned and fixed the toe to the foot properly.

They sprinkled the skeleton with the healing Water of Life, mixed with powdered bark from the red restoring larch tree. The first time they sprinkled flesh came on the bones, the second time Húnkuvai was like a man sleeping, the third time he was living and well.

Then Huragin and Isbegin went home with their father, and all feasted for many days.

VARHAN TULAI HUBUN

ONCE there were two brothers,—the elder Albat Mergin Hubun, the younger Varhan Tulai Hubun. The elder had a wife named Deri Sisin (Steel File), the younger was not married.

"Let us try and see which of us is the stronger," said Varhan to his brother one day.

They went to the shore of the Yellow Sea, and there found a stone as big as a great stallion. The elder brother raised this stone to his girdle and sank in the ground to his waist. Varhan, the younger brother, raised the stone, swayed it thrice, and hurled it into the Yellow Sea. Then they went home and began to shoot with arrows. Albat Mergin took an arrow with forty edges and said to it:

"Beyond the thirteenth mountain is an elk and his mate. If I am to live, kill them; if not, let them live."

The arrow did not strike the elk, but chanced on a hundred and eight headed and thirteen horned Mangathai, went in at the side of his sixth rib, and killed him.

Varhan, the younger brother, sent his arrow beyond the twenty-third mountain and killed two elks there.

"Thou hast conquered," said Albat Mergin, "thou mayst not live on as hitherto."

Varhan cut his forehead, opened it, and took out a book. In the book he read that the most beautiful woman in the world was Shandagan Sagai, daughter of Esege Malan, and that she was to be his bride.

Beyond a certain mountain, where she pastured with thirteen asses, was a milk-white mare, with her colt going after her. The colt was ninety fathoms long and dark gray in color. Varhan Tulai led home this colt, fed him for thirty days, saddled him, and started to ride to the sky and find there the yurta in which lived Shandagan Sagai, the beauty of all the world above and below.

He rode long and fast till his horse was wearied; then he turned him into flint, put the flint in his pocket, made himself a wolf, and raced on and on. Traveled as a wolf till he was tired; then he took his own form again, and rode on the dark gray colt till at last he reached an opening, the door through the highest point in the sky. This door is called Sinbur Ulai Tolgai.

Varhan Tulai went through and saw on the other side the end of a great yurta; then he went farther and saw the whole yurta. It was splendid and so immense that it reached up till it touched a second sky. When he came to this beautiful yurta he went in, and there in the seventy-fifth chamber found Shandagan Sagai.

"Whence hast thou come?" asked she, "and whither art thou going?"

"I am the son of Galtun Umri. I am going to find a bride, I am looking for Agin Nogón." Shandagan Sagai made tea then from a silver kettle, and they drank together.

"I have traveled far," said Varhan Tulai, "I am tired; something troubles; something irritates my head. Look in it." He put his head on her knees. Her fingers, searching through his hair, gave him wonderful pleasure, and he fell asleep. All at once she screamed. Varhan sprang up and rushed out. There were seventy-four doors besides the outer door, seventy-five in all. He shut these, and there were ninety-five chambers before him. He closed every chamber tightly; then made the house very small, as small as a little box, put it on his horse, and with Shandagan Sagai inside raced away swiftly.

Esege Malan had three Shalmos (invisible spirits) in his service, three attendant spirits, who went around through every place, watching all the time and looking in all directions very quickly. These Shalmos saw that the house was gone, the daughter gone, all things gone. They hurried to Esege Malan and told him.

Esege Malan opened his doors and saw Varhan Tulai stealing his daughter away,— saw him far off, hurrying, racing with all speed. He called the three Shalmos and sent them to bring to him a perfect fool. They brought the fool quickly, and Esege Malan said to him: "I brought thee, thou fool, for this purpose. A man came and stole my yurta, with my daughter and all her property. Do thou hurry, hasten, overtake him, catch him, kill him, and bring back my daughter."

"Give me means and help," replied the perfect fool.

Esege Malan sent three hundred champions with clubs, three hundred more with hammers, and three hundred with sharp swords, to help the fool. They went swiftly and were gaining on Varhan Tulai. He was on earth now, hurrying always. His horse was untiring, but the fool and the champions were gaining, coming nearer each moment; so Varhan rose in the air with his horse and rushed to a high country at one side.

The fool and his men lost the trail, but the fool knew what to do. He rose in the air also. "I will fly too, but stay ye here," said he to his nine hundred helpers. They passed the night at the place where he left them. During the night they burned up all the trees in the forest around, and their horses ate up all the grass, and since that day nothing has grown there.

The fool saw Varhan at a great distance. When he had almost caught up with him Varhan turned himself into an old man and sat down near a spring of pure water. He had made a hut there, and a woman was sitting inside; the woman was Shandagan Sagai.

Varhan, with a girdle of the inner bark of a larch tree around his middle, seemed very poor. This trick did not mislead the fool, however.

"What manner of man art thou, who has stolen the daughter of another and with her his house and goods?" asked he. "What right hadst thou to do this?"

They sprang at each other, closed, and began to fight, and they fought for nine days with little rest for breathing. At last the fool threw Varhan Tulai over three mountain ranges, then rushed after him, and when he came up, he asked:

"With such small power how couldst thou think to be a hero?"

Varhan had sunk to his waist and was hardly living, but when he heard these jeering words he grew terribly angry; he rose out of the earth, and as he rose he overturned one hundred and fifty acres in a circle around him.

"Though thou art a perfect fool, thou hast thrown me across three mountain ranges," cried Varhan; "now I will throw thee so far that thou wilt never be seen again!" That moment he seized the fool and threw him over seven mountain ranges. He sank eighty fathoms through the earth and stayed there.

Varhan Tulai returned to his hut by the spring, took Shandagan Sagai with all her property, and went home. He found nothing there; his yurta was gone, his cattle gone, all was gone. There was nothing where the yurta had been save one black raven and one yellow fox. Near by was a hitching-post with these words on it: "Under this post are ten pots of tarasun and the flesh of ten sheep. Eat the meat and drink the tarasun. We have been taken from our home, and are captives of a hundred and eight headed Mangathai. Find us, and save us."

Varhan ate and drank and then went to rescue his people. He traveled till he came to a bottomless swamp and a dense forest. He passed both. Beyond the dense forest he saw his brother's stallion, with one eye out and a broken leg. He made his own horse poor, a little, gray, wretched creature, and himself a miserable, starving old man with hair sticking out a whole foot through his cap and finger-nails growing out through his gloves.

He went farther and saw seven hundred of his brother's bullocks, six hundred sheep, five hundred goats, and only one he-goat. Farther still he saw two dogs; two wolves ran up to fight with the dogs. Varhan killed both wolves and went farther. Next he met four young men on four red horses. Each man had an iron whip.

"Whither are ye going?" asked Varhan.

"We are herdsmen," said they; "we run after cattle."

Varhan waved his whip thrice; the horses were fettered and the men were tied to their saddles. Farther on he saw the hundred and eight headed Mangathai walking along.

"Whither art thou going, old man?" asked the Mangathai.

"I am one of Tudai Khan's herdsmen looking for his cattle. I have come to see if they are with yours. I am dry; hast thou nothing to drink here?"

"Thou knowest much," said the Mangathai, "knowest thou where Varhan Tulai Hubun is? If thou knowest tell me."

"Of course I know. He was killed long ago by the perfect fool. What a great man Varhan Tulai was, a bony fellow! It would take three days to walk over his bones."

"This moment I will spit something," said the Mangathai. He spat out a big stone. "I will give you this stone to keep. Go home and put it away carefully," said he. "While you have the stone no one will offend, no one will harm you. I must go after my cattle."

Varhan Tulai broke the stone against a tree, and a box covered with tin fell out. He opened the box, sixteen little birds were in it; thirteen he killed and three he put in his pocket. Then he went to find the Mangathai's yurta while the Mangathai was off hunting for his cattle.

The Mangathai's wife was at home, an angry woman with an ugly face. On one of her knees Varhan's brother was sitting; on the other was Deri Sisin, Albat's wife. Whenever the Mangathai woman went out they had to go with her.

"Why did you make my brother and his wife your servants?" asked Varhan, as he pushed the woman over and caught hold of his brother and Deri Sisin.

"My husband will come quickly and pay you for this!" screamed the Mangathai's wife.

"He will not come to me, for I am going to him," said Varhan. Then with a horsehair rope he bound her securely, and leaving his brother and sister-in-law, went to find the Mangathai. While he was going he squeezed to death the three birds that he had in his pocket. When he reached the Mangathai he found him dead.

Varhan brought dry trees and burned the body. Then he made a wooden mill and ground up the larger bones of his enemy, turned all into ashes and scattered the ashes everywhere.

"Which will you have, seventy tree tops or seventy good horse tails?" asked he of the Mangathai's wife.

"I could make firewood of the tree tops," said she; "I could make ropes of the horse tails."

He took seventy tree tops, made a stake of them, put her on the stake, impaled and killed her; then he brought her to life again. Next he took seventy horses, tied her to their tails, and tore her into seventy pieces. After that he put the seventy pieces together and made her alive a second time; then he impaled her on a stake again and left her there. He searched the house carefully. In one chamber he found an iron cradle; in the cradle an infant, the son of the Mangathai. Varhan seized the boy and threw him against a corner of the chamber to kill him.

"Oh, no!" cried the child, "you cannot kill me to-day." Varhan threw him to the second corner.

"No," cried the boy, "you cannot kill me to-day." He threw him into the third corner.

"Oh, no!" said the child, "you cannot kill me to-day."

"What shall I do to kill this creature?" thought Varhan. "Dig me a hole twenty fathoms deep," said he to his men, and put all the wood into it that you can find about here."

It was done, and down deep in the hole a great fire was built; then they threw the young Mangathai into it.

"Oh, how pleasant and comfortable it is here, so warm and nice!" cried the boy; and he began playing with the hot coals.

As nothing could be done to kill the child, Varhan went to take counsel of the thousand Burkans. They gave him four chains. "Fasten these chains," said they, "to his hands and feet and take him to a place in the forest where there are four trees; chain him to those trees. Near the trees build a house. Inside the wooden house make an iron one, inside the iron house a lead one. Pack all the space between the wooden, the iron, and the lead houses with ice; when you have done that stay inside the lead house for nine days. During these nine days we will make a dreadful heat, and the boy will burst."

Varhan built the houses; then he and his brother and his brother's wife took refuge in the lead house, while the Burkans made such a terrible heat in all the country around the Mangathai's house where the boy was that he became dreadfully swollen and at last burst.

When the nine days were over Varhan and his brother came out of the lead house, burned the body of the Mangathai child, scattered the ashes, took all of the cattle and wealth of the Mangathai, and went home. When Varhan reached his yurta his wife was gone; she had fled back to Esege Malan, her father.

Varhan started on a second journey to the sky. While he was on the way up Shandagan's father saw him, and going to Hohodai Mergen (thunder), he said, "Strike that Varhan with a thunderbolt and kill him." Hohodai did as Esege Malan commanded, and Varhan fell to the earth; the sun and the moon fell with him, and it became dark in every place.

The thousand Burkans held a council and said to Esege Malan "You must send messengers to bring back the sun and the moon. We cannot live in this way."

Esege Malan sent three hundred heroes with three hundred horses and three hundred crowbars to raise the sun and the moon, but the heroes could not raise them and went back.

Esege Malan now called the seven heavenly smiths from the sky and sent them down with their forges; he sent also the three hundred heroes, and this time each hero carried a hammer ninety ponds in weight. The smiths were to heat up and the heroes to hammer. They worked a whole month, but accomplished nothing; everything they did was useless.

All this time there was darkness everywhere. At last the thousand Burkans held a second council. There was one very great sage, Zarya Azergesha (hedgehog). They sent this wise old Burkan to Esege Malan, and he said:

"Bring to life Varhan, whom thou hast killed, and delay not; give Shandagan Sagai to him. Are the sky and the earth to be in darkness because of thy daughter?"

Esege Malan said, "I will give him my daughter immediately." And that moment he summoned Herdik Shubun (the eagle), and said:

"Take my daughter to the place where Hohodai Mergen struck her husband with a thunderbolt. Take with you. a bottle of the Water of Youth and Life. Pour the water on Varhan's body and bring him to life again."

Khan Herdik did all that Esege Malan commanded. Varhan Tulai Hubun sprang up alive and well, and that instant the sun and the moon rose to their places in the sky.

Varhan went home with his wife, collected all the people, killed sheep and cattle, and made a grand wedding-feast.

"I have been traveling for a long time," said Varhan to his wife; "I am tired and want to sleep. I want to sleep four days and four nights. Do not rouse me, unless evil people come and there is great need; then strike me on the left thigh with your fist."

He lay down and was soon sleeping soundly. After two days a woman rushed up to the door. "I am afraid of your dogs!" screamed she. "Let me in! let me in! I am your neighbor!"

She was a Mangathai woman who had come to steal away Varhan; but Shandagan Sagai, thinking that she was a neighbor, let her in, brought a silver kettle, made tea, and gave her honey, then went out for a moment to get tarasun, leaving the woman with Varhan, who all this time was sleeping behind seven curtains.

When Shandagan came back the strange woman was gone. Varhan was gone also. Albat Mergin, his brother, went in search of him. He followed the woman's trail till he came upon a sixty-three headed Mangathai.

For seven years Albat Mergin fought with this Mangathai, and during those years Vardan's wife had two sons; the elder was called Altin Shagoy, and the younger Murgun Shagoy.

The boys grew very fast. When they were nine days old a ten-year-old ram's skin was not large enough to make a coat for either one of them. Soon they became wonderful marksmen and great hunters. There was a company in the country near by, youths who arranged to shoot at a mark three versts off; no one could hit at that distance except the two brothers. "We hit! we hit!" cried the others. "Why say that when ye know that it is we who hit?" asked the brothers.

The youths were confused and angry. One of them spoke up and said:

"If ye are such men to shoot why not rescue your father from the Mangathai?"

The brothers had never thought about having a father, but now they went home and asked their mother if a Mangathai woman had carried off Varhan Tulai Hubun, and was. he their father?

"Vorhan Tulai was your father," answered Shandagan Sagai, "but he died before you were born."

They did not believe this, and when they could not find out where their father was they went to the field and made a plan there.

"Go into the house," said the elder brother; "the kettle is boiling. I will cry from outside that the calves have sucked the cows dry; our mother will hurry out. Then you cry from the house that the water is boiling over. We will run in, take the cover off the kettle, seize her and hold her hands down in the water till she tells where our father is."

The younger brother went into the house and was talking with his mother, when suddenly the elder brother, who had remained in the field, cried: "Mother, come quickly! The calves are sucking the cows dry, we shall have no milk!"

The mother hurried out, but had not reached the field when the younger brother cried from within the house: "Oh, mother, come quickly! The water is boiling over and putting out the fire!"

Shandagan Sagai rushed back, and the elder boy followed as though to help her. When she was inside the house the two brothers seized her hands and held them in the hot water. "Tell us where our father is," said they.

"Thy father's ashes are where his sons' ashes should be," replied she angrily. They put her hands into the water a second time, and she told them everything, for the water was very hot.

Then the two brothers took their weapons and started away on foot. They went to the boundary of their father's land, took twelve tapers in their hands, and implored the Burkans for horses. They prayed one day and night, holding the twelve tapers. The second night they put twenty tapers on the ground and prayed for three days and three nights. On the fourth day, in the morning, they saw four bay horses near them, and on the saddle of each horse was a hero's outfit. They mounted two of the horses and rode away, leading the other two. After riding for a long time they met their uncle, who was on his way home.

"I have killed the sixty-three headed Mangathai," said Albat Mergin, "but have seen nothing of my brother, Varhan Tulai Hubun."

"Varhan Tulai is our father," said the two brothers, "and thou art our uncle." The uncle turned back then and went with his nephews, and they rode straight to the house of the Mangathai. They saw no one there, but found tracks going into a forest. They followed the tracks, went on and on, till at last the boys found their father. On his head was a wheel ninety poods in weight, and eight iron spikes were sticking into his body, four in his right side and four in his left side.

Albat and his brother seized seven young Mangathais and bound them, bound their mother also. Then they took the wheel from Varhan's head and drew the spikes out.

Near by was a great, broad, level-topped mountain where four roads crossed. At the crossing were eight immense larch trees. To this place they brought the young Mangathais and their mother and tied each, with a strong hair rope, to a larch tree. Then they nailed their heads, feet, and hands to the tree trunk and took the ropes away.

A barrel was placed before each Mangathai, and by each barrel hung a blunt knife and a pair of dull scissors. On each tree were these words: "Whoso passes, man or woman, must cut a bit of flesh from the body of each of the eight hanging here. Let every woman cut with the scissors and every man cut with the knife. Whoso fails to cut will be nailed to a tree as these eight are nailed."

They left the Mangathai woman and her seven sons at the cross-roads, turned the Mangathai's house bottom upward, took all that she had, went home with it, and lived there afterward, rejoicing.

ALTIN SHAGOY

TO a forest at the foot of a mountain came a man seventy years of age and a woman who was sixty. They cleared a small space there, and the man cut down trees to build a yurta. When the yurta was finished they lived in it, and soon the old woman gave birth to a son who was silver below the waist and gold above it.

In two days after his birth the skin of a two-year-old sheep was too small for the boy. In three days the skin of a three-year-old sheep was too narrow for him.

The two old people had a very scant living. They had only one cow, and the cow had not milk enough for that boy three days old. The father and mother began to scold their young son.

"What a glutton thou art!" said they.

In five days the boy said to them, "I am your only child, and ye are not able to nourish me; what would you do if there were two or three other sons?"

"Such as thou art there can never be. To pour milk on the ground or give it to thee is all one. Thou hast never enough, no matter how much we may give thee."

"Ye are mistaken," said the boy; "a bigger glutton than I am may be given to you. Ye grudge me milk from a cup, but if one were born who would eat your cow up what would ye say then?"

He drew from his mother's breast also.

"When I drink a little from the breast I am satisfied," added the boy.

"Though young, he understands," said the parents in alarm. "Let us throw him out! Let us be rid of him!"

"Throw me out if ye wish," said the boy, "but if ye do that, take me far away to a mountain; do not throw me out near by. There, far away, I will ask food of the Heavenly Burkans."

The father and mother thought their son was making sport of them beyond forgiveness and that they must get rid of him.

"Oh, an evil, a very evil child was born to us!" said the father and mother.

A lofty mountain stood opposite. The father took his son to that mountain and left him on the summit. The child cried for one half of twenty-four hours, then turned to the thousand Heavenly Burkans, and asked:

"Why make parents who will not nourish me? Since ye have made them who have thrown me away, give me food and clothing, give me a horse and an outfit." He cried till he fell asleep. When he woke the next morning he was in a room in a strange yurta. Many people were there, and herds of horses, and many cattle were pasturing on the meadow near by. The boy went out, looked around, came back, and passed a second night.

When the father took his son to the mountain the child could not walk. The next morning the parents, looking at the mountain and wondering what had become of the boy, noticed the beautiful yurta and marveled that it had appeared there in one night.

"Some enemy of ours has come, surely to kill us in the end," said they. "Let us go up to the mountain. Let us give an offering to the Burkans. Our son must be dead by this time."

They did not go to the mountain; they made no offering to the Burkans.

The boy stayed nine days and nights in his yurta; he walked through all the rooms in it. On the night after the eighth day he found a book. This book, which was as big as a common door, had fallen in through the smoke-hole. The boy read the book, and understood all. It was written that he would be a great khan. It was also written what land would be under his power, and his name, Altin Shagoy, was given there. He read three and a half nights and as many days as nights. In the book it was stated that all his people and all his herds were in good condition.

Soon Altin was as if ten years of age, and he said, "Now I must count all my people, my cattle, and my herds of horses."

His mother now gave birth to a second child, a real glutton, a terrible eater. People brought word to Altin that his father and mother had a daughter, that they had killed their one cow to feed her, and were suffering from want,—that his mother was dying of hunger.

Altin commanded to drive ten bullocks to his father's yurta, and he went himself with the men who drove them. He helped to prepare meat for his mother, then took her and his father and sister to his own yurta.

"Ye thought me a glutton when ye threw me out," said he, "but now ye have a real glutton."

The young sister was terrible; she cried, cried night and day, and when not crying she was drinking milk. Altin read in his book, and found that the child must be named and have a cradle. He called together the people, gave a great feast, and had his sister named with proper ceremony. She was quiet after that, she cried no more; her father and mother had peace and rest.

"I must count my cattle," said Altin, when he was the size of a boy thirteen years of age. His steed, given by the Burkans, was on the mountain Tiphen Ulan Hada. He went to that great mountain on foot, reached the base of it, climbed and climbed. At last he stopped, for he could go no farther. He turned into a falcon then and flew up,— flew for three days, flew till he came to the summit.

On that mountain stood a golden-trunked, silver-leafed aspen tree. At the foot of that tree the Water of Life gushed forth. The horse was not there. Altin drank water, turned into a reed and waited. At midday the horse came to drink. On the horse was the whole outfit of a hero.

It never rains on that mountain and never snows there. When the horse come toward the spring he stopped on a sudden, before touching the water. "What is this?" asked he. "There is an odor of flesh here. It smells of man. No man should be in this place."

The horse did not know that his master was born yet. "No man but my future master has the right to be here," said he, looking around everywhere. Seeing no one, he began to drink. From the reed Altin became himself and seized the bridle. The horse was so frightened that he ran and dragged Altin, dragged him a day and a night, around that great mountain.

"If thou wish to kill me," said Altin, "kill me quickly. If thou wish to save, stop at once. If not I shall be dizzy and die very quickly."

The horse stopped, and Altin mounted. Unused to being ridden, the beast rushed away, ran one day and one night around that flat-topped red mountain. At last, after twenty-four hours, running, the horse said, "Now I am ready for the saddle."

"What magic hast thou?" asked Altin.

"I have this magic. If one puts a cup of milk on the fire I can run three times around the world before it boils. What strength hast thou?"

"I am so strong that none can conquer me. How are we to go down this mountain?"

"Shut your eyes," said the horse. "Hold fast, very fast to the saddle, bind both your ears with a kerchief. If you do not your head will be dizzy. I will go back one mile, run with all my speed, spring into the air, and alight on the earth safely."

When they were ready the horse went back, then rushed toward the edge of the mountain. Altin held fast, heard nothing, felt nothing, and found himself at home on his own mountain, right in front of his yurta. He tied the horse to the hitching-post; then he saw his sister. She was walking already. "Whence hast thou come, brother?" asked she, and she went toward the horse.

"Come not near this horse," said Altin; "he might kill thee."

"Why should the horse kill me? I ought to be friendly with my brother's steed."

She walked around, looked at the horse carefully, then went to her father and mother. "Oh, my brother has a fine steed," said she. "He is fat and big and must be very strong."

The father went out, and when he saw the horse he was so terrified by his size that he fell to the ground without sense. When he recovered he was so weak that he could not rise; he crawled into the yurta on his hands and knees.

Altin drank, sat on his horse, and rode to count his herds and his cattle. He drove all the animals into an immense meadow, counted them for three days and nights, but could not finish. On the fourth day he discovered that three years before the best mare in his herd had had a colt; that colt was gone. They searched for bones to see if a wolf had eaten the colt, but could find none.

At last on the north side of the meadow they found a trail. A thief had stolen the colt. Three brothers lived off in that direction, and Altin thought that they had taken it; so he rode to their yurta and tied his horse to their hitching-post. The post would not stand, came out of the ground. Altin took an arrow, thrust it into the earth, and tied his steed to it. Then he went into the yurta and upbraided the three brothers, stamped with his feet till their yurta was quivering.

"Did ye think that that colt was without an owner?" shouted he. "How did ye dare to take what was mine?"

He went out of the yurta then and saw his colt in a pen with two other young horses. The colt was tremendous to look at, immense, like Altin's own saddle horse. The three brothers spoke up now very boldly.

"Shout not so loud!" said they. "If you wish war we are ready. There is a place not far from here called Taimi Sagán Her (Open White Steppe). On that steppe are five very large pine trees; there we can see who is the strongest."

Altin mounted immediately and rode to that place. He made a fire, let out his horse, and lying down to rest, fell asleep. That minute he turned into stone. The three brothers followed Altin and said to one another as they traveled, "If he is sleeping we will finish him quickly."

They found him lying on the ground asleep, and they shot at him with three arrows. Altin made no move. He woke, took his own form, and thought that fleas from the dust had been biting him. Seeing the brothers, and finding the arrows by his side, he inquired:

"What kind of persons are ye, who try to kill a man while he is sleeping? Ye will never be able to do that to me, for when I am asleep I am stone. How have ye planned to attack me,—all three at once, or one after another? Will ye meet me with arrows or with wrestling?"

"I will go against thee alone," said the elder brother. "We will wrestle and we shall see who is stronger, thou or I."

Gods which Guard the House from the Outside
Olkhon Island. *Page 85*

BURIAT GODS, OR REPRESENTATIONS OF THEIR GODS
OUTSIDE ONGONS. *Page* 85

BURIAT GODS, OR REPRESENTATIONS OF THEIR GODS OUTSIDE ONGONS.

That moment Altin seized the boaster by the back of the neck, whirled him three times around his own head, struck a pine tree with his body, and killed him. The second brother came now. Altin treated him in the same way; killed him as he had his brother. Next came the youngest. He was very strong, almost the equal of Altin. The two struggled three days and three nights. Each bit away all the flesh from the front of the other's body and tore off all the flesh from his back. They made ditches in the ground with their feet as they wrestled. Crows and magpies flew in from the north and the south, carried the flesh away, and ate it.

On the fourth day Altin threw the third brother, who before death spoke these words: "In vain have I fought with thee, but I fought for the sake of my brothers." Then he died.

Altin pulled up three pines by the roots and burned the three brothers. He went then to their yurta, turned it bottom upward, and took all their people, property, and cattle, and went with his own three horses to his yurta on the mountain.

"I have counted my horses and colts," said he to his father.

"All is finished; I will go now and seek a bride for myself."

"Thou shalt do that," said his father and mother. "We are old; it is time for thee to marry."

For three days Altin read in his book. "Gal Núrman Khan, thy bride's father, lives in the far South," said the book. "His daughter's name is Gagurái Nugún; she is thy bride."

Gal Núrman let no one come near him, and never slept day or night except a moment just before daybreak; how was Altin to go to such a man, how was he to leave his sister, how was he to leave his father and mother, who were old now and helpless? He collected the people to ask advice of all who were above ten and less than fifty years of age. He put out food and drink and told what he wanted. "I am going," said he, "to find a bride. What man will manage while I am gone?"

One old sage, eighty years of age, who chanced to be there, said: "Though I am old, I have wisdom. This is my advice: take a lettered man from the people; let him manage in thy place."

"Where can I find such a person, a good man?" asked Altin.

No one spoke, till at last the old man said: "I have a son of twenty years who knows seven languages. He may manage the country for thee."

Altin sent three horsemen to bring him. "The khan asks you to come," said the messengers. The young man was in one shirt; "I am khan for myself," said he. "I owe your khan nothing; I taught myself with my own father's means, I took nothing from any man, I am not in debt to any one. But since the khan calls I will go." He put on a black shuba, black trousers, a cap, and fishskin shoes; then he went to Altin, who came out to meet him, took him by the hand, and led him into the yurta. "What wilt thou eat?" asked Altin. He had drink placed before the young man, and next the book which he himself had read.

"If thou finish this book in three days," said Altin, "I shall believe that if thou art here in my place it will be as well as if I were here myself. If thou canst not finish, it will be worse."

The young man began to read. He finished in season.

"Thou art wise," said Altin. "Thou art here now in my place, and I will leave thee. When I come back thou wilt go to find a bride for thyself."

"I cannot stay here," said the young man. "My mother is seventy years old and my father is eighty. Who will nourish them? I have no brothers."

"Bring thy father and mother to this place," said Altin; "be my brother."

"My father's yurta and my own affairs are dearer to me than all other things," said the young man. "I had never a thought to leave them."

"I am going away for nine years," said Altin. "Leave thy parents at home and visit them from time to time. Send them food and clothing. Take from my things whatever may be lacking in thy yurta."

The young man consented, not wishing to offend Altin Khan.

"I am satisfied," said Altin. "But when I am away I need to know that thou art well. Canst thou give me a sign?"

The young man gave his own silver ring. "If I am well and in health," said he, "the ring will glitter. If I die it will fall into two parts. Give me a sign also."

"I will show thee thy dwelling-place first," answered Altin, "and then give thee a sign." After he had showed him a yurta aside, he gave him an arrow and said: "Keep this arrow carefully. If I die it will rot. If I live it will be as it now is."

Altin was ready to mount when on a sudden he thought of something he had forgotten, and called out, "I have not summoned the people to wish me good fortune." He summoned them, then placed out meat and drink in plenty. They gave good wishes, and he went toward the South, unattended.

"I can go mightily if you wish," said Altin's steed. And he rushed forward like a strong wind. Soon he was at the boundary. The sun was high when Altin left home, but he was on the boundary at midday. Taking tobacco, he smoked. "We can work well together," said he to his steed.

About evening they came to three roads, and a yellow fox crossed before them. "How dost thou dare to cross my road?" called out Altin, as he let fly an arrow, which cut the fox in two. The hind part sank in the earth and cried to Altin:

"I shall tell the Heavenly Tengeris what thou hast done to me." And the head and fore part flew to the sky.

Altin rushed forward rapidly, but if he did a heavenly hero came down from the sky and stood before him. This hero's name was Tiyil Büge Tengeri. He rushed straight at Altin, struck him across the breast, cut him in two, and seizing the upper part flew to the sky with it; the lower part he left where it fell.

"I did this," said he, while flying, "because thou hast killed my one daughter. I sent her to earth on no evil errand; she went to find and dig lily roots."

When his master was gone Altin's horse stood still and dropped tears. "Cry, or not cry," said he at last, "I must do something." And he changed himself to a falcon. "I will go now," thought he, "and ask the one who made me why my master has been killed. That wretched fox cuts the road to people; what right has she to cause a man's death? I will make her take up to heaven what is left of my master."

The falcon flew to the sky, straight to Zayasha Zayan Tengeri, who had made him, and told what had happened. "There will be a council," said Zayasha, and he sent at once for the thousand Heavenly Burkans.

"Who dared to kill the man whom I made?" asked he, when all the thousand Burkans were assembled the next morning at daybreak. They told him, and then summoned Tiyil Bilge and sentenced him to bring the lower half of Altin's body to the sky. "Thou hast not done right," said they; "thy daughter was to blame altogether. She has led an evil life on earth and has no right to cut across people's roads."

Tiyil Bilge went down to the earth and got the lower part of Altin's body three days after he was killed. It was still there near the cross-roads.

Altin's sister came to the sky now; she complained bitterly, and asked the Burkans who had dared to kill her brother.

Tiyil Bilge took the two parts to the heavenly smiths. Seven days and nights they worked over Altin. Hardly could they bring him to his right form again. They could not put the breath back; the thousand Burkans had to do that, and start life anew in him. Then Altin commanded his sister to go home without delay. She turned into a raven and flew to the earth.

"Must I fight with any one on the way?" asked Altin, as he left the Burkans.

"No, thou wilt go forward with good fortune," said they. "Thou wilt go to thy father-in-law. Opposite his yurta, on a very high mountain, is a golden aspen. There is Water of Life at the foot of that tree, and on the top of the tree sits a white cuckoo as big as a horse's head. This bird knows all that is done in the sky, everything thought out there by the Burkans. She can bring the dead to life and give riches to poor people; she has immense wisdom, this cuckoo. Drink of that Water of Life, give some to thy horse, and ride forward next morning. From here to that mountain are golden stairs." Altin reached the mountain and never stopped till he stood by the golden-trunked aspen tree. He dismounted, then drank of the water, gave some to his horse, made a fire, and ate silver leaves from the aspen. Whoso ate of those leaves was not hungry or cold thereafter.

Altin looked straight south and saw the immense yurta of his father-in-law. It was a whole mile in length, enormous in size, and so high that its roof touched the sky. He slept well that night, and rising very early, went down the mountain to the great yurta. He rode up, tied his horse to the hitching-post, and hurried in. Gal Núrman had just risen. Altin walked up to him and said:

"A greeting from me to thee, father-in-law."

"What sort of a fellow art thou, who hast come to me without invitation?" asked Gal Núrman. "How hast thou dared to appear here? No one may come to me, either on foot or on horseback!"

"Thy daughter is to be my wife. This has been settled by the Heavenly Burkans and depends on them."

"If that is true," said Gal, "thou canst see her. She is beyond seventy-seven doors; go to her."

The doors were of iron, strong and heavy. With a kick Altin opened each door. When he reached the seventy-seventh chamber a maiden was sitting there. She was very beautiful, she shone as the sun shines in the day and the moon shines during night hours.

"How didst thou open the doors?" asked she. "No one has ever before had strength to open them. My father has never let any one pass. How didst thou pass?"

"I am Altin Shagoy; thou art my bride; that was fixed by the Heavenly Burkans, and recorded in my book of life. I have seen thy father, and he sent me to hear what thy wish is."

"I do not credit thy book," said the maiden. "I know not if thou art telling me truth or art lying. Perhaps thou hast come for my beauty, with the desire to deceive me. As to my father I do not trust him in anything. Art thou really to be my husband? But I will read in my book and discover."

She had in her bosom a small book, the size of a man's palm. She took it out and read: "Thou art to marry Altin Shagoy." When she read that she commanded to bring food and drink and began to entertain Altin.

In the morning Gal Núrman cried outside Altin's door. "Thou art sleeping long!" Altin went out to his father-in-law. "Why sleep so long?" asked the khan.

"I came from afar and was weary; why should I not sleep?"

Gal Núrman entertained Altin, and then sent him back to his bride in the seventy-seventh chamber. At sunrise on the second day Altin rose and went out immediately.

"Why sleep so long?" inquired the father-in-law. "Didst thou not rest? Couldst thou not rise earlier?"

"When I am tired I am more tired the second than the first day."

"Come and drink and eat with me," said the khan. "I am going to give thee my daughter, but I have a yellow dog on a distant mountain. If thou bring that dog, thou canst take her to thy yurta; if not, thou'lt not get her."

Altin went to his bride, consulted with her, asked her how he was to get the yellow dog.

"No one can get that dog," said she. "Better go back to thy yurta. Many and many a bridegroom has come here and lost his life in trying to bring that yellow dog to my father."

"I think that thou wilt aid me in getting the dog."

"How can I aid thee? I can do so only in one way. Through my magic thou wilt be able to live without sleeping."

"I shall go in every case," said Altin, "and shall bring back the dog."

He went then to Gal Núrman, and said, "I am going for thy dog." And he rode away northward very swiftly, never stopping till he came to the Black Sea. There, near the coast, was a single great pine tree. On the tree were three beautiful maidens; the first one was crying, the second was laughing, the third was singing.

"How is this?" asked Altin. "Why are your minds so different?"

"We are the daughters of Khan Herdik Shubun (eagle). Our father warred three years with Mogoi Khan. At the end of that time Mogoi broke our father's wings. We sent him to be cured at a place on a distant mountain. Now Mogoi Khan wants to eat us while our father is gone. He will come to-day and eat my sister who is crying, to-morrow he will eat my sister who is singing, and the third day he will eat me."

"Where does Mogoi Khan live?"

"In Hara Dalai (the Black Sea), directly opposite. When he comes out the whole sea roars and rages. He has two heads, and one great eye in his chief head. That eye is as big as the moon. If thou canst send an arrow into it thou wilt kill him immediately. But to send such an arrow is terribly difficult. If it brings back even one drop of blood thou wilt die, without rescue."

"Leave this place, save yourselves!" said Altin. "Do not wait for him." They would not move; they stayed there. Altin left his horse in the field near the pine tree, and went on foot toward the sea, taking with him his bow and arrow. Near the place where Mogoi was to come out of the sea Altin became a reed. Soon the sea began to roar and rage, and he saw Mogoi Khan coming. Altin drew his bow, and aimed at Mogoi's one eye.

"Bring not back a drop of blood, wipe thyself clean," said Altin to the arrow.

The arrow went straight into the eye, and tore Mogoi Khan's head into many small pieces. The arrow did not return. It could not, it was bloody.

Altin took his own form, and ran back to the three sisters, ran swiftly. But Mogoi Khan was terribly poisonous. All Altin's hair fell off, and for one mile around each spear of grass withered up.

"I have conquered your enemy," said Altin to the sisters.

"Whither art thou going?" asked they.

"I did not come to save you," said Altin, "but to get the yellow dog for Gal Núrman Khan. I wish to see your father, Khan Herdik; perhaps he can help me." They made no answer at first; then the eldest sister said:

"I should be thy wife, but since thou art wooing the daughter of another khan it would not be proper to talk of that. But remember, I will be thy son's wife. Our father is helpless and cannot aid thee in any way."

Altin rode to that mountain from which golden stairs reach the sky. He went up those stairs on his steed, went to the heavenly smiths for hoofs, chains, and fetters. "We have no time to make those things," said one of the smiths. "We work always for Esege Malan."

"May thy bellows burst! May thy hands not rise! And be thou crooked!" cried Altin in a rage. All happened as he said. He went to each one of the other smiths, got the same answer always, and cursed them all in the same way.

The first and second and third smith cried: "Come back! Come back! Recall thy evil words, and we will do whatever is thy wish."

He restored them, and they worked quickly, made everything well, made all that he asked for. Altin took the hoops, chains, and fetters, went down the golden stairs on horseback, and went then to the mountain where the yellow dog lived.

Five days and nights was Altin climbing that great mountain. He was thinking always: "Which is the better time to seize the dog, morning or evening?" Just before daybreak he reached the summit of the mountain. He put his horse in his pocket as a flint chip, became a raven, and going in search of the dog, found him sleeping.

"If I am well, let all these chains, hoops, and fetters fasten to him!" chanted Altin, as he asked aid of the Burkans. That moment all those chains and fetters were on the dog. The dog woke up, fettered. He sprang, ran, pulled. No good in all that! He could do nothing; he was bound beyond loosening. The raven was there near him as he struggled. "I have heard that Altin is born," said the dog. "He must have come. He must be here; no one else could do this to me!"

"Altin has come indeed," said the raven. "I am he."

"Let me off," begged the yellow dog. "I will go with thee, or dost thou wish to kill me? Free me. Let us be friends."

Altin took his own form and mounted his steed. He let hoops and fetters drop and led the dog by the chain. He was near Gal Núrman's when he met two men on the road. The two said:

"Let the dog loose. That is Gal Núrman's command; he has sent us to meet thee."

"Gal Núrman would not believe me if I went to him without the dog; he would make me go again on this long journey. Ye must be strange people and think me very simple. Eat up those two men and their horses!" said Altin to the yellow dog.

The dog ate them straightway.

Altin reached the yurta of Gal Núrman, tied his steed to the hitching-post, tied the dog to the right corner of the yurta, and went to his father-in-law.

"I have brought the yellow dog," said he. "Come and look at him."

Gal Núrman looked out of the door, saw the dog, and was so frightened that he fainted and lay there without motion. Altin shook him till he brought him to his senses. "See what thy valor is," said Altin; "thou art afraid to even look at the dog. I went to him, captured him, brought him to thee. The dog has a dreadful appetite; he can eat up all thou hast, destroy all thy property in one day."

"Thou hast brought the dog, now thou must get rid of him. He may eat up all my people!" said Gal Núrman, in great alarm.

"Have the wedding to-morrow, and I will send the dog home."

"I will have it," replied the khan.

Altin gave the dog one half of an ox, and said, "Eat well and go back to thy mountain."

"Call the people together," said Altin. "Let the wedding be to-morrow, for I must hurry home." Then he went to his bride.

"Where wert thou? What hast thou seen and done?" asked she.

He told her how he had climbed the golden stairs, how he had got chains, hoops, and fetters of the heavenly smiths, had fettered the yellow dog, and brought him to her father.

"Thou hast said nothing about the three sisters on the pine tree. When shooting the arrow thy command to it was to return to thee. Why did it not come back? I know about those sisters and what they said. One said that she would be thy son's wife."

The next day was the wedding. There were many people, and they had much meat and drink. Ravens and magpies had their fill.

On the fifth day Altin and his bride were at his own yurta on the mountain. And then the young man whom he had left in charge went for his bride; but that is another story.

YERENTE KHAN AND HIS SON SOKTO

YERENTE was ninety-five years of age, and his wife, Untun Duryai, sixty. Though they lived in an immense stone yurta, they had neither son nor daughter.

Yerente owned thousands and thousands of cattle, but for fourteen years he had not thought to number them. At last he went to count all his herds, and on counting found that he had lost one light bay stallion and eighty-five mares with colts and without colts. When he learned this he began to shed tears.

"I am old, I have no children," lamented he, "and now I have lost my best horses. At Dalantai lives a Mangathai of seventy-seven heads. He is the thief; he it is who has stolen my horses." And Yerente went home weeping.

"Why art thou weeping?" asked his wife, Untun Duryai.

"I am not weeping," replied Yerente. "The wind made my eyes smart and made the tears flow."

They sat down to eat and drink.

"Though I was not weeping," said Yerente, "I have lost many mares and a stallion. I must look for those horses at once, I must find them."

"Why do that to-day?" asked Untun Duryai. "You must not go now, you must stay with me."

"I will go without delay," said he; "soon I shall be too old to go, I shall not have the strength to travel."

He made ready immediately, put on his trousers of bull-skin (there were seventy-five skins in that one pair of trousers); then he drew on boots of fish-skin, put a silver belt around his body, a silk shuba over his shoulders, and a sable-skin cap on his head. Next he took a quiver and all that belonged to it, ninety-five arrows. Then he drank spider oil. He had no need of food for ten years after drinking that oil. When ready, he opened his iron storehouse and led forth a red bull with horns sixty fathoms long, took a rope of rawhide, put it through the bull's nose, sat on the beast's back, and rode away westward.

Yerente rode far, rode to a certain mountain beyond the boundary of his land, and there found his mares and his stallion. The right eye of the stallion had been dug out, his right front leg had been broken. Yerente cured the stallion and sent the beast home; with him went the eighty-five mares with colts and without colts. Then the old man rode farther on the red bull to find the Mangathai and take vengeance.

After a time he met two young men on horseback; they had iron staffs in their hands and were looking for a herd of lost horses. He called to them and said, "I can tell ye where that herd is."

"How couldst thou know, old man? Thou art lying." And the two laughed at him as he sat on the long-horned red bull.

Yerente was enraged at their ridicule. He sprang from the bull, seized the young men, tied each to the tail of the horse which he had been riding, lashed the horses, and sent them rushing homeward over the sandy steppe.

Then he rode farther on his red bull. When he reached the top of the mountain he stopped there and looked around on all sides very sharply, thinking where it was best to go. He saw on the horizon a yurta which seemed to touch the blue sky; it was shining and splendid. Near the yurta stood the Mangathai's stallion. This stallion was black, except a white spot on the right side of his rump.

"Rise up!" called the stallion to his master. "Some one is on Onhoy Undir Ushin; it must be that an enemy is coming."

The Mangathai came out in one shirt to look; then he sprang on the stallion and rushed to the mountain.

"Why didst thou take a herd of horses from me in my old age?" asked Yerente.

"Thou art old; so I was free to take them and keep them, and now I will tear thee into small bits!" said the Mangathai, springing from his black stallion and rushing toward the red bull.

Yerente slipped off the bull and went toward the Mangathai. They approached each other sidewise and came together fiercely. Each with all his ten fingers tore bits of flesh from the other. The stallion ran at the bull and bit his spine. The bull drew back, freed himself, and rushed with his long horns at the stallion, fought with him, pierced him through the breast. Then the bull rushed at the Mangathai, pierced him, raised him on his horns, and killed him.

On the bull's back was the horse's head. The horse had bitten into the bull so fiercely that he could not let go, and when he died his head was torn from his body. Yerente took the head away now.

"The Mangathai's property is of no use to me," said he, and he rode home on the back of his red bull.

All were well at his coming, but two days afterward Untun Duryai gave birth to a son and a daughter. Yerente summoned the people. He put tarasun and meat before them on the first day; on the second day he placed the infants in a cradle and asked for men to name them.

A gray-haired old man from the North named the boy, called him Sokto Khan. A gray-haired old man from the South named the girl Agüi.

Yerente sent home the first old man with honor, gave him trousers and a shuba, gave him the marrow bone of an ox. The gray old man gave Sokto a cane. The second gray old man received trousers, a shuba, and a marrow bone, and he gave Agüi a magic stick. Each of the midwives got a silk shuba and a carcass of beef. To the woman who received his son he gave a gold ring; to the woman who received his daughter he gave a silver ring. The two women gave each child a silver ring. All the people went home then, well satisfied and happy.

When ten days had passed the children were as if ten years old, and a ram's skin was too small as a coat for the boy to wear. At this time Duryai said to her husband:

"Go and get for me the flesh of a wild goat. I am tired of common meat."

The old man had a red stallion ninety fathoms long. This stallion was far from the yurta, pasturing, with thirteen wild deer, in the mountains. Yerente took his flute and played on it very sweetly; with this music he summoned the red stallion, and it ran home quickly. Yerente put a silk saddle-cloth on the stallion, then a saddle of silver; he put a silver bit in its mouth and silver trinkets on the saddle. Then he mounted, took bow and quiver, and went to hunt.

The first day he found nothing, the second day no more. That evening he prepared to spend the night in the forest. "I am old," said he to himself; "that is why I see no game!"

The third day he killed many goats, took fifteen of them on his red stallion, and started homeward. When halfway to the yurta the horse sank to the earth on his knees and began to listen. The old man grew angry at the stallion; he thought he was lazy and began to beat him. "Why stop half-way?" cried he.

"Thou hast lived to old age without gaining wit or wisdom," said the stallion. "Why beat thy horse?"

"Why dost thou stop?"

"I stopped for a reason, and now I will tell it. While thou wert away hunting game thy wife went to Orhoy, raised the Mangathai to life, and brought him with her to thy yurta. At this moment he is hidden there behind seventy-seven closed doors. They have pots of poisoned tarasun to give thee. Thou art to drink first of good tarasun; in the second pot will be poison. Thou wilt be drunk from the first pot and poisoned from the second. The moment thou art home let me out, take off the bridle, saddle, and all that is on me. Let not thy wife touch my bridle. Thy wife wants to kill thee and me. Drink not what thy wife gives. If thou drink thou art dead. More good I cannot do thee. Thy fate is told. Later on I will help thy son and daughter."

When they reached the yurta Untun Duryai came out to meet Yerente. "How long thou wert gone! Thou hast wearied thyself for nothing. Give me the horse. I will help thee, I will tie him to the hitching-post."

"I have never let any one tie my horse; I will do that myself," said Yerente.

He unsaddled the horse quickly and let him out. "Be as fat as possible," said he to the stallion. Yerente went into the yurta. Duryai took him by the hand, commanded to skin the goats and dress them. All things were made ready; tarasun was brought in quickly. Duryai gave Yerente one cup after another, and soon he was drunk. "Let me have more drink!" said he.

"I do not know that there is more tarasun," said the woman. "If there is I will bring it."

Duryai was in high spirits; she brought another pot of tarasun. Yerente drank all from the pot and was senseless. The poison came out in blue and red flames through his mouth and his nostrils. As her husband lay there, Duryai called to the Mangathai: "Thy enemy is dead now, come out to me!"

The Mangathai came out, but Yerente was not dead. He sprang up, and the two fought; the old man fought his false wife and the Mangathai as well. They struggled for three days and three nights. Yerente was beginning to overcome the Mangathai.

"Why didst thou raise me?" cried he to Duryai. "Better lie where I was if I must suffer a second time. Better lie dead in peace than be punished in this way."

Duryai took blue grains of barley and threw them at the feet of the Mangathai, chanting words while she scattered them. The Mangathai grew stronger; then she threw red barley grains at the old man's feet and chanted; he grew weak and stumbled.

On the fourth day Yerente was very feeble, and the Mangathai finished him, choked him, killed him. The two put his body in a cask with ninety-five iron hoops on it and rolled the cask into the Hara Dalai (Black Sea); then they feasted.

"Thou must kill thy son and daughter," said the Mangathai; "they may avenge their father's death on me."

"I cannot kill my own children," said Duryai. "If thou wish thou mayst kill them."

"I have not the strength in me to do it, I have fought so many days with thy husband. I will rest, and then I will see to them."

In the night the red stallion broke into the yurta, stole Yerente's son and daughter, and ran away southward to the flat top of a high mountain.

The Mangathai and Duryai went in pursuit.

The red stallion galloped far and very fast. They could not overtake him, and he saved the two children. On the top of that mountain was the Water of Life.

"Let us go back," said the Mangathai. "What can that horse do alone? What good is a horse without a master? What good is a knife without a handle?"

The red stallion gave living water to the children. He found there by the spring an iron horn, from which they drank. He kept them three whole years on the mountain. From the north came rain in summer, and for that reason the right side of the stallion was covered with moss; on his left side the hair fell off from heat. For three years the children played; after that the horse said to them. "Ye are large enough now, I may take you down to the valley. If ye are lucky ye will prosper."

They went down the mountain, and then hand in hand wandered farther. Soon they came to a large open place, where there were eighty-five immense pine trees. Beyond the trees was a splendid yurta which shone like silver. Near the pine trees Sokto made a shelter for his sister. "Stay here," said he, "till I come"; and he went to the high silver yurta. Inside he saw a Mangathai with a hundred and eight heads, and his wife, a very tall woman.

"Whence dost thou come? From what country?" asked the Mangathai. "Thou must be some khan's son."

"People say, I know not if truly, that I am the son of Yerente Khan, that I was taken from my father when an infant."

"Thy father was my great enemy. I am glad that thou hast come. I have need of thee."

Straightway the Mangathai struck Sokto twenty-five strong blows; then he shut him up in a stone storehouse and gave him a little strip of black bread to eat. Sokto had passed many days in that storehouse, when some khan, a friend of the Mangathai, was taking home seventy-five casks of tarasun. The khan gave tarasun to the Mangathai. He drank and grew talkative.

"I have the son of Yerente Khan shut up here. I gave him twenty-five blows of a rod and a bit of black bread. This will do for him daily till I kill him."

"I have no sons; better give him to me," said the khan. "Such a little fellow can do no harm."

"If I do not kill him he may become my enemy."

The khan gave the Mangathai half a cask of tarasun to drink and begged again for the boy.

"Let me have all thy casks of tarasun and take him," said the Mangathai at last.

The khan took the boy home and shouted at the gate, "I have brought a son with me!" His wife was very glad; she took the boy into the yurta and said:

"I will summon the people to a feast and adopt him."

All the people came, and while the feast was going on the boy began to cry. They fondled him and tried to quiet him. On one side stood the new father, and on the other the new mother. "Why cry?" asked they.

"There were two of us," said the boy, "I and my sister. I left my sister in a shelter; I know not whether she is dead or alive."

The khan had four black horses brought, and he went with men to find the sister. Sokto went with them. They rode swiftly, and never stopped till they reached the shelter. Agüi was not there. They found ashes which were warm, and Sokto cried, "She must be alive, and not far from here."

They looked for tracks and found them. The time was early morning. The tracks led to a valley near by. There was dew on the grass, and they found Agüi drinking dew, which she gathered on her palms. Her face and body were covered with sores from the bites of insects; she had no clothing whatever. They gave her milk from home, one spoonful. The khan took her in his arms and carried her; when half-way to his yurta he gave her a spoonful and a half of milk. At the gate he cried out:

"I have brought thee a daughter!"

The khan's wife was very glad. She ran out, took the child in her arms, and carried her into the yurta. Then they called all the people and had a new feast, which lasted nine days and nine nights. During that time the brother and sister grew large and beautiful.

In the stable was a splendid gray colt. "This colt will do for my son," said the khan; and he made a bridle of red cloth, and reins of the same stuff. Sokto cared for the colt; he was fond of horses. When a year had passed he said to his new father:

"Show me thy shuba and trousers; I want to see thy clothing and weapons."

The khan brought his trousers made of seventy elk skins, and boots made of fish-skin. Sokto was two inches thinner than his father, but the boots just fitted. Next they brought a splendid silk shuba, a silver girdle, and a sable-skin cap, as big as a haycock.

"Now bring my bow and all my weapons," said the khan.

Sokto put on the clothes and stood there in his father's splendid outfit. "Be not angry," said he to the khan. "I must go to see the place where I was born; after that I will come back."

"Thou art too young," replied his mother. "Thy years are not many. Thy steed is young also. Better wait one year, even."

"Once he has planned to go, let him go," said his father. "We should not stop him."

Sokto mounted, and started on his journey. He rode far; at last he let his horse out to graze. Then he prayed to the thousand Burkans. "Why create a man and leave him without a proper steed?" asked he.

Immediately the Burkans gave him a steed ninety fathoms long, with ears nine ells high, an outfit of arms, and a splendid dress. He turned out his little horse, put his father's dress and weapons under a rock, and mounting the great new steed, went straight to the hundred and eight headed Mangathai who had flogged him.

Sokto was now a hero, and the Mangathai was terrified when he saw him.

'Thou hadst power and didst flog me," said Sokto. And he caught the Mangathai by his waist and throat and pushed him toward the pine trees. He took ninety-nine spikes and spiked him to the biggest pine; then he took ninety-nine hoops and bound him to the pine with them.

"Thou wilt neither die nor be free. Thou canst never free thyself, and another will not free thee. Thou wilt stay here forever," said Sokto. Then he left him and went toward the yurta; when one verst from the place he sent an arrow at it, saying to the arrow:

"Destroy the yurta and kill the wife of the Mangathai." The arrow went through the center of the yurta and hit the woman. She gave premature birth to a son and died. The child sat on the floor and cried, "Only three days from now was the time for my birth."

Sokto threw the boy into a furnace and made a big fire there. The next morning he was playing with live coals. "In what a nice, warm sleeping-place thou didst put me," said he.

Sokto got more wood, made a bigger fire. The child was alive the following morning. The third night Sokto watched and saw water flowing into the furnace on to the infant and keeping him cool. A tube came from the sky to the furnace.

"Three days were left me to be born," complained the boy, "and nine days later I was to be ready for battle."

The fourth night Sokto cut the tube and the child was consumed by the fire.

The young hero then took the Mangathai's property and went home to his father's yurta. All was silent there. He left everything he had brought and went off to the great house where his mother and the seventy-five headed Mangathai lived. He called to them from outside.Untun Duryai recognized his voice.

"Whoever has a son," said she, "will never perish! My son has come!"

She touched the Mangathai with her cane, and both went out. "Which do you prefer," asked Sokto, "a sharp stake or a square stone?"

"We want nothing of either," replied they. "We wish thee for our son to take care of us."

"Come," said he. "Walk out here before me. I will find a good place for you." He took them to where three roads met; on one side was a great pine, on the other an immense larch tree. He nailed the Mangathai to the larch tree with ninety-five spikes, and his mother to the pine tree with ninety-five other spikes. He left two great casks near them; by one cask was a dull knife, and by the other a blunt pair of scissors, and on the trees he wrote these words: "With the dull knife every man who passes must cut a piece of flesh from each of these two who hang here, with the blunt scissors every woman who passes must cut a piece of flesh from them also. If not they will be treated like this Mangathai, and this woman."

He turned the Mangathai's yurta bottom upward, and drove away all the cattle. When he reached his father's yurta he saw no one. He went straight to his birthplace. The snow that had fallen there was untouched and unmelted. No living thing was in sight. An iron storehouse stood near the great yurta. "What can be in there?" thought Sokto, the hero.

The red bull was in that iron building; he had lived on his cud all the time he had been confined there.

"Thanks to thee," said the bull. "But for the son of my master I should have perished."

Sokto let the bull out to graze; then he went to Hara Dalai, the Black Sea, where his father's body was in a cask. He turned himself into a large fish, and soon he met a still larger one and asked: "Why is this water so muddy, and why does it smell of blood? If thou wilt not clear the water Abérga Zgohun will summon thee."

"Whence art thou?" asked the larger fish.

"I live near the Gazada Dalai," replied Sokto.

"Go home; when thou art gone I will cleanse this sea."

Sokto took his own form again. Near the seashore was a mountain. He went to that mountain and waited. The sea stormed thrice in three days; the third time it hurled the cask out, threw it a whole verst from the water.

Sokto came to the shore and beat the cask open, but found nothing in it save bones. He brought water from nine springs, washed the bones with nine waters. From nine places he got juniper and burned it for incense. Next he took Water of Life from the spring on the mountain and washed the bones three nights with that water; then Yerente became alive and as well as ever. On the way home they met the red stallion.

"Through thee," said the red stallion, "I have suffered much, and thy son and daughter have also suffered greatly. Though I advised thou wouldst not listen; from this came all the trouble."

The stallion seized Yerente by the neck, and shook him three times fiercely. Then they went to the khan's yurta.

"I never thought that thou wouldst be such a hero," said the khan's wife to Sokto. The next morning all came together,—two fathers, one mother, one sister, and one brother.

"If I say a word will ye be willing that I accomplish it?" inquired Sokto.

"We will listen to all that thou sayest," answered his mother.

"Once my father was a khan. I should like to have all my buildings on the boundary between the lands of both my fathers."

"It is difficult to do that," said the khan. "The buildings on both dominions are large and numerous. Thou wilt be old before thou canst move them all."

"No, I can do it in one night if ye say so."

"Do what may please thee," said the mother.

That night Sokto sat at home, went nowhere. From evening until midnight he prayed to the Heavenly Burkans. At midnight he fell asleep. When he woke the next morning every building was on the boundary. The khan assembled all the people at the new place and feasted.

"Now I wish to find a bride," said Sokto.

"Without a wife it is impossible to be," replied the people.

"Thou shouldst read thy book of life," said his mother.

He opened his midriff and found the book in his liver. He read this book for three days and nights,—at night by torch-light, in the day by sunlight. At times he cried, at times he sang songs.

"In the south country lives Gul Khan, and he has a daughter, Goye Gohûn Duhe; she is thy bride," said the book.

Sokto began preparations for the journey. He kept his horse, the red stallion, standing on ice for three days and three nights, gave him hay and a little water. This was to make his hoofs strong. Then during three days and three nights the horse stood on sand. "Now we may go!" thought Sokto.

"Brother," said Agüi, "thou art going far away; give me some sign by which I may know how thou art, whether dead or living, slain or in health."

"I will give you this sign," said he. "Outside, at the southeast corner of the yurta, grows a golden-trunked aspen tree with silver leaves. On the twigs of that aspen tree thousands of little birds will be twittering. These birds will speak in their own way; from them news may be heard through knowledge of their speech. If I die the tree will rot and fall, and the birds will fly away. If I am well the tree will be green and beautiful, and the birds will increase in it. Here is another sign," said he, taking; an arrow and putting it by his sister's bed: "if I am well this arrow will be red and increase in beauty; if I die it will fade and grow ugly."

"Thou hast done well," said Agüi. "By these signs I shall know all about thee. I will give thee a sign." She handed him her gold ring. "If I am alive and well, this ring will glitter; if dead or ill, or married in spite of my wishes, the ring will be ugly and dim."

Sokto assembled all the people, placed before them drink and meat in plenty, and asked them to wish him success and remember him. "I will bring a bride home to you," said he, in parting.

An old man, gray bearded to the knees, wished him good health and success on his journey.

Sokto set out on a gallop, rode till he reached another kingdom, then halted, for right before him was a spring. He took out his pipe and burned tobacco to the spring; then he threw tobacco into the water. He named all the thousand Burkans and asked for a favoring journey.

Then he rode farther, rode beyond the boundary of the kingdom. Soon he heard the tramp of ten horses and the voices of ten riders. He reined in his steed. "Are those enemies or good people? A man should accomplish his purpose," said he to himself. "Why should I fear? Those are people like me!"

He hurried on, turned himself into eleven young heroes on horseback, made just such a tramping and sound of voices as that which he heard, only greater.

Soon after he met a big red-faced man. Each tooth in his head was as large as a spade, and in his ears were rings as big as a cart-wheel. He was riding on a light bay horse, whose body was eighty fathoms long and ears sixteen inches high. When they drew near they gave greeting and passed; then they halted and turned toward each other.

"From what place art thou?" inquired Sokto.

CONTENTS OF "GOD BAGS." Page 85
Pieces of cloth and silk on which are sewn tiny figures
of men cut out of tin

CONTENTS OF "GOD BAGS."

Pieces of cloth and silk no which are sewn tiny figures of men cut our of tin

BURIAT HOUSEHOLD GODS. *Page* 41
Andrei Mihailovitch's house gods

BURIAT HOUSEHOLD GODS.

Andrei Mihailovitch's house gods

"I am going to Yerente Khan," said the big man. "I have heard that he has a daughter, Agüi Nogun Duhe; I want her for a wife, but though I have heard of her, I know not where to find her. I have been told that a hero is her brother. Whence art thou, and what is thy name?"

"I am Nashin Huimer Hubun. I have also started to find my bride, Geye Gohûn Duhe, but she is far away."

They took a friendly farewell. "Go thy way; I go mine," said each to the other. "May we succeed, and our wishes be accomplished."

The big man found Yerente's yurta at last, and declared his wish without waiting.

"I am not willing to marry thee," said Agüi. "My brother has gone for his bride. I will not marry before he does. I will marry thee when the time comes, if thou wilt do one thing that my brother does. Off in the field is a stone the size of a bullock; throw that stone over thy shoulder, from the place where it lies to this yurta. If thou do that, I will marry thee; if not, I will never be thy wife."

He went straight to that stone, raised it to his waist, but could raise it no farther, and let it fall, then he mounted his steed and went home without speaking to any man.

Sokto rode on till he came to a great iron yurta. In front of the yurta were twenty-five horse skulls on stakes; crows had eaten the flesh from each one of them. Outfits, weapons, and dress were fastened there also. He stopped, changed his horse into a flint chip, put the chip in his pocket, changed himself to a weasel, burrowed under the house, passed through the floor, and came up to see who lived in that great iron yurta. He saw a hundred and eight headed Mangathai sleeping; near his principal head lay an axe, his feet were fixed against the wall firmly; from his mouth blue and red flames were quivering.

The weasel stole up, hid the axe, sprang at the throat of the Mangathai and cut it through; he crept out, then became Sokto again and the flint chip became the red stallion.

"Boast not of killing the Mangathai," said the stallion, "no blood is sold cheaply by any man. This will be a great Shaman place hereafter."

Sokto mounted his steed, rode farther and met a twenty-five headed Mangathai on a gray stallion.

"How didst thou ride by my father's yurta, which no man ever passes on foot or on horseback?" asked the Mangathai.

"As I rode past I saw twenty-five horse skulls on stakes. A black raven was croaking, and a young fox was walking about there. The place is deserted."

"Is it long since you left your father's yurta?"

"Three years ago I had the first wish to marry. I am going for my bride, Geye Gohun Duhe."

"I should like to know who killed my father. I will find him wherever he may be," said the Mangathai as he rode away.

Sokto took an arrow and shot it behind himself saying: "As sure as I am alive and well do thou slay this twenty-five headed Mangathai and his horse." The arrow killed the Mangathai and his horse and came back to the quiver.

Sokto went farther, and saw three roads. Between two of them was a shed and in it a terribly wrinkled old woman. She had but one eye and one tooth in her head.

"If thou art the son of a good father," said she, "stop. If the son of an evil father pass on without stopping."

Sokto halted, looked in, and saw tarasun in a silver goblet. "I am tired, O my grandmother, give me tarasun to drink. I am on a long journey, I am weary and thirsty."

She gave the tarasun. He saw worms in the goblet, hundreds of them, but did not like to refuse the tarasun given him. "What good tarasun!" said he, "but give me more, O my grandmother. There is not enough for a drink here, give a good large gobletful. Be generous. Why so stingy? O my grandmother, give me more, give me a plenty."

She smiled and went to the rear of the shed. This time she brought out three gallons in a strong roomy vessel. He placed the vessel on the saddle. "I am at fault," said he. "Before I drink bring your pipe, I will give you tobacco." When she turned to go for the pipe he threw all the tarasun on her, then galloped off very swiftly.

She hurled after him a scraper twenty fathoms long which was used in tanning leather. Then she fell down and that moment seven acres of land were covered with foul worms. All the land covered by the tarasun was burned up immediately. The scraper followed Sokto; he felt it coming. He made a great stone mountain behind him and waited on the other side of that mountain to see what would happen.

He waited three days and nights, then the scraper pierced through the mountain and came out on the other side. Sokto seized it and broke it. Then he traveled on till he came to a light bay stallion eighty fathoms long and ears eight ells high; near the stallion lay a young man whose flesh was almost eaten off by worms from his body. The horse had dug the earth deeply and was very lean. Sokto let out the horse to graze. The rider lay still and motionless, though he was not dead yet.

"Thou art my comrade," said the stranger, "thou wilt bury me. I passed an old witch at the roadside, drank of her tarasun, and the worms from it have almost devoured me. I am the son of Shur Galgûn Khan. I set out to find a bride. My name is Shurak Taiji Hubun."

Sokto brought water from nine springs, washed the young man, burned juniper from nine places, and cured him. The two were great friends now. Sokto went farther and came to a meadow. In that meadow was a multitude of frogs, some of them as large as a three-year-old bullock.

"Do not let that traveler pass," said one of the frogs to another. Sokto turned his horse into a flint chip and himself into a black frog as big as a young bullock, so that the others should not know him; then he moved forward slowly. He moved for nine days and nights through that frog-covered meadow. When he was on the other side he took his own form again. "Why did ye let him pass?" asked some of the frogs when they saw him safe beyond their boundary, and they were very angry.

Farther on was a second meadow covered with snakes of many kinds. "Let not that traveler pass," said the snakes to one another. "If he crosses this meadow we will kill those snakes which let him pass."

Sokto went back some distance, made his horse a flint chip and himself a snake like the snakes of that meadow. He spent seven days and nights among those hostile, venomous snakes, passed by them unobserved and then became a man again. The snakes were terribly angry and had a furious battle when they found that Sokto had crossed the meadow.

He went farther till he saw a mountain which touched the sky. He rode to the foot of it and found many bones there and skeletons. He measured the horse bones; they were three times as large as the bones of his own steed. He measured men's bones; they were three times the size of his own. He wept for nine days and nine nights. The mountain was so steep that no man could climb it. At last his stallion said:

"Be calm, there is no use in weeping! Go back one day's journey and tighten my saddle girth. There is a hair on the end of my tail from which three hairs grow. Take that hair and put it under thy arm. It has magic power in it. Hold to me firmly."

Sokto went back one day's journey. "Now," said the horse, "I will rush with all the might in me, and spring to the top of that mountain."

He did so. On the top, at the very edge, was a stone as big as an ox. The horse's forelegs were beyond that stone and he held to the edge of it. It was easy to fall and hard to hold. "Throw that hair out in front of me," said the horse.

Sokto threw the hair. That moment the stone disappeared; out in front was a good level road through a valley and farther on a broad forest. They passed the valley and were soon on the mountain top, where there was a golden-trunked, silver-leafed aspen tree. At the foot of the tree was the Water of Life, and a silver cup was hanging from a branch of the tree. Without the cup no man could drink at the spring or take water out of it. Sokto drank and gave water to his horse. Then the horse began to graze, and Sokto kindled a fire, made a bed of the saddle-cloth, a pillow of the saddle, lay down and slept soundly.

The next morning when he rose his horse had changed greatly; he was fat and strong. Sokto himself felt stronger and better and planned how he was to finish his journey. Beyond the mountain were the lands of his father-in-law. He mounted and rode toward them.

On the boundary Sokto made his horse gray and lean, made himself decrepit, white bearded to the knees, old, and wretched. Then he rode toward the yurta. Five horses of various colors were tied to the hitching-post. Five splendid young men had come to get brides and had entered the beautiful yurta. Sokto tied his poor, miserable, gray horse to the hitching-post, and walked into the yurta.

"A greeting, father-in-law!" said the wretched old man.

The five young heroes laughed as he said this. "What sort of bridegroom art thou, poor old fellow?" asked they.

"Who art thou, old man?" asked the khan.

"Why talk to me in this way? What a strange father-in-law! Thou hast five daughters, they should choose their own bride-grooms. Assemble the people to-morrow, let each daughter choose the man who pleases her."

The daughters were behind seventy-seven doors at this time. The next day the khan assembled the people and entertained them. He gave his daughters five marrow bones. "Choose thy bridegroom," said he to each daughter. Each was to give a marrow bone to the man whom she selected.

The five sisters went out together and four gave bones to four of the five young strangers. The fifth, who was the youngest sister, would not give hers to the fifth stranger, but threw it toward the old man, and ran away quickly. All wondered at this and were sorry for the fifth young man who was left without a bride.

The khan gave four fine yurtas to the four young strangers, to the fifth bridegroom, the old man, he gave a shed made of hay. "Ye will live here," said the father-in-law.

The next morning he called out the four sons-in-law and said: "I am tired of eating common meat, kill some wild goats for me." To the old man he said nothing. The old man's bride went to her father:

"I will send my husband to hunt," said she.

"Why send that old fool?" asked her father, "he will knock against a tree and kill himself."

"Let him kill himself if he wishes, I am ashamed to be the bride of that old man."

The four went out to hunt wild goats, and the old man went also. He made his horse lame. The beast could hardly move he was so crippled and wretched. They reached the forest. The four young strangers hunted all day, but found no game. The old man killed only one goat; when he shot it he said: "Let the whole body be poison except the entrails; let the entrails be the cure." Then he sat down in the forest by a fire which he had made. The four came to him. "Have ye killed anything?" asked he. "No, hast thou?"

"One small goat and I don't know how to skin it." They skinned it for him. "Divide the meat into five parts," said they. He divided it; gave them the clear meat, and kept the skin and entrails. They carried the flesh to their father-in-law. The old man's bride cooked the entrails and took them to her father. She found him sick, swollen, very ill, and complaining:

"I ate meat and am sick from it. Why bring entrails? Dost thou wish to kill me?" cried the khan in anger.

"Thou mightst even taste, even catch the odor!" urged the daughter.

He took a spoonful; found it good, took a cupful, was cured, became well altogether.

The next morning he called the four bridegrooms and said: "Go again to hunt but bring me the entrails this time." Before they left the youngest daughter came to her father. "I will send the old man to hunt," said she.

"Do not send him, his horse is lame. That old fellow can kill nothing."

"Let him go," begged the daughter; "if something happens to him I shall not be sorry."

The four young bridegrooms laughed, ridiculed the old man.

He grew angry at their laughter and jokes and when they reached the forest he kindled a fire and sat down by it. "Go ye to hunt," said he. "I will stay here by the fire." He killed another goat. When he sent the arrow he said: "Let the entrails be poison and the meat the cure."

"What have ye killed?" asked he of the four when they came in the evening. "Nothing," said they.

"Though I have killed one big goat I will not divide this time," said the old man. They insisted on division till at last he said: "I will divide if each of you will give me a finger's width of skin from his neck to the end of his back." They agreed to this. The old man cut the strap, then they took the entrails and left him the clean meat.

The four daughters cooked the entrails and gave them to their father. He ate them, and grew very sick; was swollen to the size of a three-year-old bullock and began to cry: "My end is coming, my end is near! I must die this time!"

The old man's bride cooked clean meat and brought it to her sick father. "Why bring me meat?" asked he. "I do not want it." She bowed down to him, entreated: "Try a little." The meat was very savory. The moment the khan ate a mouthful he was well again.

On the third morning he called the four bridegrooms and said:

"To-night my big gray mare will have a colt. Will ye watch her? She has had three colts in three years and each one was stolen from me."

The four agreed to watch. The old man's bride heard of this and said: "I will send my husband to watch with them."

"No need of him," said the father. "Why send that fool?"

"I can spare him," answered the wife. "I am not sorry for him. Let him kill himself if he wishes." "Send him then," said the father.

The herd was in a valley, and the five bridegrooms went there. A heavy frost came down in the night and the air was very cold. They built a fire and the four sat by it shivering. The old man was not cold.

"Warm yourselves," said he to the four, "I will go to the other side of the valley." He went, found the gray mare, turned himself into a reed and watched to see who it was that stole the colt each year.

At midnight a fifty-five headed and fifty horned Mangathai came. The mare had her colt. The reed shot the Mangathai with an arrow, killed him, took the colt and placed it with the mother. Then he collected sticks, made a fire and burned the Mangathai. The ashes from his bones filled ninety-seven bags. Then the old man made a windmill, ground all the ashes in the ninety-seven bags and let the wind bear the ashes away. All was finished by morning. The four bridegrooms knew nothing of what had happened. At dawn the old man was by their fire. They were nearly frozen, almost dead from cold. He gathered wood, warmed them, then asked:

"What have ye seen during the night? What have ye been doing?"

"We have seen nothing. What hast thou seen?"

"I have seen a fine thing. I have seen who it is that steals the colts, but I will not tell you." They urged and begged. At last he said: "Give me four straps from the flesh of your thighs, then I will tell."

They looked at one another. "We must give the straps," said they. They cut the straps and gave them. "I saw," said the old man, "only this—that a shadow, a bird or something, I know not exactly what, took the colt and swallowed it. That is all I saw."

The four returned, appeared before their father-in-law and said: "At midnight came a shadow, or a bird, or something of that sort, we are not sure what, and swallowed the colt. We could not shoot it."

"For three years the same thing has happened," said the khan. "Go home now and eat." When the four had gone the old man came.

"What are thy four sons-in-law doing?" asked he. "Are they shooting? Do they kill anything?"

"My four sons-in-law saw last night how a shadow swallowed the gray mare's colt. But thou, old man, what art thou doing?" "Nothing, but getting straps."

"Let me have them," said the father-in-law. "What kind of straps are these?" asked he, as he looked at them.

"I got those straps from thy four sons-in-law. They went to kill goats, killed none. I gave them clear meat, and kept the entrails. Thou wert sick from the meat, and wert cured by the entrails. Then I gave them entrails for straps from their backs; thou wert sick from entrails, and wert cured by the clear meat."

"Thou art wiser, it seems, than the four, and have better understanding than any one of them. How didst thou get the other four straps from the bridegrooms?"

"For telling them that a shadow, or bird, seized the colt. I did not tell them what really happened. I will tell thee the whole truth. A Mangathai came in the night; I shot that Mangathai, and killed him. The colt is alive now, and any one may see it at the place where I killed the Mangathai."

"Thou art the son of a khan, and thou art young," said the father-in-law. "Be kind and take thy own shape." The father-in-law bowed down a whole day, and begged: "Tell the truth. Tell what thy name is." At last the old man said:

"My name is Khan Sokto, and I am the son of Yerente Khan."

"Why didst thou not tell me thy name?"

Sokto gave no answer. The father-in-law summoned the four bridegrooms, made them show their backs and thighs, tried the straps and saw that they fitted.

"Ye cannot be my sons-in-law," said he. "Ye cut up your own bodies, and might cut up my daughters." And he drove them away that same evening.

The next day a splendid feast was given and it lasted nine days and nights, for Sokto was young now and had his own form.

"Prepare the wedding quickly," said Sokto. "I must go home to my father, my mother, and my sister."

"Near the Gazada Dalai," said the khan, "is Yellow Dog. Get that dog for me, and we will have the wedding immediately. If not we will not have it at any time."

Sokto went to his bride and told her all. "What does thy father wish to do with me?" asked he.

"No hero can get Yellow Dog," said the bride. "Better go home than try. It is impossible to get it. Though many men have gone for it no man has ever come back. Find some other bride; there are many maidens in other lands."

"I will not go home," said Sokto. "I will go for Yellow Dog. It is unknown whether I shall die on the way, or come back, but I will make the trial." Then he went to consult with his horse.

"Thou must go to the sky," said the horse, "and tell Esege Malan; take advice of him. The seven heavenly smiths may help thee."

Sokto made his horse into a flint chip, and went to the sky as a gray falcon.

"What hast thou to do?" asked Esege Malan. Sokto told what the task was.

Esege Malan ordered the seven smiths to make an immense chain for the dog's neck, heavy fetters for his feet, and two iron hoops to confine his mouth.

Sokto went to the smiths and they made all that was needed. While they were forging Sokto chanted: "As I live and am well this chain is to give Yellow Dog to me." He went through the heavens to where Yellow Dog was; he could not go on the earth, could not find him. He saw the dog from the sky. When above the shore of the Frozen Ocean he threw the chain, fetters, and hoops, and chanted: "If I am victorious let this chain fasten around Yellow Dog's neck, let the fetters fasten on his feet, and these two hoops confine his mouth. If I am not victorious let them drop to the earth and be harmless." As he spoke they fell on the dog and captured him. Sokto then rushed down to the earth. The dog whined, dashed about, but could do nothing. Then he stopped, and said:

"In all the world there was no magic that could harm me. I have heard that Khan Sokto is born; a great hero must he be, for no other could bind me in this way. O Sokto, if thou wish to conquer, conquer quickly. If to kill, kill me now. If to help, help this minute."

That moment the chain became laxer, the fetters dropped off, the hoops loosened. Sokto sat on his horse; led the dog to his father-in-law's yurta, and tied him to the hitching-post.

"Such a dog is not needed here!" screamed the khan. "Take him back to where you found him!"

"I cannot take him back," said Sokto. "He eats a whole bullock at a meal."

The dog heard the conversation and said to Sokto:

"Give me enough to eat, and I will go back to my own place alone. I fear nothing on earth. For ten years I shall be a great friend to thee. If any trouble happens between thee and thy father-in-law I will be on thy side."

Yellow Dog ate much; he ate a whole ox and went home to the edge of the Frozen Ocean.

At Sokto's wedding all the people feasted nine days and nine nights. "What will you give me as a present?" asked the bride of her father. He gave her a bay horse, ninety fathoms long, his ears nine ells high, with a saddle of silver and housings of silk. They mounted, and the people followed them. Sokto showed the road to the company. He tied to his horse's tail a larch tree so thick that nine men could not encircle it. "When I halt on the road," said he, "it means that we are to smoke, when I make a circuit with the tree it means a night camp.

He traveled swiftly and in nine days was at home. All were well there, and they were waiting for him. He summoned the people; meat and drink were set out for all; but they waited for those who followed. In three days they arrived and then every one feasted for nine days and nine nights. At the end of that time the guests went home, and Sokto and his wife lived on as people live usually.

Now Narin Huimer Hubun, the big man, who could not hurl the great stone, came a second time for Sokto's sister.

"What is thy business, and why hast thou come?" inquired Sokto.

"I have come to ask for thy sister."

"What is thy reason for thinking to get her?"

"Esege Malan said that I was to have her as wife."

"I believe thee," said Sokto. "But thou must remain three years with me, help me in making lists of my people, and counting my herds and cattle. I am terribly tired. For twelve years I have been traveling and struggling. I need thy assistance."

Narin Hubun agreed to this, and aided in counting the herds. At the end of three years Sokto said to him, "It is time for thee to have thy own yurta." Then he invited the people and the next day began a wedding which lasted nine days and nine nights; at it ravens and magpies ate all they wanted. The whole world ate, and was glad.

"I took care of thy yurta for twelve years," said the sister, "what wilt thou give me for a present?"

Sokto had a bay horse eighty fathoms long, which had been trained for eight days.

"Take this horse," said he, "and ask nothing of another person. I thank thee for thy care of my yurta while I was struggling with Mangathais, and winning my bride."

Sokto's sister mounted and rode away with her bridegroom, contented and happy.

ALAMALDJIN AND HIS TWIN SISTER HANHAI

ALAMALDJIN BOGDO and his twin sister Hanhai were born in Iryil of a father who was seventy-five years of age and a mother who was sixty.

After the twins were born the father called all the people to a feast of three days' duration. At the feast he took two marrow bones and asked for a man to come forth and name the boy. One old man named him, and received one marrow bone. An old woman then named the twin sister, and got the second bone.

In ten days the skin of a ten-year-old sheep was not big enough for Alamaldjin. When the boy was three years old his father taught him to reckon. When the child played with other children he said always that he would be khan.

This life continued till the boy was eleven, then he hired men to quarry stone, and he built a yurta one verst long, and so high that the roof, which was of silver, seemed to touch the sky. There were seven thousand windows below, and nine thousand windows above. All the outside was covered with silver, and it was finished inside with gold. There were seventy-seven immense chambers in that yurta.

Alamaldjin had many cattle and many people; and he lived in splendor. Fine roads went from his yurta to all places. When seventeen years of age he was so wise and famous that the people made him khan.

For thirteen years his tattles and herds had been uncounted, now he determined to have them counted. The khan had two uncles; he summoned them, and they came on bay horses. He took both by the hands, led them into his yurta and feasted them. "I have no time to count my herds," said the nephew, "will ye do this counting for me?"

They began, but in three days they could not finish counting, there were so many cattle. At last they finished. The cattle in front were very thin and uneasy, those behind very fat and well satisfied. The two uncles cried out when they saw this. They went to their nephew and asked him to choose other pastures. He was not willing to do so.

"My father's cattle did not suffer," said he. "How is it that my cattle suffer?"

"Our nephew does not believe us," said the two uncles, and they went then to hang themselves. "I will not let this come to pass," said Alamaldjin, and he stopped them. "I will go in search of new pastures, and find them."

Alamaldjin had a brown steed ninety fathoms long with ears nine ells high. This steed was in the Altai Deda, beyond mountains, at pasture with thirteen wild deer. He might have called the steed with a whistle, but he did not wish to do that, so he sent his two uncles to bring him.

The uncles went to the Altai Mountains, found the horse, but were dreadfully frightened at sight of him, and came back without him. "Let us go home and hang ourselves," said they. "Our nephew laughs at us, and pays no heed to the advice which we give him."

Alamaldjin blew his whistle; the horse and the thirteen wild deer heard the call. They had pastured together thirteen years, and the thirteen deer said: "We may be lost if we go, but we wish to go with thee."

Altai Deda, the place where they had lived in company, was very beautiful. The water was sweet, the grass an ell high, and the deer did not like to leave it. "Go not," said they to the steed. "Stay thou with us, we are afraid to be without thee." They did not wish to lose the horse; they did not like to leave the mountain.

"Fear not," said the horse. "If I perish the water will dry up, and the grass wither. If I am well all will be as it now is. Have no fear, I shall not perish."

The horse lay down and rolled; some of his hair fell out, as much in bulk as a big stack of hay. "If enemies come," said he, "get under this hair and hide there, ye will be safe from them. If I am well the hair will last many years. If I am lost it will vanish. But I shall not be lost, and this hair will remain here. If ye grieve for me, smell the hair, and ye will be cheerful."

They agreed now to stay in the Altai Mountains.

The horse ran toward his master at full speed, came at the summons of the whistle; rushed to the hitching-post, stood and neighed there.

Alamaldjin hurried out in a single shirt. In one hand he held a bridle, in the other a hair rope. He put a bit in the mouth of his horse and tied him to a hitching-post. The horse stood there three days. Alamaldjin gave him nothing to eat, and only spring water to drink. Then he led him to a sandy place, tied him to another post, left him three days on the sand; next he tied him to a post in an icy place, left him standing on ice three days; that was the last preparation.

Alamaldjin now placed on his steed a silk saddle-cloth and a silver saddle. Then he made himself ready. He wore trousers made of fifty elk skins, shoes of fish-skin, a silken shuba with seventy-five fastenings, a silver belt, and a cap of sable. He took a bow and a quiver with ninety-five arrows. He drank worms, after which he had no need to eat for twenty-five days; then he mounted and rode away swiftly. His uncles were glad.

He rode far, rode into another country, and saw on the edge of the earth an immense iron building which rose to the sky. He made his horse small and wretched, and himself old and full of wrinkles, a Shaman. He reached the great iron building. He tied his horse to a hitching-post, then tried to find a door to the building, but could not, and he broke in the southwest corner of the yurta. Inside was a Mangathai of a hundred and fifty heads. The Mangathai sprang up, and shouted, "Who art thou, who hast dared to break into my house in this manner?"

The Mangathai took his axe, forty fathoms broad, and sharpened it, but when he heard that the strange old man was a Shaman he threw the axe aside. Then it turned out that the right eye of the Mangathai had been struck by an arrow and was injured.

"It is well that a Shaman is here," said he, "my eye is sore."

"It is not difficult to cure thy eye," said Alamaldjin; "let me look at it. Three years ago some one struck thy eye with an arrow; thy sight is poor, there are many worms in thy eye at this moment."

"True," said the Mangathai.

"I will cure thee quickly," said Alamaldjin. "I am afraid thou art so big that a strong remedy is needed. Wilt thou endure it?"

"I will."

The Mangathai brought a hair rope ninety fathoms long. "I will lie down; do thou tie me to the four corners of the chamber, and fasten me so that I shall not move."

Alamaldjin tied him firmly, took a great pot, put it on the tripod of the central fire, then filled the pot with lead. When the lead was melted, Alamaldjin said, "Look at the sky with thy sound eye, count the stars in it. Look to one side with thy sick eye."

The Mangathai did so, and Alamaldjin poured the whole kettle of molten lead into the well eye. The Mangathai felt dreadful pain; he trembled, pulled, roared. Alamaldjin found three iron doors closed; he broke them and rushed out. He saw a yellow goat on the road with horns three ells long. The khan turned himself into a flea and sat on the goat's ear contentedly.

The Mangathai tugged at the rope, pulled three times, tore it to bits, and rushed out to find the Shaman, but could not see him. The goat ran to the Mangathai and butted him. The Mangathai saw a little yet with his injured eye. The goat butted him a second time; he fell, hurt his forehead, and was terribly angry.

"That goat never came near me before," said the Mangathai to himself, "now when my eye is gone he butts me."

The Mangathai made an iron wall with his magic, a very high wall, so the Shaman might not save himself. Then he took the goat and threw him over the high enclosure. The flea stayed in the goat's ear till he was outside, then it became Alamaldjin. Alamaldjin mounted his horse and called to the Mangathai, "Well, is thy eye any better?"

"It is better, thanks to thee. For reward I will give thee this axe!" And he threw the axe over the wall at Alamaldjin, intending to kill him. The axe did not hit Alamaldjin. He picked it up, stuck it in the wall of another yurta, and said, "Stay here till I come, see that this Mangathai does not leave that house and enclosure. This place will be mine hereafter; my pastures will be here."

All the Mangathai's magic, all his strength, was in that axe.

Now Alamaldjin went home. The two uncles knew what had happened to their nephew. They killed ten sheep, made many kettles of tarasun, and went out to meet him. They stopped at Red Mountain, built a shed there, and waited.

When the nephew appeared they went to meet him. "We are here to greet thee," said they; "we have brought a feast with us."

Alamaldjin was angry, "Why have ye come? why bring a feast? why can I not go home alone?"

"We did this as a mark of respect, because thou hast conquered a great Mangathai."

He tied his horse to a tree and went into the shed with his uncles. First they gave him ten pots of tarasun. He emptied them all and became very gladsome. Next he ate ten sheep. "Is there no more tarasun?" asked he. They gave him a small keg of tarasun mixed with poison. He drank of it, and fell to the ground. Blue and red flames came from his nostrils.

"Though ye have killed my master, I will not yield to you!" said the horse, and he broke away and rushed home. He reached the yurta, ran to the hitching-post, and neighed very loudly.

Alamaldjin's sister came out, embraced the horse's feet, and fell to crying, "How is thy master? where is he?"

"My master is dead at the boundary; thy two uncles have killed him." Hanhai mounted and rode to the boundary quickly. Her brother's body was lying in the shed; she found no one there with it. She tied two silk cloths around the body, and wrapped it up carefully. Not far away was Red Mountain; she buried her brother at the foot of that mountain and went home. In her brother's yurta was his book; she read this book and learned from it how to guard against death, and how to bring the dead back to life. This is what the book said:

"Far away, on the opposite end of the earth, is an impassable swamp, in the middle of that swamp is a golden aspen with silver leaves, at the foot of that aspen tree is the Water of Life. On the top of the tree sits a cuckoo. If any one goes there the cuckoo will help them; the water will heal and bring the dead back to life again."

The sister put on her brother's dress, took his weapons, mounted his steed, and rode away swiftly. At the end of six days she was near the impassable swamp. She made her horse a flint chip, and put him into her pocket, then she turned herself into a raven.

It was forty versts from the edge of the swamp to the living water. She had a small keg and flew to the place. The water flowed up out of the earth sweet and pure. The cuckoo was not there. The raven drank of the water, and then filled a small keg. After that she turned into a reed and watched, waiting for the cuckoo.

At midday the cuckoo flew home and drank water. The reed seized the bird by the neck, grasped her tightly.

"Let me go!" cried the cuckoo; "or if thou wish to kill, then kill quickly. Art thou Hanhai?"

"I am," said the sister. "I have come for thee to save my brother."

"I will go with thee," said the cuckoo. Then both flew back to where Alamaldjin was buried. There the sister took her own form and prayed to the Heavenly Burkans for three days. On the third day the ground opened and Hanhai drew out the body. It was in good condition, except the right shoulder-blade; a fox had dug into the grave and carried off that shoulder-blade. Hanhai told the cuckoo to watch the body while she herself followed the trail of the fox.

She went to Shara Dalai (the Yellow Sea) and found the fox there. She had the shoulder-blade in her mouth when Hanhai met her.

"What art thou doing with that shoulder-blade?" asked the sister.

"I took it to a Shaman to have him soothsay. This is the third day that I have a headache. The Shaman knew that it was thy brother's and sent me back with it. I am going now to where thy brother is buried."

"What right hadst thou to take the shoulder-blade from a dead man? Who gave thee permission?"

"I hunted the world over, but could not find a shoulder-blade of man or beast. Passing thy brother's grave I knew by the odor that a corpse was lying in it, then I made bold to take the shoulder-blade. I will give it back to thee. Do not beat me."

Hanhai took the shoulder-blade and forgave the fox. Then she returned and found the cuckoo guarding her brother. She put the shoulder-blade in its right place and poured the Water of Life on her brother's body, which took on its own form again quickly. The cuckoo began to sing, began at his feet and sang till she stopped at the crown of his head. Then Alamaldjin stood up well and said, "How long I have been sleeping here!"

Alamaldjin and Hanhai went home. They took the cuckoo with them, and gave her good entertainment,—entertained her one day.

"We shall be friends from this time, and forever," said Alamaldjin when the cuckoo was going. "Be thou kind, and assist us."

"I will," said the cuckoo, "whenever the need comes."

"I am going out to hunt," said Alamaldjin on the following day to his sister.

"Hunting is good," said Hanhai, "but thou shouldst rest ten days at least."

"Why rest? I shall hunt on my own land." And he rode away quickly.

In the forest he met a woman as tall as a pine tree—the wife of that Mangathai whose eye he had put out, and who was dead now. She had been hunting for Alamaldjin.

This woman held in her hand a scraper ten fathoms long,—the scraper was for dressing rawhide.

"Oh, look!" called she, "see how many men are coming behind thee!"

He looked around. She hit him on the back of his neck, and he fell with head on the right side of the horse, and body on the left. The horse ran toward home. The Mangathai woman followed the horse, but failed to catch him.

"What good is a horse without a master? What good is a wife without a husband?" cried she as the horse rushed away from her.

Again the horse neighed loudly at the hitching-post. Hanhai ran out, embraced his feet, and cried: "Where is my brother?"

"The Mangathai's wife has killed thy brother in his own forest."

Hanhai put her brother's dress on, mounted his steed, and rode off to meet the Mangathai woman. Rode straight to her; she knew by her magic power where the tall woman was. Hanhai turned herself into a man; the Mangathai woman did not know her. As Hanhai passed the tall woman she called out to her, "Whence comest thou, O woman? Who art thou?"

"I am the wife of a Mangathai."

"What art thou doing in this forest?"

"I have lost a flock of sheep, a herd of horses, and many cattle. I have asked every one where to look for them, but cannot find them. But look around!" cried the woman on a sudden, "see how many men are behind thee!"

"Let them stay behind me, they are my people. Look behind thyself! There are twenty Mangathais coming against thee!" said Hanhai.

The tall woman forgot herself, looked, and Hanhai dealt her such a blow with her strong, sharp whip that she took the woman's head off. The Mangathai's horse ran away. Hanhai followed on her swift steed, caught him, brought him back, and killed him. She gathered wood and burned up the horse and the Mangathai woman.

Hanhai then went to find her brother. First she found his head and then his body; she put them together, wrapped them in two silk cloths, tied the bundles to the saddle, and went to Red Mountain, where her brother was buried the first time. She prayed one day and one night to the Heavenly Burkans, then buried him deep, far from foxes and other animals.

Then Hanhai went home, searched the book, and read in it: "In the west lives Gazar Bain Khan. He has a daughter, Nalhan Taiji Basagan; she is the only person in all the world who can raise Alamaldjin the second time. But to raise him she must become his wife; she must marry him."

When Hanhai finished reading she cried, "I am a maiden; how can I go to that country?"

She read the book three days and three nights and then prepared to go. She put on her brother's clothes, took his weapons, mounted his steed, and rode to the boundary.

"All is left behind," thought Hanhai; "what will become of the people and the cattle, who will protect them?" But she had immense magic power, and by that power she made a great iron wall around the whole country; then she made a flat dome of silver above it. Over the silver she put earth, and made grass and trees grow out of it; so that her brother's whole country, with the people, flocks, herds of horses, cattle, and everything that was in it, was hidden and unseen by all the world outside. On the east she left small, secret apertures to let in the sunshine. Then she rode westward swiftly in search of Nalhan Taiji Basagan.

Hanhai went far, rode three weeks, till at last she saw a great white stone yurta. She rode up to the yurta, and found ninety horse skulls on ninety stakes, and on ninety other stakes ninety outfits of men and horses. She stopped her steed and shed many tears.

With women hair is long, but thought is short. She stood a while thinking, strengthening her heart, and then she said to herself, "Once I have started on this business I will go to the end of it."

She made her horse a flint chip, put the chip in her pocket, turned herself into a skunk, burrowed under the yurta and into it. Burrowed forward, peeped up at last through the floor, and saw a Mangathai sleeping. He had seven hundred heads on his body, and seventy horns on the heads.

"I have never heard," thought she, "of a Mangathai with so many heads; this must be the greatest, the father and chief of all Mangathais."

Near the Mangathai lay an axe eighty fathoms broad. Hanhai became Alamaldjin, seized the axe, roused the Mangathai, and said to him, "I have come to thee with battle!"

He woke, strove to rise; she hewed his central head off with the axe, which was full of magic. "Cunning people have come; this is the end of me!" these were the last words of the seven hundred headed Mangathai.

Hanhai made a forest by magic, and on one of the largest of the trees she wrote, "This will be a sacred forest henceforward;" then she mounted and rode away.

Next she met a twenty-seven headed Mangathai on horseback.

"Why art thou riding through my father's land?" asked he. "No man passes on foot or on horseback and remains alive after that. I will hurry home, read in my book, and see who killed my brother by magic. I will hunt and slay the one who killed him." As he turned to go home Hanhai sent an arrow after him, saying to the arrow, "If thou kill that Mangathai and his horse come back to me." The arrow came back and said to her, "The Mangathai and his horse are dead."

Hanhai rode on, but soon met another Mangathai, this one had seventy-seven heads, and called out, "What kind of man art thou, and from what country?"

"People call me Alamaldjin Bogdo," said she.

"I have heard," replied the Mangathai, "that such a one was born. Art thou he?"

"I am."

"My father and I wished to go to-morrow and kill thee," said the Mangathai, "and now thou art here of thyself. That is well! Thou hast killed many already, but I have finished better than thou art. What work will there be with thee? Get down from thy horse!"

Hanhai slipped down quickly. They sprang at each other and the struggle began,—a dreadful struggle, with teeth and with hands. Three days and three nights they fought. There was no flesh left on the Mangathai; all his ribs and bones were visible. On the fourth day he fell. He roared terribly. Hanhai went to a larch tree, opened it, cut off some of the Mangathai's heads and thrust him in there. With magic power she hooped the tree up with ninety-five hoops, all of them iron; killed the Mangathai, killed his horse, and went farther.

Soon she met a Mangathai with five hundred heads, fifty horns on the heads and a goat-skin thrown over his shoulders.

"Thou hast killed my father and two brothers; whither now?" shouted the Mangathai, springing from his horse. "I will tear thee into bits!"

"Very well," answered Hanhai, coming down from her steed. They rushed at each other, fought nine days and nine nights without stopping. Ravens and magpies flew in from the north and the south and called out to them: "Fight on, good heroes! Fight on! Give us flesh, give us plenty of it."

"We can do nothing by wrestling," said the Mangathai. "Let us use arrows now. I will go to the southwest, thou to the northeast mountain and shoot from there."

Hanhai consented. They were to rest for one day.

The Mangathai had arrows as big as a larch tree. Hanhai rested near a forest. Two elks came into view; she killed both. Then she made a fire, took a pine and a larch tree for spits and roasted the elks. She rose up at sunrise and ate the animals.

The Mangathai signaled to begin. "I must shoot first," cried he.

"No," said Hanhai; "I came in search of thee, I will shoot first."

"I will never agree to that!" screamed the Mangathai. "Thou hast killed my father and two brothers, now it is thy wish to kill me!"

"Shoot!" said Hanhai, and she lay down. The Mangathai's arrow hissed and roared as it flew toward her, but she turned instantly into a very hard stone and the arrow broke in two on that stone. She became Hanhai again, thrust the broken arrow into her saddle, and signaled to the Mangathai, "Thou art not able to hit me, thou hast only hit my saddle."

"I missed," said the Mangathai, "but do not shoot at me to-day, shoot to-morrow."

"Am I to wait days to please thee? I will shoot now!" cried Hanhai, and she sent a magic arrow. That arrow shivered the Mangathai into fragments, broke him into small pieces. Hanhai went then to the broken body of the Mangathai. His horse did not run away, but stood weeping there near his master. Hanhai killed the horse, collected wood, and burned master and horse into ashes.

After that she rode farther; rode swiftly, till she came at last to two seas, where the land between was only one ell wide and rose one ell above the water. The sea on the right was a poison sea, the sea on the left was a sea of fresh water. Hanhai halted, and said to her steed, "Thou canst not pass this sea." She made flint of him and turned herself into a swallow, then she flew on, flew for three hours, reached the other side, then turned herself and the horse back to their own forms.

There was a very high mountain on the road straight out in front of them. At the foot of it were blind, crooked, lame, and deformed people, people with every ill possible, and the bodies of dead men and of dead horses. There were mounds of those bodies, piles of them, hills of them. When Hanhai saw these heaps of bones of the men and horses that had fallen while trying to climb the great mountain she asked her steed, "Canst thou cross this mountain or not?"

"I cannot cross, as thou knowest," said the horse.

She made a flint chip of the horse, put the chip in her pocket, turned herself into a squirrel and ran up the mountain. She ran on and on till her paws were nearly gone, till she had climbed one third of the mountain, and was falling; then she caught on a tree and became a skunk. As a skunk she went up the second third with great difficulty; then became a swallow, and flew the last third of the way. Three days and three nights and the half of another day was she flying till she dropped on the summit, and lay there without stirring for one whole day and a half of a day. Then she revived and looked around. Right there in front of her was a spring of the Water of Life, Youth, and Health. A gold goblet hung from a bough of the tree by a chain of pure silver. Hanhai drank, gave her horse to drink, and then made a fire.

The next morning she felt stronger and better. She drank again from the water of the spring. After that she looked and saw far away the great yurta of Gazar Bain Khan; she saw also his countless cattle and horses. The yurta was immense, a verst long, a great white house of silver, glistening and glorious, straight out southwest from her.

She mounted immediately and rode to the house of Gazar Bain Khan. Three horses were tied to a hitching-post near it. She tied hers also and entered. Three splendid young men had entered before her.

BURIATS — HUSBAND AND WIFE IN THE HAYFIELD, OLKHON ISLAND. *Page* 116
Their implements for turning and raking grass

BURIATS—HUSBAND AND WIFE IN THE HAYFIELD, OLKHON ISLAND.

Their implements for turning and raking grass

REPRESENTATIONS OF BURIAT GODS. *Page* 121
These are held sacred in each Buriat household

REPRESENTATIONS OF BURIAT GODS.

These are held sacred in each Buriat household

"A greeting from me to thee, father-in-law!" said Hanhai.

"Whence hast thou come, a son of what khan art thou?" asked Gazar Bain Khan.

"I am Alamaldjin Bogdo. I have heard that thou hast a beautiful daughter, Nalhan Taiji is her name; I have come to ask for her. In my book it is written that she must be my bride."

"These suitors here came earlier; they have not spoken yet. Why dost thou hurry so?"

"I had no thought to wait for them or for others. I tell at once what my wish is."

"We came to ask for thy daughter," said the three young men.

"She will choose whom she likes; I will not force her," said the father.

"Are we to wait here or go to her?"

"Spend the night here. To-morrow I will call all the people. Let my daughter come out then and choose him who may please her."

Next day there was a feast. Nalhan Taiji, who was behind forty-three doors in the forty-third chamber, came out. Her father gave her a goblet of wine and a marrow bone to give to the man who pleased her most. "Here are four bridegrooms," said he, "give these to the one you like best."

She looked a number of times at the four, and at last gave the bone and the wine to Hanhai. When the choice was made the people and the suitors went away

"Go to thy bride and rest; thy horse will be cared for and fed," said the father-in-law.

Nalhan Taiji was waiting in her chamber. Drink, food, and all things were ready. They sat there and feasted till night was near, then Hanhai sprang up. "I must go now," said she, "I may not stay with thee longer. Since my horse is enchanted, it is impossible to stay."

"It cannot be! On that horse thou travelest, how can thy stay here affect him? What sort of bridegroom art thou to leave me thus?"

"Only let me go home on this horse, then I will leave him. I

will send him back to the Altai Deda, where he pastures in the mountains with thirteen wild deer. In all this world he is the luckiest and best horse for the road. No ill is possible with him, but misfortune would happen in a moment were I to break his enchantment, which is this, that no man fully married may ride him. Not only should I die, but my wife would die also."

Nalhan Taiji believed her bridegroom now; she let him go from that forty-third chamber. The next morning his father-in-law called him: "I will give thee my daughter, but thou must do something for me: bring me a quill from the wing of Khan Herdik, I wish to write with it. If thou bring not the quill I will not give my daughter."

"How is this?" asked Hanhai. "I have barely ridden to thee, and now must I go to another country?"

"Do as may please thee. Bring me the quill or thou wilt not get my daughter."

"I will go, but let me see Nalhan Taiji."

Hanhai went to her bride. "I am going on a long journey," said she; "thou must help me in some way."

"Thou wilt meet no hindrance on the journey; but Herdik Khan will delay in giving thee the feather. This is the second year that he is fighting with Mogoi Khan. Thou wilt not get the quill till the war is ended."

"I cannot wait till the war is ended," said Hanhai. "I must go at once and thou must assist me."

"Thou wilt not feel hunger or need much sleep. I cannot give thee other assistance," said Nalhan Taiji.

Hanhai rode away swiftly. On the fifth day she came to an immensely high mountain. On that mountain stood a great pine; ten men could not embrace it. On that tree lived Khan Herdik and his two daughters.

"Whence dost thou come, good youth?" asked the daughters of Hanhai.

"I am Alamaldjin Bogdo, I have come on business to thy father."

"Art thou a khan? Was thy father a khan also?" asked Khan Herdik's elder daughter. "Our father is at war with Mogoi Khan. He is near the Icy Ocean, but thou canst go to him."

Hanhai set out for the Icy Ocean, and when she reached it Khan Herdik had arrived three days earlier. She found him on a great pine tree near the ocean shore. Hanhai bowed down to Khan Herdik. "A greeting from me to thee!" said she, and then told him the cause of her coming.

"I cannot give thee a feather now," said Herdik. "In four days I must fight with Mogoi Khan. If thou help me I will give thee my feather."

Hanhai agreed, made her horse into a flint, put him in her pocket, became an eagle herself, and sat there on the pine tree with Herdik.

"Mogoi Khan comes out of that valley," said Khan Herdik. "He has two heads, and between the two is a shining white spot; if thou hit that spot he is dead. I will fly away with thee then and give thee a quill."

On the fourth day Mogoi Khan came out of the Icy Ocean and came through the valley straight toward them. If Mogoi Khan conquered, he was to get Khan Herdik's daughters. If Khan Herdik conquered, he would have Mogoi Khan's daughters.

When Mogoi Khan was near enough Hanhai saw the white spot, sent her arrow into it, and killed Mogoi, then took her own form. Herdik Khan put her on his back and hurried to his daughters at the pine tree, and there they feasted three whole days.

"Thanks for thy aid. Take the quill," said Herdik. "Tell thy father-in-law that he will hardly lift that quill to write. But thou and I will be friends in the future."

Hanhai returned to her father-in-law. On the sixth day she reached his yurta, tied her horse to the hitching-post and left the feather leaning against the corner of the yurta. The great building bent till it was near falling.

"Misfortune will come from this quill! It will break down my yurta!" cried Gazar Bain Khan. "Take it away! Take it back to Khan Herdik!"

"Have the wedding and I'll take it." Hanhai turned then to Nalhan Taiji: "I have brought the quill, now your father does not want it, and asks me to take it back."

"You need not take it back yourself; make it small, tie it to your arrow, and tell the arrow what to do."

Hanhai did as her bride advised. "Do no harm to Khan Herdik," said she to the arrow, "only return the feather to him."

The arrow did as commanded and came back again. The next day the people had all assembled for the wedding when a female Shaman cried out: "What a misery! Our khan is crazy to give his daughter to a woman!"

The khan was frightened and sent for Gazari Ganek, a champion, to try the bridegroom in a contest. Hanhai hurried to her steed. "What am I to do now? How am I to hide my bosom?"

"Bind two silk kerchiefs around thy breast and tie them tightly crosswise. All will be well then."

"What answer can I give if people ask why I do this?"

"Say that thy breast was injured by thy horse, and thou must keep it bound in this manner."

Gazari, the champion, did not seem so very heavy or tall, but he was strong and stalwart. Hanhai dismounted, took off her outer dress and stood in wrestler's trousers. Her horse whispered to her, "I will snort and raise a cloud of dust; then seize him, hurl him high above thy shoulder, and drive him deep into the earth before thee."

When she went out to wrestle people asked, "Why is thy breast bound?"

"My horse hurt me on the road and I had to bind up my breast."

"That may be so," said the people.

The two closed; their strength was nearly equal. The horse snorted, raised a terrible dust. Hanhai seized Gazari, hurled him high above her shoulder and dashed him to the earth. He fell head downward, and went into the ground to his shoulders. She grasped his legs, pulled him out and threw him to one side.

"What kind of champion is this?" asked she.

The champion was very heavy, nine horses drew him away. "I say that this bridegroom is a woman!" cried Shorgo, the Shaman. "Let four men go to the sea and swim with her; they will find out then what she is."

Four men hurried off to Narin Dalai (Narrow Sea). Hanhai mounted and rode to the shore. The men were already in the sea when she came in sight. The horse snorted. The waves rushed high upon the shore and spray was dashed everywhere. Hanhai undressed while the waves were roaring madly; no one could tell whether she was man or woman. She swam out very far from shore, swam quickly around the men, passed them. No one could come near her or catch her, she swam with such swiftness. At last she swam in directly to shore. The horse snorted. Again the waves rose high. Waves and thick spray were around her, and before the men could come to shore she was out, dressed, and on horseback.

"What shall we say?" asked the men of one another. "Shall we say man or woman when the khan asks us?"

"Of course say man," replied one of the four. And all agreed to say man.

The khan asked the four, "Is the bridegroom a man or a woman?"

"A man," said the four.

Again Shorgo sang out: "This is a woman, this is no man! This is a woman, this is no man!"

Hanhai now made a gray wolf by magic. Not far from the khan's yurta a herd of five hundred horses were grazing. The gray wolf sprang at the horses. When they saw the great creature they were frightened and ran, stampeded to the yurta. There was great terror among the people; they had to follow and kill the gray wolf. Shorgo, the Shaman, was left alone. Hanhai slipped into the place. There was a large barrel of sour milk standing near. She seized the witch and put her head first into the barrel.

When the khan came back from killing the wolf the bride-groom took the Shaman woman by the feet and stirred the milk with her as with a stick.

"How is this?" asked Hanhai. "Instead of wood you mix milk with an old woman. You stir milk with people's bodies!"

"What a wonderful thing!" exclaimed the khan. "I left this old woman here alive and well. How did she fall into the milk barrel?"

"I suppose," said the bridegroom, "that she crawled into the milk from fright when the wolf was running after the horses."

"But what shall I do with her now?" asked the khan. "This woman was a Shaman; people may think that I killed her; they may say so."

"They will say so, surely," said Hanhai. "But give me thy stallion, I'll mount him, and carry the old woman off to her own yurta very quickly."

The stallion was brought. Hanhai, who had driven a nail into each of her boot heels, mounted and took the old woman. Shorgo, the Shaman, swayed like a drunken person as the stallion rushed forward. When Hanhai reached the old woman's yurta she called to the Shaman's three daughters, "Come out and take your mother; she is drunk!" Then she drove a nail into one side of the horse with her heel. The girls ran out. The stallion, made wild by the prick of the nail, sprang aside quickly; threw both the old woman and the bridegroom. The bridegroom fell under, was senseless, seemed dead; the horse ran off home madly.

Hanhai lay motionless; she waited to hear what the daughters would say. All three began to cry. "If only our mother had died it would not have been so bad, but now the khan's son-in-law is killed, what will happen? What will become of us?"

After a while the bridegroom recovered. "It appears," said he to the old woman's daughters, "that I only fainted, but maybe your mother is killed."

"We were only weeping for you. We can outlive the loss of our mother," said the daughters.

Hanhai went back on foot to the khan's yurta. The khan was glad to be freed from the suspicion of killing the Shaman woman. "Now, father-in-law, we must have the wedding immediately," said Hanhai.

The wedding began again on the morrow, and lasted nine days and nine nights. "What present will you give me?" asked the bride of her father, when she was ready to go home with her bridegroom.

The father gave her a horse ninety fathoms long with ears nine ells high. The mother gave her a silver goblet; the brother a silk, magic kerchief, which had power to bring a dead man to life and make a poor man rich.

The young couple started for home, and the people followed. Hanhai fastened a larch tree to her horse's tail, and rode on ahead to show the places for rest, refreshment, smoking, and night camps.

On the seventh day Hanhai was almost in view of her hidden kingdom. Before she came up to this covered country she said to the young wife, "I must hurry home before thee; I am sure there is bad management. I must put things in order, and make ready to receive thee. Follow on my trail." She hurried quickly to the boundary, removed the iron walls. The silver dome, the grass, and forest all vanished.

Then, instead of going home directly, Hanhai rushed off to her brother's grave at Red Mountain, raised the body, and took it home with her. There was nothing left save the skeleton; this Hanhai put in the yurta, which the bride must enter first, and then the guests who followed with her. She put the bones on the floor near the door, turned herself into a fly, sat in the room, and waited.

The guests rode up quickly. Hanhai's father and mother were so old now that they did not leave the yurta. Bride and guests entered. The skeleton was on the floor before the bride.

"How quickly thou art asleep!" said the bride, and raising the blanket she saw the skeleton, and was terribly frightened. Hanhai, who had undressed before turning into a fly had thrown the clothes near her brother's skeleton. The bride had power, was possessed of great magic. "Since things are thus they must be cured," thought she, and stepped thrice over the skeleton. Then she took juniper leaves, put them into her silver goblet, burned them, and walked thrice around the bones while the leaves were burning. Next she threw leaves and coals into the fire, and covered the skeleton head with the goblet turned bottom upward, then she waved her kerchief thrice, saying each time before she waved it, "How long thou art sleeping!" The third time that Nalhan Taiji waved the kerchief Alamaldjin sprang up.

"Somehow I have slept long," said he. Immediately he commanded the people to come, and all feasted. They feasted nine days and nine nights with great pleasure.

The fly slipped out of the yurta. Not far away was a forest, and it flew there. The fly made itself into a hare in that forest. Three days later Alamaldjin, while out to look for wild beasts, saw many hare tracks. "There are hares in this place. We should trap them," said he; and he went to set traps. The next day, when he looked at his traps he found one hare caught, but alive yet.

"See what a nice hare I have caught. I will tame it, and keep it as a pet," said Alamaldjin; and he took the hare to the yurta. The hare seemed fond of Nalhan Taiji, ran after her whenever she stepped out of the yurta.

"I will go and see what is happening in my pastures," said Alamaldjin one day.

While he was away his wife began to make a silk shuba. The hare came in, stood on its hind legs, and looked at her sewing. This watching annoyed the young woman. At last she threw pincers at the hare, wounded her nose and scratched it. When the husband came home the hare was sitting near the door. "Who beat this poor hare?" inquired Alamaldjin.

"I was sewing; it came near me too often, annoyed me; I threw pincers at it," said the wife.

"Better kill the poor beast than torment it. Why torment it? I will not permit this." And he began to beat his wife, beat her soundly.

"Do not beat me!" screamed Nalhan Taiji. "I will not strike the hare a second time."

The hare ran away then, ran outside. Alamaldjin beat on, beat his wife more. She began to cry bitterly. The hare turned to a woman and went into the yurta.

"What art thou doing, brother?" cried she. "Thou art beating the wife whom I brought thee. How much have I suffered from thy folly already? How much have I passed through?" Then she told the whole story. Told how her brother had died twice; told all the wonders. Then came tarasun and a feast. There was much conversation and great joy.

"I will not go far away from thee," said Hanhai to her brother the next morning. "Make me a white stone yurta with silver roof." He did so, and she lived ever after in that white stone yurta which Alamaldjin Bogdo built for her.

THE TWIN BOYS, ALTIN SHAGOY AND MUNGUN SHAGOY

VERY, very long ago lived Hodoy Shon Mergen Khan. He had a wife named Agwi Nogón; he had also a sister, whose name we do not know.

Hodoy Khan said one day, "I will build a great white, square roomy yurta."

And he built for himself an immense house, in the upper part of which he made many windows, and in the lower part many doors. The main building was gold on the outside and silver inside. The wings and rear buildings were silver.

Hodoy Khan made bazaars, he made thirty-three of them, and thrice daily at each of these were exchanged gold and silver for furs of all sorts; sable, beaver, and ermine were offered for sale in them. He sold to twelve other khans, and to peoples of seventy-three languages.

South of his golden yurta ten thousand cattle were at pasture; thousands and thousands of people were under his hand, and obeyed him.

Hodoy loved his one sister very greatly, so he built a splendid yurta for her, with many windows in the upper part and many doors in the lower. She was not living long in this splendid new yurta when the wife of a Mangathai came to her. This woman was a lying, deceitful, old flat-nose, who began to persuade the khan's sister to marry her son, a hundred and eight headed Mangathai.

"My brother is very stern," said Hodoy's sister. "He is chief of the thirteen khans; I do not wish to disobey him. He will not let me marry; he wants me to live in this house where I am, and be near him."

The mother went away after these words. "I will put an end to Hodoy Khan," said she in her own mind. She went out to the broad steppe, the open country, and got a plant which makes all people who eat of it swell up, but does not otherwise injure them.

"Eat this," said she to the khan's sister; and foolishly she ate it. Then she began to swell up, and was terribly frightened.

"Nothing can cure you, or save you," said the Mangathai woman, "but the liver of Shara Nagóy (Yellow Dog). Tell your brother to go for it."

She went then to her brother, and said: "I am sick, very sick."

"What hast thou seen in dreams?" asked Hodoy Khan.

"I saw in a dream that Yellow Dog lives beyond nine mountain ranges, and that if I eat his liver I shall be well; if not, I shall continue to swell and shall die surely."

"I have always told thee," said the brother, "that Shara Nagóy is a great friend of mine; how canst thou eat my friend's liver?"

"I tell thee my dream," replied the sister.

The sister went home. Hodoy Khan saddled a red horse that was ninety fathoms long and had ears three ells high; he mounted, took his bow with its quiver, and rode away with all swiftness. He rode and rode, but still he was far from Yellow Dog's kingdom. Then he made his horse into a flint chip, put the chip in his pocket, made himself into a wolf, ran on and on, but the wolf could not reach Yellow Dog's kingdom. He traveled till a great swamp was before him, then he turned himself into a falcon, flew and flew far; flew over the great swamp and over a wet meadow. After that he turned himself into a fox, and raced on, raced far beyond that. Still the fox could not go to Yellow Dog's kingdom.

Now Hodoy took his own form again and went toward Ulan Hada, a mountain which seemed to touch the sky. He could not pass over that mountain, so he tried to go around it, but found at one side a stream of blood flowing down straight in front of him. This blood was from people who had fallen and killed themselves while trying to climb that mountain.

"How are we to pass this mountain?" asked Hodoy of his horse.

"We must go back eighty versts," said the horse. "Then I will rush forward with all my might. But hold thou to me firmly."

They went back; the horse rushed forward, sprang, reached the top, crossed the mountain, went down on the other side, and went farther, but could not reach Yellow Dog's land for a long time. They came to the boundary at last, and crossed it. Yellow Dog heard them approaching, and began to call to them, to attract, and to draw them on by his magic.

When Yellow Dog called Hodoy's horse stuck his feet in the earth and resisted, held back with all his strength. The wind made by Yellow Dog raised Hodoy's skirts above his head and was dragging them off. The power that drew him on was tearing the clothes from his body. Now on his horse he rose to the sky to get nails there. The seven sky smiths gave him the nails, and he nailed his skirts to the saddle behind and in front.

Yellow Dog then began to howl, and all the nails were drawn and dropped out of the saddle. All the trees in the forest round about fell to the earth from the howling. The horse could resist no longer. It rushed forward swiftly till Hodoy saw Yellow Dog's open mouth before him; the upper jaw touching the sky, the lower jaw on the earth; he moved not. Hodoy was pulled off his horse and drawn into the mouth. He grasped an upper tooth with one hand and pushed a lower tooth with his foot.

"Why come to fight me?" inquired Yellow Dog. "We were friends, thou and I; for that reason I will leave thee alive."

He placed Hodoy in a deep pit, poured living water upon him, that he might live and not die there. "Remain here," said Yellow Dog, "till a son of thine comes to rescue thee." Then he placed a great heavy stone over the pit and left Hodoy covered there, safely.

Next he turned to the horse, put all Hodoy's things on his back, and said: "If thy master has sons, or daughters, take these things to them."The horse went home, but found no one there except Hodoy's wife. The sister was gone; the houses had vanished; all was gone. The young Mangathai had taken sister, houses, cattle, people, and had left nothing behind but a poor little yurta, and Hodoy's wife, living in it. Soon after twins were born to her; their backs were of gold and their hearts were of silver. They grew so fast that three days after their birth the skin of a sheep three years old was too narrow to wrap around them.

The Mangathai by his magic knew that Hodoy's wife had twins, and he said: "We must kill those two children."

A magpie flew into the yurta, and told the poor mother that the wicked Mangathai was coming to kill her two children.

She took the boys, put them on the red horse, with provisions, and rode away to a mountain. She left the boys on that mountain and went home again quickly. Soon after the Mangathai came to her wretched little yurta.

"Thou hast two young sons," said he. "Where are they? Where hast thou put them?"

One ewe with twin lambs was left to the woman. This ewe was the last of her flock. She had taken the twin lambs and burned them.

"Tell me where thy two boys are!" screamed the Mangathai. "I threw them into the fire," said the mother, "because they were shapeless, born prematurely."

"If they were thrown into the fire there must be bones left. Where are their bones?"

"Here they are," said she, showing the bones of the little twin lambs.

The Mangathai looked at them. "These are the bones of a beast," said he, "not the bones of children," and he fell to beating her with a club very cruelly.

She would tell nothing about her sons, except that the charred bones were theirs. The Mangathai went home; then he sent seven hundred men quickly to search in all places, to hunt for the children and find them at any cost.

The men searched three days for the children. On the fourth day the whole company was at the foot of the mountain and the boys on the summit.

"Let us go down," said one boy to the other at midnight. "Let us take provisions from those men who are hunting for us."

When the boys reached the foot of the mountain the seven hundred were sleeping. The brothers took two saddled horses and two baskets of bomshoy (cream mixed with rye flour) and went back to the mountain top. They sent home the red horse, ate bomshoy, and started; rode away southward; escaped on the two small horses. The seven hundred could not find them, and went back empty handed.

The brothers rode on and on till they reached a broad meadow. At one side of the meadow was a poor little hut with a big smoke rising out of it. They tied their horses to the hitching-post and went into the hut. There they saw a gray old man, and a little old woman sitting by the fire, but no child was there.

"We are childless," said the man and the woman; "be our children. Whose sons are ye? Where is your birthplace?"

"We were born on Ulan Hada. We know not our father or mother. We are willing to be your children."

The boys let out their horses and sat down to eat. The next morning they went off with the old man to herd sheep. While following the sheep they saw wild goats racing around through the forest. "What beasts are those?" asked the brothers.

"If a man is a master at shooting he kills them; they are good to eat," said the old man. "If he is not a master he looks at them, and does nothing."

The next day the old man made bows and arrows, and gave them to the twin brothers. "Shoot," said he. They shot, and killed many goats. The old man and woman dressed and cooked the flesh gladly.

Farther on in the forest was a house. "What is that?" asked the boys of the old man and woman.

"Small boys like you must not look into that house," said the old people.

"Why not?" asked they. "Any man may look in, or he may enter."

The next day, when out herding, they left the sheep, and went into the house. Inside were two hundred men, one half of them crying, the other half laughing.

"Why are ye shut up here?" asked the brothers. "Why are some of you laughing, while others are crying?"

"Those who are crying will be eaten to-day by the Mangathai; those who are laughing will be eaten to-morrow. The Mangathai comes every day to eat people. Do ye go away quickly."

"We have no fear of that Mangathai," said the boys. "What will ye give us if we kill him?"

"One half of our gold and one half of our cattle."

"When the Mangathai comes we will be here. Shut the door, and bar it firmly. Do not let him enter."

The two boys turned into two bees, one above the door, and one at the side of it. When the Mangathai knocked the people answered, "We'll not let you in!"

"Who taught you to keep me out?"

"No one."

"If you do not let me in at the door, I'll come down through the smoke-hole!" said the Mangathai in a rage, and he started to climb to the smoke-hole, then the two bees went one into one ear, the other into the other ear of the Mangathai, and stung the brain in him till he died in great torment.

The two hundred men gathered wood, burned the Mangathai, and scattered his ashes; then they brought meat with tarasun, and feasted the brothers. The next day they gave half their gold and half their cattle to the boys, who sent all this wealth to their mother's yurta. They went back then to the old man and woman, and said this to them:

"We are the sons of Hodoy Khan. We must go to our parents. We can live with you no longer."

The old people cried, and begged, but the brothers went home in spite of their tears. They found the gold in their mother's yurta, and the cattle at pasture near by.

"Where is our father?" asked they.

"Thy father was killed long ago while away from home fighting," said the mother.

"Where was he killed?"

"I will not tell, for you are too young yet to hear of this." After that she boiled milk for them. When it was boiling they seized her, thrust her hands into the milk, and said: "Tell us now where our father is." Then she told all that the red horse had told her. "He is in Yellow Dog's kingdom where a great stone confines him," said Agwi Nogón.

The two brothers mounted their horses straightway and rode to Yellow Dog's kingdom. When they were near that great kingdom Yellow Dog heard them coming and pulled them in by his magic, and when they were close enough, he asked:

"Whose sons are ye?" They told him. "I was always a friend of your father," said Yellow Dog, "but his sister forced him to come here to kill me, so I put him in a pit, and placed a heavy stone over him. Draw him out of that pit, and take him home to his own place."

The stone was very heavy. The elder of the twins raised it a little, the younger raised it higher, with great effort, and then they rolled it to one side completely. Their father was wondrous to look at. His hair had grown out through his cap; his toe-nails had gone through his boots, and his finger-nails through his gloves. He was barely alive when they freed him.

A raven was flying from the north, it was flying toward them with great speed. When she came near, they called out to her: "Bring the Water of Life. Bring it quickly!"

The raven flew away, and wherever she found that water, she brought back her beak full, and poured it over Hodoy. He revived at once, became youthful, shook himself and stood up. "How long I have slept!" said he.

He begged Yellow Dog then to go with him and his two sons to punish the Mangathai, and kill him.

Yellow Dog agreed and they started off together. When Hodoy was near home he sent his sons to their mother, and went with his friend to meet the Mangathai. Not far from the Mangathai's house Hodoy Khan saw his own cattle, and among them a bull that in fighting had lost one horn and one eye. They met two herdsmen and asked:

"Have ye not seen any strange cattle? Ours ran away from us."

The herdsmen gave no answer. Hodoy and Yellow Dog broke the necks of those herdsmen. The two friends went on farther, and saw Hodoy's horses. Again they met two herdsmen, and Hodoy asked: "Have ye seen my horses?" They gave no answer, and received the same death as the other two.

Next they met two women driving seventy small calves. These women did not answer questions put to them, and they were killed also.

When the friends were near the house of the Mangathai they turned into two immense dogs of great strength, and became of the very same age. Everything was bright at the

Mangathai's yurta, gleaming. Guards would not let in the strange, dreadful dogs; the dogs tore the heads off those guards, and then walked into the yurta very boldly.

The Mangathai was sitting at the left side of the room, his wife was at the side opposite, and was kneading a rawhide. The dogs began smelling around.

"Such immense dogs," said the Mangathai, "must belong to a very rich man; give them something to eat. It may serve us to feed them."

When food was given the dogs fought for it savagely. The Mangathai tried to quiet them. The dogs fell on him. He rushed from the house, and ran off to save himself. The two dogs followed and attacked him outside. Yellow Dog tore him to pieces, ate him up where he killed him, devoured every bit of his body.

When Yellow Dog had finished the Mangathai, the two friends took their own forms immediately. "Now," asked they of the Mangathai's wife, "which wilt thou have as a present, seventy horse tails, or seventy sharp stakes?" She answered not a word. They took her by the hair then, and dragged her to a place where three roads met, nailed her alive to a very great larch tree, poured the Water of Life on her so that she might survive every torment, and live on for countless years, unable to die. Then they put in front of the tree two casks, on one was a blunt knife, on the other a pair of dull scissors. On the tree they wrote this inscription: "When a man passes here he must cut, with the knife, a piece of flesh from this woman's body; when a woman goes by she must use the dull scissors in cutting."

Each time that flesh was cut from the woman a new piece grew quickly, taking the place of the old one cut off by the knife or the scissors.

Hodoy now drove home all his cattle. Yellow Dog went with him, and they had a great feast; a sea of drink and a mountain of meat for all present. Then he gave half of his cattle and riches to Yellow Dog, and conducted him homeward with honor. "We shall be friends," said he, "from this day forth, and forever."

The next day Hodoy summoned all his people and said: "I have conquered the Mangathai, and these are my two sons." Among the guests was one old man, white bearded to the knees. "I will give names to thy sons if thou wish," said this old man. Hodoy gave permission.

"The elder will be called Altin Shagoy, Gold Knee Cap, the younger Mungun Shagoy, Silver Knee Cap," and so it was.

NOTES

MY collection of Buriat myths and folk-tales is small. The work should have been done years ago. I found many incomplete stories and fragments of myths, and am convinced that during the past five decades a large amount of rich Mongol material has been lost. The collection of the folk-lore of the different peoples of the world should not be neglected, for it is of great value. It is the entire stock of wisdom accumulated by the unlettered masses of mankind in all ages. Like language, it is the product neither of one mind nor a given number of minds, but of all the various groups which together form humanity. Like language, it is property bequeathed by anonymous ancestors or predecessors. As there is no nation, tribe, or group of persons without language, there is none without folk-lore, which in a broad sense is the fruit of the intellectual activity of men before they are modified by what is called education, and represents their religion, philosophy, and literature, if the latter term may be used with reference to people unacquainted with letters.

The term "Folk-lore" first appeared in 1846. Mr. Thoms, in a letter to the "London Atheneum" dated August 12 of that year, signed Ambrose Merton, proposed it, adding, "Remember I claim the honor of introducing the epithet *Folk-lore*, as Disraeli does that of introducing *Fatherland* into the literature of this country." The term has, I believe, no exact equivalent in other languages. The words more nearly corresponding to our folk-lore refer only to that part of it included in stories or tales, such as the German *märchen*; the French *contes*; the Russian *skazki*; the Bohemian *pohadki*; and the Magyar *mések*.

I think no language except the English has a word that describes the result of the whole mental activity of uneducated men. The Russians have a term as broad as the English, *Narodnoe tvorchestvo*, meaning people's creativeness. This phrase describes the activity, while ours gives the result of the activity.

The folk-lore of the great nations of antiquity, the Greeks and Romans, is lost to us in its popular form, which we can only infer from what we find preserved in literature, religion, and art. The folk-lore of the Kelts, Teutons, and Slavs has come to us preserved by the uneducated people. Keltic folk-lore from Irish and Welsh sources has entered largely into the poetry and imaginative literature of western Europe. The folk-lore of Germany has had great influence on national literature and music. By a happy chance the Scandinavian branch of Teutonic folk-lore was preserved by Iceland, and preserved in its most developed form,—one in which it more nearly approaches the maturity of Grecian mythology than that of any other folk-lore in Europe.

The folk-lore of the Aryans of India is preserved in the Vedes and the great poems, the Maha Bharata and the Ramayana, and exists in a rich growth of popular lore, only a part of which is yet collected. What there is in Persia in a modern form is unknown; of the ancient stories the *Shah Nameh*, or Book of Kings, is the great storehouse.

The Slavs, the most numerous of the Aryan race in Europe, present the most interesting field possible for the philologist, and no division of the race has a richer or more beautiful stock of folk-lore.

Folk-lore, though interesting in many directions and of the utmost value,—for taken together with language it furnishes us with a documentary history of the human mind,—is undoubtedly of most importance in what may be called its religions, meaning by religions theories of the universe and man's place in it.

The first five myths in this volume are not considered as myths by the Mongols, but as true descriptions of the Creation, the destruction of evil creatures, and the preparation of the world for its present inhabitants. They are for the Pagan Buriats what the Bible is for Christian peoples. Esege Malan is the Creator. To destroy the harmful creatures which inhabited the earth, Gesir Bogdo, his grandson, leaves heaven and is born of woman. The Iron Hero is created for the purpose of aiding Gesir Bogdo. When the earth is purified and inhabited by man, Mindiu appears.

MINDIÚ QUBUN NOYAN

The story of the birth of Mindiú Qúbun Noyan, whose father was one of the fifty-five Tengeris, is interesting as having parallels in many mythologies. The spirit of the god enters into a hailstone which falls to the earth and is swallowed by Mélûk Shin. In one version of this myth the hailstone falls on Mélûk Shin's head. In due time a son is born. This son of a heavenly Tengeri establishes the Mongol religion. He instructs the people, tells them to whom they are to pray, and what offerings are most acceptable to the gods. He consecrates the first Shamans and teaches them how to offer sacrifices.

In Greek mythology, Helena, the heroine of Troy, is the daughter of Leda and of Zeus, the over-arching heaven, with all its light. Leda after her death was raised to the rank of a divinity. No such honor was given Mélûk Shin, but her son is a god, or, at least, prayers are offered to him and he is supposed to answer them.

Among the Algonkin Indians there is a myth of the Earth-maiden who becomes a mother when looked upon by the sun. She gives birth to a daughter who is called Wakos ikwe, the fox woman. In time Wakos ikwe gives birth to a great hero, the benefactor of aboriginal man in America, the food-giver. This benefactor's name has not been changed or its meaning forgotten; he is known to be that warm air which, in fine weather, we see dancing and quivering above the earth,—that same hot, dancing air which Mother Earth gave to Esege Malan.

THE BURNING OF THE DEAD

It is almost certain that in Mongol mythology there was once a long myth about the Cuckoo from which we could get some idea of why this bird is connected with the burning of the dead. From the time that the cuckoo ceases to sing in August till its first song in spring no one who dies is burned. The Mongols do not know why this is. To questions asked the old men in the Buriat land, the answer was always the same: "Mindiú Qúbun told us when and how to burn our dead."

The cuckoo appears in many of the myths in this volume, and usually in connection with bringing the dead to life. When the Iron Hero is killed and thrown into the Black Misty Sea the cuckoo appears, and before her power the sea vanishes. When the skeleton is taken from the cask she sings as she moves around it. When she reaches the head the third time the Iron Hero springs up. When Hanhai is trying to bring her brother to life, she reads in her book that she must ask a certain cuckoo to aid her.

A Buriat will never kill or shoot at a cuckoo.

THE MORNING STAR

There was once a Mongol myth about Solobung Yubún, the morning star, but, so far as I could find, only fragments of it remain.

In the religious system of the Buriats the morning star is a great personage, the son of Esege Malan the Creator. Solobung Yubún is benevolent; if properly propitiated he will grant increase of crops and of cattle. But the offerings to him must be made at the dawn of day, and the dance in his honor must continue from sunset till daybreak.

Solobung Yubún, the Lucifer of the Latins, has in Mongol myths much the same character as in the myths of the Indians, especially in those of the Modocs and Delawares. The Modocs have a very long story which contains much valuable material. In this story the morning star appears as the attendant spirit of the sun. (Introduction to "Myths and Folk-lore of the Russians, Western Slavs, and Magyars.")

In Delaware myths the morning star often assists people by bringing daylight quickly. In Yana myths the morning star, Halai Anna, and the evening star, Paiowa, are the daughters of Wakara, new moon. ("Creation Myths of Primitive America.")

A SHAMAN STORY

The Buriats believe that the spirit can leave the body and return to it, even after having been away several days. Many of our Indian tribes have the same belief. When in the Indian Territory an old man of the Sauk tribe told me of the many countries he had seen "with his spirit," stating also that his spirit was not happy when away from the body, for it feared that something would happen to the body and it could not return. In India where this conception is universal among the native peoples, a "wise man" will say "I am going to such a village or town." He finds where his body will be safe, lies down and apparently falls asleep, then the spirit leaves the body, makes the long journey and returns. When the man wakens he describes accurately places which he knew nothing about previous to his spirit journey. The Malays do not like to waken a sleeper, lest they may harm him by disturbing his body while his spirit is away.

BURIAT BURIAL OF THE DEAD.

For three days after death the spirit remains near the body..It is lonely and sad, and is sorry to go from among the living. The Buriats think that when a mother dies her spirit hovers around in the mountains, returning to its home from time to time.

Professor Mooney of the Bureau of Ethnology notes a similar belief among the Cherokee Indians. (Journal of American Folk-lore, Vol. XIII.) "When a member of a family dies, it is believed that the spirit is loath to leave the scenes of life and go alone upon the long journey to the Darkening Land in the west."

GESIR BOGDO

The idea of a man's life being in one place and his body in another is common to many mythologies. In Mongol tales, no matter how the man is slaughtered or cut up, he does not die until his life is found and destroyed. This idea runs through Buriat mythology, and there are few myths in which it does not appear. The same conception is found in both Keltic and Slav mythology. There is a well-known Russian myth called "Koshchéi Without Death." Koshchéi was not deathless. His death was in the world but "in a place apart from him." There is a good illustration of the idea in "Phakir Chand," in "Folk-tales of Bengal," by Rev. Lal Behari Day; also in "The Herding of Cruachan," in "Folk and Hero Tales from Argyllshire," by Rev. D. MacInnes; and in the Norse tale of "The Giant who had no Heart in his Body."

The idea frequently occurs in the myths of our North American Indians. It seems to be explained by the fact that these tales deal with the adventures of non-human heroes. Whatever the names of the heroes are at present, the original heroes were not men.

Indian mythology sheds light upon this idea. There are myths which still preserve the primitive names of the characters. In a myth told me by the Warm Spring Indians of Oregon the conflict is between the North Wind and the South Wind. In a Wintu myth the heroes are Rain and Snow.

In a very beautiful myth, found among the Modoc Indians, who live near Klamath Lake, the chief personage is Winter, or Snow-maker, whose heart is hidden away at a distance. The heart is found by Winter's enemy, Heat. This enemy burns Snow-maker's heart and he dies.

When the real heroes are known we find the myth accurate and truthful. It is only when the heroes are looked upon as men and women that they perform impossible deeds,—deeds which only one of the forces of Nature could perform if it had the volition and desire of a person.

THE IRON HERO

The stubborn battles fought by the heroes of Buriat mythology are strikingly similar to those fought by mythologic Kelts. Buriat heroes often fight nine days and nine nights. They tear off all the flesh from each other's backs with their hands and from each other's breasts with their teeth, wherever they press their feet they knock out earth to the size of a calf, they make hills and valleys, "where there was a hill there is a valley, where there was a valley there is a hill."

Gaelic heroes fight till they make soft ground hard and hard ground soft, they make high places low and low places high, they bring cold spring water through hard gravelly ground. Clods the size of a bull shoot out from under their feet. Usually the battle lasts for a day and a year, and each day is a day of fierce struggle.

In Indian myths struggles for supremacy are not decided by fighting, as in Aryan and Mongol myths, but by trials of skill, strength, and dexterity. The opponents always bet their heads, and the head of the losing party is cut off at once.

HÚNKUVAI

A prominent characteristic of Buriat myths is the wisdom of the horse, which in many instances is sent from heaven in answer to prayers. These wonderful stallions of Buriat mythology are different in some respects from the steeds in Aryan myths; they have the same appearance always, whereas in Aryan myths the steed when taken from the stable or pasture is often either a miserable mangy colt or a shaggy-haired, crooked-legged mare; its wonderful power and beauty being made manifest only when in action.

The god-given stallion of the Buriats is of enormous size, and travels with such speed that "he can reach in one day a place so far distant that a boy of five years of age would be sixty when at the end of the journey, and a full-grown man would die on the road." Sometimes the horse foresees the death of his master and warns him.

The steed which the Iron Hero rides is always spoken of as "the blue stallion of the sky." In most instances the color of the stallion is mentioned, and not infrequently it is blue or red. Probably in the original story these steeds were clouds. In Hungarian myths the food of the steed is glowing coals. There are Hungarian myths in which little, if any, doubt is left that the steed is lightning. It was a steed of this kind that carried Cahal, son of King Conor, to Striker's castle, a place to which no ship could go ("Hero-Tales of Ireland").

BRINGING TO LIFE

Bringing to life is one of the most ordinary acts in Mongol as well as in other mythologies: usually where there are hundreds of skeletons and many piles of dry bones, the Mongol hero sprinkles them with the Water of Life taken from a spring near a silver-leafed aspen tree; immediately the bones assume their old connection and take on flesh, and the men rise to bless their benefactor. When the hero himself is killed, restoring life is more difficult. For several days the wife, sister, or friend must pray to the Heavenly Burkans. Often the Water of Life is far away, and to procure it a long and dangerous journey must be made. Usually the cuckoo assists. She sings around the body, beginning at the feet. When she reaches the head the first time flesh comes on the skeleton, the second time breath enters the body, and when she reaches the head the third time the hero springs up.

In Gaelic mythology, if the hero has been dead long the bones are collected, or if they have fallen into dust the dust is gathered up; some one strikes the bones or the dust with the rod of enchantment or Druidic switch, and immediately the hero rises up as well and strong as ever.

In the myth tales of the Iroquois Indians the bones of hundreds or thousands of people are found lying in a heap. The hero pushes a near-by hickory tree as if to throw it on them, crying at the same time, "Rise up! Rise up! or the tree will fall on you." The bones assume their old arrangement, take on flesh, and the multitude rise up, thank their benefactor, and each man returns to his home.

Among the Yana Indians of California there are several methods for restoring life, sometimes it is done by kicking or turning over a corpse with the foot, sometimes by boiling one hair or the heart, frequently it is accomplished by the stroke of a twig from a red rose-bush.

In Modoc mythology, when the hero has been dead many hours or perhaps days the morning star calls out to him, "Rise up! Rise up! why sleep so long?"

THE WORLD BEFORE THIS

In Mongol myths we find a conception of "a world before this world," a common conception in the Creation myths of the Indians of the Pacific coast, in some of which the idea is worked out with great detail and beauty. But the "first people" of the Wintu and Yana and other Indian tribes of the coast and of Mexico, the people who occupied "that world before this," are unlike the "first people" of the Buriats. With the Indians the first people lived for untold ages in perfect harmony, then very slowly a change came, discord appeared, and in time conflict, which grew in venom and continued till all the first people, except a very small number, were turned into the various kinds of living creatures—beasts, birds, insects, trees, plants, etc.—that are now, or ever have been, on earth.

Two enemies would meet and fight. When one was triumphant he said to the vanquished, "Hereafter you will be nothing but a ——," and he mentioned what his enemy was to be, and at once the change was accomplished.

With the Mongols the people of the earlier world were so wicked that Esege Malan the Creator, and his grandson, Gesir Bogdo, determined to destroy them. In one or two instances the destruction is accomplished in the same way as described in the Indian myths,—for example, Gesir Bogdo takes all power from the Raven; from being a great personage he makes him the insignificant bird that he is to-day, saying to him, "Hereafter you will be puny and weak, unable to harm people." The first people were not Mongols, but Marat and Mangathai, evil spirits.

ALTIN SHAGOY

Mongol, Aryan, and Indian ideas agree as to the way a father should treat the man who wishes to marry his daughter. In Gaelic myths the suitor is given such tasks as thatching a byre with bird feathers, the stem of each feather to be inwards and its point outwards; catching a steed that has never seen a blink of earth or air, etc. ("Folk and Hero Tales from Argyllshire"). In Mongol myths the suitor is sent on a dangerous journey to accomplish what is supposed to be an impossible feat. In Indian mythology similar tasks are given by the father-in-law to the new son-in-law.